✓ P9-CDY-344

Praise for the novels of Katie MacAlister

A Girl's Guide to Vampires

"With its superb characterization and writing that manages to be both sexy and humorous, this contemporary paranormal love story is an absolute delight."
—*Booklist* (starred review)

"Fantastic! It's sensual, it's hilarious, and it's a winner! Ms. MacAlister is my favorite new author."
—Suzanne Coleburn, Reader to Reader Reviews

"A book rich with humor, loaded with sexual tension, and packed with interesting, if sometimes slightly offbeat, characters."
—Romance Reviews Today

"Hysterically funny paranormal romance, oh my!"
—The Best Reviews

The Corset Diaries

"Reality TV has never been more entertaining than here as the wickedly funny MacAlister has her heroine record her hilarious experiences with the quirky cast of characters and her passionate encounters with Max in a laughter-laced diary that is a saucy, sexy delight."
—*Booklist*

"Offbeat and wacky . . . MacAlister has outdone herself."
—*Romantic Times*

"A fast-paced page-turner. A laugh-a-minute trip with stops along the way for love and acceptance. Pick it up and enjoy the ride."
—A Romance Review

"Enjoyable contemporary romance."
—The Best Reviews/Harriet Klausner

continued . . .

"This latest Katie MacAlister novel simply bubbles over with wit, fun, and hilarity. Heart tugging emotionality deftly combined with sizzling passion and tongue-in-cheek hilarity." —Curled Up with a Good Book

Men in Kilts

"With its wickedly witty writing, wonderfully snappy dialogue, and uniquely amusing characters, MacAlister's latest is perfect for any reader seeking a deliciously sexy yet also subtly sweet contemporary romance." —*Booklist*

"A fun, fast paced and witty adventure. . . . *Men in Kilts* is so utterly delightful, I read this book nearly all in one sitting." —Roundtable Reviews

"Katie MacAlister sparkles, intrigues and is one of the freshest voices to hit romance. . . . So buckle up, for Katie gives you romance, love and the whole damn thing—sheep included." —The Best Reviews

"*Men in Kilts* is filled with warm, intriguing characters and situations, and the atmosphere is fiery as Katie and her silent Ian irresistibly draw you into their story." —*Rendezvous*

"Wonderfully witty, funny and romantic, *Men in Kilts* had me laughing out loud from the first page. . . . A definite winner." —Romance Reviews Today

"This book hooked me from the first paragraph and kept me smiling—and sometimes laughing out loud—to the last page. . . . I thoroughly enjoyed *Men in Kilts* and recommend it highly." —*Affaire de Coeur*

Katie MacAlister

You Slay Me

AN ONYX BOOK

ONYX
Published by New American Library, a division of
Penguin Group (USA) Inc., 375 Hudson Street,
New York, New York 10014, USA
Penguin Group (Canada), 90 Eglinton Avenue East, Suite 700, Toronto,
Ontario M4P 2Y3, Canada (a division of Pearson Penguin Canada Inc.)
Penguin Books Ltd., 80 Strand, London WC2R 0RL, England
Penguin Ireland, 25 St. Stephen's Green, Dublin 2,
Ireland (a division of Penguin Books Ltd.)
Penguin Group (Australia), 250 Camberwell Road, Camberwell, Victoria 3124,
Australia (a division of Pearson Australia Group Pty. Ltd.)
Penguin Books India Pvt. Ltd., 11 Community Centre, Panchsheel Park,
New Delhi - 110 017, India
Penguin Group (NZ), 67 Apollo Drive, Mairangi Bay,
Auckland 1311, New Zealand (a division of Pearson New Zealand Ltd.)
Penguin Books (South Africa) (Pty.) Ltd., 24 Sturdee Avenue,
Rosebank, Johannesburg 2196, South Africa

Penguin Books Ltd., Registered Offices:
80 Strand, London WC2R 0RL, England

First published by Onyx, an imprint of New American Library,
a division of Penguin Group (USA) Inc.

First Printing, September 2004
20 19 18 17 16 15 14 13

PUBLISHER'S NOTE
This is a work of fiction. Names, characters, places, and incidents either are
the product of the author's imagination or are used fictitiously, and any resemblance to actual persons, living or dead, business establishments, events, or
locales is entirely coincidental.
    The publisher does not have any control over and does not assume any
responsibility for author or third-party Web sites or their content.

ACKNOWLEDGMENTS

Writing a book is never an entirely solitary endeavor, which is one reason I offer my thanks and appreciation to Patty Woodwell for casting her eagle eye over the French used in this book. I'd also like to thank the wonderful people at NAL: my witty editor, Laura Cifelli, editorial director Claire Zion, who read the book while Laura was away, and publisher Kara Welsh, who gave the OK to let me try something new with this series. I would also like to thank Christine Feehan for her friendship, support, and for being the inspiration for a karaoke-singing demon in Newfoundland dog form.

1

"Ezling."

"No, it's Aisling."

"Azhlee?"

"Aisling. It's Irish."

The Orly passport control man glared suspiciously at me over the top of my passport. "Your passport, it says you are American."

I rallied a smile when I really wanted to scream with frustration instead. "I am. My mother was Irish, hence the name Aisling."

He transferred his glare to the passport. "A-sling."

I tried not to sigh too obviously. I might be brand-spanking-new to the courier business, but instinctively I knew that if I showed the least sign of impatience with being grilled on the pronunciation of my name, Antoine the passport man would drag out his interrogation. I sweetened my smile, pushed down the worry that something would go wrong with the job, and said very slowly, "It's pronounced *ash-ling*."

"Ash-leen," Antoine said, his eyes narrowing in concentration.

I nodded. It was close enough.

"*Bon*, we march forward," he said, flipping through my passport. "You are five feet and nine inches tall, have gray eyes, are thirty-one years of age, unmarried, and you live in Seattle, state of Washington, America. This is all correct, yes?"

"Yes, except I think of my eyes as being a bit more hazel than gray, but the passport guy said to put gray down. Hazel sounds more exotic, don't you think?"

Antoine cocked an eyebrow at me, briefly examining the visa that allowed me to act as a courier for Bell & Sons, before moving on to the documents for the aquamanile.

I quickly glanced around, Uncle Damian's strictures on perimeter security echoing in my head: *Security is your personal responsibility; your security is not the responsibility of the police, or of the government, or any officials—your first and last line of security is yourself. Be alert and aware of your surroundings. Radiate confidence. Never do anything to indicate you are prey.*

Easier said than done, I mused as I eyed the large number of people passing through the airport. Happily, no one was paying any attention to me or the case I held. I breathed a silent sigh of relief and raised my chin, trying to look confident and in control, not at all like a courier in charge of a six-hundred-year-old small golden statue in the shape of a dragon that was worth more than what I had made in the last ten years put together.

Antoine's gaze flickered to the small black heavy-duty plastic case I clutched tightly in my right hand. "Do you have the *Inventaire Detaillé*?"

"Of course." I passed over the sheets of paper describing in French the gold aquamanile. The document was stamped by the San Francisco French consulate and included an appraiser's certificate, as well as a copy of the bill of sale to Mme. Aurora Deauxville, citizen of France and resident of Paris.

Antoine's finger tapped on the top document. "What is this . . . aquamanile?"

I shifted the case to my left hand, flexing my right fingers, being careful to keep the case out of sight, held between me and the examination table. "An aquamanile is a form of ewer, usually made of metal, used for the ritual washing of hands by a priest or other liturgical person. They were very common in medieval times."

Antoine's eyes widened as he stared at the black case. "It is a religious artifact you have?"

I gave him a crooked smile. "Not really. Rumor has it that aquamaniles were sometimes used in . . . er . . . dark practices."

He stared. "Dark practices?"

I took in his raised eyebrows and smiled sympathetically. "Demons," I said succinctly. "Aquamaniles such as this are said to have been used by powerful mages to raise the demon princes."

I didn't think his eyes could open any wider, but at the word *demon*, they all but popped out of his head. "Demon princes?" he asked, his voice a hoarse whisper.

I shifted the case again and leaned forward, speaking quickly, aware that a faint note of desperation had tinged my voice. "You know, Satan's big guns. The head honchos of Hell. The demon lords. Anyone can raise a demon, but it takes a special person with special powers to raise a demon lord."

Antoine blinked.

"Yeah, I know. I think it's a bit out there, too, but you'd be surprised what people believe. Even so, it's a fascinating subject. I've made quite a study of demons— not that I believe they really exist outside of man's imagination—and found there are whole cults revolving around the idea of demons and the power they wield over mortals. I heard there's a group in San Francisco that is trying to get a demon elected into public office. Ha ha, like anyone would notice?"

The blinking stopped. Antoine stared at me with a blank look in his eyes. I decided my little foray into joke land was probably pushing the Anglo-Franco boundaries. Not to mention that the minutes were ticking by at an alarming rate. "Yeah, well, I don't guarantee the usefulness of the items; I just deliver them. So, if everything is in order, do you think I could go? I'm supposed to get this aquamanile to its owner at five, and it's already past three. This is my first job as a courier, you see, and my uncle—he's my boss—told me that if I screw up this delivery, I'm off the payroll, and since a very stupid judge in California ordered me to pay my ex-husband alimony just because Alan, my ex, is a lazy slob who likes to hang around the beach and ogle the fake-boobed girls rather than get off his surfer ass and work for a living like the rest of us, it's kind of important that I keep this job, and to keep it means that I have to get the aquamanile to the woman who bought it from Uncle Damian."

Antoine looked a bit stunned until I nudged the hand that held my documents; then he pursed his lips as he shot me a quelling glare. He nodded toward my case. "You will open it. I must examine the object and ensure it matches the pictures presented."

I stifled yet another sigh of frustration as I fished the keys out of my bag before unlocking the case. Antoine's glare turned to an open mouthed look of wonder as I peeled back the protective foam padding and laid open the soft linen cloth that was wrapped around the aquamanile. *"Sacre futur du bordel de Dieu!"*

"Yeah, it's pretty impressive, isn't it?" I looked fondly at the dragon. It was about six inches high, all coiled tail, gleaming scales, and glittering emerald eyes. It was one of the few dragons I'd ever seen depicted without wings.

Antoine reached out to touch the golden dragon, but I quickly wrapped the linen back over it. "Sorry—look but don't touch." His nostrils flared dramatically. I hurried to sooth his ruffled feathers. "Not even the X-ray guys got to touch it. If you'll take a peek at the appraiser's valuation of the piece, I think you'll see why it's better not to."

He glanced at the appraiser's sheet and swore under his breath before brandishing his stamp on my passport and the dragon's documents. "All is in order. You may continue."

I closed up the case, locked it, and tucked the keys back into my neck pouch, giving Antoine a cheery smile as I slung the bag containing my clothing onto my shoulder. "Thanks."

"One moment—," he said, stopping me with an upraised hand. I held my breath, worried he was going to insist on something that would keep me from making my appointment with Mme. Deauxville. It would be just my luck that Antoine would decide I needed a full body search.

I tried to look innocent and friendly and not in the least like someone who would smuggle something into the country in a convenient body cavity. "Hmm?"

He glanced around quickly, then stepped closer to me, his voice dropping. "You are an expert in demons but you do not believe in them?"

I shook my head, not wishing to get into a philosophical conversation while the clock was ticking. "I'm not really an expert—I've just studied a few medieval texts about them."

"Demons are very bad."

I shrugged and edged sideways. "Not really. According to the texts I've read, they're actually rather stupid. I think people fear the thought of them because they don't know how to control them."

He leaned closer, the stale odor of cigarette smoke clinging to him, making my nose wrinkle. "And you don't fear them?"

I shook my head again, edging even farther away.

His dark eyes lit for a moment with a deep red light, making him suddenly look a whole lot more ominous than a simple customs inspector. "You should," he said, and then turned away, gesturing the next person in line to his table.

"Hoo, I guess there're weirdos all over the world," I mumbled to myself as I pushed my way through the crowd toward the exit, careful to keep both hands on the handle of the black case. My clothing and personal items I could afford to lose, but this job was my chance—my *only* chance of getting ahead since the company I worked for went belly up. If I messed this up, I'd be jobless again. With no unemployment benefits left, and a beach bum to support, I had to have work, something that would allow me to live while paying Alan the huge wad of money the court decided I owed him.

Men. Bah!

It took me another fifteen minutes to figure out the signs in the airport concourses and find where the taxis were. Beth, Uncle Damian's secretary, said Orly had signs in English, but Beth lied—not only was there no English, but also nothing I saw written on the signs matched the handy little phrases in the *French for Francophobes* book I had bought to get me through the next day and a half.

"Um . . . *bonjour*," I said to a bored-looking taxi driver who stood leaning on his car and picking at his teeth. *"Parlez-vous anglais?"*

"Non," he said without stopping the teeth-picking.

"Oh. Um. Do you know if any of the other taxi drivers *parlez anglais*? Know*ez-vous* if *le* taxi drivers *parlez anglais?"*

He gave me a look that should have shamed me, but I was beyond being ashamed of going to France without knowing a single word of French except what I found in the guidebook. I had a job to do—I just wanted it done.

"Look, I'm doing the best I can, OK? I want to go to the Rue . . . Oh, just a sec—let me look in the book. . . ." I hugged the black case to my chest with one arm while I rooted around in my bag for the French guide. *"Je veux aller à la Rue Sang des Innocents."*

The taxi driver stopped picking his teeth to grimace. "That is the worst French I have ever heard, and I have heard much bad French."

"You *do* speak English!" I said, slamming my guide shut. "You said you didn't! And I can't help it if what I said was wrong. That's what the book said."

"It wasn't much wrong, but your accent . . ." He shuddered delicately, then with a sweeping bow, opened the door to his taxi. "Very well, I will take you to the Rue Sang des Innocents, but it will cost you."

"How much?" I asked as I slid into the backseat, still clutching my case. I had the euros Uncle Damian had given me, but I knew they were only enough to cover my hotel bill for the night, two meals, and minor incidentals like the taxi rides.

The taxi driver tossed my bag into the other side and slid behind the wheel. "The journey will cost you thirty-six euro, but the ride will cost you more."

"Huh?"

He smiled at me in his rearview mirror. "By the time we arrive at the Rue Sang des Innocents, you will know how to say three things in French. With those three things, you will be able to go anywhere in Paris."

I agreed to his terms and, since I was early for my appointment with Mme. Deauxville, had him wait for me while I ran into the hotel where Beth had booked me. I checked in, dropped my bag on the bed, pulled a comb through my curls so I looked less like a crazed woman and more like a professional courier, and dashed back downstairs to where Rene and his taxi were waiting for me.

At five minutes to five, the taxi pulled up next to a six-story cream-colored building with high arched doorways and windows graced by intricate black metal grilles.

"Wow," I breathed as I leaned out the window to peer up at the house. "What a gorgeous building. It looks so . . . French!"

Rene reached backwards through his window and opened my door. I grabbed my things and got out onto the cobblestone street, my mouth still hanging open as I stared up at the house.

"You see that all the houses here are old mansions. It is a very exclusive neighborhood. Île Saint-Louis itself is only six blocks long and two blocks wide. And now, you will pay me exactly thirty-six euro, and recite for me please the phrases I have taught you."

I dragged my eyes off the house and smiled as I handed Rene his money. "If someone annoys me, I say, *Voulez-vous cesser de me cracher dessus pendant que vous parlez.*"

"Will you stop spitting on me while you are speaking," Rene translated with a nod.

"And if I need help with anything, I say, *J'ai une grenouille dans mon bidet.*"

"I have a frog in my bidet. Yes, very good. And the last one?"

"The last I should reserve for any guy who hits on me when I don't want him to: *Tu as une tête a faire sauter les plaques des egouts.*"

"You have a face that would blow off the cover of a manhole. *Oui, trés bon.* You will do. And for your meeting with the important lady, *bonne chance,* eh?"

"Thanks, Rene. I appreciate the lessons. You just never know when you need to tell someone there's an amphibian in your bidet."

"One moment. I have something for you." He rustled around in a small brown bag for a second, then pulled out a battered card and handed it to me with the air of someone presenting an object of great value. "I am available for hire as a driver. You pay me, I drive you around Paris, show you all of the sites you must see. You can call me on my mobile number anytime."

"Thanks. I don't know that I'll be in Paris long enough for a chauffeur to drive me around, but if I ever need a driver, you'll be the one I call." I saluted him with the card, then tucked it away in my wallet.

He drove off with a friendly wave and a faint puff of black exhaust. I turned back to the impressive building, squared my shoulders, and after a quick look around to make sure no one was watching me, stepped into the doorway to press the buzzer labeled DEAUXVILLE.

"I am confident," I muttered to myself. "I am a professional. I know exactly what I am doing. I am not at all freaked out by being in a different country where the only thing I know how to do is complain about frogs and insult people. I am cool, calm, and collected. I am . . . not being answered."

I buzzed again. Nothing happened. A quick glance at my watch confirmed that I was two minutes early. Surely Mme. Deauxville was in?

I buzzed once more, leaning on the buzzer this time. I tried putting my ear to the door, but couldn't hear anything. A glance at a window showed me why—the walls of the building looked to be at least three feet thick.

"Well, hell," I swore, stepping back so I could look up at the building. I knew from the instructions Uncle Damian had given me that Mme. Deauxville was on the second floor. The red-and-cream drapes visible through the slightly opened windows didn't move at all. Nothing moved anywhere on the second floor . . . or on any of the floors, for that matter. Since it was a pleasant June evening, I expected people to be arriving home, bustling around doing their evening shopping, strolling down the street, gazing upon the Seine, and so forth, but there was no movement at all in the house.

I looked down the street, the hairs on the back of my neck slowly standing on end. There was no movement on the street either. No people, no cars, no birds . . . nothing. Not even a flower bobbed in the slight breeze from the river. I looked behind me. The cross street was the Rue Saint-Louis en l'Île, a busy street with stores and restaurants, and lots of shops. It had taken Rene ten minutes to navigate a couple of blocks because the traffic and shoppers were so dense, but where I stood, the noise of said traffic and shoppers was oddly filtered, as if the whole of Rue Sang des Innocents was swathed in cotton wool, leaving it an oasis of stillness and silence in a city known for its liveliness.

"The word *creepy* doesn't even begin to cover the situation," I said aloud, just to hear something. Unease rippled through me as I held my case tightly, giving Mme. Deauxville's bell one more long ring. The skin on the back of my neck tightened even more as I noticed that the door to the building wasn't shut properly.

"Someone must have been in a rush to leave this morning," I told the door, trying to tamp down on the major case of the willies the silent street was giving me. "Someone was just late for work, and they didn't quite close the door. That's all. There's nothing foreboding in a door that hasn't been shut all the way. There's nothing eerie in that at all. There's nothing creepy about a street . . . Oh, crap. Hello?" I pushed the door open and took a step into a tiny hall. The entrance narrowed into a dark passage beyond a brown-paneled stairway that led upward. "Anyone here? I'm looking for Mme. Deauxville. Hellooooooo?"

I expected the last notes of my hello to echo up the stairwell, but strangely, my words were muffled, as if they had been absorbed into the walls, filtered by the same strange effect that kept the street outside as quiet as a tomb.

"I would have to think of a tomb," I grumbled to myself as I carefully closed the door behind me, turning to start up the stairs to the second floor. "There are times when it absolutely does *not* pay to have a good imagination."

There were two doors in the tiny hall stretching the length of the second-floor stairs. One bore a silver plate with the word DEAUXVILLE written on it in a fancy script that screamed expensive. The other door, I assumed, was a second entrance to the apartment. I stepped up to the main door, one arm holding the case tight to my chest, the other upraised to knock. Just as my knuckles were about to touch the glossy oak of the door, a wave of dread and foreboding, a sense of something being very, very wrong swept over me. The sensation was so strong, I stepped backwards until the coolness of the paneling seeped through the thin cotton of my dress. I clutched the case and struggled to breathe, my chest tight with dread. The feeling of unease that had set in as soon as Rene left swelled into something much more frightening, leaving me with goose bumps on my arms and a warning voice in my head shrieking at me to leave the building that very second, if not sooner.

Something horrible had been in that apartment. Something . . . unnatural.

"I am confident," I ground out through my teeth, and forced my feet forward to the door. "It's just an eccentric collector, nothing evil. There is nothing to be afraid of. I am a professional. I can do this."

The door swung open at the first brush of my hand against it.

I stood frozen in the doorway, the skin on my back crawling with horror as I looked down the short hall into what must be the living room of the apartment. Tiny little motes of dust danced lazily in the late afternoon sunshine that streamed through the tall floor-to-ceiling arched windows, spilling in a ruby pool on a carpet of deeper red. A bouquet of fresh flowers sat on an antique table between two of the windows, the sharp scent of it detectable even from where I stood. The ceilings were high, cream-colored to complement the robin's-egg-blue walls, the edges scalloped with intricate molding. Along one wall I could see a highly polished antique desk with a red upholstered matching chair sitting before it at an angle, as if its occupant had arisen just a moment before. Everything was lovely, beautiful, expensive, just exactly what I expected in the apartment of a rich woman who lived in an exclusive area of Paris.

Everything except the body, that is. Suspended from a chandelier, a woman's body was doubled over, hanging from her hands tied behind her back, her body swinging slightly above a black circle of ash that had been drawn on the lovely red carpet, a circle inscribed with twelve symbols. The dead woman was Mme. Deauxville; of that I was sure.

"J'ai une grenouille dans mon bidet," I said, and wished fervently that the worst of my problems were frogs.

2

I hope I get major brownie points for not racing screaming from the house as soon as my eyes caught sight of the dead body of the woman I had come halfway around the world to meet. I hope whoever controls the karma scale rewards me for *not* getting the hell out of Dodge while I could, because stepping into Mme. Deauxville's apartment while her body swayed gently in the warm afternoon sun was the hardest thing I've ever done.

OK, I admit it; I whimpered a little bit, and I left the front door ajar because something in the primitive part of my brain was insisting on an easy escape route just in case the body should suddenly spring to life and try to grab me (in the best horror-movie style), but the whimper was small, and I stopped it as soon as I realized it was coming from my mouth.

"Get a hold of yourself," I said sternly, flinching at the sound of my voice in the dead apartment. Then I flinched at the way the word *dead* rolled around in my mind. "If she's really dead, she can't hurt you. Oh, shoot, *if* she's dead . . . Uck. I suppose I should make sure she's really dead."

It took what seemed to be hours to travel the seven

steps needed to cross the short hall. I sidled around the ash circle, unwilling to disturb it, unwilling to touch the body. Surely she couldn't have survived being strung up like that? Surely the lack of movement was indicative of death? Surely I could get by without checking to make sure she was really dead?

"Poop," I said, and set my case down carefully on a beautifully embroidered antique chair. I shuffled forward, careful not to touch anything as I stopped directly in front of the body, my toes just brushing the outer edge of the ash circle. I took a deep breath, pushed down the horrible feeling that I shouldn't be doing what I was about to do, and leaned forward to feel for a pulse on Mme. Deauxville's neck.

"Non!"

Startled by the man's voice behind me, I jumped just as I reached for Mme. Deauxville, sending me plummeting toward the body, my arms cartwheeling madly. I screamed even as I tried to twist away from her, but it was a hand on the back of my dress yanking me backwards that kept me from plunging into the circle.

"Ne la touchez pas!"

"Huh?" I rubbed the goose bumps on the suddenly cold flesh of my arms as I blinked at the man who loomed before me. "I'm . . . uh . . . sorry, *non* me *parlez* French."

"American?" the man asked, his nostrils flaring as if he smelled something.

"Yeah," I answered, still rubbing my arms. I looked from him to the body, then back, the realization flashing through my head that I was alone in an apartment with a stranger and a dead body, which probably meant that he was . . .

"I didn't kill her," he said quickly, evidently reading my mind before turning away to look at the body.

I used the moment to examine him. I'm not exactly an

idiot—if I find myself in a room with a murder victim, the big, tall, dark-haired, extremely handsome guy dressed in black who positively reeks of danger and who mysteriously pops up out of nowhere is naturally going to be on the top of my Potential Murderer List.

Which meant I had to get myself and my dragon out of there before Mr. Killer decided to enjoy a double-header.

I grimaced just as the man turned back to me. Something flashed deep in his dark green eyes. "Are you unwell? You aren't going to vomit on me, are you?"

"That wasn't on my list of planned activities for the afternoon, no, but if you really insist, I suppose I could try for a hairball or something."

His head tipped to the side for a moment as he examined me from toes to nose. "I've never completely understood American humor. That *was* supposed to be a joke, yes?"

"Yes, it was." Oh, brilliant, Aisling, just brilliant. Here you are trapped in a room with a murderer in a foreign country, and all you can do is make jokes when what you need to be doing is running away as fast as you can. I took a deep breath and edged toward the chair that held my case. He moved backwards a step, effectively blocking me off from the exit. Panic, held rather tenuously at bay, rose within me. It quickly became clear that I needed to distract the handsome green-eyed murderer so I could escape.

His eyes glittered darkly at me in a way that simultaneously scared the crap out of me and made me want to throw myself on him. "Ah. Yes. A joke. I thought that is what it was."

Distraction, girl. Don't get caught up in a pair of pretty eyes, not when they likely belonged to a cold-blooded killer. "Um. I was just going to check and make sure

Mme. Deauxville was really dead." I closed my eyes for a moment, aware of just how damning that sounded. "That is, I wanted to make sure she wasn't still alive. Not that I want her to be dead, you understand. I just want to make sure that she's not. Oh, crap, it's all coming out wrong."

"You want to make sure there is nothing you can do for her," the dark man said neutrally, his voice—a sexy blend of an English accent and something that sounded vaguely Germanic to my ears—oddly flat. It sounded just the way you'd expect someone to speak if he suspected you of being a deranged killer.

"Although that really is an oxymoron. I mean, what killer *isn't* deranged?"

The brilliant green eyes considered me for a moment. "Is that a rhetorical question, or do you wish for an analysis of the mind of killers?"

I groaned. "Sorry, that just kind of slipped out. Don't you think one of us should . . . you know, check her? To make sure she's not just gravely wounded?"

He looked back at the body. I looked, as well. "You don't believe she's really dead?"

I had to admit he had a point. The body was too still, the heavy silent atmosphere of the apartment (house, street, possibly the whole world) almost smothering. I knew without even thinking about it that there were only two living beings in the apartment, and the body that hung by her hands wasn't one of them.

The man cocked his head again, then whirled around and closed the door that was still standing open. Fear flared to life with the movement. He was going to kill me! I looked around frantically for a weapon, shrieking when his hand clamped down on my arm.

"What is the matter with you? You look like you're going to pass out."

"Me? Nothing's the matter with me. I'm fine. Although, now I come to think of it, I have a horrible memory problem. I can't remember what people look like. Or sound like. Or the things they said to me, or . . . or . . . anything. So anyone who was worried about what I might have seen or heard would really have nothing to worry about at all. Because of my memory problem. It's permanent, too."

He gave me a long, curious look, then made an annoyed noise and let go of my arm as he squatted down to study the ash circle. "I told you I didn't kill her. I'm not going to harm you. Your fear of me is senseless."

What is it about scorn of any sort that makes your bravado fire up? My chin lifted at the arrogant tone in his back-to-being-sexy voice. "Yeah? Who said I was afraid of you?"

"I can smell your fear. What do you make of this?"

He gestured toward the ash circle. I glanced toward it and crossed my arms over my chest, trying to sniff the air around my armpit region without it being obvious I was doing a BO check. "It's an ash circle, inscribed with the twelve symbols of Ashtaroth. What does fear smell like, exactly?"

He frowned at the circle but didn't touch it. "Sexy."

I blinked a couple of times. (Like that was going to make me think better?) "What?"

He straightened up and turned toward me, and once again I was very much aware that I was alone in an apartment with a dead woman and a mysterious man who was much too handsome for my peace of mind. "It brings out the predator in me."

My eyes widened as he leaned toward me, his eyes a mesmerizing green that seemed to suck me into their cool depths. There was something about him that made every atom within me aware that he was a man, and I was a woman, and there were certain fundamental differences between us that my body very much wanted to explore, regardless of the fact that he might be a murderer. "Oy."

He nodded, the thick black of his lashes emphasizing the purity of the green irises. "And because of the masculine nature of my reaction, you feel threatened on a feminine level. Thus you make jokes as a defense when others might feel it inappropriate to do so."

"Are you saying there's a guy/girl thing going on between us?" Various parts of my body were pleading for just such an eventuality, but I firmly told those parts to behave themselves, and remember that the man they were lusting after was probably a murderer. "Are you saying that I'm afraid because you're a man and I'm a woman, and not at all because we're standing in front of a woman who was quite obviously murdered?"

His lips quirked. He looked back toward Mme. Deauxville. "No, I am not saying that. Is this circle closed or open?"

I looked down. It looked whole. "Looks closed to me. Um. Who are you?"

His gaze flickered around the room. "I might ask the same question of you."

"You might," I said, watching as he gave the circle a generous berth. He stopped on the other side of the body, in front of a gold-and-scarlet couch that matched the two other chairs in the room, frowning down at it. "But I asked first. So, who are you? Not that you have to tell me, but I expect the police are going to want to know, so I thought you might just want to practice your alibi on me."

He gave me another one of his impatient looks, then reached into the breast pocket of his black leather jacket and pulled out a wallet, flipping it open to flash an official-looking identity card at me. "Drake Vireo. Interpol."

My mouth hung open in fly-catching position for a couple of seconds before I realized it. "Interpol? The one that's like the international Scotland Yard? You're a detective?"

"Of a sort." He started to close his wallet.

"Wait a minute," I said, carefully skirting around the circle and Mme. Deauxville. "I didn't just fall off the stupid wagon. I want to see that up close."

He waved it toward the couch as I moved over next to him. "If the circle is still closed, how did the demon escape?"

There are times when a girl just has to have a good goggle. This was one of them. I stared, goggle-eyed. "What is it with everyone in this country, you're all demon-obsessed or something? What demon? What are you talking about?"

He made a *tch* noise in the back of his throat. It expressed all sorts of annoyance and impatience, with just a smidgen of an implied eye roll. "I am asking you what happened to the demon that was summoned by whoever drew the circle. If the circle is closed, as you say it is, then it would be impossible for the demon to leave, and yet the proof is before our eyes."

I looked at where he was pointing his wallet. Between the couch and the wall there was a black smudge on the floor, as if someone had rubbed charcoal on it. I looked at it for a moment, then back at Drake, unsure of whether he was totally and completely mad, or if I was. I decided that since I'd known him the least amount of time, he got to be *it*. "You're serious, aren't you? You really think a demon has something to do with this? I'll admit that whoever killed Mme. Deauxville did so in a manner that makes it look like the ritual destruction of a demon, but that doesn't mean that there was an actual demon involved."

One glossy black eyebrow cocked. "Ritual destruction? How so?"

I gestured toward the body, pleased that all those years spent on my little hobby finally had a payoff. "The Circle of Ashtaroth beneath her feet with the twelve symbols of summoning, the way the body is hung from her hands bound behind her, and I'm willing to bet if you bend down and look at her chest, you'll find something made of silver piercing her heart. In other words, she was murdered in the style of the first of the Three Demon Deaths, only this woman was not a demon, which really is no surprise, since demons are nothing more than fiction."

Drake looked amused. "You don't believe in demons?"

"I'll take no for five hundred, Alex. Demons don't exist outside the minds of some pretty twisted and confused people."

His nostrils flared again. If I weren't so convinced he was stark, staring mad, I'd have admitted to myself that he even did a nostril flare well. "Are you trying to tell me that despite the evidence before us, you do not believe that a demon was recently called to this apartment?"

I pursed my lips, slowly moving away from him. No quick movements; everyone knew that was the key to keeping dangerously mad people calm. Slow and easy was the plan. "OK, you know what? I'm going to just scoot over to the desk where the phone is and call the police. You can do your detective stuff while I'm calling."

"I've already called the police. They should be here in four minutes. Why do you hesitate to tell me what happened to the demon? Did you have something to do with Aurora Deauxville's death?"

I stopped before the desk, trying to figure out whether I could make it to the door before he grabbed me. My gaze dropped to the case sitting on the chair. Rats. I wouldn't be able to make it without the aquamanile. "No, I just got here. I'm a courier. I was supposed to deliver a package to her. I don't know anything about demons or who would want Mme. Deauxville dead. But as we're on the subject, just what are *you* doing here? I assume you aren't here in a professional capacity, because if you were, the homicide squad would be here, too. So, if you didn't kill her, you must have seen who did. She doesn't look like she's been dead too long."

"She doesn't *look* like she's been dead long?"

I pointed to where Mme. Deauxville's arms were bound behind her back. "Rigor hasn't set in yet. If you look at the angle between her arms and her back, you'll notice it's closing as rigor starts to take hold. That means she's either been dead for more than twelve hours, and rigor is wearing off, or it's just setting in, which means she's been dead . . . oh, maybe fifteen minutes. But I don't have to tell you that—you're a cop."

"I specialize in finding lost items, not examining murder scenes," Drake said abruptly. "How do you know so much about the stages of decomposition?"

"The Detection Channel. I'm addicted to a reality forensic medicine show on it. It's really interesting. They do autopsies and stuff. Do you know what happens to bones left exposed to the elements?"

"Yes, they turn brown."

"That's right. I thought you said you didn't work homicides?"

He scanned the room again, like he was looking for something he missed. He also totally ignored my last question, which was fine with me, because I'd rather he answered the important one. "I arrived shortly before you did, five minutes at the most. My business with her is none of your concern. She was dead when I entered the apartment."

"Then you must have heard me ringing the bell."

"Yes."

"You didn't let me in!" I said, a wee tad bit more petulantly than I would have liked, considering he was still the number-one suspect for the murder.

He tipped his head back like he was smelling the air. "Would you have if you were in my place?"

"I suppose not. So, why were *you* meeting Mme. Deauxville?"

His brows pulled together in a frown as he turned to face me fully. "I think a more important question is why you insist on lying to me. You are a Guardian, and yet you deny the facts. You deny that a demon has been here. I can feel the very air soiled by its presence, yet you deny it?" He shook his head, moving slowly toward me. "Why a Guardian seeks to lie about something so simple as a demon summoning is beyond me. You will explain yourself now."

I took a couple of steps back, toward the desk. "See, this is where you're confused. I'm a courier—I just told you that. I don't have any kids, my own or anyone else's, for whom I'm acting as a guardian."

His frown deepened. "What?"

"I'm a courier. *C-o-u-r-i-e-r.* It means someone who transports objects. That's my job. At least it *was*. There's no telling how Uncle Damian is going to react to my first delivery going to pot like this, but I have a feeling I shouldn't be planning on a raise and a promotion any time soon."

Drake moved around to the far side of the circle, his eyes puzzled as they watched me. "You smell as if you are telling the truth, but you know about the symbols of

Ashtaroth. You knew the circle was closed, and not even I can tell if a circle is open or closed. In addition, you are familiar with the rituals for destroying a demon. Only a Guardian would know such things. What game are you playing?"

I spread my hands to show him that I was innocent of whatever it was he suspected me of. "What is it with you telling me I smell? I took a shower this morning! As for the rest of what you said, I'm just trying to do my job."

"Which is to deliver what?"

I shrugged, unwilling to tell him. Despite his badge and claims to the contrary, I didn't know he *didn't* murder Mme. Deauxville. The intriguing air of danger that surrounded him certainly made it seem possible, not to mention all that double-talk about demons and their guardians. And then there was his obsession with smelling things . . ." It's just a small statue. Even if you're not a homicide cop, shouldn't you be, like, you know, examining the body and stuff?"

"I am questioning a suspect," he said, moving toward me. The calm part of my mind enjoyed watching how he walked, a sort of powerful glide, coiled strength implied, but not obvious in his fluid movements. "A statue of what? What is it made of?"

"Metal. It's of a creature, nothing special, nothing important," I lied.

His head lifted again, and I could have sworn he was scenting the air. "Gold. The statue is of gold."

I ran for the chair, just barely beating him to it. "You know what? I think I need to see your badge again. You're not doing this questioning thing right at all. You should be asking me my name and where I'm staying and whether I knew Mme. Deauxville and stuff like that, not babbling on about demons and why someone would use the Circle of Ashtaroth to summon one of the demon prince's legions, and what the small, insignificant statue I brought is made of."

"For someone who professes not to be a Guardian, you appear very learned in demon lore," he said in sort of a low growl that sent shivers of mingled thrill and fear down my spine. With a move that was too fast for me to follow, he grabbed my arm and hauled me up to his chest, one hand clamped behind me, the other grabbing my hair and pulling my head back. "Very well. We will play this game as you demand. What is your name?"

"Aisling," I said before I realized what I was doing. My body—traitor that it is—thoroughly enjoyed being smooshed up against him, fully aware of the long hard lines of his body. After several seconds of numbed bemusement, the sane side of my mind regained control. "Hey! What do you think you're doing? You can't manhandle me like this! Let me go!"

"You wished for me to ask questions—I am simply granting that wish. Where are you staying?"

"The Hôtel de la Femme Sans Tête. Let go of me!"

"Not yet. Did you know Mme. Deauxville?"

"No, I told you I was a courier. Stop holding me like this, it's not at all PC."

"PC?"

"Politically correct. Let me *go*."

His eyes narrowed on me. "A Guardian who claims she is not a Guardian, and yet who understands the steps needed to summon a demon. What a puzzle you present me. I believe it is a puzzle worth investigating." Instead of releasing me, he buried his head in my neck and drew in a deep breath.

"What on earth are you doing?" I shrieked, beginning

to struggle in earnest despite the urge to go all girly on him.

"Memorizing your scent."

"What?" I shrieked again, then realized that it wasn't just my own voice that was echoing around the room— police sirens outside the windows were growing steadily louder.

Drake pulled his face out of my neck just long enough to give me a look that left my knees weak. There was something different about his beautiful green eyes. The pupils were slightly elongated rather than round, almost like a cat's eye, but not quite as dramatic. It wasn't just his eyes, though. It was the way he touched me, the way he spoke, the way he . . . scented me. There was something not quite human about him that had my heart racing. I understood then what he meant about my fear of him—it was definitely sexually charged, but beneath that was a baser emotion—the fear of being consumed, destroyed by a being who was much more powerful than I.

With a gentle touch that belied the threat in his voice, he tucked a strand of hair behind my ear and said, "The police are here, Aisling; thus I must bid you adieu. I do not know for what purpose you are denying the truth, but I advise you to be a bit more circumspect with the French police. They are not known for their tolerance of those who dally with the dark powers."

He leaned forward and brushed his lips against mine, the warmth so quickly withdrawn that he was gone before I pulled my wits together.

"What? Hey! You can't kiss me! And what do you mean to be more circumspect? What dark powers? Where are you going—? No! Stop! That's mine!"

I lunged forward but was too late. Drake snatched up

my case and spun around, racing out the door of the apartment before I stumbled forward three steps.

Unfortunately, the three steps were directly into the circle. Instinctively I reached out to keep myself from careening into the body. What I grabbed, though, wasn't Mme. Deauxville. It was a silver object that I suspected had been plunged into her heart, an object I hadn't seen because of the way her body was hunched over. The cool metal slid easily out of her body as I staggered to the side, away from her. I stood staring at the weapon in my hand for one horrified moment. It was long, with a thick curved blade smeared almost to the hilt in blood. I recognized what it was from several of the texts I'd read on demon lore—it was a seax, a medieval single-bladed dagger that was commonly used in the ritual destruction of beings of a dark origin. This seax had a bone handle and appeared to be made of silver. It was said that only silver piercing a demon's heart could destroy it . . . when coupled with the twelve words, of course.

"A real live example of one of the Demon Deaths," I murmured, the reality of the decidedly unreal situation being driven home by the cold weight of the seax in my hand. I was just thinking about making a sketch of the arrangement of symbols so I could compare them with a book back home when noises in the hall had me gawking in surprise. A number of policemen pushed through the door, all talking at once. They stopped and looked at me in equal surprise, the look quickly turning to one of profound suspicion as they saw the dead woman next to me . . . and the bloody seax in my hand.

I sighed as I raised my hands in surrender, the police swarming forward to surround me. What was turning out to be the longest day of my life had just grown a whole lot longer.

3

"Hi. I'm Aisling Grey, in room twenty-three. Are there any messages for me?"

The hotel clerk on graveyard duty looked up from his magazine and gave me a martyred sigh before reluctantly setting down his *Paris Match* and hoisting his bulk out of the chair. "It will require me to check," he said, his voice rich with accusation.

I gave him a feeble smile as an apology. After spending the whole night explaining to the police over and over and over again who I was and what I was doing at Mme. Deauxville's apartment holding the deadly weapon that had been used to kill her, my "be a good American abroad" muscles were all worn out.

"Yes, there is one."

The clerk looked at me. I looked back at him. Neither one of us blinked. When the room started to swim, I decided to give in. "I'm sorry, it's six in the morning, but according to my internal clock, it's two in the afternoon, and I've just spent the last thirty-some hours without sleep, which means I'm more than a little bit fuzzy around the edges. Could you maybe get the message for me? So I could read it? If it isn't too much trouble?"

He sighed and shambled over to the old-fashioned wall of pigeonholes that served as the hotel's room directory, plucking a yellow message sheet from the square labeled 23. With an even bigger sigh, he gave it to me, then stood looking at me as if I were going to demand some other extraordinary act.

"Thank you," I said politely, and glanced at it. It was a message from Uncle Damian demanding that I check in and tell him how the delivery had gone. I crumpled up the note and turned toward the little elevator that the tiny but eccentric Hôtel de la Femme Sans Tête (which, I found out at the police station, means "hotel of the headless lady") boasted.

"The lift, it is not marching," the clerk called out after me, with, I couldn't help but notice, an immense amount of satisfaction. With five rooms on each floor, my room was on the fifth floor. My shoulders sagged a bit at the thought of dragging myself up five flights of stairs, but there was no help for it.

Ten minutes later I collapsed on my bed, having first rallied enough energy to kick off my sandals and peel from my body the dress that had been light and gauzy when I'd put it on, but was now just limp and blood-stained. I figured that being grilled nonstop by the police for more than twelve hours would have sent me immediately to sleep, but I ended up tossing and turning for a long time while the events of the day ran through my head like an annoying song refrain that refuses to stop.

"Oh, this is ridiculous. I'm so tired, I can't even see straight, and yet my mind won't shut up," I said, sitting up and clicking on the light next to the bed. I caught a glimpse of myself in the bathroom mirror visible through the open door—the skin around my eyes looked bruised; my hair, normally cute and curly, resembled brown straw sticking out of my head; and my skin could have doubled for the underbelly of a fish. A *sick* fish.

"Right, shower first, then coffee, lots and lots of coffee, followed by some exquisite French food, and then, after I've gathered my strength, I'll call Uncle Damian."

The pale face staring back at me in the mirror flinched at the words. The only way I could possibly imagine my day getting any worse was thinking about what my uncle would have to say to me.

"I take that back," I said out loud a moment later as I did a little spin, looking at every possible spot in the small room for a dark blue canvas bag. "Having my luggage stolen out of my room can make my day worse, too. Well, hell."

The bag was gone. The handful of change I'd thrown on the table before leaving for Mme. Deauxville's was still there, as was the airline magazine I'd filched for the article on fun things to see in Paris, so I knew I was in the correct room. But my bag of clothes and sundries? Gone, goner, gonest. The only things I had with me were my money, Rene's card, a small comb, my plane ticket, and my French phrasebook. The police had confiscated my passport, visa, and all the aquamanile documents. I couldn't leave the country, let alone go home.

A titter of semihysterical laughter burst from my lips. I thought seriously about just letting myself go and having a good old-fashioned nervous breakdown, but realized that once I started, I probably wouldn't be able to stop. Since I had no idea if the French loony bins were at all nice places, it was probably better if I skipped the whole breakdown thing and just stayed sane. "Shower," I told myself. "Sanity, shower, then food. And shopping. Cheap shopping. *Then* I'll call Uncle Damian."

My dress was still limp when I went downstairs an

hour later, but at least I was clean, my hair was combed, and I'd washed out the worst of the bloodstains. I followed my nose to the small room in the basement of the hotel where meals were served, stopping by the reception desk to inform the management that my bag had been stolen from my room.

The woman in charge didn't look very happy with me when I told her that, and I ended up wasting another twenty minutes by having to tramp up the five flights of stairs to accompany her while she examined the room for signs of a break-in.

"You must have left the door open when you left," she finally decided. "A stranger must have entered and taken your bag. The hotel is not at all liable for damages in such a situation."

I protested my innocence, but she had made up her mind, and I was too exhausted to argue with her. To be honest, I kind of wondered if the police hadn't taken it. They certainly had the time to sneak in and grab it while I was being questioned. "If someone turns my bag in, will you let me know? There's nothing valuable in it, it's just my clothes and cosmetics, but right now, they're all I have."

She sniffed and returned behind the smooth wooden desk that served as reception, giving me a disparaging eye. "There are many shops in the Rue des Mille Décès. You will wish to avail yourself of them before you return to the hotel, yes?"

I brushed at my still-damp dress and bared my teeth in what I fervently hoped was a grin. "Afraid I'll bring down the tone of the neighborhood? Yeah, I'm going shopping, don't worry. Later. After I have some breakfast."

I left her pursing her lips as if she'd like to refuse me

admittance to the dining room, but breakfast was included in the price of the room, so I trotted downstairs to a cheery whitewashed room that looked out over a petite little garden. I took a table in the corner and concentrated on consuming as much caffeine and food as one person could handle in a half hour.

By the time breakfast was finished, I'd come to several decisions. First, I wasn't going to call Uncle Damian. Not just yet. My stint in the police station had made it quite clear that although they did not have enough evidence to charge me, they considered me a suspect. Probably the *only* suspect because Drake had so conveniently skipped out.

I drew circles on the tablecloth with my spoon, my now-caffeinated mind going over the events of the evening one more time. A lot of the past twelve hours was a dulled blur, most of it consisting of me sitting around in a small, airless room waiting for a translator to show. Then Jean-Baptiste Proust, a small, balding man who was the head of the criminal investigation department arrived, and things began to happen. A call was put in to the American Embassy. My fingerprints were taken, as were samples of the blood on my dress. People asked me questions, some in English, some in French. I explained who I was, showed my passport and visa, and the invoice for the aquamanile.

"Where is this valuable artifact?" Inspector Proust asked in a softly accented voice. Everything about him was quiet, from his mild brown eyes to the neutral tones of his brown pants and jacket. I knew, however, that you don't get to be the head of a police unit without having a razor-sharp mind.

"It was stolen. Just before the police arrived."

Inspector Proust looked down at a notebook another

policeman had given him. "Ah, yes, by the man you claim was an agent of Interpol."

"I'm not claiming it; he is. He said he was an Interpol detective. He even showed me his badge, although I didn't get a good look at it. I was . . . uh . . . distracted." By the nonsense about demons, but I wasn't about to tell Inspector Proust that.

He looked at me with sad eyes. "You are aware, Mlle. Grey, that Interpol does not have detectives?"

I stared at him, my hands suddenly going clammy. "They don't?"

"No. Interpol is an organization dedicated to the sharing of information between countries only; they do not have a police force of their own."

He waited patiently to see what I would say. I didn't say anything but "Oh."

That's not all I was thinking, of course. My brain was whirring about madly, angry at Drake for stealing my dragon and fooling me, furious with myself for having ignored Uncle Damian's strictures about security. I see one dead body and what do I do? I throw away everything I know about safeguarding the aquamanile. Damn Drake. It was all his fault. Well . . . mostly his fault.

I didn't say any of that to Inspector Proust, though. I answered his questions, then the same questions asked by other members of his investigation team. Over and over again, I answered the questions, until I knew them so well, I started answering them before my interrogators had the chance to ask them.

But I never once told them that I had frogs in my bidet. I was oddly proud of that fact, too, which just goes to show you how deranged you can get when you don't have any sleep while being suspected of a murder you didn't commit. The truth is, I was certain that I was going to be tossed into some dark, dank, rat-infested jail cell and left to rot there until the U.S. Embassy was notified of the horrible events that had overtaken me, but to my surprise, twelve hours after I was taken to the police station, M. Proust strolled into the interview room and announced I was free to leave.

"Free?" I asked, blinking, my voice rough and hoarse from talking so long. I was a bit groggy from lack of sleep and food, but I didn't think I was quite to the point where I was hallucinating. Yet. "Free as in I can leave? Walk out of here? You're not charging me with murder?"

Inspector Proust made a sort of a half-shrug that I'd seen several times during the course of the night. Although he'd been awake the night through, as well, he didn't look as if he was the least bit troubled by lack of sleep. "You say you had nothing to do with Mme. Deauxville's death, so I have no grounds to charge you. Unless there is something else you'd like to tell me?"

I smiled at the question in his soft brown eyes. "I didn't kill her, honest. I don't know who did, unless Drake murdered her, and he says he didn't, but then, he lied to me about being an Interpol agent, and he stole my dragon, so how much of what he said can I really believe? Besides, he's too handsome. I don't trust handsome men like that. They think they're god's gift to women, and they go around grabbing you and kissing you and smelling really nice, and making your legs turn to mush when you're pulled up tight against them, not to mention filling your head with all sorts of really wicked thoughts about what you'd like to do to them with a small bowl of ice cream and your tongue. Well, not *your* tongue, my tongue. And speaking of that, just how did he know the aquamanile was gold?"

Inspector Proust watched me silently for a moment,

gently tapping a pencil against his chin. "François, my driver, will take you back to your hotel. I believe you are in need of sleep, Mlle. Grey. If you can think of anything else that would help us, you will please contact me at the number on the card."

I looked down at the white card that had somehow materialized in my hand. It was at that point that I realized I was not only babbling almost incoherently, but I truly was being released, as well. No ratty damp jail cell for me, woo-hoo!

"You'll let me know if you capture Drake, won't you? 'Cause my uncle is going to kill me if I don't recover that aquamanile. He's going to say it's my fault that Drake stole it, and that he'll have to reimburse Mme. Deauxville's family if I don't find it, and you know, I just honestly don't think I could ever make that much money, not with Alan—he's my ex-husband and a beach bum— leeching everything off me. So you'll tell me? If you find Drake? Or my dragon?"

A grim little smile played around Inspector Proust's lips. "You may rest assured, mademoiselle, if we meet up with a man calling himself Drake Vireo, I will notify you immediately."

"He didn't believe me," I said softly to myself as I sat in the sunny hotel dining room, the remains of eggs and croissants littering the plate before me. I checked the tiny coffeepot, poured the last bit of it into my cup, and tried to force my brain into some fruitful thinking. Two things were obvious—I had to clear my name with the police before they would let me have my passport, and I needed to find Drake and get my dragon back. Surely the American Embassy could help with the former.

"Step one, buy new clothes. Then go to the American Embassy and throw myself on their mercy." I looked in my neck pouch. The money I had left was meant to last only through that morning, no more. But I had my plane ticket. . . . Since Uncle Damian only used cash to buy such things, it meant I could cash the ticket in. That should keep me from starving. The hotel bill was another matter. I knew that Beth had paid for the first night with the company credit card—maybe I could just tell the hotel to bill the rest. It was worth a try. With the hotel and money for food and a change of clothes taken care of, I could concentrate on the two issues at hand—proving to the police that I wasn't guilty of anything other than having extremely bad luck, and getting the dragon back. I'd worry about how I would get home later.

"First things first," I said as I marched over to the lobby phone. I pulled out the grubby card Rene the taxi driver had given me and dialed the cell-phone number on it.

Ten minutes later, Rene pulled up opposite the hotel, a grin on his face that faded when he took in my rumpled, bloodstained dress. "You look as if you have just visited a foie gras factory. What has happened to you?"

"It's a long story, way too long to tell you here. Did you mean what you said? You'd be my driver for the morning for fifty euros? No limit on the number of stops and stuff?"

Rene got out of the car and opened the back door for me, his blue eyes narrowing as I fingered my neck pouch. "You will stay in Paris, yes? No drives to Marseilles or Cannes?"

I gave him a wry grin. "I don't know anyone in Marseilles or Cannes, whereas I know three people in Paris—you, a very bad man named Drake, and Inspector Proust of the criminal investigation department. I just have to hope that Drake hasn't left Paris."

"Inspector Proust?" Rene sputtered, but he didn't stop me as I climbed into his taxi. "You have had dealings with the police?"

"I said it was a long story. If we're go on the fifty euros for the morning, then would you please take me first to a nice but cheap shop so I can get out of this grungy dress? My bag was stolen, and I don't have anything else to wear. I promise I'll tell you all about yesterday while we're on the way."

He shot me a look that contained at least a dozen questions, but then got back into the car, flipping off the taxi meter. "I will take you to La Pomme Putréfiée. It is a shop run by the wife of my cousin. Berthilde will give you a special price."

"Special sounds good as long as it's cheap. Oh, before we go there, I need to swing by and cash in my plane ticket. Is that on the way?"

His dark gaze met mine in the mirror. "*Non*. But I will make it in our path. Now you will commence with your story. I am very much looking forward to hearing it."

By the time I'd cashed in my plane ticket (feeling a couple of twinges of guilt about that since I didn't pay for it in the first place) and visited the shop Rene recommended, I had made it through most of the story. The last bit was told as I stood in a curtained dressing room, trying on a couple of summer outfits, answering Rene's questions while I tried to decide between a very chic beige linen sleeveless tunic and matching pants, or a sexy 1930s-looking dress with big red poppies on it.

"What did Inspector Proust say when you told him about this man who stole your dragon?" Rene asked.

I parted the curtains and did a little twirl in front of where he sat waiting for me. "What do you think, too girly? I kind of like the poppies, but the other outfit is more sophisticated."

He did the Gallic shrug I'd seen earlier. "It is very nice, as well. Why do you not take both?"

I did a little mental arithmetic. The two outfits with accompanying underwear would eat up almost a quarter of my meager funds. Still, I was in Paris, buying authentic French clothes. . . . "What the heck, I'll just eat cheap for a few days. The answer to your question is nothing. Inspector Proust didn't seem to care anything about Drake. To be truthful"—I did a spin in front of the mirror, enjoying the way the dress flared out—"I don't think he believed me about Drake."

Rene didn't say anything. I turned back to him, my hands spread in front of me. "I'm telling the truth, Rene. I know it sounds fantastic, but it's the truth. You believe me, don't you?"

He stood slowly, waving to his cousin's wife, who was arranging a display in the shop window. "You do not have the air of a murderer. I believe you. But I am not the one you need to convince, eh? You must convince the inspector that you are telling the truth."

"Easier said than done. I don't know how to go about proving I *didn't* do something."

I waited while Rene spoke rapidly to Berthilde, who took the linen pantsuit and my stained dress, putting them both in a tote bag.

"It is difficult, yes, but there is no need for you to derange yourself. I will take you wherever you need to go, yes? And with me helping, we will solve this little problem of yours."

I paid Berthilde, thanked her, and stepped out into the sunny June morning. "I appreciate the help—I truly do—I'm just at a loss as to how to start proving that I'm innocent, and where to look for Drake."

Rene mused as we strolled down the street to where he'd parked his taxi. Paris on a sunny summer morning was a delight—if you discounted the blare of horns, the variety of music spilling from shops with doors flung wide open (no two shops seemed to have their radio tuned to the same station), and the air heavy with the smell of gasoline. Still, it was Paris, and even though I was having the worst time of my life, I was determined to embrace the City of Light.

"Me, I think in order to find out who killed Mme. Deauxville, you need to know who drew the magic circle on the floor. Once you find that person, you will prove to *monsieur l'inspecteur* that you did not do the crime."

I couldn't keep a little giggle from slipping out at the sly look Rene gave me. The lack of sleep was definitely making me silly. "This isn't some sort of mystery story, Rene. I'm not Buffy the Vampire Slayer. I'm not even Miss Marple. I'm just an extremely tired American who is probably this close to being sent to the guillotine for a murder she didn't commit. And even if I did manage to find out who killed Mme. Deauxville, my uncle will kill me for losing the aquamanile."

"Stop hitting your biscuit—we will figure it all out."

I blinked at him. (I seemed to be doing that quite a bit lately.) "Huh? Stop hitting my biscuit? What biscuit?"

His hands danced in the air as he tried to explain. "Yes, yes. Stop hitting your biscuit. Stop being angry at yourself because you cannot proceed."

"Oh. Stop beating my head against a wall?"

He made a face, pulling out his keys to unlock the car doors. "My expression is more elegant, but yes, the idea is the same. As for the situation with Mme. Deauxville and the man who stole your dragon, how do you know the two things are not related?"

I paused as he opened the door, staring at him as my tired brain hashed that idea over. "Drake said he didn't kill Mme. Deauxville. I know he lied about the other things, but he . . . he just didn't seem like a murderer. And besides, if he was, he could have killed me the second I walked into the apartment, and he didn't. But he *did* call the cops. That's definitely a point in his favor."

Rene patted my hand. "He might not have killed the old woman, but what was he doing there?"

"I don't know. I asked, but he evaded the question." My eyes opened wide as something occurred to me. Yeah, yeah, *you* probably thought of this hours ago, but hey! I'd been up all night. Cut me a little slack. "Do you think he drew the circle? He didn't act like he did. In fact, he questioned me about whether or not it was complete, just before he went off about demons being summoned by the circle."

"Demons? The circle was to attract demons? You mean the little devils?"

I got into the car. "Well . . . kind of. Technically demons are the servants of the demon lords, who are the main warriors of Hell, each responsible for varying numbers of legions. The legions are made up of demons, greater and lesser, all of whom are bound to their lords — servants, if you will, whom the demon lords can call, and who can be summoned by mortals who invoke the master's name. The demons themselves are an interesting group — according to my research, there are several different types of demons, each with specific abilities and levels of competence. One book I read claimed that not all demons were actually evil; some were simply misguided or mischievous."

Rene shot me another look over his shoulder as he slid behind the steering wheel.

I grinned. "It's my hobby. I study medieval demon texts. They're really interesting, and offer quite an insight into how the medieval mind dealt with the concepts of heaven and hell, but unlike Drake, I don't believe demons actually exist."

He made a relieved moue. "I am happy to hear so. I think, however, you have the answer to the question you asked earlier—how to find M. Drake the dragon thief. There is a strong occult society here in Paris. No doubt someone in it will have heard of him and will know how you can find him."

That made sense, but . . . "I have no idea if he's still in Paris or not. For all I know, he could have taken my dragon and run."

Rene shrugged again and yelled something that sounded like an obscenity out the window to a man on a bike who dashed in front of him. "It is, perhaps, the only lead you have, yes?"

"Yes," I agreed, feeling like I was a hundred years old. My whole body felt fragile, as if one touch would shatter me into a gazillion pieces. "It is the *only* lead I have. I really should go to the American Embassy, but I got the feeling from the police last night that they wouldn't be much help. I suppose I could call them later, after I chase down my nebulous lead. Any ideas on how I get in contact with the dark side of Paris?"

As it turns out, he did. We started out by visiting occult bookstores, but the people there didn't seem to know too much. We stopped for an early lunch (bread, cheese, and sliced ham from a small shop), then headed into the Latin Quarter, where Rene said he knew of a shop that catered to the witch trade.

A short while later I was negotiating my way down a street made dark by narrow alleys and tall buildings. The air smelled of spices and incense and something earthy that I couldn't pinpoint. Rene had dropped me off a block away, giving me directions to the shop before he dashed off to take care of a prearranged appointment.

"I will pick you up right here in an hour, yes?"

"Yes," I said. "And thanks, Rene. I'd be lost without you. Literally!"

"Just remember what I taught you to say if anyone annoys you," he said, wagging his finger at me.

I cleared my throat and tried on a little sneer that Rene said would go far. *"Pardonnez-moi, mais avez-vous un porc-epic coince entre les fesses?"*

He cackled and waved, one hand on the horn as he drove through the crowded streets.

"Yeah, right, like 'Excuse me, but do you have a porcupine wedged between your buttocks?' is going to save me from being cursed or whatever it is witches do." I looked at the directions on the slip of paper Rene gave me and started off down a dark little alley named Rue d'Ébullitions sur les Fesses de Diable, which Rene informed me with no little mirth was translated as "boils on the buttocks of the devil street."

Could my life get any stranger?

"Yes, yes it can," I said a few minutes later as I stepped into a surprisingly well-lit shop. After visiting all the dark, murky occult bookshops, shops that seemed to thrive on dirt and the merest hint of sunlight through grimy, unwashed windows, Le Grimoire Toxique ("The Poisonous Grimoire") was a pleasant change. Flowering plants lined window boxes beneath the shop's two (clean!) windows, and the inside was not only bright and cheery, but also smelled pleasantly of frankincense. The wall opposite the door was filled with the big glass jars I associate with old-time apothecary shops, each labeled with a violet tag. To the right were books and what looked like a large tarot-card section; to the left, a short, salt-and-pepper-haired woman was seated behind a long wooden counter, reading a paper and sipping coffee.

"Bonjour," I said, mindful of Rene's warning of common courtesies. *"Parlez-vous anglais?"*

The woman looked up. Her eyes were a pale, pale blue, the kind of blue you see on Siberian huskies. "Yes, I do, although I do not have much opportunity to speak it. You are American?"

"Yup."

"How delightful. I am Amelie Merllain."

I set my tote bag on the floor, reaching over to shake her hand. "Aisling Grey."

"I am most pleased to meet you. How can I help you?" A fat black Welsh corgi waddled over and started nosing in my bag. Amelie scolded her. "Cecile! That is very poor manners to show a visitor."

"Oh, that's OK," I said, pulling my bag out of the dog's reach. I set it on the counter, bending down to pat her, but the little beast snapped at me.

"Cecile!" Amelie pointed to a small maroon dog bed and ordered the dog to it. "My apologies. She is very elderly and feels that gives her the right to be surly."

"No problem. I was wondering if you would happen to know—"

"Tch," she interrupted, brushing at the counter where my clothes had spilled out of the tote bag. "Dragon scales. They get everywhere, no?"

I stared at her. With my mouth open. "I *beg* your pardon?"

"Dragon scales," she said a little louder, brushing

something off the counter. She tugged at my gauze dress that was peeking out of the bag, pulling it out and showing me the neckline. "Here, you see? Dragon scales. They are all over your dress."

I looked, my mouth unfortunately still hanging open. There was a slight iridescent powder on the left shoulder and neck of the dress. "Um . . . dragon scales?"

"Yes. You must have been with a dragon recently."

I blinked a couple of times, but you know, I think I'm going to give up on blinking as a turbocharger for my brain. It didn't seem to be working. "Dragons as in the big fire-breathing creatures with wings and an aversion to saints named George, *those* sorts of dragons?"

Amelie snorted and pushed my dress back into the bag. "Don't be ridiculous. What sort of dragon do you know who would walk about in his animal form? He would be captured immediately and put to those horrible tests the scientists so love."

"I don't know *any* dragons," I said hastily, wondering if Paris had become a city of lunatics. First demons and now dragons? Maybe my name was Alice and I had slipped into Wonderland without knowing it.

"If that is your dress, you most certainly do know at least one dragon," she said sharply, frowning at me. "Where is your portal?"

I started to blink, but decided to go for the suave look instead. I raised my eyebrows and leaned one hip against the counter. "My portal? What portal would that be?"

"The portal that you guard. You are a Guardian—it is not difficult what I ask. Where is your portal?"

"With the dragon?" I guessed.

Her frown deepened. "That is not at all wise. Dragons are not to be trusted when it concerns portals. Too much temptation, you understand. What sept is he from?"

"Who?" I asked, totally and completely lost at this point.

"The dragon whom you left guarding your portal. What is his name?"

I said the only name that came to mind, the name that had been on the tip of my tongue since I entered the shop. "Drake Vireo."

Her frown disappeared as her brows shot upward in a look of horror. "Drake Vireo? You left a wyvern in charge of your portal? Merciful goddess!"

The room spun. Seriously, the room started to spin right before my eyes. I clutched the counter and held my breath, but it didn't help.

"Do you have a chair?" I asked, sure I was going to faint.

She waved me around the long counter to where a second stool stood. "You are exhausted. Come, sit here."

I allowed her to pour me a cup of coffee, praying the caffeine would keep me sane until I could go back to the hotel room and collapse. Maybe the sleep deprivation was making me hallucinate? There was no other reasonable explanation for why I was in a city where people invoked demons and talked about dragon scales as casually as I would the weather.

"Thank you. No, black is good. Now, maybe we could take this slowly. I'm a little tired and not thinking very well. First off, do you know Drake Vireo?"

Amelie shook her head. "Not personally, although I have heard of him, of course. All the wyverns are known in our community."

"So he lives here?" Hope rose within me. All the creepy paranormal stuff aside, if she had heard of him, that meant he must be local.

She pursed her lips. "No, I believe the main lair of the

green dragons is in Hungary. But he is a frequent visitor to Paris, if that is what you are asking."

I stifled the nervous little giggle that wanted to come out. "This is probably going to sound really silly, but are you trying to tell me that Drake, Drake Vireo, about six foot two, dark hair, green eyes, gorgeous voice is a . . . well, a dragon?"

Amelie didn't smile as I expected. Instead, her eyes narrowed as she examined me. "Drake Vireo is not just a dragon. He is a wyvern. The green wyvern."

"Wait," I said, shaking my head and gripping the counter so I wouldn't fall over. "Isn't a wyvern another name for a two-legged dragon? One with wings and a barbed tail?"

"Yes," she said slowly, her blue eyes growing darker. "It is also the name for the leader of a dragon sept. His name explains that."

I rubbed my forehead. "You've lost me."

"Drake—a modernization of the Latin *draco*, meaning 'dragon.' *Vireo* is also Latin. It means 'green.' Only wyverns are allowed to use their sept color as a name."

"Can we go back to the part about Drake being a mythical creature who breaths fire and consumes virgins and all that? Because I just can't seem to wrap my brain around that idea. He was . . . He was so masculine. Gorgeous. Sexy as hell. He didn't look at all like a big scaly lizard wearing a human suit."

"Immortals do not need to wear human suits. They can change form," she said a bit scornfully, then suddenly leaned forward and placed both hands on my head, her fingers touching my temples. I was too tired to be alarmed, too exhausted to be scared. Besides, her touch wasn't unpleasant. She hummed a soft little song, her fingers gently stroking my temples.

"You do not understand of what I speak, and yet I feel in you great power, great possibilities," she said dreamily, her eyes closed as she continued to stroke my head. "You are untouched by the dark powers, and yet you were born to harness them. You are a wyvern's mate, and yet he did not claim you. You are a puzzle that has no end and no beginning."

"Whoa," I said, my muscles all stiffening at the words "wyvern's mate." "Let's just take a step back from that idea, shall we?"

She released my head and moved over to the stool, her brows pulled together in a puzzled frown.

"Look, all I want to know is where I can find Drake. He stole something from me."

She nodded. "The green dragons are thieves. That is their skill. He is their wyvern—he would naturally be a very talented thief. And you know how it is with dragons."

I raised my eyebrows.

"They hoard treasure." A faint smile curled her lips.

"Um . . . I think I'm just going to let that one go. Do you know where Drake lives?"

"No."

My shoulders slumped.

"But I know where you can find him most evenings."

I sat up straight. "Where?"

"The same place you can find anyone of consequence— G & T. It is a club on Rue de la Grande Pest—'the street of the great plague.'"

"Sounds like a lovely neighborhood. G & T . . . gin and tonic?"

"Goety and theurgy," she answered. ("Black and white magic." How fitting.)

"Thanks for the coffee. And the information," I said as

I gathered up my things, knowing I was close to the end of my energy . . . and my sanity.

She watched me walk all the way down the length of the counter to the door before she spoke up. "Aisling, a word of warning from one who wishes you well."

I cocked an eyebrow at her. Anything more would have taken too much energy.

"Do not close your mind to the possibilities. To do so will not only deny you your rightful place in this world, but it can also mean great destruction to those you love."

I glanced out through the open door to the street outside filled with sunshine and happy, dragon-free Parisians. "Don't tell me—the fate of the whole world rests on my shoulders?"

"Perhaps," was all she said.

I looked back at her, summoning up the last of my strength for a smile. "Thanks, but I've got enough on my plate right now without worrying about a bunch of stuff that doesn't even come close to being real. Maybe I'll see you again some time."

"Of that, you can be sure," she said. "I would not wish to miss your entrance into the Otherworld."

I went out into the warm sunny street without saying anything else. There was just nothing left to say.

4

"And then I said to her, Rachel, you're out of your ever-lovin' mind. There's no way in *h-e*-double-tooth-picks you'd find *me* hookin' up with a faery, especially one of the unseelie court, no matter how well hung he is. Ya just never know with them, do ya? I heard about a witch in Quebec who crossed one of the unseelie princes, and she ended up with three breasts. Can you imagine what she goes through trying to find a bra that fits?"

I paused, surprised not by the words—I'd had the whole day to come to grips with the fact that everyone in Paris was evidently either on drugs or suffering from mass hypnosis (I couldn't quite face the alternative)—but by the Texas drawl that spoke them. Soft, rather eerie music pulsed with an almost palpable beat through the club, music as smoky as the air that surrounded me. I peered through the depths to the bar, a long U-shaped wooden structure that sat in the center of the room. Nearest me a perfectly normal-looking woman in jeans and a T-shirt was chatting with a tall blonde in a slinky black dress. Neither one of them looked crazy, despite the subject of their conversation. I dragged my eyes back to the waitress as she headed over to a small table in the far corner of the room, taking a moment to give the room a sweeping glance as I followed. What I saw shocked me—everyone looked so normal! There weren't any odd creatures lurking about or people wearing pointy witch's hats and leaning over crystal balls. No tarot cards, no rune stones, no cauldrons or crystals or pentagrams. Not even one magic wand was in evidence. Without realizing I had been so tense, I felt the muscles in my shoulders relax. I don't know quite what I expected from the Goety and Theurgy club, but it *wasn't* normalcy. Dark, smoky dance clubs, however—oh yes, those I knew.

"Thanks," I said to the waitress as she waved toward a table and shoved a small menu in my hands.

"You will please to read the rules. English is on the behind," she said in a heavy French accent.

"Rules? Oh, like the cover charge and stuff? Sure." I flipped the menu over, and the sane world I so desperately clung to quickly took a nosedive.

G & T IS A NEUTRAL GROUND. PLEASE FOLLOW THE RULES:

1. No summoning minions of any form, persuasion, or origin.
2. No wards are to be drawn within the club, either protective or otherwise.
3. Glamours are strictly prohibited. No exceptions will be allowed.
4. Patrons who squash imps will please scrape up the mess and deposit the remains in the imp bucket.

BEINGS AND ENTITIES WHO DISREGARD THE RULES WILL BE SUMMARILY DEALT WITH BY THE VENEDIGER.

"Ooookay," I said, wondering for the millionth time that day when life would return to my previously scheduled program. I glanced up at the waitress. She was clearly waiting for something. "Er . . . I agree?"

That was evidently it, because she nodded and headed toward the bar.

I sat back, leaning against the chair as I took a few deep breaths, struggling to come to grips with some very profound thoughts. Amelie was right. What I thought was unreal had turned out to be very real. Even six hours of sleep back at my hotel hadn't been able to wipe away the knowledge that Something Had Changed. Whether it was me or the world, I didn't know, and at that moment, I didn't care. All I knew is that I had been sucked into a weird version of Wonderland, but that didn't mean I couldn't hold my own. So demons were real, and dragons looked like handsome men with scrumptious bodies and droolworthy voices, and faeries had mammary fetishes. So what? I was still me, and I was a professional. "I am confident. I am self-assured. I am in control—"

"Are you? How very nice for you. I've never been in control. I've found the world is just so much nicer if you let it go by without bothering too much about it."

A young woman with masses of waist-length curly blond hair stopped in front of me, her blue eyes twinkling with delight. "Did I startle you? I'm so sorry. I didn't mean to, but I heard you speaking English, you see, and it's rare we see Americans in G & T, let alone American Guardians, so I thought I would say hullo. Hullo!"

"Hi," I said. "Er . . . you're English?"

"Yes, Welsh actually, although I can't speak the language. May I?" She gestured toward the chair opposite me.

"Sorry, please do."

She sat, arranging her diaphanous sea-green skirt carefully around her as she smiled a nice, normal, pleasant smile. I couldn't help but wonder what she was . . . wood nymph? Water sprite? Sacrificial virgin?

"My name is Ophelia. Now, don't laugh, Mum was a Shakespearean scholar."

I smiled in return, relaxing. She couldn't be anything *unnatural*. She was too nice. "I think Ophelia is a pretty name. I'm Aisling."

"Hullo, Aisling. As for the name, it could be worse— my sister is named Perdita. That's her over there, talking to the Venediger. You look a bit lost. Is this your first time?"

"In France, in Paris, and in this club, yes," I said with a nervous laugh. "Does it show?"

"Only when you smile," she answered. "Well, what can I tell you about G and T? You've read the rules, so you know that this is a neutral ground. Practicers of both the light and dark powers are welcome here because everyone agrees to put their differences aside while in the club. It really is a pleasant place, although you have to watch out for the satyrs after they've had a few drinks. They get a bit grabby."

"Grabby?" I asked, making a silent promise to myself right then and there. No matter what weird things people said to me, no matter how many fantastical concepts were thrown my way, I would be calm and professional. I wouldn't gawk, I wouldn't stare, I wouldn't freak. Brazen it out, that was going to be my motto. Later, when I had time to sort through things, no doubt everything would become clear.

Yeah, like *that's* going to happen.

Ophelia wiggled her hands in a recognizable boob-grabbing motion. "Grabby. Other than them, the rest of the regular crowd are fairly well behaved. We have to be—the Venediger wouldn't allow any breach of the rules."

"The Venediger? Uh . . ." Already I was regretting my promise to play it cool, but I was in too deep to go back to being clueless.

"You really are new, aren't you? The Venediger is the most powerful mage in France. He's a tyrant, really. It's not right one man having so much power, but there's not much any of us can do about it. The word *Venediger* is actually German—I think it means 'man from Venice,' not that Albert is Venetian, but he clings to the old ways. Albert Camus is his name, although most of us just call him the Venediger. So much easier to remember, you see."

I didn't see, but I'd just sworn to brazen this through. I was sure that later there would be time to have that quiet nervous breakdown I had contemplated earlier.

Ophelia evidently saw my confusion, because she gave me a sympathetic pat on the shoulder. "Just remember that he's the one person in all of France with enough power to keep everyone in line. You do not want to cross him."

That sounded more than a little ominous. I looked curiously at the man standing next to the woman she pointed out as her sister. He was dressed in a long navy frock coat with matching pants and a beautifully embroidered gold vest. It was a strangely elegant, very old-world ensemble. He was middle aged, probably early to mid-fifties, going bald with his shoulder-length black hair caught back in a ponytail. He looked polished and moderately narcissistic, but certainly not like the most powerful mage in France.

I didn't blink over the thought of a real mage, either, which says a lot about how well I was brazening. That or

I was completely insane and totally out of touch with reality . . .

"So, where is your portal?"

"Oh. Um. Well, I'm portal-less." Her eyes opened wide in stark surprise. "For the moment," I added quickly, not wanting her to think me careless. Where exactly did these portals lead to? And did I really want to know?

Her eyebrows resumed their previous position. "Closed it, did you? You must be a very powerful Guardian if you can close a portal to Abaddon."

"Actually, I'm not really a—"

"Well, *that* was interesting. Feelie, you're not going to believe what the V told me about that imp outbreak in Versailles." A woman who was clearly Ophelia's identical twin (but with shorter hair) grabbed a nearby chair and swung it around to our table, setting her glass of white wine down and flashing me a bright smile. "Hello, I'm Perdita. You're a Guardian? Pleased to meet you."

"This is Aisling, Perdy. She's American, and she closed up a portal."

Perdita looked over the rim of her wineglass with frank astonishment. "You didn't! Goddess above! I don't think we've ever met a Guardian of your sort of caliber."

"Oh, I can just about guarantee you that," I said with a laugh, and would have cleared up the misunderstanding (just what *was* a Guardian?) but at that moment a tall, handsome, green-eyed dragon-snatching . . . er . . . dragon walked into the club. I stood up, waving away the waitress who came over to take my order. "Oh, he is going to be *so* sorry he ever tangled with me!"

"Who?" both Ophelia and Perdita asked, craning their heads to see who I was glaring at.

"A very nasty man with light fingers," I growled, grabbing the handbag I had purchased after my long nap. "His name is Drake Vireo."

Perdita started to stand up, but gave a yelp at my words, hurriedly sitting back down.

"Drake?" Ophelia asked, her eyes huge. Both sisters grabbed my arm as I started past them. "Goddess help you!"

Perdita tugged at my sleeve. "Aisling, you don't want to mess with him. He's bad news, very bad news. He's the green dragon's wyvern, you know."

"I know," I said, giving them both a smile. It was nice to feel that someone was in my corner . . . whatever that would end up being. "But he doesn't scare me. Much."

"But . . ." Perdita glanced at Ophelia, then back to me, her voice a hushed whisper. "What do you want with him?"

"He stole something of mine," I answered. The sisters just stared at me. I remembered what Amelie had said about the green dragons being thieves. Evidently no one was surprised by the news that Drake had robbed me. I straightened my shoulders, patted Perdita's hand until she released my sleeve, and said, "Don't worry—I'm not going to do anything stupid. I'm just going to make him give it back."

I thought their eyes were going to bug right out of their heads as I stormed off to the far curve of the bar, where Drake stood with his back to me as he chatted with two redheaded men.

"Well, if it isn't Puff the Magic Dragon," I said to Drake's back. I didn't speak loudly, but the second the words left my mouth, a hush fell over the entire club. Even the music stopped, as if by magic.

And what a discomforting thought *that* was.

Drake's shoulders stiffened at my words. He slowly

turned around, his eyes shining with a brilliant green light in the smoky darkness of the club. Figuring a best defense was a strong offense, and not wanting to admit that all of a sudden everyone's warnings about wyverns were scaring the bejesus out of me, I took a step forward and poked him in the chest. "You have something of mine, Drake. I want it back. *Now."*

"Aisling." His voice was just as wonderful as I remembered it, deep and rich, and as soft as velvet brushing against my skin. I shivered at the undiluted effect of it at close range. "I had not expected to see you here."

I pulled myself together enough to give him a disgusted snort. "I'm sure you didn't. I want my aquamanile back."

His eyes narrowed. His nostrils flared. The air of danger that surrounded him—so palpable, I could almost touch it—thickened. The people surrounding us surreptitiously moved back several paces as if they were expecting trouble. I wished I could join them. I felt as if it were high noon, and I'd just stepped into the main street of Tombstone, my trusty six-shooter at my side.

His voice swept over me again, deep with warning. "You are a very good actress. I actually believed your act earlier. I shall not make that mistake again."

I lifted my chin, my insides quaking. I was about to pick a fight I knew I couldn't win. Sometimes I truly am an idiot. "It wasn't an act. I've had a very informative day. I've learned about dragons and Guardians and imps and faeries, but all that is irrelevant. I want my dragon back, Drake. We both know you have it. So, for that matter, do the police. If you don't want me to call them up and tell them where to find you, you'll give it back to me."

A smile flirted with his lips. Dangerous lips, I reminded myself as my heart started beating faster. He might be a dragon, he might be someone whose name instilled fear in other people, but boy howdy, he sure turned my crank. "Are you by any chance threatening me?"

I lifted my chin even higher. "Only if you intend on making things hard."

His gaze raked me as he took in the pretty poppy dress. "*Things* are already hard, sweetheart."

My knees almost melted at the double entendre, but I stiffened them and reminded my libido that he was a thief who had cruelly stolen my aquamanile and left me at the mercy of the gendarmes. "I doubt you're going to die from hauling a little wood," I said, purposefully misinterpreting his statement. "Let's stick to the point, shall we? You have my dragon. I want it back."

"I am immortal, Aisling—I cannot die. You, however, are refreshingly mortal." As he spoke, his fingers slid around my neck until his hand was gripping me in a hold that was borderline strangling.

The silence in the club was so thick, you could have cut it with a piece of toast.

"You can huff and puff and breathe fire on me all you want, Drake," I said, my voice hoarse as his fingers slowly squeezed the air from my windpipe. I kept my chin up, my gaze firmly on his. "I'm not going to back down. I am not afraid of you."

"No? We shall see about that, shall we?" He moved closer, and every nerve in my body screamed a warning, but I just stood there as he pulled me to him, his arms hard as steel behind me, his mouth swooping down to claim mine. One part of my mind protested the fact that he was kissing me in full sight of everyone in the bar; the other part felt a moment of fear flare to life as I understood the true relationship between a dragon and his fire.

Heat burst through me the second his lips touched mine, the flames of his desire scorching me, licking along my skin until it started infernos within me. Pinpricks of sweat formed along my brow and spine as his fever consumed us, wrapping me in a searing cocoon of fire that stripped the air from my lungs. His tongue touched mine, and the heat that swept through me started to boil my blood. My flesh caught fire. Smoke from my body and the incandescent shimmer in the green eyes before me obscured my vision. I was dying, burning from the inside out, Drake's fire setting every atom within me alight.

Just as I knew I was literally going to burst into flames, something miraculous happened. A door within my mind opened, a door I didn't know was there, one tucked away in the dark recesses of my consciousness. The door opened, and suddenly I had leashed the fire, controlled it, changed it from a destructive element that was meant to consume me into something that added fuel to the desire that flared between us. I turned the fire back on Drake and began to kiss him in return, reveling in the power that was flowing through me as if I were a conduit. He jerked but didn't stop the torturously wonderful touch of his mouth.

Everyone was still watching us, I knew, but that didn't stop me from leaning into Drake and rubbing my hips against him, fitting all my soft curves to the hard planes of his body. I wanted him, all of him, his fire and his body and his soul, right then and there, and I hate to imagine what would have happened if Drake hadn't had the strength of purpose to pull back from me. Unable to look away—let alone *think*—I stared into his eyes, seeing the flickers of our shared fire in their emerald depths mingled with something that looked very much like surprise, surprise that quickly changed into speculation. Slowly, atom by atom, the fire he'd started within me dropped down to a simmer.

"I believe that round goes to you," he said softly, his voice thrumming through me, threatening to stir the newly banked embers.

I untangled my fingers from his hair and took a step backwards, extremely aware of the voyeurism that I had paid no mind a moment ago. "Yeah, well, maybe you'll think twice about messing with me again," I said with bravado I didn't feel, gritting my teeth over the shakiness of my voice.

The man Ophelia had named the Venediger appeared at my elbow. I turned to face him, grateful to have someone else to concentrate on. He didn't look at all the tyrant sort, as the sisters claimed, nor particularly powerful. Self-assured and confident, yes, but a tyrant? Hardly.

"Drake, you will do me the honor of introducing me to your companion."

It wasn't a question; it was a command. And with it a wave of his power washed over me, making me gasp for air. Maybe *tyrant* wasn't such a bad description after all. As I caught my breath, I couldn't help but notice that with his words, life in the G & T returned to normal. The music resumed. People started talking again. Waitresses floated through the crowd with trays of drinks and food. The wave of people swelled around us again, leaving us an island of three.

"Aisling Grey, may I present Albert Camus, better known to the immortal community as the Venediger. Aisling is newly arrived in Paris."

The Venediger made an odd sort of formal bow over the hand I reluctantly held out. "I bid you welcome. It is a distinct pleasure to meet you, Aisling. It is not often my humble premises are graced by a wyvern's mate, especially not one who is also a Guardian."

"Do I have a great big *G* painted on my forehead or something?" I asked, rather peevishly, true, but I really had been through a lot in the last twenty-four hours. "I don't even know what a Guardian does, let alone why you people think I'm one, but this I do know—I am not anyone's mate, *especially* not Drake's, so you can just get that idea right out of your head."

"You withstood the dragon's kiss," the Venediger said mildly, but as his pale gray eyes settled on me, I squirmed uncomfortably. An aura of power surrounded him, a leashed power not unlike what I felt with Drake, only the Venediger's was . . . *harsher.* Less refined. Crueler and much, much more scary. "Only a mate could do that. It is clear to everyone what you are."

"I'm glad someone thinks they know what's going on, because I sure don't," I grumbled.

He made another little bow. "As I said, you are welcome at Goety and Theurgy. I am in your debt for providing my patrons with such an entertaining show. It has been a very long time since we've had the opportunity of seeing a wyvern claim his mate."

I blushed at his reference to our little smoochy session, but didn't have time to set him straight before he moved off.

"I am *so* not claimed. I'm not a mate, either," I called after him. He ignored me. I turned back to Drake, dreading the look of mocking assuredness that I knew I would see in his eyes. A man like him—one who knows he's drop-dead sexy—couldn't help but gloat over the fact that he had really rattled my chain.

I gritted my teeth and raised my eyes to his, but he was looking at me with a puzzled expression that was 100 percent gloat-free. His brows pulled together in a little frown. "You are telling the truth. You truly do not understand who you are."

"On the contrary, I know exactly who I am. It's you guys who seem to be confused. In case you need it spelled out to you, I'm a robbery victim. I am also a murder suspect, thanks to you. Since you are responsible for both situations, you're going to fix things, starting with returning my dragon."

He turned toward the bar and signaled the bartender. "What will you have to drink?"

"Dragon's blood," I snapped vindictively.

He tipped his head as he considered me, his slow smile turning my legs to mush. "Really? Guy, two Dragon's Bloods."

I stared openmouthed as the bartender returned with two wine glasses filled with a liquid so dark red, it was almost black. "You're kidding, right? That's not really . . . er . . . blood?"

"No. It's a beverage favored by my kind, however."

I sniffed at the glass. It didn't smell like anything other than spiced wine. I took a small sip, gasping as liquid flames burned down my throat, quickly warming my stomach, the heat from the wine flowing out through my veins to every point in my body. "Holy cow," I croaked, blinking back the tears that formed. "That's potent. What's in it?"

"You don't want to know," he said, grasping my elbow and steering me to an empty table in a dark corner. "Now, perhaps we can discuss what you desire of me."

I sat, aware of a distinct sense of loss when he removed his hand from my arm. To distract myself from the unwanted temptation he posed, I lifted my glass again, this time just dipping the tip of my tongue into the liquid.

"Oh, great, now my tongue's gone numb. If I find out this has something harmful in it, you're going to be history."

He grinned. "Nothing harmful."

I relaxed and took another sip, braced for the roar of fire that flooded my body.

"Not to dragons, that is. I've never heard of a mortal drinking it and surviving."

The fire from the drink seeped into my blood, pooling low, in my groin. "You know, it's not so bad this time. Maybe I'm getting used . . . *What do you mean no mortal has survived drinking it?*"

He shrugged. "Just what I said."

I set the glass down carefully. (I had a notion that if it splashed over onto the table, it would eat right through the wood.) "Do you mean to tell me that you let me drink something poisonous and you didn't bother to warn me?"

"You asked for it. It would have been rude of me to deny you what you wanted."

"Yeah? And if I asked you to help me jump off the Eiffel Tower, would you do it?"

He did the cute head tip again. I gritted my teeth and fought the desire to grab his head and kiss him. "Are you likely to ask me to help you jump off the Eiffel Tower?"

"No, but—"

"Then it does not matter what I would do. Why have you sought me out?"

I breathed heavily through my nose for a few seconds, trying to get a grip on the anger and lust and frustration that were all mixed up inside me. "I. Want. My. Dragon. Back."

"It's not yours, though, is it? You told me you were just the courier, delivering it to Mme. Deauxville. She is the rightful owner. What right do you have to it?"

"More than you have!" I snapped. "I want it so I can return it to her family. God only knows why you want it."

He sipped at his drink. "It's pretty. I like it. It's mine now. Besides which, it is the Anima di Lucifer. I cannot relinquish it to anyone who does not appreciate its true history."

I frowned. "The *what* of Lucifer?"

"*Anima.* It's Italian. The name means the 'blood of Lucifer.' The aquamanile is one of three objects known as the Tools of Bael."

That could mean anything or nothing—the folks during the Middle Ages were awfully fond of giving impressive, dread names to innocent objects in order to increase the perceived value of the object. I had a sudden, awful thought. "It's not . . . uh . . . a family relic, is it?"

He raised his eyebrows.

"It has green eyes, like you. I thought maybe it was a family heirloom that someone sold and . . . Oh, never mind." I felt stupid even saying it, noting in a distant part of my mind how far I'd come since the morning before when I had no idea that such things as dragons really existed.

Drake leaned back in his chair, his fingers rubbing along the top of his wineglass. It was a strangely erotic move that had me squirming in my chair. I took another sip of my drink, embracing the fire that roared through me.

"What do you know about dragons?"

"They're big, scaly, four-legged creatures with wings who terrorized small villages until a virgin was offered up as a sacrifice."

His grinned again. "I do miss the virgins."

I had an almost overwhelming urge to kick him.

His grin deepened, but there was something serious in

his eyes, another warning. "The most important thing you should know about dragons is that they protect what is theirs. A dragon would never, under any condition, part with any of his treasure."

"*Never* is an awfully uncompromising word," I said, my heart sinking. I knew it was going to be hard getting the aquamanile from Drake, but the look in his eye told me it was going to be harder than I thought.

"Not as uncompromising as I," he said, his eyes dancing with silent laughter.

I took a deep breath to lessen my almost overwhelming desire to punch him in his obstinate but sexy jaw. "While we're on the subject of pigheaded men . . . dragons . . . whatever you are, let's have a little discussion about what you were doing at Mme. Deauxville's house. I know that story about you being with Interpol was a bunch of bull, so don't even bother trotting that out again."

"I was with Interpol—for a bit. They seemed to take exception to the fact that I was using their resources to organize my rare-arts acquisition program." I stared a question at him. He waved it away as if it were no matter. "They couldn't prove the charges, but once you have been tarred with the brush of international thievery, it is hard to regain their trust."

"That goes without saying. Did you draw the Circle of Ashtaroth?"

"Why would I want to do that?" he asked, neatly avoiding the question. "What did the police say to you?"

I smiled. I was on to him now. He used provocative questions to distract me whenever I wanted information from him, but two could play that game. "Not much. Did you draw the circle?"

His eyes darkened. "If I did not know whether it was

open or closed, is it likely I drew it? What happened to the demon that was summoned by the circle?"

I ground away a few more layers of tooth enamel over his nonanswers. "I have no idea. Despite studying a few medieval manuscripts on the subject, I'm hardly a demon expert."

"You are a Guardian, even if you are untrained. It is in your nature to control demons. Surely you could feel that one had been present on the scene?"

I remembered the feeling of dread, that something was very wrong as I approached Mme. Deauxville's door. "Maybe," I said, determined not to be distracted by his questions. "If you didn't draw the circle, who did?"

His gaze flickered away from me. "What makes you think I would know that?"

"Call it a hunch. Do you know who drew the circle?"

He shrugged and sipped his wine.

"Look, I know you're all hot on this big, bad, power-ful dragon kick, but this is important. The police think I killed Mme. Deauxville, but they can't hold me, because they don't have any proof that I did, and I don't have the time to wait around until they realize that I'm not guilty. I have to figure out who did kill her so I can get my pass-port back and go home. So would you stop playing the macho games and answer my question? *Please?*"

"I do not see the advantage to me to give you what you want. Perhaps if you had something to barter for the in-formation, I might be willing to give it to you."

I clamped my teeth together to keep from calling him every name I could think of. "I had a valuable antiquity, but you stole that."

"Yes," he said calmly. "What else do you have?"

His gaze caressed the low neckline of my dress, where the upper slopes of my breasts swelled above it. I ground my teeth some more, the sane part of my brain not wanting to make the bargain he was hinting at, but not seeing any other choice. We won't go into what the insane part wanted. "I have me."

His eyes shifted to my breasts, blatantly ogling me now. Despite the embarrassment of having to offer myself as a barter, my breasts tightened at the thought of what it would be like to have his hands on them. Or his mouth.

"That is true," he said in a sexy drawl rich with innuendo. "However, I am not sure that what you offer is worth the price you ask."

Fury rose within me, fury like nothing I've felt before. It was all I could do to keep from throwing the remains of my drink in his face. "You arrogant, conceited, egotistical, presumptuous—"

His eyes glittered dangerously as he leaned forward, stopping my words with the warning in his glance. "You really do not have the slightest idea of who I am, do you?"

I leaned forward as well, until we were almost nose to nose. I made the meanest eyes possible at him. "I know you're a nasty little thief who stole my dragon."

Anger roared to life in his eyes. I swear a faint curl of smoke drifted out of his left nostril. "Mate or not, you go too far, Aisling."

I stood up, took a big swig of the Dragon's Blood, allowing its fire to give me the strength to walk away from the man I wanted simultaneously wanted to throttle and kiss. "Fine. Be that way. You know, of course, that I'm going to do whatever it takes to get my aquamanile back."

He inclined his head in acknowledgment. "You are free to try."

I gave him a sharp nod in return and started to leave.

"Aisling," he said, stopping me as his voice caressed my flesh. I shivered again, rubbing the goose bumps on my arms away as I turned back to look at him. He was so handsome, so damned handsome sitting there that it almost took my breath away. "You do understand that when I say that I will protect what is mine, I mean everything, not just treasure."

Oh, yes, his meaning was crystal clear. Various parts of my body wanted to celebrate the look of possession in his beautiful eyes, but I am made of sterner stuff. I lifted my chin and gave him as disdainful a look as I could muster, turning on my heel as I said, "In your dreams, dragon boy!"

5

I thought of storming out of the bar on the exit line to end all exit lines, but I caught sight of Ophelia and Perdita on the opposite side of the room and decided I could use a little advice. As I started toward them, I noticed a strange phenomenon—rather than having to push my way through the dense throng of people as I had when I went over to Drake, the crowd parted before me. It was almost as if they were intimidated by me, afraid of me, moving respectfully out of my way.

It was also as if no one wanted to touch me.

I plastered a friendly smile on my face and kept it there while the Red Sea of club-hoppers parted before me.

"So, who's game for a drink?" I asked as I stopped next to Ophelia and Perdita. The two women looked at me like I had an extra head. "I know I sure could use one."

I plopped down in my chair and gave both sisters a bright smile. Ophelia glanced at Perdita. Perdita blinked at me.

"What?" I asked, wondering if I had something hanging out of my nose or an equally embarrassing affliction.

"You didn't tell us you were also a wyvern's mate. I heard that the dragons were . . . you know, different. Down there. So different that they hurt women when they do it. But you're his mate, and you don't look like you've suffered," Perdita finally said, her voice just barely above a whisper. I leaned forward to hear her over the low throb of music. Both women jumped backwards in their chairs.

I sat back in mine, feeling more than a little hurt by their reaction. Damn Drake and his show-off kiss. The first normal people I meet, and he makes them think I'm a freak. I caught the waitress's eye as I said, "I'm *not* a wyvern's mate. All that is nonsense. As for the other stuff, I wouldn't know, although Drake looks pretty normal to me, if brooding, sexy, makes-you-want-to-drool guys are what you call normal. Hi. Can I have another one of those Dragon's Blood drinks? Thanks. As I was saying, Drake is having a bit of fun at my expense, nothing more." OK, OK, I didn't quite believe all that—the kiss we shared had something other than just attraction going for it, but I needed time and quiet to think about what happened. Until I figured it all out, denial was going to be my best friend.

The sisters watched with pursed lips as the waitress hurried back with a glass of the fiery wine. I savored a sip of it, rolling it around in my mouth, wondering what sort of spices were used to give the wine such heat. I had to admit that I was growing to enjoy the flash fire that blasted through me with each sip.

"Are you sure?" Ophelia asked, doubt clearly evident in her eyes. "It looked to us as if Drake had given you his fire, and you withstood it. Only a mate would survive such a test."

"Well, I'll be the first person to admit that he's proba-bly the champion kisser of all Europe, but just because we have a little attraction thing going on, doesn't mean that I'm a dragonette. Now, what I want to know is how you can defeat a dragon."

Both ladies blinked in surprise at me.

"Defeat—," Ophelia squeaked.

"—a dragon?" Perdita finished.

I nodded.

"Defeat Drake?" they said together.

I glanced over Ophelia's shoulder and across the room to where I could see Drake still sitting at the table I had left. The two red-haired men had rejoined him, one of them speaking avidly, his hands waving in the air as he emphasized some point. Drake was watching me, his expression unreadable at this distance, but I did see as he lifted his glass in a silent toast. I lifted my own, draining the contents in a brazen show of defiance.

"Hooooaaaaah," I gasped, clutching my neck when the almost full contents of the glass set fire to every molecule in my body. Tears streamed down my face as I struggled to put out the inferno within me, and it wasn't until I opened that magical door in my mind that I gained enough control over the internal blaze to allow air to enter my lungs again.

"OK, that was stupid," I wheezed, wiping tears off my cheeks. Ophelia and Perdita sat silently staring at me, their own glasses stopped halfway up to their mouths, their eyes huge.

I glanced beyond Ophelia to Drake to see if he noticed my unfortunate reaction. He was smiling. Damn. I looked back to my tablemates. "Hoo! Has a bit of a kick, that drink does. Where were we? Oh, yeah, you guys were going to tell me how to best a dragon."

Perdita set her glass of wine down. "We were? Aisling . . ." She glanced to her sister.

Ophelia's gaze slid off my face as I looked at her, too. "What Perdita is trying to say is that we don't know how to defeat a dragon."

"You don't? Rats. I was hoping you'd help me. Drake has a small statue that he stole from me, and I really need to get it back. I'd be happy to pay for any help," I hinted broadly.

Both women were shaking their heads before I had finished speaking. "It's not that we wouldn't like to help you," Ophelia said.

"But we can't," Perdita added. "We're not strong enough to take on a dragon, especially a wyvern, double especially the green wyvern."

A little frown tugged at my eyebrows. "Powerful? You mean you two are . . ." I waved my hand around the room in a vague manner.

"We're Wiccans, didn't you know?" Ophelia asked.

Perdita nodded. "Pagan, of course. We would never condone any magic that was tainted by a dark power."

"Of course," I said, confused, but unwilling to admit it. I felt stupid enough, like I had stepped into the middle of a game where everyone knew the rules but me.

"People who dally with the dark powers are no better than those they use," Ophelia said somewhat righteously.

Perdita nodded. "Worse, since they have a choice."

Whatever. I wasn't about to get into a metaphysical discussion of the right and wrong of light and dark magic. "So I take it you do know someone who is powerful enough to take Drake on?"

The sisters exchanged another glance. I could read the reluctance in their eyes.

"Please," I said, allowing the desperation I felt to creep into my voice. "This is very important to me. Drake seems to think the whole thing is a game, but if I don't get that statue back, I'm never going to get him to help me."

"Help you?" Ophelia asked, looking as confused as I felt. "I thought you said he stole something of yours?"

I sighed and briefly explained about the murder and my visit with the police. "There is a chance my uncle may not fire me outright if I don't have the dragon aquamanile to hand over to him, especially if I tell him that not even the police could recover it, but there's no way I'll be able to get Drake to tell me what he knows about the murder unless I have something he wants, which means I need to get the blasted thing back so I can force him to tell me. That's the only way I'm going to be able to clear my name."

"But you're his mate," Perdita said. "Why don't you just ask him to help you?"

I ran my fingers along the stem of the wineglass and decided I had to shove my protective denial aside for a few minutes. "I don't know exactly what is going on between me and Drake, what it means to be a wyvern's mate, but I do know that he's not going to help me unless I bribe him to do it. And since I don't have anything of value"—I ignored the faint blush that arose when I remembered how he scorned the offer of my body—"I have to first acquire something he wants. Since the aquamanile is rightfully my responsibility, that seems like the logical thing to use. The problem is, I don't know how to go about taking something away from a dragon. That's why I asked you if you know of someone who does."

Perdita pursed her lips, slipping Ophelia an unreadable look. "There's only one man powerful enough to do what you ask."

I raised an eyebrow in silent question.

"The Venediger," Perdita said.

A little curl of fear shivered down my spine as I glanced over to where the Venediger held court at the open end of the bar. I remembered the touch of his power, the feeling that he could easily overwhelm me, and the shiver grew to dread. "Um."

"Of course, he will demand a price for his services," Perdita pointed out.

"Oh? I have a little cash," I said slowly, ignoring the fact that I had spent almost all of it. I was very uneasy about the thought of turning to the Venediger. There was something about him that didn't feel . . . right. Drake, for all his arrogance and maddening attitude, at least felt like he wouldn't chew me up and spit me out.

Which is probably the stupidest thing I've ever thought. Of anyone in the bar who posed a threat to me, Drake was numero uno.

Perdita laughed. Ophelia just looked worried. "The payment the Venediger will ask of you isn't one of money," Ophelia said softly, her fingers worrying a napkin. "Truly, you don't want his help. His powers are . . ." She looked at Perdita for help.

"Dark," Perdita said. "Do not venture down that path, Aisling. As one who has sealed a portal, you have triumphed over the dark horde. Do not now give yourself to one who will damn you."

I didn't say anything for a moment. I didn't quite know how to tell them that I wasn't a practicing Guardian, hadn't sealed a portal, and for that matter, didn't really know what they were talking about. Instead I gave in to the worry nagging my mind whenever it thought about the Venediger. An idea that had slowly been growing in my mind every since my conversation with Drake might be the answer to my problem. "You're right. I can do this without him. Thanks for all the advice, ladies. I greatly appreciate it."

"What are you going to do?" Ophelia asked as I gathered up my bag, extracted a couple of euros for the drink, and stood up.

"I'm not sure yet, but I'm bound to think of something. It was lovely meeting you both. I hope to see you again soon."

They exchanged glances again, Ophelia being nominated to speak as I started to leave. "You're not going to do anything rash, are you?"

"Rash? Me? The queen of circumspect? Don't be silly," I said, smiling reassuringly at them, then without a single glance toward the corner that Drake dominated, headed out into the night to raise my first—and hopefully last—demon.

I know what you're thinking; Aisling summoning demons? The woman who just a few hours before would have laughed herself hysterical if the subject had been raised? Well, needs must as the devil drives and all that. I was hesitant to beg the Venediger for help, so I had to do something myself to get the aquamanile back, and since everyone kept telling me I was a Guardian, I figured I might as well start acting like one.

I just wished I knew exactly *what* a Guardian was.

Once I returned to the hotel, I placed a very expensive international call to Beth, my uncle's secretary, who also happened to be my closest friend.

"Bell and Sons," Beth answered the phone in her best professional voice. I glanced at the clock. It was 11:20, which meant it was just after three in the afternoon in Seattle.

"Hey, chicky, it's me."

"Aisling? Girl, where have you been? Damian is going out of his head. We got a call earlier from a policeman in Paris who says you were involved with the murder of Mme. Deauxville. What on earth is going on?"

I pulled a pillow behind me as I sat back on the bed, shuffling the many phone messages that were waiting for me when I returned. There were six messages from Uncle Damian (I tossed those away—I wasn't ready to face his wrath until I had the aquamanile), three from the U.S. Embassy saying they needed to get in touch with me regarding my status in Paris as an undesirable (so much for help from that quarter), and one from someone named Wart who claimed that once I had a taste of his forked tongue, I'd never go back to dragon again. *That* message I set aside to burn. "Beth, if I told you what was going on, you wouldn't believe me. Honestly, this has been the worst couple of days of my life, and frankly, it doesn't look like it's going to get better soon. What did the police tell Uncle Damian?"

"Not much. I got the idea they were fishing for information about you more than they were telling him anything. What happened?"

I gave her a brief summary of the events.

"Good golly, Miss Molly, you really have been busy. What can I do?"

That's what I like about Beth—she doesn't waste time hashing over useless stuff. She gets right to the point.

"First, you can tell my uncle that I didn't kill anyone, and I'm going to do everything in my power to get the aquamanile back from the man who stole it."

"Damian said the police mentioned that you claimed it had been stolen."

"Yeah, well, they don't want to believe me, and considering the guy who stole it, I don't entirely blame them. But it was stolen, and I'm going to get it back."

I didn't tell her that I planned to use the statue to tempt Drake into helping me, but hey, international calls were expensive. I couldn't mention everything, now, could I?

"I'll tell him. Is there anything I can do here?"

"Yeah. I need to you to drop by my apartment and grab a transcription of one of the medieval texts I read last summer."

"This is hardly the time for a little light reading, Ash."

"Don't I know it." I gave her instructions on where to find the transcription and read the hotel's fax number off the informative brochure that I had picked up in the lobby. "Fax me the chapter on summoning a demon, 'K?"

"What?"

I sighed and rubbed my eyes. Despite the strength the fiery Dragon's Blood had given me, I was bordering on exhaustion. "I don't have time to explain the hows and whys now, Beth. Just fax me the chapter."

I spent a few more minutes reassuring her that I hadn't lost the wits remaining to me and finally hung up, collapsing on the bed, asleep even before I could turn off the light.

The dream started sometime around dawn. I thought at first I was dreaming about walking into a darkened G & T, but quickly I realized that I was back in Mme. Deauxville's apartment, a soft, silvery light from the streetlamps shining through the open curtains doing little to pierce the darkness. The air was musty and warm; the flowers on the table I'd seen before were still scenting the room. In the center of the room the circle of ash remained, but thankfully Mme. Deauxville's body was missing.

"What am I doing here?" I asked aloud.

A shadow separated itself from the wall and resolved itself into Drake's form. He glided toward me, the light casting the lines of his face into harsh relief while the rest of his body remained in shadow. "I called you here."

"You're a dream," I said, unsure if I really was dreaming, or if I had somehow been transported to the scene of the murder. "You're not real."

"No? Perhaps not. Or perhaps the line that divides reality and fantasy has become blurred in your mind."

His hands slipped up my bare arms. I looked down at myself, surprised by the touch of his hands on my bare skin. I was wearing an absolutely gorgeous cream-colored satin-and-lace negligee, one that emphasized my good points and hid the bad ones. "Now I know this is a dream. I don't own a nightgown like this."

I slipped effortlessly into his arms with just the slightest tug of his fingers on my shoulders. He was wearing a black silk shirt that felt like cool water beneath my hands.

"Perhaps that particular gown is part of *my* fantasy," he admitted with a roguish smile, his fingers dancing along the exposed flesh of my back, trailing fire with every touch.

I leaned closer to catch that elusive, spicy scent that seemed to cling to him. "Are you saying that this is real, then?"

"It's as real as you want it to be, sweetheart," he murmured against my collarbone, his lips caressing my skin. If I thought he had magic fingers, his lips were candidates for the Houdini Hall of Fame.

"Really?" I breathed, allowing my fingers to do a little walking of their own. He groaned as I slid my hands down the silken contours of his chest. "Then maybe you'd like to talk about why you were at Mme. Deauxville's last night?"

His chuckle was a bit rusty, as if he didn't use it very much. "You don't give up, do you?"

"Not when my freedom is at stake." I swirled my fingers lower, over his belly. Beneath the material of his shirt, his stomach contracted. "Did you have an appointment with her?"

He discovered the sweet spot behind my ear. I arched into him, my mind threatening to completely give itself over to the pleasure of his mouth on my flesh. "Not with her, no."

It took every ounce of willpower to keep my mind on the questions I wanted so desperately for him to answer. "Did you draw the circle?"

"Dragons can't summon demons," he whispered into my neck just before he sucked my earlobe into his mouth. My knees buckled. His arms tightened behind me, holding me up as I let my hands drift lower, over the tight front of his black jeans. Beneath the zipper he twitched.

"Do you know who did draw it?"

He breathed a groan into my ear. "If you touch me there again, this dream will become more real than you can imagine."

I was tempted—oh, how I was tempted. My fingers hovered just in front of him, but I needed answers, so when sanity sank through all the desire and need and lust that were swirling through my brain as they tried to blot out rational thought, I payed attention to it. I reversed my hands and sent them upward instead, mapping out the terrain around his rib cage. "The circle?" I asked again.

His teeth scraped gently along the curve of my ear, his breath harsh and hot on my skin. "No, I do not know who drew it."

There was a slight inflection on the word *know*. He might not know for certain, but I was willing to bet he had a good idea of who was responsible for the circle, possibly for the murder, too.

"Who do you—?"

He cut off my question by kissing me. Unlike the kiss in the bar, this time I knew what to expect, and I reveled in the heat he poured into me, allowing it to flow between us like a completed circuit. I melted against him, his fingers digging into my behind to pull me tighter. He was aroused, his body aggressive and hard against mine, his fingers everywhere in touches that became progressively more insistent. I tugged the tail of his shirt out from his jeans and slid my hands under his shirt to feel the muscles of his back.

He moaned into my mouth, a moan I felt all the way down to my toenails.

"You cannot touch me like that and expect me to remain in control." The warning in his voice was heated, as heated as my blood, which I swore was about ready to boil as his lips moved down my jaw to my neck, pressing hot kisses into my flesh. "If you do it again, I will not be responsible for what happens."

A shiver of pure desire rippled down my spine as he bent me backwards and licked the valley between my breasts. I clutched handfuls of his hair, trying to decide what I wanted to do—give in to the desire that was roaring through me like his fire, or remain fully in control of the situation, not to mention my life.

"What the hell—this is just a dream," I said, my voice shaky as his mouth moved in hot circles around one satin-covered breast. "That makes this nothing more than a fantasy, and I refuse to feel guilty about fantasies."

Drake lifted his head, his eyes glowing green in the faint light. "I'm so glad you refuse to feel guilty. Fantasies should always be encouraged, especially when they involve me."

"Arrogant dragon. Too much talking," I murmured as I tugged on his hair until his mouth was where I wanted it. I claimed it, welcoming the flash of dragon fire that filled me when my tongue rubbed alongside his. My hands slid down the sleek muscles of his chest, pausing for a moment to tease two impudent nipples.

His breathing went choppy as I slithered down his chest, kissing a path along his collarbone, then down the middle of his chest. I ached to touch him, kiss him, taste him, my body tight and gathered as if for a leap, but our standing position was too awkward to maintain for long.

I kissed my way back up to his jaw, nibbling on his earlobe for a moment before growling into his ear, "In my fantasies there's a long, wide chaise where I can comfortably frolic upon your body. A red velvet couch. With gold tassels."

"Something like this?" he asked, sweeping me up into his arms and turning to the long, wide red velvet chaise bearing a number of silk pillows with gold tassels that was hidden in the shadows. He laid me gently on the chaise, standing over me for a moment, gazing at me with eyes that had gone a dark forest green.

"Exactly like that, except you're the one on the bottom."

His hands strayed to the buckle of his belt. "Are you sure, Aisling? Once we begin, I will not be able to stop. It is the way of the dragons to possess their mates fully. You must be certain this is what you want."

I stretched with the sensual languidness of a well-fed cat. It was just a fantasy, nothing but a dream created by the frustrated attraction I felt for Drake. Surely indulging in a little healthy brain sex couldn't be bad? "Yes, I'm certain."

If there was a land-speed record for getting out of tight jeans, I'm willing to bet that Drake broke it. One moment he was standing over me, scorching my body with his green-fire gaze; the next he was naked, hard and aroused, crawling up the couch to part my legs. "I can smell your desire," he said in a low voice that seemed to rub itself against me. His head dipped to kiss my belly as his hands slid up my thighs, spreading them. "It matches my desire, my need. You are my mate, Aisling, but I will show no mercy to you, for tonight, I will make you truly mine."

The shiver that swept over me had nothing to do with fear, and everything to do with arousal. Drake pushed the satin nightgown up, kissing in the wake of the frothy lace that hemmed the bottom. His mouth was hot and aggressive on my stomach, moving higher as he bared my breasts, the hot brand of his body singeing my flesh wherever we touched. His tongue swept over one aching nipple, followed by the gentle sting of his teeth as he tugged on the tender flesh. I arched beneath him, mindless to everything but the touch of his mouth and hands, my body weeping silent tears of desire as I dug my fingers into the heavy muscles of his behind, trying to pull him closer, tried to merge myself with him.

"No," he whispered, his mouth hovering over my other breast. I groaned as he lathed that breast, his hands and mouth stroking and teasing me into a frenzy of need. "The first time, I must take you as a dragon's mate. After that, we can make love as humans do."

I rubbed myself against him, my legs closing around him in a desperate, overwhelming wave of passion. "I don't care how we do it—I just want you inside me, Drake. Deep inside me. *Now!*"

He rose up, his knees on either side of my legs. I stared up at him, part of my mind marveling at the beautiful, masculine sight he made, the other part wondering just how he expected to make love with my legs trapped between his. He snaked a hand beneath me, pulling my hips upward, his fingers curled around one thigh, parting my legs just enough to suddenly possess me with his mouth. I was growing familiar with the heat of his dragon fire flaring through me when we kissed, but the heat that roared to life from this most intimate kiss had me literally screaming with pleasure. Flames licked my sensitive flesh as his tongue probed, swirled, and sucked, leaving me breathless and writhing in his grip. Before I could do so much as catch a breath, he pulled two fat gold silk pillows beneath me, flipping me over so my belly rested on the pillow, his body covering me completely with his hard heat.

"You are mine, Aisling," he said just before he spread my legs and thrust into me, his teeth biting into the flesh of my shoulder at the same moment. I was pinned, helpless, unable to move, Drake's body heavy on mine as he moved within me, long, deep strokes that seemed to touch every part of me. The tension that had started building with his first touch wound tighter and tighter as his movement rubbed my breasts, aching and swollen, against the abrasive texture of the velvet chaise. I made one half-hearted attempt to move, but the resulting growl of refusal came not from his throat, but from deep in his chest, and I knew that the hold he had on my shoulder was his way of keeping me submissive. I've never been one to take pleasure where I couldn't give it, as well, but I was too overwhelmed by Drake's possession to complain. He seemed to sense my compliance because he became more forceful, licking my shoulder and neck, his body pumping hard and faster into mine, stretching me, filling me, pushing me beyond what I though were normal human limits of tolerance, and into a realm of flame-licked ecstacy.

Just as I trembled on the edge of an orgasm I knew would be unlike anything else I'd known, Drake tilted me to the side, his mouth on my collarbone as he rammed into me with enough force to knock the remaining pillows to the floor. My body exploded in a conflagration of heat and rapture, mindless of the burning flame that seared my flesh beneath Drake's mouth. His shout of triumph rang in my ears as we burned bright together, for a moment seemingly made of fire rather than flesh and blood.

I drifted for a while after that, not quite sure whether I wanted to come down from the high he had driven me to, but eventually I remembered how to breathe, and my brain decided to go back to work again. I opened my eyes and found that I was draped across Drake, the dampness of his chest and ragged nature of his breath a testament that he had enjoyed himself as much as I had.

I pressed a kiss to the center of his chest, then slid off him, scooping the satin of the nightgown up from where it had landed on the floor with the pillows.

Drake's eyes opened as I pulled it on.

"That was truly the most amazing thing I've ever experienced," I said, leaning over to nip his bottom lip. "It goes without saying that you have fulfilled every wild fantasy I could ever imagine. Thank you, Drake."

A slight frown wrinkled his brow as he rose from the chaise, starkly masculine even in his resting state. "It will always be this way between us. You are my mate."

"I'm not sure what I am other than sated within an inch of my life. No wonder you guys are immortal—if this is how sex is normally, you'd die of extreme pleasure if you weren't. As much as I'd like to stay and see if I can't rustle up another fantasy, I have to let my brain get some sleep so it's nice and sharp tomorrow. If you recall, I do have a murder to figure out. I don't suppose you'd care to offer me any advice about how to find the person responsible for drawing the circle and killing Mme. Deauxville?"

"I have answered three questions tonight, and that is all you are allowed," Drake said, tugging me against his body. I melted against him, my curves cushioning his hard lines, his hands pulling me up against proof of his renewed vigor. The dragon fire swept through me, threatening to consume me until I returned it to him.

He pulled his mouth from mine, stepping backwards away from me, and I would have followed him and claimed another one of his mind-searingly wonderful kisses, but he slid back into the shadows, the green of his eyes glittering from the blackness for a moment before it dissolved into the night. "Look to the circle, Aisling. The answer you seek is there."

I awoke to the echo of his darkly sexy voice in my head, my heart beating madly as if I'd just run up all five flights of stairs, the taste of his burning kiss still on my lips, my body still humming with pleasure, deep, secret parts of me still quivering from the memory of his invasion.

"It was just a dream," I told myself, trying hard to push down the desire to call him back. "A really, really erotic dream, but still just a dream. Nothing more. Not real at all. Just a figment of your oversexed imagination."

My voice was reassuringly solid in the gray light of the dawn.

"Just a dream," I said again as I flipped my pillow over to let the cool linen dampen my dream ardor.

When I woke up two hours later, I was wearing a cream-and-lace negligee that I didn't remember buying.

Here's a little hint for those of you planning on summoning a demon: Don't stint on your supplies. If you don't invest in quality products, you run the risk of getting one of the lesser demons. Think runts of the litter.

Being in a frugal state of mind, when I arrived at Amelie's shop the following morning with the sheets of instructions on demon-summoning that Beth had faxed me, I scorned the more expensive items and settled for what I was sure would be equally viable (and much cheaper) substitutes. Amelie didn't question me at all on my purchases until I piled them on the counter.

"Chalk, purified water, salt, ash, a compass, and a copper wax stick. Copper? Are you sure?"

I nodded. Everyone knew those medieval guys were more than a little bit gold obsessed. As long as the stick looked goldish, the demon wouldn't know I hadn't used actual gold.

"This ash is not dead man's ash," Amelie said, turning the label to face me.

"Yeah, I know, but ash is ash."

She pursed her lips, and her glance flickered toward the bottle of water. "Holy water is more beneficial, I believe."

"It's also more expensive," I said, reading over the faxed sheet. "Oh, do you have a copy of *The Book of Sacred Magic* by Abramelin the Mage? My copy is back home."

Silently she plucked a small book off a bookshelf and handed it to me.

"Thanks. That's everything, then."

She eyed me for a moment before moving to an antique cash register. "I hope you know what you're doing."

"You and me both," I said under my breath, then gave her a toothy grin when she looked questioningly at me.

Two hours later I chalked a circle about three feet across on the carpet in my hotel room, being careful to leave a break in the circle so it wasn't closed. I finally understood what it was Drake had been asking me when he wanted to know if the circle at Mme. Deauxville's was closed or not.

"Too bad I didn't read the instructions on how to summon a demon until now," I mumbled to myself as I used the salt to retrace the circle widdershins. "Maybe I could have figured out whether or not that circle had been used. Ah well. Onward and upward. Let's see . . ." I gnawed on my lower lip as I read the slightly blurry fax. I'd begged Beth to copy a chapter out of one of the books I seldom looked at because it consisted solely of recipe-like instructions on summoning various demons, something that until now was strictly an academic rather than practical interest.

"Add a pinch of dead man's ash to a tablespoon of holy water, mix thoroughly, bake until done, frost if desired." I snickered to myself and then looked back at the sheet, tapping it as I read. "Trace the twelve symbols of one of the demon lords with a scribe of gold, followed by the four symbols of the demon you wish to summon using the ash of a branch that has lain across a grave. Well, I'm going with a copper wax stick and plain old ash rather than a gold scribe and dead man's ash, but I'm sure it'll be good enough. Now, who shall I try for?"

I pulled out the book I'd purchased at Amelie's and browsed through the listings of demon lords and the demons who made up each of their legions. There were eight demon lords (also known as the princes of Hell), each of whom had their own strengths and weaknesses. Since this was my first time summoning up a demon, I felt that it was better to go with one of the lesser lords. The one who caught my eye was called Amaymon—he was supposedly known for his fiery, poisonous breath.

"Sounds right up Drake's alley," I said, flipping through the chapters to find one of Amaymon's demons. "Hmm. 'Effrijim: one who quivers in a horrible manner.' That doesn't sound too scary. Beats the pants off of the demon who's known for decaying in liquid putrefaction."

I drew the demon lord's symbols with the copper stick, hoping while I did so that the symbols would come out of the rug with a little soap and water, then used the ash to draw the demon Effrijim's symbols. "All right, showtime," I said, preparing to close the circle. According to the instructions, it was very important that the circle be closed properly . . . which meant blood. I took the pin from the complimentary hotel sewing kit and pricked the end of my finger, closing the circle with a smear of blood.

The second the blood touched the carpet, the air within the circle began to shimmer. The hairs on the back of my neck stood on end in response, the hum of charged power within the circle so disconcerting, I came close to rubbing out the chalk lines in order to destroy whatever it was that I had started, but I thought of Drake and Inspector Proust and Beth and even my Uncle Damian, and knew I had to finish it.

Standing before the circle, I used the compass to align myself so I could call up the quarters. I turned first to the east. The book said to draw a protective ward, but I had no idea what that was, so I just sketched a peace symbol in the air. "Guardian of the towers of the east, I summon you to guard this circle."

Turning south, I drew a peace symbol for that direction as I spoke the appropriate words. "Guardian of the tower of the south, I summon you to guard this circle."

I repeated the process for the two remaining quarters, finishing with the words that would summon the demon to me. "I conjure thee, Effrijim, by the power of thy lord Amaymon, also called the bringer of fire, creator of all things poisonous, to appear before me now without noise and terror. I summon thee, Effrijim, to answer truly all questions that I shall ask thee. I command thee, Effrijim, to my will by the virtue of my power. By my hand thy shall be bound, by my blood thy shall be bound, by my voice thy shall be bound!"

There was a blue crackle of static in the air; then a noxious thick black smoke poured out of the circle. I crawled toward the window, coughing and hacking, throwing the windows open wide, leaning my upper body outside to drag deep, gasping breaths of air into my lungs. Wisps of black smoke wafted over my head, slowly dissipating into the afternoon breeze that came up from the Seine. I coughed out the last of the demon smoke, then turned back to the room, waving the smoke out of my way so I could see my demon.

A black dog sat in the circle. A large hairy black dog. One that slobbered.

"A dog?" I said, plopping in a surprised heap next to the window. "I summoned up a *dog?*"

"I'm not just *any* dog," the animal snarled, its pink tongue flashing as it spoke. My eyes widened as I realized that the words came from its black lips. "What, are you, blind? I'm a Newfoundland! That's like royalty among dogs!"

The dog was talking to me? "Uh . . . you're a *Newfie?* You're a demon who's a *Newfie?*"

The demon sniffed in an irritated manner and licked its shoulder. "We prefer the word *Newfoundland,* thank you."

I summoned up a polite demon Newfie? I shook my head. Something was very wrong here. "Demon, what is thy name?"

"Jim," it answered in a surly tone.

I closed my eyes for a moment. Oh, wasn't that just fine and dandy. I risked my eternal soul to summon up a demon, and I got Jim the Newfie. "Jim? That's it, just Jim?"

"Well, the whole thing is Effrijim, but I prefer Jim. Effrijim sounds a bit girly."

I nodded. I mean, what else could I do? Argue with it?

Jim. I had a demon dog named Jim. I looked at the sheets Beth had faxed me. Maybe she had left out a page and I'd missed a step?

"This place is pathetic," Jim said, looking around at the hotel room with a sneer on its doggy lips. "You're like, what, a pauper?"

"This is a three-star hotel, and my financial status is of no concern to you," I said absently, flipping through the sheets. It looked like I had done everything correctly . . . perhaps it was the few shortcuts I'd taken on supplies that left me with what appeared to be the bottom of the barrel, demonically speaking. "You're sure you're a demon? You're one of the demon lord Amaymon's servants?"

Jim rolled its eyes. "An extremely handsome and impressive specimen of the Newfoundland breed materializes in the middle of your shoddy hotel room, and you ask if I'm a demon? Oh, I can tell my time with you is going to be one long joyride."

I thinned my lips at it. "Look, I've got enough problems in my life without a crabby demon trying to lay a guilt trip on me. Just answer my questions."

The demon's face took on a martyred look. "Yes, I'm a demon."

"And you're one of Amaymon's servants?"

Surprisingly, it looked away and gave an embarrassed doggy cough. "I was."

"Was?" I pounced on the word. "Was? As in . . . *was?*"

"You're a regular Einstein, aren't you? Yes, was, as in Amaymon kicked me out of his legions because of an unfortunate incident when a leviathan tried to mate with him." I just stared at it. Jim made an annoyed face. "It was just a joke! But try telling that to one of the princes of Hell. They have absolutely *no* sense of humor."

"Oh, great." My shoulders slumped. "You're a delinquent demon. A Hell dropout. A demon without a cause."

"No one asked you to summon me," Jim said with dignity. "I'm just out of favor for a bit. I'll be back, just as soon as Amaymon can sit down again."

A little headache throbbed to life in the front of my forehead as I looked at Jim. A sticky line of drool dribbled out of one side of its mouth as it looked back at me. I could send it back to where it came from, but to be honest, I didn't think I had to strength to see what else I would summon up. Hard as it was to believe, I could end up with something worse than Jim.

"Let's get a few things straight here, demon. My name is Aisling. I'm your master. You will do my bidding without resistance, complaint, or undue shedding."

Jim scratched at its ear with its back leg. "You wouldn't happen to have a flea collar around, would you? I just know I've picked up fleas from this dive you live in."

I ground my teeth. I'd been doing a lot of that since I arrived in Paris. "It's a nice hotel in a very expensive area of Paris, and there are no fleas. Now, my first command is for you to lead me to where Drake Vireo, the green wyvern, lives. It's somewhere in the city, so it shouldn't be too much of a challenge for you."

Jim looked around the room. "I'm hungry. You got anything to eat here, or do you plan on starving me back to Abaddon?"

I rubbed my forehead. The headache was getting worse. "Then, after you find where Drake lives, you can help me acquire an object of mine that he has."

Jim stood up and shook itself. Long strands of slobber went flying everywhere. "Hoo, feel like my back teeth are floating. Shake your stumps, sister. I need to go out."

"After you have served me, I will return . . . you *what?*" I stared at it. Weren't demons supposed to follow orders rather than give them?

It walked over to the door and looked pointedly over its shoulder at me. "Do I have to *spell* it for to you? Fires of Abaddon, the sorts of Guardians they produce these days, it's a disgrace to the memory of the old times. When I think of the sort of quality Guardians who used to summon me up . . . Walkies! I need to go walkies! *Comprendez?*"

If there's one word I never expected to hear a demon utter, that word was *walkies.* "Wait a minute, wait a minute, this does *not* make sense! Walkies? You're a demon who says *walkies?* No demon says *walkies;* that's undemon-like! And how come you know who Einstein is?"

The dog had a jaded look on its face. "Just how many demons have you met?"

"Well . . ." I thinned my lips again, refusing to admit

that I had been a demon virgin before it had been summoned. "That's neither here nor there. Why don't you sound like a proper demon? Why don't you talk like something from one of those medieval texts? You've got to be, what, five hundred years old? A thousand?"

"Closer to three thousand, although I don't think I look a day over two thou."

"Three thousand years? You're three thousand years old?" My jaw just about hit the floor in amazement.

"All quality demons are that age or older," Jim said smugly. "And just because I've seen a couple of millennia doesn't mean I don't keep up with the times. There's not a lot to do in Abaddon once you get past the 'doing your demon lord master's bidding' business. We go for long stretches of time with nothing to do but torment the lesser demons, and even that pales after a few centuries. That changed once you mortals came up with TV. Brilliant idea, that."

I stared at the dog, my mind still having a hard time wrapping itself around the thought that Jim was as old as he was. "You watch TV? In Hell? *Television?*"

I couldn't believe it was possible, but the demon looked offended by the note of disbelief in my voice. "What, you think that just because we're demons, we don't like to stay current with world events? You think we don't like to be entertained? *We're demons, not Nazis!*"

I sat in the middle of the room, stunned and trying to absorb the fact that I'd summoned up a TV-watching demon while it wandered into the bathroom. The crash of a large ceramic object hitting the floor brought me out of my daze.

"Well, that experiment was a failure," Jim said, emerging from the bathroom with toilet paper stuck to one of its back paws. "You'll want to get the maid in before you go in there. Had a little trouble with my aim. There's more where that came from, too, so unless you want to explain to the hotel about *le lac du peepee*, I'd suggest you take me out and let me do this doggy-style."

My mind still reeling, I got to my feet.

"Whoa, would you look at my package!" Jim stopped next to the door, doubled over as it looked at its groin. "I'm a demon studmuffin! The babes are going to love me—oh yes they are! After you take me for walkies, I want some food. Raw meat sounds good. This is France, right? You think I can get some horsemeat? Used to love the stuff. Come on, come on. I don't have all day! Chop, chop!"

I opened the door and let the demon out, wondering as I followed after it what I had done to deserve this.

6

"You're doing this on purpose." I bent and used a plastic shopping bag to retrieve yet another of Jim's offerings left on the velvety green of the Tuileries. "This is why they call you a demon, isn't it? You're tormenting me with poop."

Jim, ignoring me, lumbered over to a small shrub and watered it.

I disposed of the bag in a proper receptacle. "Can we go now? You've pooped four times—you can't possibly have anything left inside you."

"Oh, like I enjoy dropping a load out in the open where anyone can see?" Jim snarled. "What sort of a demon do you take me for?"

"One who is going to have a quick visit to the neuterer if you don't shape up and get with the program," I said through my teeth. "And lower your voice! I told you there is to be no talking out in public."

Jim essayed an injured sniff, but allowed itself to be escorted toward the path that led to the north side of the busy Paris park.

"Wait a minute," I said, looking down on its front. "Where's your drool bib?"

My little demon in fur pursed its lips and tried to look innocent. "What bib?"

I spun around and searched the wide open green area we'd just visited. "The one I bought at the pet store. Jim, so help me, if you deliberately lost it—"

"Excuse me, I'm a demon! I'm the dread servant of a demon lord! I bring fear and loathing to all mortal hearts! Demons *don't* wear drool cloths!"

"Demons who slobber all over themselves do. I do not have the time to stop every five minutes to mop you up." I rustled around in my bag, pulling out a second bib that I had wisely purchased at the same time I bought Jim a collar and leash. I tied it around the demon's neck. "Don't lose this one! Now, let's go find Drake's lair. Which direction should we go?"

"How should I know? I'm just a walking drool bib."

I stopped walking and grabbed Jim by the fuzzy black ear nearest me. "Listen here, you horrible little minion of Hell—"

"Abaddon," Jim said.

"What?"

It gave me an impatient look. "Abaddon. Don't you know anything? We who serve the dark masters refer to home sweet home as Abaddon, not the other word."

I glanced around quickly to make sure no one saw me talking to my dog, then made squinty eyes. "Why?"

I swear Jim shrugged. "Names have power. The one you keep tossing around has more power than most. I would have thought that as a Guardian you knew that, but I forgot that I've been bound to the Forrest Gump of Guardians. Lucky, lucky me."

"Right," I said, losing the remainder of my patience. "You have made me waste two whole hours while I ran around finding food that you would accept, not to mention undergoing a detailed tour of the Tuileries while you peed on every available shrub—"

"I like to pee. It's fun. We don't get to do anything like this back home."

I ignored the interruption, keeping a wary eye out for eavesdroppers. "—as well as dropped demon ploppies everywhere, which *I* had to clean up, so now it's time for you to do the job I summoned you to do—find Drake's lair. Which direction is it?"

A mother and her two little kids strolled by, the woman pausing to say something harsh to me. I had no idea what her problem was until I looked down to find Jim writhing in apparent agony, making the most tortured face a Newfie could possibly make.

I released Jim's ear and patted it on the head as I told her, "Don't pay any attention to it—it's trying to drive me insane."

"Sounds like a short trip," Jim muttered just loud enough for me to hear as the woman snarled something in what I was willing to bet was gutter French before she stormed off.

"Oh, thank you so very much. Just make me look like the type of a person who beats up on dogs!"

"You held my ear *hard*," Jim accused.

"You're a demon!" I all but shouted, wanting to tear out my hair in frustration. "You're used to eternal torment, *not* that I was holding your ear hard. So stop complaining, stop stalling, stop creating distractions and *do the job I brought you here to do!*"

"I don't suppose you'd care to swing by another *boucherie* for a morsel more of that prime-aged beef you bought me this morning?"

I let the demon see in my eyes its fate if it didn't do what I wanted.

Jim sighed and plopped down in an unhappy slump. "I can't."

Another group of children was approaching. I tugged on the leash, heading to a quiet area next to some trees. "You can't what?" I asked when we were far enough away so we couldn't be heard.

"I can't find the wyvern's lair."

I counted to ten to keep from strangling Jim, not that I was entirely sure I could since it *(a)* wasn't technically a living being and *(b)* was approximately the size of a small pony, and thus strangling with my bare hands would be difficult.

Through still-clenched teeth I said, "But not completely out of the question. Why can't you find Drake's lair?"

Jim rolled its eyes. "Because I don't know where it is! Do I look like I have the phone book memorized?"

"You're a demon. You have demonic powers. I may not be the savviest Guardian around"—*that* was the understatement of the year—"but I do know that demons have all sorts of abilities, and surely one of them must be to find someone who is being sought."

"In a normal situation, yes," Jim said, looking longingly at a bank of rhododendrons. I jerked on the leash to remind it that I was waiting. "But my case is a little different. I . . . eh . . . don't have any powers."

The last sentence was spoken so softly, I thought I'd misheard. "You *what?*"

It glared at me. "I don't have any powers, OK? Amaymon stripped me of them when he cast me out of his legions. You want to rub a little salt into the wound? Go right ahead. I'm just a demon; I don't have any feelings."

"You don't," I agreed. Jim sniffed and turned away as if tears were imminent. I reminded myself that demons might take the form of a human (or if they were particularly deranged, a dog), but they weren't really human. They didn't have feelings that could be hurt with mere words. "You can stop pretending you're crying, because I'm not buying it. Oh, geez, will you stop? You're making me feel like the biggest bully on the face of the earth."

I pulled a tissue out of my bag, wiping up the doggy tears that Jim had somehow managed to manufacture.

"You yelled at me."

I tried to take a deep, calming breath, but it came out a semihysterical laugh. "If anyone ever told me that a demon would make me feel guilty about asking it to do the job it was summoned to do, I'd say that person was a grade-A lunatic."

Jim gave me an accusatory look.

I raised my hands in surrender and staggered over to a shady bench to collapse with defeat. "I give up—I just absolutely give up. I asked Drake nicely to give me back my dragon, and he refused. I asked him a few questions, and he gave me the runaround for answers. I summoned up a demon, and I got a demon that's been kicked out of He . . . Abaddon. Why am I trying anymore? I should just go to Inspector Proust and save him the bother of hunting me down, because he's sure as heck going to lock me up and throw away the key when I can't prove my innocence."

Jim sat next to my feet. "You want me to find some balloons for this pity party you're having?"

"Go away," I mumbled, my head in my hands as I tried to work up a few tears of self-pity. They wouldn't come, damn it. "Just go back to wherever it is you came from, and leave me alone."

"I can't leave. You're my master, remember?"

"I'm freeing you."

"Doesn't work that way."

I looked up at the demon. "Oh, right, I have to conduct the release ritual. I can't do it here. You'll just have to wait until I get back to the hotel."

"Whatever. No hurry. I'm enjoying being out. As you can imagine, we demons don't get around much. Last time I was in Paris, they were beheading everyone. Ah, how I miss the good old days."

I sniffled a couple of times, sighed once or twice, and gave up on feeling sorry for myself. I never could do it well. "Well, poop. And no, I didn't mean that as a command."

Jim made a husky sound that I took for laughter. I shook my finger at it. "Don't even think of trying to be nice to me—I can't take it right now."

"Nice? *Moi?*"

The expression of astonishment on Jim's furry face was so amusing, I couldn't help but giggle. "Right. Let's get down to business, then. If you can't help me find Drake, I'll just have to manage it myself, although how I'm supposed to do that is beyond me at the moment."

"You could look in the phone book," Jim suggested, lifting a big paw to examine it.

"Dragons don't list themselves in phone books," I said dismissively, an idea blossoming as I spoke. I thought about it for a while, gave it a long, hard look, and decided it was a good one. "Drake told me that the answer I sought was in the circle, so I'm going to take him at his word. Come on, Demon Jim. We're going back to the scene of the crime."

"Give me a couple of minutes. You're not going to believe what I found I can do," Jim said, its voice muffled as it engaged in a bit of groinal hygiene.

"The ew factor on that is borderline vomit territory," I

said, tugging on its leash until the great furry black head emerged from the depths of its crotch. I ignored the glazed look in Jim's eyes and got to my feet, heading out of the park and toward the nearest Metro stop. "Come on, you'll like the Metro. As a dog, you've got carte blanche to smell strangers' crotches."

"Really? That's something, although not nearly as good as licking my own—"

"When we get to Mme. Deauxville's house," I interrupted, not wanting to hear the rest of that sentence, "I want you to look around and see if anything strikes you as odd. Drake was convinced that a demon was summoned by the circle. Maybe you can tell me who it was."

A half hour later we crossed the five-arched stone Pont Marie bridge from the right bank to the Ile Saint-Louis, and turned onto the Rue Sang des Innocents. The street was back to normal, I was pleased to note, no longer in the grip of whatever it was that had left it so lifeless and quiet.

"Remember, you're a dog whenever people are around," I said a bit nervously as we approached Mme. Deauxville's building.

"The words *demon* and *stupid* aren't interchangeable," Jim said, in a bit of a pout because a woman on the Metro objected to having her butt snuffled.

"Just remember that," I warned, and taking a deep breath, pushed on the buzzer for the name above Mme. Deauxville's.

"Allô?"

"J'ai une grenouille dans mon bidet," I mumbled incoherently, praying the person whose apartment I buzzed would assume something was wrong with the intercom and open the door for me. Luck, for a change, was with

me, because without any further interrogation or questions about frogs, the door clicked open.

I hustled Jim up the carpeted stairs in case the person on the third floor came out to the landing to see who was buzzing them. I stopped just long enough to tap on Mme. Deauxville's door, making sure no one was inside before hurrying down the tiny hall to the back door.

"Bet it's locked," Jim said.

"Hush. Of course it's locked, but I am not my father's daughter for nothing," I said, breathing a sigh of relief. The lock on the back door was an older one, not a dead bolt. I pulled out my maxed-out credit card and used it.

"You've got to be kidding," Jim said, disbelief rampant in its eyes.

"Nope. Daddy was a locksmith. The best locksmith in Santa Barbara. The things he taught me would astound you."

"I doubt that," Jim started to say, then closed his fuzzy lips when I swept open the door with a grand gesture. "Hrmph. You *do* know that what you're doing is illegal?"

"I'm suspected of murdering a woman I don't even know," I hissed, waving the demon into the dark, musty room, checking the hallway before closing the door. "Breaking and entering is the least of my worries. This must be the laundry room. The living room is to the left. Don't touch anything!"

The delicate tinkle of glass hitting linoleum was the answer to my command.

"Jim!"

"Sorry. Thought it was something to eat. When's lunch?"

"So help me, if I live through this . . . ." I crept on tippy-toes through a tall-ceilinged bedroom with a four-poster bed swathed in white and gold gauze, a color scheme that was carried throughout the room. An antique gold fainting couch sat along one wall, a huge ebony armoire opposite. Bouquets of near-dead lilies were scattered around the room, making the musty air even mustier with their heavy decaying scent. The curtains were drawn, but the closed apartment retained the heat of the day.

"Antiques, very nice. This is what I call proper living, not at all like the pit of a hotel room you've been happy in."

"Shut. Up." I opened the door to the living room cautiously, my nose wrinkling with the stale smell of the room. "OK, no one's here. That's the circle. Drake wanted to know if it was opened or closed. What do you think?"

"You're the Guardian. You should know."

I thought momentarily about grinding my teeth, but decided the dentist bills weren't worth the satisfaction it would give me. I crossed the room and squatted down next to the circle, Jim beside me. "I'm kind of new to the Guardian business." Jim snorted. I ignored the snort and held my hand above the circle. The air around it tingled slightly. I examined the ash circle, noting that the salt had sunk deep into the fibers of the carpet while the ash remained on top. "I think it's closed. It feels . . . active. Unfinished. Almost as if it's waiting for something."

Jim nosed around the couch, pausing to sniff the black mark on the carpet that Drake had pointed out.

"Was that made by a demon?"

"Not any demon I know," Jim said, moving over to look out the tall windows.

I sat back on my heels, more than a little surprised by the answer. "It wasn't a demon? Are you sure?"

The look Jim shot me spoke volumes. "I may be powerless, but I'm not totally inept. That mark wasn't made by a demon. Take a look at it yourself. It's just charcoal, not demon smoke."

I crawled over to it, swearing to myself. If a demon hadn't actually been summoned by whoever had killed Mme. Deauxville, then someone wanted it to *look* like one had been called. But that didn't make sense, because I had felt that something was wrong even before I entered the apartment, so a demon must have been here. I looked at the black mark on the carpet feeling totally at sea, completely overwhelmed by forces I couldn't even begin to understand. Why had I thought it was such a good idea to tackle this strange new world when I was almost completely clueless?

Pride, that's why.

"Brazen be damned, I'm going to ask for some help," I swore, kneeling by the circle to make a sketch of the exact arrangement of the symbols in the small notebook I'd borrowed from Amelie. Once that was done, I stared down at the circle, unsure of what else I was supposed to see in it. Drake sounded so positive when he said I'd find the answers in it.

"Can a Guardian tell who drew a circle?" I sat back on my heels again as I considered the ashy markings.

"An experienced Guardian, possibly. A neophyte like you?" Jim stopped looking out the window long enough to shake its head. "Unlikely."

I gnawed my lower lip for a few seconds. "Could a Guardian tell what specific demon was summoned by the circle?" I couldn't imagine how knowing what demon was summoned would help me, but it was the only other thing I could think of.

Jim didn't even bother looking my way. "If she couldn't, she's not much of a Guardian."

"Really? How, exactly?"

Jim sat and started licking its belly. I averted my eyes quickly in case it decided to give its personal equipment another spit bath. "You summoned a demon, and you don't know how you did it?"

I gave a mental sigh. "I really hate it when everyone answers my questions with questions."

The demon glanced at me before returning to its belly wash. "We're just trying to swing the scale from clueless to merely incompetent."

I ignored the comment and studied the circle, thinking back to the circle I drew to summon Jim. Suddenly I sat up straight. "The demon's six symbols! That's how I can tell which demon was summoned."

"Give the girl a cigar."

"But this circle doesn't have anything but the twelve symbols of Ashtaroth." I chewed my lip again, searching for signs that the six demon symbols had been rubbed out. There were none.

Jim gave a huge martyred sigh. "If you're any sort of a Guardian, you should be able to feel which demon was summoned by opening yourself to the possibilities."

"The possibilities?" I glanced from my furry demon and to the circle. "Er . . . how do I do that?"

"What am I, the headmaster at a Guardian school? I've got better things to do than hold your hand." Jim got up and started down the tiny hall toward the bedroom.

"Hey! Where are you going?"

"To drink out of the toilet, since you seem to forget that this magnificent form I have taken needs both feeding and watering."

"Don't touch anything else!" I warned, then looked back at the circle, muttering under my breath about demons who wouldn't answer a question when it was put to them. "Open myself to the possibilities. How the heck am I supposed to know what *that* means?"

I remembered the door in my mind that had opened when Drake gave me his fire, and decided to see if I could do the same without being lip-locked with the sexiest dragon in Western Europe. "Guess it's worth a try. I can't do anything worse than fail."

I closed my eyes, my hands outstretched toward the circle. After a few moments of clearing out the everyday hustle and bustle of thoughts that made up my mind, I settled down to opening myself up to the room. Slowly the muffled noises of Paris outside the apartment, the sounds of Jim drinking at the toilet, and the musty, closed smell of the apartment all faded into the background as the circle dominated my thoughts. As I swung the mental door open, I was amazed all I had felt before was a slight tingle around the circle—the power contained within it was enough to make the hairs on my arms stand on end. Even with my eyes closed, I could see it, much clearer in my mind than when viewed with mere eyes. It was as if opening up myself had flipped on a switch that gave me a tremendous clarity of vision. I looked down at the circle and saw clearly that the six demon symbols were drawn with salt, not ash, and like the salt of the circle itself, the symbols had sunk into the depths of the carpet.

"Bafamal," I said, the name coming to my mind with a surety that made me believe it even though I had not recognized the demon symbols. "This circle was drawn to summon Bafamal, but he did not answer the summons."

"Why?"

The voice was Jim's. I turned blindly toward the windows around which Jim had been sniffing. I could feel echoes of the demon, as if its presence had violated the room. "Because it was already here. It left by the window."

As the words sank into my brain, the door in my mind closed. I opened my eyes, almost disappointed with what I saw. The colors of reality were dull compared with what I had just seen, the edges and contours not quite so defined. Just as I was mourning the loss of my super brain-vision, realization of what had happened struck me. "Hey! I really *am* a Guardian! Not that I know exactly what a Guardian is, but I'm whatever they are, I'm one."

"Well, duh," Jim said. "You think just anyone can summon up a superior demon like me?"

I frowned. "According to the books I read, pretty much anyone *can*."

"The lesser demons, yes, but not a demon of my quality," Jim sniffed righteously.

I let that comment go without the answer it deserved. "The demon Bafamal left by the window," I said, getting to my feet and going over to examine the window. I looked out, surprised by what I saw. "There's a fire escape here."

"No!" Jim said in mock surprise.

"I'm quite serious about visiting the neutering clinic, you know," I said, but without any heat as I examined the window. There were black splotches of powder all over it where the police had fingerprinted the woodwork. I unlatched the window, pushing it open. "One has to assume that a demon must have a reason for escaping through a window rather than just disappearing in a puff of nasty-smelling smoke. Come on, Jim. Let's see where this leads."

I waited until Jim left the apartment, closing the window as best I could from the outside, hoping no one would notice that it was unlatched. The end of the fire escape nearest me led to a ladder that went up, not down. I turned and walked the length of the building to where a metal ladder could be dropped down halfway to the ground. I examined the ladder, noting that the police had fingerprinted it, as well. Point one for Inspector Proust. "Interesting. So the demon escaped out the window rather than just going back to He . . . Abaddon. Now I just need to find out when and why Drake was in the apartment and whether he saw the demon. Or the killer. I wonder if Drake came in by the window, as well?"

"Why would he?" Jim asked.

I shrugged. "I don't know, but then, I don't know why Drake was here in the first place if he isn't the murderer. And I'm still not sure he's not."

"Are you going to stand there and debate the issue all day, or can we get down?"

Jim was peering over the edge of the fire escape. There was a definite look of unease on its face.

"Scared of heights?" I asked.

"Don't be ridiculous. I'm a demon. The only things we're scared of are the demon princes and the dark master of them all."

"That sneer doesn't quite cut it." I grinned but took pity on Jim as I slid the ladder into place, quickly climbing down it. "Last step's a doozy—be careful," I said, rubbing my knees that had protested the four-foot drop.

"I don't suppose you'd even *think* of offering to catch me?" Jim asked from the top of the ladder.

"You must weigh at least a hundred and twenty pounds. The answer is no. You're a demon—you can't feel pain. Jump."

"Doesn't mean I want to ruin this nice form by breaking my legs," Jim grumbled, but it managed to head down most of the steps before jumping to land beside me.

"Any ideas which way the demon would have gone?" I asked, looking down the shady alley that ran the width of the building. I peered into the shadows, trying to determine whether a demon would have been likely to run that way.

Jim didn't answer me.

"Look, I'm not asking you to be actually helpful or anything, but you could offer me a bit of advice once in a while. I don't think that would kill you." I turned around to glare at Jim and came face-to-face with the mild brown eyes of Inspector Proust. "Gah!"

"And *bonjour* to you, too," Inspector Proust said. His eyebrows raised a fraction as his warm eyes considered me. "You will forgive my impertinent curiosity, Mlle. Grey, but I am unable to keep from asking if you often find yourself receiving advice from dogs?"

I looked down at Jim, who was sitting with an unusually smug look on its face, madly trying to come up with an excuse for being there, but it wasn't any good. My mind had evidently gone to lunch, leaving me holding the proverbial bag. And Jim's leash. Next to the fire escape that led up to the apartment of a murdered woman.

One whose death I was suspected of causing.

"Poop," I said. And meant it.

7

"Perhaps you would care to take a stroll with me?" Inspector Proust asked in a voice that held a note of steel beneath the polite veneer.

"Down to the police station?" I asked miserably, falling in alongside him as he ambled toward the end of the street, where a couple of benches overlooked the Seine. Jim walked next to me, thankfully silent. I made a note to buy the biggest hamburger I could find in Paris for Jim . . . if I managed to keep from being thrown into jail. I couldn't help but wonder if the French still used the Bastille. Thoughts of the guillotine weren't even worth contemplating.

"I have no intention of taking you to the station. Not unless you desire me to do so," Inspector Proust answered. He strolled along with his hands clasped behind his back, just as if we were two old buddies taking a lunchtime walk together. "I have been looking for you this morning. I wanted to speak to you. I see you have acquired a dog."

I glanced quickly at Jim. "Well, it . . . *he* sort of found me. He's a stray, homeless, one no one wanted, so I thought I'd take him in until I can find someone to take him off my hands." Not entirely a lie, but not entirely the truth, either.

"Ah. Most commendable of you." We reached the benches. He waited politely until I seated myself before sitting down next to me. "You permit?"

I nodded my head when he pulled out a package of cigarettes, then shook it when he offered me one. "We are having very nice weather this week, yes? So nice it seems strange to me that a visitor to Paris would desire spending her time inside rather than out seeing the many pleasing sights there are to see."

I squirmed a bit until I realized what I was doing. Either he was going to arrest me, in which case squirming wasn't going to do me the least bit of good, or he was going to pump me for information, and my squirming might be interpreted as an indication that I was not telling him the truth. "You want to know why I was in Mme. Deauxville's apartment just now?"

"If you would not object to telling me."

"I kind of thought you would be curious." I thought briefly of lying, but my ex-husband once told me I was the world's worst liar, so I figured the truth would have to do. "I wanted to look at the circle that was drawn beneath where Mme. Deauxville was hung."

"Ah, the occult circle, yes. Why did you wish to examine it?"

I slid him a quick glance. "I thought if I had a good look at it, I might be able to figure out who killed her."

His eyebrows raised. "Much as I appreciate your help, I must point out that the Criminal Investigation Department has a full roster of policemen and investigators employed. Your time, perhaps, would be better spent in other endeavors."

I played with the leash, avoiding meeting either Proust's or Jim's eyes. "Such as?"

"An explanation of what ties you have to a lady by the name of Amelie Merllain."

"Amelie?" I frowned at him. Why on earth was he asking about Amelie? A nasty suspicion started to form in the back part of my mind. "She owns a shop in the Latin Quarter. Other than visiting her shop, I don't have any ties to her."

"Indeed. And yet you visited the shop twice yesterday."

"That was . . . I was . . . I just needed . . ." I stopped, unable to tell him my last visit was to procure demon-raising supplies.

Inspector Proust looked at me with gentle sorrow, as if I'd let him down somehow. "I see. Perhaps instead of answering these so troublesome questions, you would care to discuss your relationship with the gentleman known as Albert Camus?"

"The Venediger?" I asked, surprised.

Proust inclined his head. "I believe that is one of his aliases."

"You've been following me!" I jumped to my feet so I could glare down at him.

He did the Gallic shrug I was starting to think I'd have to learn, it was just that expressive. "Did you think I would allow you to wander freely?"

I sat back down and thought about that for a few minutes. "I suppose you have a point, although I don't like it. I'm not guilty of the murder—I've told you that."

Inspector Proust puffed on his cigarette for a few minutes as we both watched a barge drift by. It was surprisingly pleasant sitting there, a tranquil and peaceful corner of Paris. Although we were approaching midday, the breeze from the river kept it from being too hot, and as the now-familiar cacophony of sounds that was Paris seemed a long way away, our little spot seemed almost a haven.

"I do not think you killed Mme. Deauxville," Inspector Proust said suddenly. "I have examined your movements most stringently, and I do not believe you would have had the time to murder her and hang her between the time you arrived and when the police descended."

I hadn't realized I was holding my breath until he said that. I let it out, relaxing against the back of the bench, more than a little surprised to find he believed me innocent of the murder. "That's not an admission that you believe I'm telling the truth, but I'll take it."

"However, I have not ruled out the possibility that you are working in cooperation with the person who did murder her," Proust added.

Jim made a noise that sounded strangely like it was a laugh. I tugged on the leash as a warning. "Well, hel . . . er . . . heck. I don't suppose you'd care to just take my word for it that I didn't?"

"I would prefer proof absolute," he said in a careful neutral tone.

I sighed. "I'd give it to you if I had it."

He continued to watch the river for a few minutes. "What did you find in the circle during your visit to Mme. Deauxville's apartment?"

I glanced at him out of the corner of my eye. He looked almost disinterested, as if he were simply passing the time talking about something innocuous, like the weather. Now I had to lie, or else he'd think I was stark, staring mad. "Not much. There was salt in it as well as ash."

He nodded, waiting for me to go on. I fidgeted, trying

to pick out things I could safely tell him. "Whoever drew the circle followed the formula for summoning Ashtaroth, a demon lord."

"A demon lord, how very unusual." If his voice were any more bland, it would be tapioca. "Why would someone wish to do that?"

"You got me," I answered, giving a little shrug of my own. It wasn't nearly as effective as his, but it felt good nonetheless.

"No, I do not have you, but I could if I feel strongly enough that you are not being entirely honest with me."

I glanced at him again to see if he was joking. Serious brown eyes looked back at me.

"Oh. Uh . . ."

"For someone who is new to Paris, you seem to have made quite an entrance in the occult underground society that is so popular in the Latin Quarter."

Oh, lord, had he seen me playing kissy-face with Drake in G & T?

"One might almost say you were comfortable in such a society, as if you were expected."

"I didn't know a soul here until I arrived," I said honestly. I chanced another glance at him. His left eyebrow was cocked in outright disbelief.

"If that is so, I would be forced to say that you have made yourself familiar with certain individuals exceptionally quickly."

He *had* seen Drake and me kissing! Damn. "Um . . ."

Proust flicked his cigarette to the pavement, grinding it out with his heel as he stood up. "A word of advice, if you will permit it, mademoiselle."

"Whatever turns your crank," I said as I stood up, too.

"It is an English poet, I think, who said that all that

glitters is not gold. Me, I say that which looks innocent is often the most corrupted."

With those parting words, Inspector Proust patted Jim on the head and strolled off down the cobblestone street toward Mme. Deauxville's house.

"Well, how do you like that? Was he talking about me, do you think? Or something else? And if so, who? Or what?"

"How would I know? I'm just a homeless stray no one wanted that you so kindly took in," Jim answered. "He petted me, you'll notice. You could do more of that. Wouldn't hurt you any."

I made a face. "May I remind you that you're a demon, not a dog, and it is commonly held that those things that we mortals find enjoyable—like petting—are loathsome to demons?"

"All I said was that you could do more of it," Jim said with great dignity, lumbering over to pee on a nearby trash can.

I thought about what I needed to do next. Even though Inspector Proust said I was off the hook for the actual murder, it was obvious he thought I was involved somehow, which was not going to get me my passport back. I still needed to find out who drew that circle, and although I had a clue in the name of the demon that was present, it wasn't enough to give me the answer.

"I bet Drake knows, the rat fink."

"I thought he was a wyvern."

I turned to Jim, patted it on the head, and even gave its ears a quick fondle. "Stop groaning, people will hear you."

"Dogs groan when you rub their ears," Jim said with a sour look.

I grabbed the leash and headed toward the Pont Marie.

"True, but they don't mumble 'Oh, yeah, mama, that's the spot right there!' while they're doing it. Any ideas on where in Paris a wyvern would be likely to keep his lair?"

"Phone book," Jim said.

I shot it a look. "That's just stupid. Drake is a powerful dragon, a wyvern, an immortal. He wouldn't be in a phone book like normal people."

"Just because you're immortal doesn't mean you don't want people to call you," Jim pointed out.

"Fine, I'll look, but it's a waste of time," I grumbled as I changed course to stop by a pay phone. "You could be trying to help me by thinking of all the likely spots that a dragon might . . . Well, I'll be damned."

"Told you," Jim said smugly as I stared down at the phone book page. There was Drake's name, big as life.

"I am *so* in over my head," I said with a sigh as I wrote down the address. I toyed with the thought of simply calling him up, but that would take the surprise out of me showing up on his doorstep demanding my aquamanile. Not that he was going to give it to me if I just asked . . .

"Inspector Proust mentioned Amelie. I wonder if I should talk to her. If he thought she was someone important, maybe she can shed a little light on the murder, or at least who might be likely to call up Bafamal. Or I could go straight to Drake's and try to sneak in. Or I could swing by the G & T and see if Ophelia and Perdita might be there."

"Who?"

"They're sisters, Wiccan sisters. I met them at G & T."

"Oh. Or—and this is a much better plan—you could take me to lunch and feed me."

"You just had breakfast," I said absently, trying to think what would be the logical next step. The problem was, logic didn't seem to be on speaking terms with me anymore.

"That was hours ago," Jim complained. "I'm hungry. This form needs to be fed. *Frequently.*"

"You did that well," I told my furry demon as we strolled toward the road. "That plaintive note in your voice was particularly heartrending."

"It's wasted on someone who doesn't have a heart," Jim snapped.

I laughed—which should have been worth some major karma points, because my life was anything but amusing—and patted the big black head that bobbed alongside me. "Poor little demon. All right, we'll have a quick lunch, but it has to be fast. I've got to get that aquamanile back."

We ate in a small café, then feeling pressured, I gave in to temptation and called Rene to see if he was free for a few hours.

"You desire help finding your missing dragon?" he asked. "I will aid you. I know a great many people in Paris. Where are you?"

"Near the Pont Marie."

"I will meet you on the Right Bank. I can be with you in fifteen minutes. Then we will make our plans, yes?"

"Sure, although I think I know where the dragon is. The trouble isn't going to be finding it, it's going to be . . . uh . . . liberating it."

"*Ah, bon? Viva la libération!*" Rene said, hanging up after giving me instructions about where he would collect us.

"Remember the rules," I warned Jim as Rene pulled up a short while later. "You're just a dog. No laughing, no disgusted snorts, no rolling your eyes, and *no* talking."

"You really are a control freak, aren't you?" Jim asked as I opened the car door.

"You look *très bon* today. No blood on your dress! This is good, yes?" Rene said over his shoulder, his eyes widening as he saw Jim follow me into the taxi. "You have a pet?"

"Uh . . . yeah. A stray dog. I found him. Here's the address for Drake—"

"A dog? That is not a horse?" Rene said with a chuckle as he pulled out into traffic.

"If I were a horse, I wouldn't fit in this ratty old taxi, now, would I?" Jim asked.

Rene made an inarticulate sound and slammed on the brakes. Behind us, the squeal of tires on pavement could be heard, quickly followed by the prolonged honking of horns and a great deal of profound swearing.

"Jim!" I yelled, grabbing its ear.

"Ow! You're hurting me! You're my witness, Rene. This is animal abuse. She could go to jail for this, right?"

Rene turned around in his seat, his eyes huge as he looked from me to Jim. "You . . . you are not . . . what is it called, the person who speaks through a doll?"

"Ventriloquist?" I released Jim's ear and sat back with a heartfelt sigh, ignoring the sound of some really ticked off people behind us. "No, I'm not. You're not hearing things, it was Jim who spoke."

"A dog?" Rene choked and turned red.

"You see?" I whapped Jim on the shoulder. "This is why I told you to keep quiet. Now you've upset poor Rene."

"You said he was a friend of yours. Who was it who said 'Love me, love my dog'?"

"You're not a dog. Rene, why don't you pull over somewhere. I'll explain it to you then."

"How is it the dog he is talking?" he asked, ignoring my suggestion.

"Jim's not really a dog. It's a demon. It just took a dog's form."

"A demon?" I didn't think it possible, but Rene's voice went up an octave. "One of the little devils?"

"A demon formerly of the legions of Amaymon," Jim said with a sniff, turning its head to look out the window.

"Rene, can we please get moving?" I pleaded. "There's a huge line of traffic behind us. I can explain—"

"You said you did not believe in the little devils, and yet you have one here?"

"Yeah, well, I changed my mind."

Rene looked at Jim for a few more moments, then shrugged and turned back to the steering wheel, saying, *"A lui le pompom."*

"What was that?" I asked, relieved we were moving again, although if Jim had done as I asked, I wouldn't have had to explain to Rene about it in the first place . . . I glared at Jim and pinched its shoulder.

"To him the *pompom*. It means . . . *heu* . . . he ate the cake."

"Takes the cake, yes, I know what you mean, but really, Rene, you don't have to worry about Jim. It can't hurt you. It's powerless."

"Well, just tell everyone, why don't you?" Jim huffed. "Shall I rent you some billboard space? Maybe book you some time on the local news station for maximum coverage?"

"You should be counting yourself lucky I don't drop you off at the nearest pound, you big blabbermouth." I gave it a glare just to let it know I wasn't pleased. "Be quiet, and stop causing problems."

"I'm a demon," Jim mumbled. "That's what we do best."

I narrowed my glare until it had laser accuracy. Jim sniffed again and looked pointedly at the handle for the car window.

"Honest to Pete, what I have to do for you . . ." I leaned over and rolled the window down enough so Jim could stick its head out. "Oh, Rene, I think I may be followed by the police. I hate to say this because it sounds so cheesy, but do you think you can lose them?"

Rene snorted, his eyes lit with pleasure. "The police? You do not even have to ask, *ma vieille branche.* It is done."

"What's a *vieille branche?*" I asked Jim as Rene spun the car around a corner and wove his way through traffic. I didn't honestly expect Jim to know, but I was willing to do anything to distract myself from the death-defying manner in which Rene plunged through traffic in his attempt to shake the police tail.

"Old branch. It's slang for 'friend.' You came to a country without even bothering to learn the language?"

"It's my first job. I'm going to take classes once it's over," I muttered, annoyed that I had to defend myself to a demon.

After that I closed my eyes, deciding it was really better if didn't see how close to death I was with each spin of the steering wheel. I clung to the armrest, saying, "I'm really sorry you had to learn about Jim this way, Rene. I hope it doesn't shake you up too much. I'm kind of stuck with having a dog until I can send it back."

"Non." I opened my eyes long enough to see in the rearview mirror as Rene pursed his lips. He took a deep breath, flipped off another taxi driver who swerved into

our lane, and finally said, "It is not the deal big. You have a dog who is also a little devil, eh, me, I do not mind."

"That's remarkably accepting of you. It took me hours to get to the point you're at after just a few minutes."

"I'm French," Rene said with another shrug. "We are superior, yes?"

"Absolutely," I said with a smile, one that stayed on my face until we pulled up outside the address listed for Drake.

"We are here, and the police, they will not know where we are," Rene said with great satisfaction.

"Um," I said, looking at the courtyard. A private courtyard, one with a fountain. If I thought Mme. Deauxville's building said expensive, this one screamed *millionaire*.

Rene whistled as he took in the beautiful pink stone building set back behind the courtyard. "This man who stole your dragon, he has much money?"

"I'm going to say the answer to that is a resounding yes." I got out of the taxi and gave myself over to a few seconds of blatant gawking. "Can you wait, or do you have to go run rich tourists around?"

He reached for his cell phone, his eyes still on the house. "I will call my friend to take my afternoon appointment. I think I should come with you."

"Geez, Rene, I don't want to make you lose out on good pickings from tourists."

He waved me forward, already speaking into his phone.

"So, what's the game plan?" Jim asked as we skirted the fountain.

I just knew someone was going to ask me that. Unfortunately, I hadn't yet thought of a reasonable answer. "Well . . . I don't really have one."

Jim groaned. "Don't tell me you're just planning on walking in the front door?"

"Er . . . maybe. Unless you have a better idea?" I stopped in front of the two large doors and gnawed my lower lip. The courtyard was completely deserted. There wasn't even a shadow to be seen flickering behind the lace net curtains that hung in all the windows, lace curtains that I suspected were there to keep prying eyes from seeing too much rather than for decorative purposes. The thought of Drake picking out lace curtains for his house was just too much for my brain to handle.

Jim rolled its eyes. "This is a dragon's home. You think they survived for centuries by letting in anyone who wants to stroll in and have a look around?"

I hated to admit it, but that made sense. Drake would hardly be likely to leave the aquamanile lying around where I could easily get at it. "Right. What do you know about dragon's lairs?"

"I don't know any dragons," Jim answered, smelling at a large potted plant. "Thus I don't know anything about their lairs."

"No peeing on anything that looks nice," I warned, then chewed my lip a little more as I considered the problem. What was good for Mme. Deauxville's might be good for Drake's house. "I suppose we could sneak around the back of the house and see if I can't find us a way in. Then we'll reconnoiter."

"Reconnoiter, yes, that is a very good plan," Rene said as he tucked his cell phone into his pocket. "I like that. I am very good at the reconnoiter. Where do we commence?"

A couple more gnaws on the old lower lip, and I came to a decision. "Rene, I don't think it's a good idea for you to come inside with us. Even though Drake stole my dragon, and I'm just getting it back, technically it is a crime to break into his house. I wouldn't want you to get into any trouble."

"Feh," Rene said, waving away the possibility of trouble. He tapped his chest, giving me a knowing look as he did so. "I know the way of things here. You do not. And the demon, he is not very bright, *hein*? So we commence."

We commenced. I felt bad about Rene, but didn't think I could talk him out of it, and to be honest, I felt more secure with him along. I'd just have to see to it that he didn't get his kindness to me paid back with trouble.

"You get to be the watchdog," I told Jim as we approached one of the three ground-floor doors recessed in the back of the building. The back opened onto a dark, dusty alley that appeared abandoned. I studied the lock on the door for a second, almost smiling at it. I knew this lock; it was even easier to open than the one at Mme. Deauxville's.

"Watchdog? What does that mean?" Jim asked.

"Bark if you see anyone. Or anything suspicious. Or my aquamanile. You know, be a watchdog."

Jim rolled its eyes. The lock clicked open as I worked my credit-card magic upon it. Rene pursed his lips again at the sight of the door opening, but he didn't say anything as I slipped inside.

"Looks like a utility room of some sort," I whispered as Jim and Rene followed. I crept to the opposite door, opening it just a crack as Rene gently closed the outer door. Light from a hallway illuminated a few occasional tables and a couple of green embroidered chairs. From the right, I could hear the faint sound of conversation— a TV, I was willing to bet, coupled with the sound of crockery clinking a comfortable, homey sound. "That's the kitchen down there, to the right," I whispered. "Which way do you think—up or down?"

"Up," Rene said. "There is less chance we will see someone upstairs if the common rooms are on this floor, yes?"

"Works for me," I muttered as we skinnied down the hallway to where a large staircase curved upward, its elegant sweep of dark oak gracing an already stunning hall. "Is that linen paneling? It looks antique—"

"Aisling!" Rene hissed, halfway up the stairs. "Now is not the time to be a tourist."

Reluctantly I stopped myself from admiring the beautiful paneling. "Sorry. Coming."

I started up the stairs as Jim paused to sniff the air. The sound of voices was louder here, as was the smell of grilling meat. "Food!"

"You had your lunch," I said, tugging on its collar. "Come on. If everyone is eating, we can look around without being seen."

We hurried up the carpeted stairs, alert to anyone who might suddenly pop out of a room, but we saw nothing. Well, that's not strictly correct—we saw room after room of gorgeous furnishings, artwork that looked original (and valuable), works of art that should have been in a museum—but people? Not a soul. There was no aquamanile, either.

"Man, I had no idea there was so much money to be had in the dragon business," I said as I followed Rene and Jim into a bedroom decorated with an Oriental theme, all black lacquer and bright blues, greens, and golds. I was positive it was Drake's bedroom, which gave me an odd thrill as I looked around. The room was absolutely breathtaking, but not as breathtaking as the view seen from the terrace a solid wall of windows overlooked.

"Wow, this is absolutely astounding. What a gorgeous view. What a gorgeous room. What a gorgeous house."

"But it is not finding us your dragon," Rene pointed out.

"True." I kept my eyes firmly away from the huge black-and-gold bed that dominated the room and thought about where the lair would be. "We could look on the floor above, or the ground floor, but call it a hunch, I'm willing to bet that Drake's lair is in the basement. That's where I'd put something I wanted limited access to."

"I agree most strong," Rene said.

"Right. Back downstairs we go."

We slipped out of the bedroom and, after listening for a moment at the top of the stairs, decided the coast was clear. We descended with a minimum of sound and crept back to the side hall. "Where do you think the door to the basement is?" I whispered to Rene.

He pointed to the left. "That door."

I looked at the door. It didn't look any different from the two others. "Why that one?"

"It has the keys."

He was right. There was a key strung on a blue piece of string hanging around the doorknob. I snatched the string off the knob, surprised to find that it turned freely.

"Maybe the key is for something else?" I asked. Rene shrugged. Jim looked bored. Aware of the sounds of habitation in the kitchen, I hurried into the room. "Point one for us," I whispered as I felt around for a light. It clicked on to show us standing on the landing of a narrow flight of stairs that led downward. "Good call, Rene."

He looked pleased. "I told you I would be most helpful."

"I never thought you wouldn't be, but at the first sign

of trouble, I want you out of here. Jim and I can take care
of ourselves."

"We can?" Jim asked doubtfully. I didn't say anything.
What was there to say? I felt just as doubting as the
demon sounded, but I was determined to keep Rene from
being dragged any further than he already was into the
hideous mess my life had become.

Silently, or as silently as we could be considering the
wooden stairs cracked and groaned with every step, we
made our way to the bottom, where another closed door
was set into a stone wall. This one was padlocked shut.

"Voilà," Rene said. "That must be his storeroom, yes?"

"I imagine so. You'd think a man who had hundreds of
years to learn basic security would be a bit more careful
about his priceless objects," I whispered as I used the key
on the string to open the padlock. "All those pictures and
vases just sitting around upstairs, and just one lock on
this door? Uncle Damian would have something to say
about that." I set the lock on the floor, carefully opening
the door.

Two things should have become readily apparent to
you by now: First, I'm not the brightest bulb in the pack
when it comes to obvious things, and second . . . well, it's
the same as the first.

"Woof," Jim said as a light automatically turned on
when the door to the lair swung open. Rene sucked in his
breath and muttered something I didn't understand. I
clutched the door, blinking at the sight before us. It was a
treasure trove, pure and simple. There was gold everywhere—real gold, not fake gold. Gold plates, gold gob-
lets, gold statues . . . Drake's lair was a room filled with
display cases and ornate wooden cabinets, all housing objects of gold. "Have you ever seen anything like this?" I
whispered, walking slowly into the room.

"Arf."

"Never," Rene breathed, following me. I stood in the middle of the narrow, low-ceilinged room, my mouth hanging open as I looked from case to case.

"I can't even begin to calculate what it's all worth. . . . Hey, there's my dragon!"

"Bow wow."

I hurried over to the wooden cabinet that faced the door. Each one was individually lit within, the soft light carefully focused to highlight the objects nestled on the shelves. On the top shelf of the cabinet in front of me two objects sat on black velvet—one was my dragon aqua-manile; the other was a gold goblet similarly decorated with a dragon coiled around the stem.

"Bark, bark," Jim said behind me.

"Jim, what's your problem?" I asked as I reached out to open the glass-fronted door.

"I think perhaps *I* am the problem," a smooth, silky, extremely sexy voice said behind us.

"Oh, crap," I swore, letting my hand drop.

"You are in France. The correct word is *merde*," Rene corrected gently.

"Sorry. *Merde*." I turned to face Drake, trying to summon an innocent smile, not that it would do me any good. It didn't. The expression on his face left me wishing I'd taken my chances with the Venediger.

8

"Hi, Drake. Long time no see. We were . . . uh . . . in the neighborhood and thought we'd stop by and see how you were."

"Did you? How very generous of you. And your companions are?"

I waved my hand toward Rene. "This is Rene, my taxi driver. He doesn't know anything about what's going on."

"Doesn't he?" Drake turned his attention on Rene, eyeing him carefully for a moment before lifting his hand. A flash of blue like a concentrated ball of lightning shot from him to Rene, leaving me with big black spots bobbing before my eyes.

"What have you done to him?" I yelled as soon as the spots disappeared enough for me to see. I ran over to where Rene was slumped unconscious against one of the cases. "My god, you've killed him!"

"How bloodthirsty you are. I had no idea your lovely exterior hid such a cruel nature."

I sent him a glare that should have burned the hair right off his head. "I'm not the one who just killed an innocent man! You are going to pay for this, Drake. So help me, you are going to pay!"

Drake sighed and shook his head in mock sorrow. "Such a suspicious mind you have. I did not kill him. I merely sent him to sleep for a while. The fewer witnesses to what is about to happen, the better."

Relief filled me even as I recognized just how ominous his words were. I made sure that Rene was just out, and when I was satisfied that Drake told the truth about zapping him, moved so I had my back to the case holding the dragons. Drake glanced toward Jim.

"That's Jim."

"Her demon," Jim said, strolling over to Drake. "But if you're as powerful as you look, I can be *yours* instead."

"Traitor," I whispered, taking a step backwards. Although the main part of my brain, the functioning part, knew I was caught and how, the little daredevil section of my brain said that if I could just grab the aquamaile, I could run for it. True, the odds weren't in my favor, but there was still a chance I might be able to get by Drake if I could get Jim to distract him by attacking.

OK, it was a *very* small chance. But I didn't have much choice, now, did I?

I took another step back, my fingers brushing against the brass handle on the front of the case. Drake was giving Jim a look that had the demon backing away as it mumbled, "It was just a suggestion. Sheesh."

"Would it surprise you to know that I've been expecting you?" Drake asked, leaning back against the door, his arms crossed over his chest. "The police were here earlier, asking many questions about you and my alleged visit to Mme. Deauville's apartment. I, as an upstanding businessman, naturally expressed horror and surprise at accusations such as you have evidently leveled against me. The police seemed very satisfied of my innocence when they left, but somehow, I knew you would pay me a visit.

The memory of my highly detailed, erotic-beyond-my-wildest-dreams fantasy about him the night before was potent enough to make me shiver at odd moments during the day, but seeing him in the flesh took my breath away. I used a few moments to admire the hunter-green silk shirt he wore (the color matched his eyes perfectly) and the marvelous way it caressed the muscles of his arms and chest, as well as the tight fit of his black leather pants. He really was gorgeous, enough that my tongue cleaved to the roof of my mouth for a moment. I engaged in a little decleaving while swallowing hard a couple of times, my fingers busy as they opened the case behind me, quickly closing over the cool metal shape of a dragon.

"Were you? How prescient of you. Would it surprise you to know that I've got my aquamanile?" I crowed triumphantly as I whipped the gold object around in front of me. I pointed at Drake and used my best demon-ordering voice to say, "Effrijim, I command thee by thy lord Amaymon to attack him!"

Jim sat down. "You have *got* to be kidding."

Drake smiled, amusement clearly visible in his eyes. I wanted to scream. Why did nothing ever go right in my life?

I marched over to Jim and shook the aquamanile at him. "You are supposed to be my demon, mine to order, mine to give commands. I gave you an order. I'm in a desperate situation here. Drake is likely to kill me if you don't help me escape. If I die, no one is going to buy you hamburgers anymore. *Now* are we on the same wavelength?"

Jim made a pouty face. "He's not going to kill you—you're his mate. Dragons mate for life; they can't kill their mate or their own life ends."

I looked at Drake. He was still smiling. "Is that true?"

He looked me over carefully, his eyes lingering on my breasts. My mind went off on a little excursion remembering what it felt like to have his mouth on my flesh. I smoothed down the taupe linen tunic while I reminded myself that what had passed between us had been a dream, not real . . . even if the nightgown *had* been.

"You claim you aren't my mate."

"No, I meant that if I were—and I'm not saying I am—but if I were, is it true you can't kill me without corking off, too?"

The amusement in his eyes turned to outright laughter. "The demon does not lie."

"Whew," I said, breathing a huge sigh of relief. "That's nice to know. Hoo! I was worried there for a minute that you were going to get a bit testy over me having my aquamanile back, but I don't have anything to worry about if you can't hurt me—"

"I didn't say I couldn't hurt you—I said I couldn't kill my mate. As far as I'm aware, you have not agreed that you are my mate; therefore, were I to take exception to the fact that you have broken into my house with the intention to rob me, I could do so without any repercussions."

I clutched the aquamanile to my chest as I squared my shoulders and sent him as offended a glare as I could rally. "I do *not* like you."

"At this moment I'm not exceedingly fond of you, either." Drake straightened up, striding toward me, his hand outstretched for the aquamanile. "You will return my treasure now."

I clutched it tighter, moving backwards as he continued forward. "No. It's mine. I've stolen it back from you. If you want it, you're going to have to agree to help me, because there's no other way you're going to get it from me."

He backed me up until I was against the wall, the coolness of the stone seeping through the thin linen of my tunic. "You little fool, I allowed you to enter my home. Do you really think I have learned nothing about security in all my hundreds of years of existence?"

"You heard me," I accused, breathlessly aware of every inch of his body as he leaned against me, the dragon caught between us.

His fingers trailed a line from my ear down my neck. It was an oddly gentle touch. "It's called closed-circuit TV, sweetheart, and it can be found in every room of this building. As can the silent alarms on all the doors and windows, the pressure-sensitive floor alarms, and the thermal detectors that alert me to anyone who enters the house. If you had gone into the room beyond my bedroom, you would have seen the monitors that show me what's happening in every room."

"You have thermal detectors?" I asked, my mind going all girly as he tucked an errant curl behind my ear.

"I have many of them."

"Oh." My heart sank as I accepted the truth. We hadn't been fooling Drake at all. See? Not the brightest bulb. "I didn't see any of those."

Drake smiled his slow, sexy smile at me. "I knew sooner or later you would try to take the aquamanile back, so I decided to make it easier for you."

"Why?"

His hands slid up my waist, slipping under my crossed arms to head for the no-man's-land made up of my breasts. "Perhaps I wanted to lure you into my home. You liked my bedroom."

"It's very . . . you," I gasped as his thumbs rubbed across my breasts. The familiar fire was back in his eyes, a fire that warmed me to my toenails, a fire that set my whole body alight, but I was a woman determined. I kept a firm hold on the aquamanile as Drake pulled me tighter against him. "I thought you said you weren't fond of me?"

"I don't have to like you to want you," he murmured as he pressed his mouth against the pulse point in my throat. My knees threatened to give way under the erotic touch of his tongue against my flesh. I wanted to be offended by his statement, but in truth, I was not terribly happy with him at that moment, and yet he was stirring things deep in my soul that no one had stirred before. I was far from perfect, but I would not add hypocrite to my list of failings.

"Does he have his hand on your boob?" Jim asked, watching us avidly. "Is he copping a grope? 'Cause that's what it looks like from here."

"Go away!" I frowned over Drake's shoulder at Jim. It shot me a sour look but lay down and rested its head on its paws. "Drake, why did you *really* let me in?"

"Questions," he said, nuzzling my collarbone. My spine went all boneless as the cool silk of his hair brushed against my jaw. What is it about men's hair that makes it so sexy? "You always have questions."

"That's because you won't give me the answers, although you were almost a chatty Cathy last night before we . . ."

I stiffened the second the words left my lips, and not just because Drake's right hand slid around to my derriere. I hadn't meant to mention the dream, not since I was still confused over what was real and what wasn't. Although that nightgown was awfully real this morning. . . .

"I will always answer questions if you present me with an inducement to do so," he said, kissing a hot, wet path down toward my chest.

"An inducement?" I asked, my blood starting to simmer. He hadn't acknowledged the dream had been real, causing that tiny little part of my mind that worried it had been reality to sigh with relief. "What sort of inducement? Like money?"

"Mmm," he said, taking little nibbling bites that had me arching against him. His fingers slid down the line of buttons on the front of the tunic, his tongue snaking into the valley between my breasts. My knees gave out completely. "That's not what you offered last night."

"Last night? Oh, my god, it was real? When we— uh—that was real?" Embarrassment filled me at the thought of the things I had done with him, but that faded quickly as his mouth moved over me. My mind warred between the desire to give myself over to the burn he was generating within me and the almost desperate need to escape the desire he represented.

His tongue touched the spot on my collarbone where he had burned me in the dream. "Do you really doubt it was real?"

My mind decided it didn't want to cope with the fact that I had jumped the bones of the first handsome dragon I met a day after meeting him, focusing instead on what Drake was doing to me now. "You mean that's all it would take to get you to answer my questions—sex? Hot, steamy dragon sex? Hoo, you're not going to— Are you going to—?"

"I told you that after the first time we would make love

as humans do," Drake answered, his tongue a brand on my quivering flesh.

"Wow!" Jim said. "Wish I had a camera. The blackmail potential of this is enough to keep me in burgers for the next millennia."

"Jim!" I squawked as Drake's hand slipped inside my bra.

"Yo! Right here. Wow. I can't believe he's doing that in front of me. This is better than cable TV."

"Can't you make him go to sleep, too?" I asked Drake.

"He is your demon to command," Drake murmured against the swell of my breast.

My mind kept telling me I was stupid to just stand there and let him seduce me. My body overruled my mind with a majority vote. "Oh, yeah. I forgot that. Jim, I command you to close your eyes. And turn around. And don't listen to us."

"Party pooper." Jim grumbled.

My breast heaved a couple of times in Drake's hand as his long fingers stroked the swollen flesh, his mouth kissing a line over to the nipple that was screaming for his touch. I waited until Jim obeyed me before I looked at Drake.

His eyes glittered with arousal and want and leashed power, and I knew that if I did not stop him, things would go much further than I anticipated. The dream might have been shared between us, but what we were about to do was indisputably real, with very real repercussions . . . repercussions I wasn't sure I wanted to face. "This mate business . . . How do we know if I really am your . . . mate?"

"Only a true mate can survive a dragon's fire," he said as his teeth closed gently over my nipple. I clutched his hair and arched upward, my body and soul on fire, but it was a wonderful sensation, one that left me craving more.

"That's it?" I gasped, part of my brain surprised I could still form words. The other part was busy directing the fingers of my left hand as they unbuttoned Drake's shirt.

"That is what a dragon's mate must do. . . . A wyvern's mate must also prove herself to the sept."

"Uh . . . prove herself how?" I slid my hand inside his shirt, my fingers tingling with the heat of his skin. His muscles rippled as I mapped out the wonderful terrain of his chest and abdomen.

"A challenge is set. The mate must triumph over it or be rejected." He kissed a burning path over to my other breast, tugging my bra down so he could tease that breast with long strokes of his tongue. His voice was harsh, rough like crushed velvet. "You taste of my fire. You taste of desire. You taste the way a mate should taste. Come to me, Aisling. Give yourself to me again. Mate with me as mortals do."

His words were blunt, but they sent a shiver of pure arousal down my spine. After the things we'd done in my dream, I had no right to become suddenly prudish, but Drake was completely different from any man I had known. It wasn't just his power; it was the way he made me feel totally and completely feminine. He might be a dragon in human form, but he was the most masculine person I'd ever met.

His tongue burned me as it flicked over my hardened nipple, and I almost said yes, I almost threw caution to the wind and agreed to be whatever he wanted me to be just to taste again the promised fire in his eyes, but this was more than just a fantasy—there was something missing that I just couldn't ignore. There was arousal in his eyes, there was desire and the knowledge that we would bring each other ecstasy, but there was no affection.

"You don't like me," I whispered into his hair, a tear sliding down my cheek. Surprise flashed across his face. "And to be honest, although I really enjoyed the dream, and want to do lots and lots of things to you, many of which involve my tongue, I'm not . . . I don't . . . I'm not in love with you."

His emerald gaze didn't waver, but his eyes opened wider, the disbelief in them almost enough to make me laugh. "You do not sleep with men unless you are in *love* with them?"

"You don't have to say the word like it's something dirty."

"What we did last night did not involve love."

I tightened my lips. "What we did last night was not real, not in the sense that matters. As for love—so I don't sleep around, so I happen to believe that people should care about each other before they have sex. Lust and physical attraction are all well and fine as a fantasy, but there is more to be had than just wild, fiery, incredibly fabulous sex, you know."

His eyes grew dark. It was amazing how his irises grew brighter or darker with his emotions, but I didn't have the time to ask him how he did it before he spoke. "You are the only woman in all of time who was born to be my mate, the one woman to whom my life is irrevocably linked, the woman whose death will bring my own, and you believe I don't care about you?"

I raised my chin. "There's a big difference between self-preservation and true affection. Since right now part of me is so angry that I want to bean you with this aquamanile, I think it's probably better if I leave. With my friends. Unhurt." I added that last bit just as a reminder.

His gaze burned into mine for a few seconds, the flames of his anger licking along my skin. I opened the magic door in my mind and embraced the fire. He stepped back from me, and my entire body wailed a dirge at the loss. I tucked myself back into my bra and, still clutching the aquamanile, buttoned up my tunic.

Drake raised an eyebrow until he looked like he was the poster boy for irony. "And just how do you expect to keep me from taking the aquamanile from you?"

"I am a Guardian," I said with a great big bucketful of confidence that I didn't come even remotely close to feeling. "I have power of my own. You mess with me, you'll be sorry."

His lips quirked. "I believe someday that statement will be true, but today?" He glanced at Jim, who was lying by the door, its back to us. "Today I believe I will dare your wrath."

I'd like to point out that I had no choice. I really didn't. I'm not a violent person normally, but I knew without a doubt that if I didn't disable Drake, he'd simply take the aquamanile from me. If I had the aquamanile, he'd be pissed at me, but he'd agree to anything I asked in order to get it back. So I knocked him out.

Actually, I think I just stunned him. He wasn't expecting that I would take his move toward me as a classical situation of attack from the front, but one of the things Uncle Damian had insisted that I do was take a course on self-defense. So I kneed Drake in the noogies, stabbed at his eyes with the fingers of my left hand, and brought my right hand—and the heavy aquamanile—down on his head. He hit the floor with an astonished look on his face.

"Jim, up, help me with Rene," I yelled, not waiting to see how badly Drake was hurt.

"Oh, now you want to recognize me again— Fires of Abaddon, what did you do to him?"

"I want you to carry Rene upstairs and out to his taxi."

"Pardon me, you evidently have me confused with a pack mule. I'm a demon, *not* a form of transportation."

"You're a huge dog who can probably bench-press me and Rene put together, but don't worry, I'll be helping you. Lord, he's heavy."

With Jim's dubious assistance, I managed to drag Rene so he was partially draped over Jim's back.

"Ow! My back!"

"Shush," I said, running over to Drake, sliding two fingers along his jaw to find his pulse. It seemed a bit sluggish, but nothing too serious. There was no blood, which gave me hope he was just stunned. I turned him so he was on his back, pulling a cushion off a chair in the corner and tucking it under his head before turning back to Rene. The aquamanile I stuffed in my purse, slinging the strap over my head so it crossed my chest. I picked up Rene's legs. "Come on, let's go."

Jim groaned, but it staggered forward. I halted us once we got out of the lair, spending a few precious seconds to snap the padlock onto the door. I had a feeling it wouldn't stop Drake, but the lock might slow him down long enough to let us escape.

In the end, I didn't have to worry about leaving the house. Drake, secure in his ability to control me by himself, had evidently sent his minions elsewhere, because we didn't see a single person as we dragged Rene's body up the stairs, and we made *a lot* of noise.

"How do you know if you've broken your ribs?"

"You haven't broken any ribs," I panted halfway up the steep stairs. "Can't you go any faster?"

"I'm not a beast of burden," Jim snapped. "I think my spleen just imploded."

"Shut . . . up . . ."

"Fine, but you just remember this when I have to be on dialysis for the rest of my life."

"That's . . . man, he's heavy, how many steps are left? . . . Your kidneys, not your spleen."

We made it to the top and took a moment to catch our respective breaths before dragging Rene to the small utility room and the door I had forced. We had almost reached the door when Jim staggered into a collection of mops and brooms and other assorted cleaning tools that sat in a bucket, with the result that all three of us were immediately entangled. Jim fell, Rene slid off Jim's back, and I yelped when a broom slammed against my head.

"Sorry," Jim said.

"I'm going to get . . . ow! . . . you for this." I had gone down on my knees, half falling on Rene when a couple of brooms tripped me. I grabbed my purse from where it had fallen and hoisted Rene's chest onto Jim, grabbing him by the waist to help drag him out the door.

"You're not related to the Three Stooges, are you? 'Cause I could swear this escape thing is one of their routines."

"You . . . stay . . . here . . . with . . . him," I wheezed as we emerged into the dark alley, ignoring Jim's idea of witticism. I pushed Rene against the building and fished through his pockets until I found his car keys. "I'll get the taxi. Don't let anyone take him!"

"How am I supposed to stop anyone without any of my demonic powers?"

"You're in the form of a dog, so start acting like one! If anyone shows up, bite them!"

"Might be fun," Jim said thoughtfully as I staggered off down the alley toward where Rene had left his taxi.

By the time I returned, Rene was beginning to regain consciousness, but I wasn't about to hang around outside Drake's house until he was fully sober, so I stuffed the Frenchman into the back of the taxi with Jim and got the heck out of there, mindlessly following streets until I felt we had enough distance between us and the wyvern's mansion. With a sigh of relief, I pulled into a multistory parking building.

Twenty minutes later I was trying to concoct a story that sounded believable without spilling too much. Rene might know about Jim, but Jim was harmless. Drake was another matter, and I had a feeling he wouldn't be too happy if Rene knew too much about his identity. In this instance, ignorance was most definitely bliss.

"I didn't see a second man," Rene complained as he rubbed his head. "You said he was behind me?"

"Yeah, there was a . . . uh . . . secret passageway that opened up behind you. Drake's henchman clobbered you when you weren't looking."

Jim snorted.

Confusion and wariness took turns in Rene's eyes. "I don't feel the bump anywhere. If he hit me on the head, I would have the bump, yes?"

Jim snorted again.

"Did I say he hit you? I meant he karate-chopped you. You know, whacked you right on that nerve thingy in your neck that knocks people out. It was very fast. I'm not surprised you don't believe it, and Jim, if you snort one more time, you're off to the vet's office for a little snipping."

"And they say demons are nasty," Jim said, gazing innocently out the window at shoppers going to and from their cars.

"Ah. But you escaped?" Rene asked, still looking a bit confused.

"Yeah, well, I had to crack Drake on the head with my aquamanile. At least I have *that*," I said as I patted my purse.

It felt remarkably light for a bag that was suppose to contain a six-hundred-year-old chunk of gold.

"Merde!" I yelled as I frantically dug through the purse. I didn't have that much in it, but even emptying it on the seat next to Rene showed what I feared with a sick, sick feeling in my gut.

The aquamanile wasn't there.

I wanted to cry. "I had it, I had it in my hands, I put it in my purse. . . . Oh, crap, I must have lost it in the utility room when you knocked all those brooms down on me."

"It wasn't my fault. Rene was heavy. I could hardly walk," Jim protested.

Much as I would have liked to blame the loss of the aquamanile on Jim, I couldn't. I didn't think it had purposely careened into the brooms. Demon or not, it was obeying my command to carry Rene outside. Losing the artifact was just bad luck.

"Now what will you do?" Rene asked, a concerned look in his nice brown eyes.

The urge to cry was strong, but I knew all tears would do was leave me with red eyes and a runny nose. Instead, feeling very much the martyred Saint Aisling, I set my mind to being proactive.

"I suppose Drake made it out of the room and has found the aquamanile by now." I had to swallow back a big lump at the thought of the lost dragon, but I never was one to cry over spilled aquamaniles. "So going back to take it is out of the question. What I need is someone who's an expert with dra—uh—" I glanced at Rene. "—Drake. I think, if you feel OK to drive, that I'd like to go back to La Pomme Putréfiée."

"What is there to help you?" Rene asked curiously as he slid into the driver's seat.

"Amelie knows Drake," I fibbed. She knew *about* him, I was sure, and that was good enough for me. Perhaps she knew of a dragonish Achilles' heel. "I'm sure she'll help me."

"Famous last words," Jim intoned from the backseat.

9

"What is it with you and dumps?" Jim asked as we strolled through the door to Amelie's shop. "This place looks like a reject from a Harry Potter knock-off."

"Shh! Don't be so rude—Amelie will hear you." I glanced quickly around the room, grateful that Amelie wasn't present to be insulted by my demon. I unsnapped the leash and made squinty eyes at Jim. "And just what do you know about Harry Potter?"

"Oh, Harry's very big in Abaddon. Is that cat's toes I see over there?"

"Ew!" I said, staring in horror at a shelf full of jars containing what I had assumed were a variety of innocent herbs and such. "Cat's toes? That's horrible!"

Jim made a disgusted face. "Grow up. Cat's toes is a fern."

"Oh." I shot the jar Jim was snuffling a suspicious glance, then turned back to the store. "Hello? Amelie? It's Aisling. Anyone home?"

"I will be only one moment, Aisling," Amelie's voice called out from a back room. "Cecile is just returning from her constitutional."

"Who's Cecile when she's at home?" Jim asked, moving its investigation to a rack of books.

"Amelie's Welsh corgi. Now, listen to me—I don't want you embarrassing me, OK? Just remember that I hold the key to any and all future meals, and keep your lips zipped unless I ask you a question."

Jim cocked its head to the side and considered me. "You'd fit right in Abaddon, you know. You're got the demon lord bossiness down pat."

"I have nothing of the sort—," I started to say, then became aware of Amelie standing next to a curtained doorway. I gave her a watery smile. "*Bonjour*, Amelie."

"*Bonjour*. I see you have successfully summoned . . . a demon?"

I upped the wattage of my smile, painfully aware of the blush that rode my cheeks. "Yes, well, the summoning went a bit . . . awry. This is Jim."

"Yeah, hi, whatever, I'm not allowed to speak unless Her Holiness there permits me. . . . Fires of Abaddon! Baby, baby, baby!" Jim's eyes almost bugged out of its furry black head as Cecile waddled into the room. Jim did an odd little shimmy toward the surprised-looking Corgi. "Are you one hot mama, or what? Hey, baby, who's your daddy?"

"Oh, god," I said, slumping down onto one of the stools that sat next to the long counter.

Amelie looked from the dogs to me. "I do not understand—the demon named Jim wishes to know who Cecile's sire is?"

"No," I said, my hands over my eyes. Just how much worse could things get? "I think it's enamored with your dog. It tends to forget that it's not really one, as well. Which, actually, is one of the things I want to talk to you—Jim! That's rude!"

Jim didn't even look abashed at being caught sniffing Cecile's rear. "Dogs do it." I swear Jim waggled its eyebrows at Cecile. "Hey, honey, you wanna sniff mine?"

"Right, that's it, out!" I ordered, pointing to the door.

Jim looked shocked. "Out? You can't send me out there! I'm a valuable dog—someone will steal me!"

"If I'm lucky."

"*Well!*" Jim huffed, and sat down next to Cecile.

I turned back to Amelie, who stood with a puzzled frown watching Jim. "I'm sorry about that. Jim's a little . . . odd."

We both ignored the snort that came from Jim's direction.

"Yes, I believe I understand what you're saying." She waved toward a small brass-fitted coffeepot. "May I offer you some coffee?"

"Thanks, I could use it."

"I should tell you that I'm not entirely surprised to see you," she said as she poured us both cups of coffee.

"Why? Oh"—I inclined my head toward Jim—"you mean because of my little friend in dog fur? You were right about skimping on supplies. You can see what the result of *that* was. Big-time screwup."

"Of that, I am not entirely sure," she answered, looking thoughtfully at Jim, who was licking Cecile's ears. I pretended not to notice. "I have always felt that Guardians summon the demon who is most deserved by them. But it was not because of the supplies that I expected to see you. You have heard about the happenings at G & T?"

I dragged my mind away from the ghastly contemplation of what horrible deeds I had done to deserve Jim and shook my head.

"The police, they went to the club and questioned everyone there."

"Questioned them? Why?"

She watched me over the rim of her cup. "It is said that the police were looking for you."

"Me?" I squawked, splashing coffee everywhere. "Oh, I'm sorry. Do you have a cloth—? Thanks. They were looking for me? Are you sure? I've already talked to the police, just this morning I talked . . . Oh. Inspector Proust mentioned he had been looking for me. "

She did the feminine version of the Gallic shrug as I mopped up the spilled liquid with a dish towel. "That is what I was told. The police who interviewed the Venediger reportedly questioned him most closely about you."

"Oh, no," I said, staring into the remainder of my coffee. It was strong and black, just the way I liked it, minute beads of oil dancing along the gently steaming surface. I knew that Inspector Proust had had me followed—he all but admitted that—but I had no idea he would go so far as to bother people at the G & T. My shoulders slumped as I wondered how angry the Venediger was.

"My informant said that the Venediger has put the word out that you are to be brought to him immediately," Amelie said, evidently reading my mind.

Yikes! "Brought to him? As in kidnapped? Is he that angry?"

Her black-eyed gaze didn't waver one tiny little bit. "The Venediger does not look kindly upon people who bring the *l'au-delà* to the attention of the police. Everyone has been told to look for you. Everyone."

"*L'au-delà?*" I had a horrible, sick feeling in my stomach.

"It means . . ." Her hands fluttered for a moment while she tried to find the words. " 'Otherworld.' It is the name of our society, those of us who practice magic, and those of you who manipulate the dark forces. The police do not tolerate us well. It is part of the Venediger's job to keep us far from the notice of the authorities, thus his anger with you for jeopardizing our safety."

I didn't quite know what to think of being lumped in with the dark-force-commanding group, but there were other things, more important things to worry about, things like just what the Venediger had planned for me. "You're saying that kidnapping isn't out of the question?"

She nodded.

"Lovely. Now I have the whole of the Paris Otherworld after me. You know, I didn't think my day could get much worse, but somehow, it has. I almost hate to ask this, but are you going to turn me in to the Venediger?"

She looked down at the cup in her hands. "I am a *guérisseur,* a healer. I owe no allegiance to the Venediger, nor do I practice magic—not the type that could be influenced by him. So no, I will not turn you in, although if you will accept a morsel of advice—"

I smiled. Advice I was getting great huge gobs of of late.

"—it would, I think, be better for you to see the Venediger on your own terms rather than be presented to him as a bounty . . . or worse."

I pushed my coffee aside, no longer able to swallow anything. I didn't want to think what would be worse than being dragged to the Venediger as bounty. "You think I should turn myself in to him?"

Her gaze flickered away from me. "He is not the police, although he serves that function in *l'au-delà* of France."

My stomach, already wadded up into a tiny little ball, turned to lead and dropped to my feet. "Gotcha."

"Why is it, I wonder, that the police are so interested in you?"

I looked up from my slump against the counter. Amelie's face was one of bland innocence, no expression visible. "Well, it's no secret. If the police are going so far as to question the Venediger, you'll probably hear about it. I'm . . . um . . . kind of involved in a murder."

"The death of Aurora Deauxville," Amelie nodded.

I sat up straighter. "You know about it?"

Amelie waved her hands in an expressive gesture. "Everyone in *l'au-delà* knew Aurora Deauxville. She was an amateur, one who had pretensions but no true ability. She frequented G & T, as well as my shop and shops of the Wiccans. She called herself a mage, but I do not believe she even knew what a mage truly was."

"Hmm. Do I take it she was not well liked in *l'au-delà?*"

"I do not think it was so much a matter of her not being liked—she paid very well for consultations, for supplies and manuscripts. People tolerated her perhaps, but they respected the power of her money."

"Really? I thought . . . I assumed . . . I mean, if you've got the sort of power that can call up demons and cast spells and stuff, I'm surprised you'd be swayed by something so mundane as money."

She laughed, her eyes crinkling in delight. "There are very few wealthy inhabitants of *l'au-delà*. Only the very oldest immortals are what you would call rich, and that is because they have had time to accrue their wealth over the centuries, rather than because of their powers."

"Oh." That made for some interesting thinking. "Maybe I am going about the solving-the-mystery thing all wrong. Maybe rather than forcing Drake to tell me whodunit, I should investigate the murder like a detective would. . . . Naw. I'm no detective. Give me the easy way every time. Not that forcing Drake to tell anything is easy."

"I imagine it would be very difficult if he did not wish to oblige you," Amelie agreed without asking what I was talking about.

I gave her a feeble smile. "Drake is also involved in the murder of Mme. Deauxville. At least, I think he is. He won't tell me what he was doing there, or what he saw, or what he knows. He's so darned frustrating!"

Amelie laughed again and got off the stool to pad barefoot over to a beautiful antique glass-topped rosewood box sitting next to the cash register. She unlocked it and withdrew a small green object on a gold chain. "I believe you have more need of this than I have to profit from its sale."

I stared down at the green jade dragon. It was about three inches tall, highly stylized, obviously Oriental in origin, the curved tail of the dragon forming a figure eight around the body. Touches of gold on the head and body and tip of the tail made the piece glow with a brilliance that isn't usual in jade. "What is it?"

"It's a talisman. Its provenance is unclear, but I believe it was created by one of the dragon septs, possibly the green dragons."

"It's so pretty," I cooed, wanting like mad to touch the beautiful dragon. My fingers positively itched to feel it.

"It is. It is also something that I suspect you could use, given the present difficulties you find yourself in."

I gave in to temptation, allowing the tip of my finger to trace the sinuous curve of the dragon's body. It felt warm, not cool like jade normally feels. "It's much too valuable for me to accept, Amelie, although I greatly appreciate your generosity in offering it to me."

"It is not a gift I offer easily," Amelie said, pressing the jade dragon into my hand. "But it is one that I feel is right."

"But, it's valuable, and I don't have a lot of money—"

"To refuse a gift that is sincerely offered is to give great insult," Amelie said briskly.

I looked at the green dragon. It felt . . . vibrant. As if it had its own energy. It hummed silently in my hand. "Thank you," I said as graciously as I could, slipping the chain over my head. The talisman hung between my breasts, a warm, oddly comforting weight.

Amelie nodded her approval. "What is it you came to consult me about?"

I looked up from running my finger around serpentine dragon's tail. "Huh? Oh. Well, I was wondering if you knew whether dragons have an Achilles' heel. So to speak. Something I could use to force Drake into telling me what he knows about Mme. Deauxville's murder."

She made a thoughtful face.

"No Achilles' heel?" I guessed.

"None that I know of. The only one who might have the power to force a wyvern to do something he does not want to do . . ." Her voice trailed off into nothing.

I sighed and picked up the cup of coffee again. "Don't tell me: The only one who can get the upper hand with Drake is the Venediger."

She spread her hands in a gesture of impotence. "He is the only one."

"Great. So now I'm going to have to go crawling to him on my belly to apologize up one side and down the other, as well as beg for his help—which will cost me heaven only knows what, if Ophelia and Perdita were right—all while he's so pissed at me that he's put a contract out on me."

"Contract?"

I waved away the question as I climbed off the stool, gathering up my bag and Jim's leash. "Doesn't matter. I think if I'm going to have to grovel, I'll do it without my furry little friend. I'd better get back to the hotel and figure out how to do the release ritual."

Jim, who had licked Cecile's ears to the point that they were frothy with dog slobber, frowned at me as I waggled the leash meaningfully, but the demon managed to drag itself from the corgi.

"Time to eat?" it asked hopefully.

"No, time to go to the hotel and send you back to your fiery little home."

Jim sat and gave me an odd look. "You can't send me back. I told you that you were my master now."

I snapped the leash on its collar. "Yes, I know. I'm your master because I summoned you, but you belong to Amaymon, so it's back you go."

"Geez, what do I need to do, use semaphore? I told you I was unclaimed."

Amelie sucked in her breath, and with that sound I had the first inkling that something else was about to go very, very wrong with my life.

"You said that Amaymon kicked you out of his legions, but that he'd take you back in a bit," I said slowly. With much portent.

Jim made a face. "Yes, but before that could happen, you summoned me. You bound me to you. That means you're my master now."

The inkling turned into a full-fledged flood of horror. *"What?"*

Jim grinned; I swear it grinned at me. "It's just you and me, sweet cheeks."

"It can't do that, can it?" I asked Amelie with more

than a little bit of desperation evident in my voice. "It can't refuse to go back? All I have to do is conduct the ritual, and it's gone, right?"

She shook her head. "All demons belong to a lord; that is the nature of their existence. If you summoned one who had been cast out, it would become your demon. Unless you did not command it so?"

A wild hope arose within me. I looked at Jim.

"Do the words 'My name is Aisling. I'm your master' ring any bells with you?"

My heart joined my stomach as it turned to a leaden ball and promptly dropped to my feet. "Oh, god. This means . . . This means I'm . . ."

"Yes," Amelie nodded gravely. "You are now officially a demon lord."

Oddly enough, I didn't collapse or burst into tears or have a hissy fit, or even throttle Jim right back to Abaddon, even though I really wanted to do all those things. Instead I drank a few more cups of coffee while Amelie looked through her extensive library for any help there might be in getting rid of an unwanted demon.

"I'm afraid that short of destroying the demon, there is nothing you can do. I do have one piece of good news, though," Amelie said.

"Hit me with it—I could use some good news," I said as I gathered up my things to leave.

"You are the only Guardian in existence who is also a wyvern's mate *and* a demon lord."

"Guess I'm just lucky that way, huh?"

Her lips twisted in a smile. "*Luck* is one word for it, yes."

I waved good-bye and trotted out to find a taxi to take me to the address she had given me.

"Metro's cheaper and has the added benefit of crotches right at nose level," Jim said as I walked toward a main street where Amelie said I'd find a taxi stand.

"You are in such hot water right now, I don't think you need to be saying anything, especially on a street where people might hear you."

"You're the one who's on the Venediger's hit list, and *I'm* in hot water?"

I stopped listening to Jim, concentrating on what I'd say to the Venediger when I met him, polishing up my apology for the police closing down his bar (even though that wasn't technically my fault), and trying to form a request for help with Drake that wouldn't involve me selling him anything I was attached to, like my soul.

By the time the taxi pulled up outside the four-story building in a quiet neighborhood in the fourteenth arrondissement, I had my groveling down perfectly. Trees lined a street almost empty of traffic as children ran up and down, romping on the sidewalks, dodging little old ladies with black scarves and mesh bags. The Venediger's gray stone building looked like any other in Paris, complete to the ubiquitous black scroll wrought-iron railing that graced the bottom third of every window. Twin white French doors were set back into a recessed entrance.

"Looks nice," Jim said as I paid the taxi driver. "Maybe he can put us up? It would be a nice change from those dives you like to hang around."

I shuddered. I didn't even want to think about staying with the Venediger. I had a feeling it wouldn't be at all healthy. "Effrijim, I command thee to keep thy piehole shut until I inform thee otherwise."

Jim, unable to refuse an outright order, glared at me. I smiled at it, patting its head as I pressed the buzzer. "Why didn't I think of this before? Silence, sweet silence."

Jim lifted its leg and peed on the side of the entrance-way.

"Bad demon, bad!" I scolded, quickly straightening up from where I was about to try to rub Jim's nose in the puddle when the door opened. A pretty brunette stood in the open doorway, her bright pink lips pursed in what I suspected was a perpetual pout as she looked first me, then Jim over. She was wearing the sort of black leather straps and fishnet ensemble I had always thought meant bondage queen. All the important parts were covered—just barely—but the rest was left open to inspection. *"Oui?"*

"Bonjour. Parlez-vous anglais?"

"Yes," she admitted rather grudgingly. "What is it you want?"

"I would like to see the Venediger."

Her hand tightened on the door, almost as if she thought I was going to force my way into the house. Ha ha, oh ha. Almost made me laugh, that idea did.

"It's important," I added.

"He's meditating. Not for anything is the Venediger disturbed when he is communing with his guides."

"I have a feeling he won't mind being disturbed by me," I said with much loftiness, not a single ounce of which I was feeling. "My name is Aisling Grey."

Her eyes widened at my name; without a word she stepped backwards, waving me inside, which alternately pleased me (I was special!) and scared the crap out of me (the Venediger must really want to see me to allow his meditation time to be disrupted). Jim at my heels, I followed her through a surprisingly light, airy living room to a lovely small garden at the back of the house. Pink Lips gestured toward a small wooden structure in the back of the garden, situated next to a tall brick privacy fence. "He is in the gazebo."

"Thanks," I said. "Um . . . excuse me, but what's your name?"

Suspicion filled her eyes. She took a step backwards. "Why do you ask?"

I raised my hands to show I was harmless. "Politeness. I thought it would be nice to know who you are."

"My name is my own," she said, snapping off the words. She turned on her heel and marched back into the house, slamming the door behind her.

"Sheesh, what did I say? Why wouldn't she tell me her name?" I asked Jim.

It blinked its eyes at me.

"Oh for heaven's sake . . . you can speak again."

The answer to that permission was a rude gesture made with a big hairy paw. I tugged on the leash as we started across the yard. "Very clever, Mr. Pottypaws. Answer my question: Why did that girl get all bristly with me when all I did was ask her name?"

"I told you once—names have power."

"Uh . . ."

Jim heaved one of his (many) martyred sighs. "If she told you her name, you could have used that against her."

"You're kidding."

Jim flared its nostrils, not an easy feat for a Newfie. "Do I look like I'm kidding?"

"Hmm," I said thoughtfully as we strolled across the lovely velvety green lawn toward a white gazebo. Nothing about the structure was what I thought of as a traditional gazebo—a circular covered wooden deck with seats going around the perimeter. This building was made of wood, all right, whitewashed wood, but the windows were standard size and bore tinted glass panes. There was also a solid-looking door. The fence beyond the gazebo was at least ten feet high, made out of solid red brick.

Evidently the Venediger liked his privacy even in his backyard.

I took a deep breath as I stopped before the closed door, mentally running one more time over my apology and plea for help. "OK, I can do this. I'm a professional. I'm in control. I have a demon, and I know how to use it."

"Do you have a history of insanity in your family? 'Cause I think what you're about to do is downright stupid."

"Comments from the peanut gallery are entirely optional," I said, raising my hand to knock on the door. The second my knuckles struck wood, the door opened. Slowly. With much creaking. I stood in the open doorway, my hand still raised to knock as I gazed inside. Evidently there were skylights, because the closed gazebo was filled with light shining down in beautiful golden beams.

Light that caressed the figure of a man hanging upside down.

Light that shone off the highly polished handle of the seax that had been plunged into the man's chest.

Light that glinted off the blood pooled below, captured in the black-etched symbols of Ashtaroth.

Jim pushed against my leg to peer inside. "Well, now, there's a sight you don't see every day."

"Voulez-vous cesser de me cracher dessus pendant que vous parlez," I said, my heart pounding wildly.

"There's the spitting-in-my-face saying," Jim said softly to itself.

"J'ai une grenouille dans mon bidet!" I growled.

"And the frogs."

"*T'as une tête a faire sauter les plaques d'egouts,*" I wailed.

"Face like a manhole cover. Can *merde* be very far behind?"

"*Merde!*" I bellowed.

"You can say that again," Jim said.

10

"Why does this keep happening to me?" I wailed, waving my hands around wildly. "Why, why, why? What am I, a dead body magnet?"

"You want everyone in the neighborhood to hear you, keep it up," Jim advised, looking over its shoulder toward the house.

"Ack!" I shoved Jim inside the gazebo and closed the door behind us. "Don't touch anything. Oh, my god, he's been *killed!*"

"Looks like the same setup as the other place," Jim said, nosing around the circle. "Smells the same, too."

I wrung my hands, my mind whirling like a hamster chained to a wheel, forced to run around and around and around without stop. "He's dead! The Venediger is dead! Right in front of me, he's *dead!*"

"Yeah, I think we've established that. Are you hysterical?" Jim asked. "Should I slap you upside the head?"

The threat of being slapped by a demon allowed me to get a grip on myself (although it was a close thing there for a few seconds). I took a few deep breaths to get some much-needed oxygen heading toward my hamster-on-a-wheel brain. "OK. I'm in control. I'm confident."

"But are you a professional?" Jim asked.

I circled the upside-down body of the Venediger, gnawing on my lower lip as I examined him. "He's hanging by one foot. His hands are bound to his sides. He has a knife in his heart. Oh, *merde,* this is the Second Demon Death, isn't it?"

"Yup. All the classic signs, right down to the summoning circle beneath him."

I reached across the circle to place two fingers on the Venediger's hand. It was cooling, but not yet cold. He hadn't been dead long, maybe a half an hour. As I took my hand away, an object fell from his grasp. Without thinking, I picked it up. It was about the size of a silver dollar, a flat, round, dull gray-striped stone that was chased in gold, a paper-thin golden dragon limned onto the back. "What the heck is this?"

"You asking me?"

"No," I said slowly. I turned the stone over in my hands, unsure of what I should do with it. It felt heavier than it looked, and made the tips of my fingers tingle. "Power. It has power. Since it was clutched in his hand, more than likely it was the Venediger's, but the dragon is the same style as the one on my aquamanile and the chalice I saw in Drake's lair. Didn't Drake mention something about the aquamanile being one of a set of three?"

I gnawed on my lip for another moment, then tucked the stone into my bra for safekeeping. If it turned out to be nothing, I could easily return it. If it was valuable, perhaps I could use it to charm Drake into helping me. "Besides, the Venediger's dead, so it's simply a matter of finders keepers."

"Oh, yeah, *that* sounds ethical," Jim said dryly.

I ignored the demon as I paced around the body again before squatting on my heels to look closely at the circle, being careful not to touch it. "It looks like it's been drawn with a marking pen."

"Wood floor," Jim pointed out.

"Oh, yeah. At least it's easy to see the demon symbols. Bafamal again."

"Popular guy. Gets around a lot. Likes disco. Favors shiny Italian suits when it dons human form," Jim said helpfully.

"Hmm." I bit back the urge to run away from the dead body, from Paris, from *everything,* and instead held my hands close to the circle as I closed my eyes and opened myself up to the power within it. The light in the gazebo as viewed through my inner sight was so brilliant, it made me flinch. Mentally I looked around the room, but there was nothing to see but the body, the blood, and the circle. "The circle is closed, but no demon was summoned. Bafamal was here, though."

"Went to ground." Even with my eyes closed, I could see Jim nosing around a faint black smear on the wooden flooring. "Don't suppose you can feel who drew the circle?"

I dragged my sightless gaze back to the circle and allowed myself to really *see* it. There was something about it that felt . . . familiar. "It's someone I know, someone I've met since I came to Paris, but who it is . . . I can't see. I just can't see." A finger of ice chilled my back, making me shiver. "I know this: It's someone with a truly evil soul."

Jim looked toward the body of the Venediger and pulled a face. "That pretty much goes without saying."

"Darn it, I can almost feel who drew the circle. I must not be doing something right. If I can just concentrate enough . . ." I pictured my magic door, pictured it opening as it had when I channeled Drake's heat, when I felt the power of his fire as it burned through my body, giving me strength, giving me energy.

"Uh . . . Aisling . . ."

"Shh, I'm concentrating." I embraced the dragon fire, shaping it, molding it, turning it from a force that took life to one that created it.

"Aisling, I think you should see this."

"Just a sec—I'm almost done." Drake's dragon fire was the key to my power, about that I was sure. I took the shaped energy I had drawn from within me and gave it form.

"How do you like your dead man, rare or well done?"

I opened my eyes, once again aware of a vague sense of loss as I was confined to just normal sight.

The gazebo was on fire.

"What the hell?"

"Abaddon, not—"

"Crap on rye!" I interrupted, stared at the flames licking at the back wall of the gazebo. "Didn't I *tell* you not to touch anything?"

"I didn't do that—you did. The minute you started breathing heavy and doing your Mme. Aisling stuff, the fire started."

"Criminy dutch," I snarled as I got to my feet, coughing as the smoke from the fire stung my throat and eyes. "Why does everything happen to me?"

"I don't think now is the time to debate the catastrophic nature of your life. Now is the time to get out of here before we become barbecue."

"I think you're right, but not only because of the fire—I'm more worried what Inspector Proust will think. He might know I didn't murder Mme. Deauxville, but he is *not* going to be a happy camper if he finds me here. Oh, blast, Pink Lips!"

"Maybe she won't say anything," Jim suggested as I opened the door a couple of inches to scan the garden.

"You think?"

"Naw, I was just trying to make you feel better."

"Oh, you're a big help."

"All my masters tell me that."

The fire was gaining strength, the bench beneath the wall now burning steadily. I squinted through the growing smoke at the Venediger. "Shouldn't we try to get him down?"

"It's him or you, chicky."

"I vote me."

"For once, I'm with you."

I waved Jim forward, slipping out the door and closing it carefully. I paused for a second, then turned back and with the hem of my tunic wiped the doorknob clean.

"Prints," I told Jim as I shooed it toward the house.

"The building is about go bonfire, and you're worried about fingerprints?"

I shot it a glare. "I bet you if I searched hard enough, I could find a do-it-yourself neutering kit."

Jim looked thoughtful. "Point taken."

I hesitated before the flagstones leading to the patio. "I wonder if we should call the police. It feels wrong to just leave the Venediger hanging there. After all, if Pink Lips tells Inspector Proust I was here, and I didn't raise a fuss about finding the body, won't he think I'm involved?"

Jim took the edge of my tunic in its mouth and tugged me sideways along a narrow crushed-stone path that ran the length of the house. "You don't think you're involved now?"

"Yeah, but maybe I should call the fire department—"

"*Halte!*" A masculine voice yelled from the house. A man in a policeman's uniform stood in the doorway looking in my direction. He turned and gestured to his left, where two other men came around the far side of the house, both in plain clothes. I recognized one of them as being on Inspector Proust's CID team. The man in the uniform paused in the doorway and pointed at me. *"Arrêtez-vous où vous êtes!"*

"Jim!" I yelled, spinning on my heel and taking off in the opposite direction, heading for the non-police side of the house. "Help me!"

"Make it a command," it yelled at me.

I stopped long enough to bellow, "Effrijim, I command thee as thy sovereign master to attack the men who would stop me . . . but don't hurt them seriously, and don't let yourself get hurt, either, OK?" before darting down the crushed-rock path toward the wooden fence that met the brick one. Behind me, Jim started woofing in proper dog tones. I stopped at the gate, struggling with the catch, suddenly worried about Jim. All I saw of him was a giant black blur as he jumped the men. One of the plainclothes detectives was running away, talking into a handheld radio. The uniformed cop was on the ground, writhing. Jim was snapping and growling at the second detective.

"Jim, heel!" I yelled, then threw the gate open and raced out of it. I made it the width of the house when I ran into a six-foot-tall broadleaf hedge that merged seamlessly with the front corner of the house. Behind me Jim panted, the sounds of yelling coming from the back garden.

"Crap!"

"Merde," Jim said.

"Whatever. I'm going through the bloody thing." I shoved my way into the hedge, instantly getting snagged on a gazillion little branches. My tunic tore, the chain holding my talisman got stuck on a branch, my hair got caught, horribly sharp branches scraped my bare arms and face, but I continued through it, losing only a sandal in the process. I was breathless and covered in leaves and dirt when I lunged through to the other side, taking only a second to note the police cars lining the house's drive.

I turned my back to them and started limping in the opposite direction, wiping the smoke and dirt from my eyes, plucking branches and leaves from my hair, braced and ready to take off if anyone so much as breathed in my direction. Jim mumbled something about ruining a beautiful coat as it followed me. I held my breath as we walked to the corner and took a sharp left, but there were no whistles, no sirens, no yelling, no police pounding down the pavement after me.

I looked at Jim. It was covered in branches and leaves, too, dirt smudging its muzzle. I plucked the bits of debris off it, trying to keep the shaking that suddenly swept through me to a minimum.

"Heel?" Jim asked in a caustic voice. *"Heel?"*

"Sorry, it was all I could think of." I took a shaky breath. "I think we're safe."

As the words trembled on my lips, a glossy black limousine sped around the corner, slamming on its brakes to come to squealing halt two feet away from me. I stared in dumbfounded surprise as a red-haired man leaped out of the car, jerked open the back door, then without so much as a "Hi, how are you, mind if I kidnap you?" grabbed me by my now-grubby waist and tossed me inside. I crashed onto the lushly carpeted floor, my nose banging into a pair of expensive, highly polished Italian shoes. Jim squawked as it was tossed in behind me.

"Good afternoon, Aisling."

I followed the feet up to legs, then higher to well-

muscled thighs. I knew that voice. I knew those thighs—
sort of.

I pushed myself off the feet and faced Drake, Jim leaning up against my back. "Drake Vireo, fancy meeting you
here."

Drake cocked a glossy black eyebrow. "That's just
what I said to myself when I saw you standing at the
scene of yet another murder."

I put my hands on his knees and used them to hoist
myself up to sit on the comfy leather seat next to him.
Just as I was going to ask him how the devil he knew
where I had been, he said something in a language I
didn't even come close to understanding. One of the red-
haired men nodded. The car swooped into driveway,
backed up, and headed in the direction we had just come
from.

"What language was that?"

"Hungarian," Drake answered, leaning forward to
look beyond me out the window at my side.

"Hungarian? Is that where you're originally from,
Hungary?"

"Yes." A siren grew louder, and I realized that we were
driving down the Venediger's street straight toward the
mass of police cars with their blue flashing lights. The
police more or less blocked the street, one uniformed cop
directing traffic around the obstructions.

Drake gave another command, and the car came to a
halt. Over the hedge I could see the gazebo as smoke bil-
lowed out its top. Several people stood around the burning building, one man hauling a garden hose over to it,
others just standing helplessly. Pink Lips was there,
clinging to the arm of one of the plainclothesmen.

"Did you do that?" Drake asked quietly, watching as
the flames licked up the side of the building.

"No! It was Jim!"

"Me?" Jim gasped. "I did nothing of the sort."

Drake looked at me, his eyes almost black. "You ordered your demon to set fire to the Venediger's body?"

"It wasn't like that—it was an accident. I was thinking about your fire, and . . . and . . . I guess it got out of control."

Drake snapped an order, and the car backed into another driveway, turning around to leave the way we came. His lips pursed, Drake looked at me as if he was trying to figure me out. I lifted my chin, painfully aware that my arm was bleeding, my eyes were burning, and there were bits of broken branches in my hair. "If I get your passport back, will you leave?"

"What?" I stopped wiping at a trickle of blood running down my upper arm to stare at him.

"If I get you your passport, will you leave the country?" Drake pulled a handkerchief from his pocket and gently wiped my arm where blood was beading up in a couple of spots.

"How can you get my passport back?"

He shot me a quelling look. "I am the wyvern of the green dragons. It wouldn't be that hard."

"Oh. Yeah. I forgot about that whole thief thing for a moment."

"I believe it would be best for all if you were out of the country," he said, turning his attention to the scratches on my other arm. His touch was tentative and careful, as if he were handling an object of great value. "If you promise to leave Paris, I will bring your passport to you."

I had to think about his offer for a minute. If all I truly wanted was to go back home, it might tempt me, but now there were other things to think about, things like honor and my pride and . . . Oh, who am I trying to fool? Drake was one of the things, too, although I still didn't know exactly what I wanted to do about him. "No. I wouldn't go home if you gave me my passport, not so long as Mme. Deauxville's murder is unsolved, and now the Venediger . . . Hey! How did you know he was dead? How did you know I found him? How did you know I was even there? OHMIGOD, *you* killed him, didn't you?"

"Kill him?" Drake snorted, tucking the bloody handkerchief back into his pocket. "Why would I kill him? I was working for him. With him dead, I won't get paid."

I don't know why, but Drake's admission was the very last thing I was expecting to hear. "You *worked* for him? You, a wyvern? What had he hired you to do?"

"I don't believe that's pertinent." Suddenly his eyes narrowed as he turned fully to face me. "Why do you smell of gold?"

My mouth hung open a moment as I stared at him. "You can smell gold, really smell it?"

"Yes." He leaned toward me, sniffing the air around me, his face coming to a halt in front of my bosom. "You have gold. Let me see it."

I clasped both hands to my breasts. I had tucked the jade dragon inside my blouse so it nestled between my breasts, a warm glow that radiated pleasure. There was also the gold-limned stone, the one I thought might be brother to the other two pieces Drake held, but it had slipped down underneath one of my breasts. "If I show you, you'll just steal it from me."

"Possibly. But I'll steal it for certain if you don't show me."

I gave him my very best fulminating glare. "Well at least you're honest about your dishonesty." With an annoyed grimace I tugged on the chain until the jade dragon popped up. I held it up so he could see the gold bits on it. "It's a talisman, and you can't have it. It was given to me."

Drake's nose twitched as he carefully eyed the dragon. "Jade?"

"Yes. It's *mine.*"

"Hmm." He peered closely at it. "Eighteen-carat gold, approximately two hundred years old. Chinese in origin, judging by the style of the head—the Chinese always insisted on giving us those silly fringy bits on top. Not terribly valuable. Very well, you may keep it," he said, sitting back against the seat.

"How very generous that is of you," I said acidly, tucking it away under my tunic, secretly pleased that he hadn't sussed the fact that I had another bit of gold tucked in my bosomage.

"I thought it was," he said placidly. "What were you doing at the Venediger's?"

"Ironically enough, I was just going to ask you that very same thing, along with half a dozen other questions, beginning with why you have snatched me off the street when I was making a perfectly acceptable getaway, and ending with why you were lurking outside around the Venediger's gazebo if you didn't kill him."

Drake waved the questions away. "The answers to your questions aren't important. Why did you go to see the Venediger? Did you not know he had placed a bounty on your head?"

I reached over and pinched the skin on the back of his hand. Hard. "I see you are confused about how this game is played. Conversation consists of give and take—"

He twisted in the seat and grabbed me around my waist, hauling me up to his chest.

"Oh, goody," Jim said from where it was lying on the

floor. "I get to see another show. I just love it when he gets all manly with you. You think maybe he's going to rip your bodice or something?"

"Jim, I order you to be quiet," I said.

"Shut up," Drake told Jim at the same time, his eyes burning into mine. "Now, would you like to discuss the rules of the game?"

"Stop doing that," I protested, my bones melting under the look of wanton desire he was sending me.

His fingers trailed across the back of my neck, causing wave after wave of pleasure to ripple down my spine. His head tipped toward mine, his lips just a hairbreadth away. My back arched, forcing my breasts to rub against his chest, his breath hot on my mouth. I parted my lips, unable to resist the lure of his mouth for another second—

"Damn," he swore, pushing me back onto the seat.

"What?" My body, so close to going up in his flames, protested the rejection.

Drake rubbed his nose. "It's that gold you're wearing. It's distracting me. Take it off."

And alert him to the fact there was more gold on my person? Huh-uh. "Thank you, I believe I'll keep it on. Amelie said it was a talisman against dragons. I'm beginning to see why she thought it was important I have it. Now, let's get back to this conversation thing—where are we going? I hope it's somewhere we can talk, because I'm quite serious when I say that I have a lot of questions for you."

His eyes glittered darkly. "What makes you think I will answer them? I have the aquamanile back that you attempted to steal from me—"

"The one you stole from *me.*"

"—and although your jade talisman is distracting, it's

not valuable enough to tempt me. What do you offer me in return for answers to your questions?"

Why was it that having just a simple conversation with Drake made me feel as if I was juggling fire torches? I gnawed my lip for a moment, then decided that offering him the stone I had taken from the Venediger was the only thing I had to barter with. "What about the third piece that matches my aquamanile and that chalice you have?"

His beautiful green eyes widened. I grinned at the look of surprise on his face, one that was quickly wiped away and replaced with his usual savoir-faire. "You have the Occhio di Lucifer?"

"The *what?*"

"The Eye of Lucifer. That is the name of the third Tool of Bael. It is a lodestone bound in gold. You have it?"

I spread my hands wide, fervently hoping he'd buy my innocent act and not rip off my tunic to nose around my boobs. "Do I look like I've got it? You'd know if I had, wouldn't you?"

"Yes," he said, rubbing his nose again. The avid light in his eyes died down a fraction, but not much. "Then you know where the Eye is?"

"Maybe," I said coyly. "But I don't understand the name. Why is it called the Eye of Lucifer? And isn't that name you gave it Italian?"

Drake leaned back against the seat, his eyes watchful. "Yes, it is Italian. The Tools of Bael consist of the Anima di Lucifer—Blood of Lucifer—that is the aquamanile, and the Voce di Lucifer—the Voice of Lucifer—which is a gold chalice."

"You have that, as well," I said, thinking of the dragon-stemmed chalice that had sat next to my aquamanile in the display cabinet at his house.

"Yes. The third is the Occhio di Lucifer. The Venediger had that." He looked at me with speculation rife in his eyes. "If you have it, you must have taken it from him."

"Who's to say I did? And if I did, who's to say what I did with it?" I answered as mysteriously as I could. I needed to get him off the subject of what I could have done with a small stone in the short amount of time that passed while I was running from the gazebo until he nabbed me. "What were these Tools of Bael used for?"

Drake frowned for a second; then his brows relaxed into their normal smooth lines. "I keep forgetting that you have not yet discovered your full powers as a Guardian. The Tools of Bael were forged by a powerful mage during one of the Crusades. His intention was to use the power the Tools would give him to aid England's King Richard, but as soon as he had created them, a rival mage stole them and turned the Tools against him."

"But what did the Tools do? And who is Bael?"

Jim did an antsy sort of up-and-down jump. I narrowed my lips at it. "You may speak if you have something worthwhile to contribute."

"Everything I say are pearls of wisdom," Jim answered, then hurried on when it saw the warning in my eye. "Bael is the first principal spirit in Abaddon, the leader of all the princes. He rules sixty-six legions and often takes the form of a man with a hoarse voice."

"Oh, you mean Beelzebub. Right. Gotcha. So these Tools of Bael tap into his power?" I asked Drake. He nodded. "Wow. I imagine having access to the head of all the demon lords is pretty powerful stuff. What were the Tools used for, exactly? I mean, an aquamanile, a chalice, and a lodestone don't seem to have too much in common."

"Ritual," Drake said, looking away.

"Think sacrifices," Jim said with much pleasure.

My stomach turned. "Ah. OK."

"Blood sacrifices," the demon added, as if I didn't get that part.

"Yes, thank you. I gathered that."

"Of innocents."

"Innocents?" I asked it, afraid of what its answer would be.

Jim's lips twisted. "Children."

"Pull over!" I yelled at Drake, my stomach roiling. He took one look at my face and snapped a command to the two guys up front.

I made it to a space between two parked cars, but just barely, aware of Drake's presence behind me as I vomited my lunch into the sewer. Life, I was pretty sure, could not get any stickier.

I am so often wrong about these things.

11

"Say what you will about you—and I can say a lot, despite having known you for only a couple of days—you really have a fabulous house. Is this all stuff you've stolen over the years?"

Drake shrugged as I set a lovely Grecian bowl back onto its pedestal. I took the shrug to mean yes. The room he called his library could have doubled for a museum, so full of antiquities was it. It gave me an odd feeling to know that he was old enough to have seen most of the objects when they were new. I moved over to stand in front of a triptych depicting Saint George about to stab his lance into a writhing dragon. "One of your ancestors?" I couldn't keep from joking.

"No, that was one of the red dragon sept," he answered in all seriousness.

I gaped, looking from the triptych to him. "You mean Saint George really *did slay* a dragon?"

"Of course." Drake walked over to an ebony sideboard holding a variety of cut-glass decanters.

"Wow." I looked back at the picture. "So what was it like back then? The Middle Ages, I mean?"

Drake gave me a disgusted look as he brought me a

glass filled with a deep red wine. "I wouldn't know—I wasn't alive then."

"Oh, really?" I took a tentative sip of the Dragon's Blood, its now-familiar burn a comforting heat, one that effectively singed out the last remnants of my nausea.

Drake's digusted look got a whole lot more disgusted. He did the nostril-flare thing as he asked, "Just how old do you think I am?"

"Well, let's see. . . ." I strolled around him, enjoying the opportunity to look him over without appearing to ogle him (which, of course, was what I was doing). He was dressed in a navy suit this time, although as soon as we arrived at his house, he shucked the suit jacket and tie, and rolled up the sleeves of his cream-colored shirt. As I circled him, I had to clutch my hands together to keep from allowing my fingers to go exploring. "I'd say . . . hmmm . . . five hundred years?"

"Five hundred!" Drake snorted.

I raised my eyebrows in mock surprise. "Four hundred?"

"I am exactly three hundred and eighty-nine years old, although I have been told that I don't look a day over two hundred."

I smiled at the outraged expression on his face. "Sorry, I didn't mean to offend. You're right—you don't look that old. I'm surprised that you're so young, though. You're just a widdle bitty baby dwagon, aren't you?"

"Hardly that," he said with another disparaging look.

I strolled over to admire a fabulously detailed ivory-and-ebony-framed dartboard. The darts in it were hand-painted with ornate dragons, trimmed in gold, each one fletched with peacock feather flights. "Pretty. Do you play?"

"Extremely well."

I put the dart I was examining back in its ivory socket. "Darts seem a little tame for a dragon almost four hundred years old."

"Any game can be made exciting if the stakes are right," he answered, waving me toward a chocolate-colored leather sofa.

"I suppose so. Are you sure Jim is going to be OK with your minions?"

"They're not minions—they are members of my sept. And your demon will be fine with them," he answered as he sat next to me, one arm snaking out to haul me up to his side. I thought of protesting the possessive move, but the truth was, I enjoyed being snuggled up next to him. And as long as I had to interrogate him, I might as well be comfy, right? Right.

I hadn't noticed much during the trip to Drake's house after having ralphed up my guts in the street, but once I arrived, I couldn't help but be impressed once more with just how fabulous his house was. Drake sent Jim off to the kitchen with Pál and István, his two red-headed buddies who I gathered also served as some sort of body-guards, both of whom Jim immediately began ingratiating itself with.

"So, let's get right down to the negotiating."

Drake looked like he was going to say something, but inclined his head toward me instead.

"First, the ground rules: You answer my questions, however many I want to put to you, honestly and completely. You agree to help me discover who the murderers are of both Mme. Deauxville and the Venediger. Once we find that out, I tell you where you can find the Eye of Satan."

"Lucifer."

"There's a difference?"

Drake sipped his drink. "One of semantics, perhaps. Names—"

"—have power. Yeah, yeah, so I've gathered. Do you agree to the rules?"

He set down his glass, pulling me close. His breath was warm on my cheek as he nuzzled my jaw. "Do I have a choice?"

"Lots of them," I said, squirming, although whether it was to get away from him or closer to him was not quite clear in my mind. That thought, however, made me curious about something. "What . . . uh . . . what exactly did you *do* with the virgins?"

"What virgins?" he asked, his hand sliding up my thigh.

"The ones you said you missed so much," I answered, stopping the hand before it could slide under my tunic. There would be no touchy-feely business while I hid the Eye of Lucifer in my bra.

He pulled back a couple of inches, unexpected amusement making his eyes dance. "Unfortunately, by the time I was born, very few villages were offering up virgins as a sacrifice."

"Really? What did they give you instead?"

He glanced toward a cabinet that held a variety of jeweled daggers.

"Oh. Ah. Well, I suppose gold and jewels and valuables are better than a virgin any day, eh?"

"That depends on the virgin," he answered, his hand trying to slide under mine.

"Sorry, gropage isn't part of the rules," I said, firmly pushing his hand away. "Do you agree to the terms?"

He sighed and sat back, his fingers trailing down my bare arm. I shivered at the heat that just his fingertips could generate. "Very well, although I must warn you, I do not like my women dominant."

I snorted at that comment (which was all it deserved) and settled in to get serious. "Right, let's begin with Mme. Deauxville. What were you doing there?"

Drake sipped at his drink, stalling as long as he could before he answered. "I told you that the Venediger hired me. I was at Mme. Deauxville's to fulfill the duties that I was hired for."

I pinched his wrist. "We'll be at this all night if you answer all my questions that evasively. Now, spill."

He frowned at me. "It does not come easily to me, this interrogation. I am the wyvern of the green dragons. I am not a person to be treated thusly."

"You're also arrogant, domineering, and sexy as all-get-out, but that doesn't change the rules. You agreed to answer *completely*."

Emerald fire burned hot in his eyes. "You push me too far, Guardian."

I smiled and flicked my tongue across the tip of his nose. "I haven't even *begun* to push you, dragon. Now let's get on with it."

A tiny wisp of smoke drifted out of one nostril. Drake's jaw was so tight, I was surprised he could talk at all, but talk he did. "I was hired to retrieve the Blood of Lucifer from Mme. Deauxville. I arrived early, having been misinformed about the time you were due to deliver the aquamanile. When I arrived, she was dead."

Without thinking, I laced my fingers through his, resting our joined hands on his thigh. "Hmm. If you didn't kill her, who do you think did?"

He tossed back the remainder of his drink. "I assumed the Venediger did. Bafamal was one of the demons he frequently used. The murder had all the signs of being his handiwork, but for one thing."

"What was that?" I asked, my thumb tracing circles on the back of his hand.

"He would never have spent the money he agreed to pay me to do a job he intended on doing himself."

"Oh, yeah, I see your point. So who do you think killed her?"

"I have no idea." His green eyes turned to me. "I had rather thought you would be able to tell."

I grimaced. "I couldn't. When I tried to figure out who drew the circle beneath the Venediger, the gazebo caught on fire." I frowned, remembering the powerful feeling of controlling Drake's fire. "Why was I able to feel your fire when you weren't with me?"

His gaze flickered to the side. "You are my mate. One of the abilities of a mate is to channel fire."

"But I shouldn't have been able to do that if you weren't there, right?" Something so obvious that you probably thought of it eons ago struck me. "You *were* there, right there. You were at the Venediger's house. That's how you knew I showed up, how you knew I had gone into the garden to see him."

"I was just leaving when you arrived, yes. I remained to see what you would do when you discovered the body, but unfortunately István had discovered that the police were on their way. I decided retreat would be a better choice than to stay to see what you would do."

"You didn't miss much of anything other than me setting the building on fire." And finding the Eye of Lucifer, of course. "Why did the Venediger want you to steal the aquamanile? Why didn't he just buy it from Mme. Deauxville?"

Drake turned our hands so that his fingers were

stroking mine. It was an extremely erotic feeling, although I couldn't for the life of me figure out why. "She was his rival."

"Rival?"

"In the sense that she acquired an object he desired, yes. She believed she was the reincarnation of a great mage, but in truth she was deceived."

"And the Venediger? He really was a great mage?"

Drake shrugged, his fingers moving up my arm.

"So the Venediger was trying to gather together the Tools of Bael. Did he know you had the Voice of Lucifer?"

"No. I was going to negotiate for the sale of that after I had acquired the aquamanile. He already had the Eye. I knew he would give anything to gain the last of the three."

I peered suspiciously at him. Something he said didn't make sense. Drake had mentioned that he held on to what was his. As avidly as he reacted to the sight of gold, I didn't believe for one moment that he'd give up such a glorious piece as the Voice of Lucifer for mere money. I couldn't help but wonder if he had been planning on double-crossing the Venediger, planning to steal the Eye of Lucifer from him once he had the other two pieces. But if he had intended on doing so, that would mean he meant to use them. But for what purpose? "If the Vendiger was such a powerful mage, why would he need the Tools of Bael. What would that do for him?"

Drake laughed and tugged me closer. I leaned bonelessly into him, aware again of the wonderful feeling of his heat, of the spicy scent I knew was him and not cologne, of the sensual feel of his leg and hip pressed against mine. "Sweetheart, why does anyone want power? To conquer, of course."

"Conquer what?" I looked up at Drake, noting absently that he had adorable earlobes.

"With the power of Bael joined with his own? Anything. Nothing would be out of his reach. Europe, the Eastern Hemisphere, the world, mortal and immortal . . . it would all have been his."

A shiver of dread skittered down my back. What made sense for the Venediger also made sense for Drake. He was a powerful wyvern. If he could use the Tools to draw on the power of Bael, was there anything he couldn't do, any treasure he couldn't take?

"No one should have that sort of power," I said firmly.

"No? It is a point many would dispute. Come," he said abruptly, standing and pulling me up.

"Come where? I'm not done questioning you."

"Am I not allowed occasional respite?" he asked, his eyes full of dark laughter again. He tugged me toward the door to the hall.

"What sort of respite?" I couldn't help but think of that big black-and-gold bed upstairs.

"Dinner. I'm hungry, and after emptying your stomach, I assumed you would be, as well."

I was a bit ashamed of the smutty direction my thoughts were taking as he led me out to the hall and up the curved staircase I had crept along earlier in the day. "Oh, dinner, yeah, that would be nice. . . . Hey! Your dining room isn't upstairs."

His fingers ran around the edge of the armhole of my tunic. "I assumed you would prefer to change into something less stained."

I twitched myself out of his grasp. "Oh. Yes, I would, but my clothes— Oh, blast it!" I stared up at Drake, dismay filling me at what I'd forgotten. "The police! They know I was there, and they must have gone back to my hotel by now. I'm a wanted criminal! Proust is never going to believe I'm innocent now. They probably even have an arrest warrant out for me. What am I going to do? I can't go back to my hotel or they'll arrest me. My things—"

"I will provide you with whatever you need," he answered, leading me down the hall, in the opposite direction of his bedroom, I was pleased to note. Well, perhaps not completely pleased . . .

"Really? Do you keep a supply of women's clothing and undergarments available just in case of drop-ins? Wait—maybe I don't want to know the answer to that."

Drake grinned a grin of absolute and complete smug male delight. "Jealous, sweetheart?"

As a dark, brooding, and incredibly sexy man, he was nearly irresistable to me. But playful Drake almost did me in. Immediately I went into full scorn mode. "You wish."

"You don't lie very well, do you? As for the other, I have already offered to retrieve your passport. If you will not take it and leave the country, there is little else I can do other than provide you a safe haven," he said as he flung open the door to a room I hadn't visited earlier. The room was decorated in varying shades of blue and gold. On a very comfortable looking bedspread with a lapis-colored satin cover a variety of women's clothing had been placed. "Just to set your jealous mind at ease, I had Pál pick a few things up for you while I was showing you around the house. He had to estimate your size; if anything doesn't fit, let me know and I'll have him fetch the appropriate replacement. The bathroom is through that door," he pointed to a door next to a large wardrobe. "I thought you might want a shower before dinner. If you need me, the intercom is here."

I looked at the electronic panel set next to the door. "Um . . . you said you have closed-circuit TV in all the rooms. . . . "

He nodded toward corner. I peered across the room. A small, unobtrusive camera was attached to the ceiling, a tiny little red light glowing as it watched us. Drake pushed a button on the intercom panel. The light on the camera faded into darkness. "The green button turns the cameras off."

I looked at the camera suspiciously. "How do I know it doesn't just turn the light off? How do I know you're not some strange pervy man who likes to videotape women undressing?"

Drake laughed and put his hands on my hips, turning me to face him. "If I wanted to see you undress—and I'll admit, it's a thought that gives me pause—I wouldn't have to resort to using a camera to do so."

I went all breathless and weak-kneed, which was pretty much my standard response to Drake whenever he was closer to me than fifty feet. "Oh, yeah? You're awfully sure of yourself."

For a moment his eyes were filled with longing, and I knew he was absolutely right. If we weren't both making the effort to keep our desires safely leashed, we'd be rolling around that big bed of his at that very moment. "Don't be too long. I'm very—" His gaze roamed over me. "—hungry."

The door clicked quietly closed behind him as I stood in the middle of the room and hugged myself. "I am *so* out of my depth with him," I said softly.

The sound of my voice reminded me that I had things to do, important things, things that did not involve mooning over a dragon in a male form that made great huge puddles of slobber gather in my mouth. I checked the clothing on the bed, approving of the two lightweight dresses, a sleeveless silk blouse styled very like my tunic, and a pair of white gauze harem pants. Pál got full marks for getting darn close with the size of the clothes (including a pair of espadrilles that fit perfectly). There were also three sizes of both bras and undies, one of which was mine, so I added bonus points to his tally as I trotted into the bathroom to take a fast shower.

After I threw one of the dresses over the camera. I wasn't taking any chances with Drake.

12

A cold, wet nose rubbed against my cheek, dragging me from a very erotic, very detailed dream involving Drake, me, and a container of yogurt. Lemon yogurt. My favorite, especially when consumed in the manner Drake was feeding it to me.

"Mmmmm. What? Who . . . oh, Jim. What are you doing here?"

"I know you're heading for forty, but I didn't think old age would be catching up to you so quickly."

"Huh?" I rubbed my eyes, pushing myself up on one elbow to glare at my hairy little demon.

It glared right back at me. "Have you forgotten that you got down on your dimpled knees and begged me to stay in your room so as to protect your chastity from the big bad dragon?"

"My knees aren't dimpled," I said irritably. I was enjoying my dream about Drake. If I couldn't taste the forbidden fruits he posed in reality, at least my subconscious deserved to have a good time. "And I didn't beg you, I commanded, and the only reason I commanded was because Drake kept trying to seduce me last night."

"Really? I didn't see that. He didn't even touch you after dinner."

I blushed. It hadn't been an easy thing to sleep in the same house as Drake, knowing his lovely, warm, enticing body was sleeping just down the hall from me. "He didn't have to. He just sat there oozing sensuality at me, the rat fink. Besides, I figured it was safer for everyone if you spent the night here. István was ready to gut you after you tried mating with his leg. What on earth possessed you to do that?"

Jim looked over my shoulder, a mildly embarrassed look on its face. "I wanted to find out if it was as good as I thought it would be."

I wouldn't ask, I wouldn't ask . . . .

"It was," Jim said.

"Right, I've heard enough. Now I feel all icky," I said, climbing out of bed. "I'm going to take a shower—then I'll take you for walkies."

"Eh . . . you better take me out now, unless you want to be explaining to Drake why there are some pretty bodacious pee stains in this carpet."

"Great, just what I need, an incontinent demon," I grumbled as I pulled on the pants and tunic from the day before. I snatched up the leash and waved Jim out of the room, stopping by the kitchen long enough to ask István (who was sitting at the kitchen table sipping coffee) for some plastic bags. The furious look he shot Jim made me glad I'd kept the demon in my room during the night.

We returned twenty minutes later with me muttering about Jim being nothing but a walking poop machine, and the demon grousing about who it had to bribe to get some food.

"I'll take you down for breakfast as soon as I've had a shower," I said once we were back in my room. I pulled off the tunic top, casting a quick glance over to make sure my dress was still covering the camera. I started to undo my bra. "Turn around."

"Oh, please. I'm a demon," Jim said with a roll of its eyes.

"I know exactly what you are, and I'm not getting naked in front of you. Turn around."

"You really have issues, you know that?" Jim turned its back to me. I peeled off the bra, grabbed some fresh clothing, and with the lodestone that had been under my pillow all night, headed toward the bathroom.

"Just what am I supposed to do while you're taking your time in there?" Jim asked plaintively as I was about to close the bathroom door. "Other than starve to death, that is. I know how long you women can take in a bath-room."

"Comments like that are not going to make me hurry. Go . . . oh, I don't know, go explore. Just don't touch anything or get into any trouble, and if you have any brains in that big furry head of yours, stay away from István!"

I made my morning ablutions, taking the time after-wards to use a pair of manicure scissors I found in a drawer to make a slit in the double-lined cup of my bra, sliding the lodestone into it. The stone was so flat, it couldn't be seen, although I had no doubt that should Drake's hand go awandering, he'd feel the large round stone instantly. "I'll just have to make sure there's no touchy-feely business going on, that's all," I said to my-self as I did a twirl in front of the steamy bathroom mir-ror. The gauze dress Pál had selected fit almost perfectly. I slipped on the espadrilles, tidied my bedroom, and was about to go find Jim when the door burst open and the demon dashed into the room, its eyes wild.

"Thank the fires of Abaddon you're done!" Jim panted.

"What's wrong? Why do you look so frightened?" My breath caught in my throat as my heart started galloping. "Oh, god, the police aren't here, are they?"

"No, it's worse than that," Jim said, turning back to the door.

My heart settled down into its normal rhythm, the horrible suspicion that Drake might have turned me in evaporating even as I drew a breath. "Don't scare me like that! What could possibly be worse than the police?"

"You'll see. Come on."

"If you're dragging me somewhere to see another dog you've fallen in love with—," I warned as I followed Jim down the hallway, past the big staircase and into the wing that housed Drake's bedroom.

"Are you kidding? I'm a demon, not a two-timer. My heart belongs to Cecile."

"You don't have a heart," I pointed out. "I thought you were on the verge of starving to death."

Jim stopped in front of a door and gave me a scornful look. "There are some things more important than feeding your face, Aisling."

That stripped the grin off my lips. If Jim thought something was more important than having breakfast, it would have to be something tantamount to the apocalypse.

"Isn't this Drake's room?" I asked, looking at the closed door.

"No, we passed that. Go on in."

I wetted my lower lip, suddenly nervous. "What's in there?"

"I can't tell you," Jim said softly.

"Why?"

"Just go in."

I gave Jim a steely glare. "If this is some sort of a setup between you and Drake—"

"Fires of Abaddon, will you just *go in!*"

I put my hand on the door, a familiar feeling of dread swamping me, stripping the air from my lungs with its intensity. "Oh, no, not—" I threw the door open. The room must have been the communications center that Drake had mentioned earlier, because it was filled with a bank of computers, monitors showing various parts around the house and grounds, and one big control panel laid out like a soundboard.

Oh, and one demon in a shiny, electric-blue suit.

I stared speechlessly at the demon in man form that swiveled around in its chair to look at me. It looked like a man, a rather handsome man with high cheekbones and elegantly coiffed blond hair. It even had a tiny, discreet earring. What the devil was a demon doing in Drake's house?

"What is your name, demon?" I asked.

It smiled. The monitor nearest it went snowy. "You know the rules, Guardian. You didn't summon me, so I don't have to answer any of your questions."

I looked back through the open doorway to where Jim sat in the hallway. "Do you know who this is?" I asked.

"Yep. But if you are expecting me to tell you, I can't. That's another one of the rules—no narcing on fellow demons."

"I could command you to tell me its name," I said.

Jim shook its head. "Still wouldn't be able to tell you. You really do need to read the rule book."

I made an exasperated noise. Jim cleared its throat. "However, nothing says I can't give you a hint. . . . Think about the demon you've been chasing."

"Bafamal?" I asked, turning to look at the demon-man. "You're Bafamal?"

The demon snarled something as it stood up. Jim flinched. Two monitors flickered, then died.

Bafamal? What was it doing here in Drake's house . . . ? The penny dropped. I stared in horror at the blond demon as all the pieces came together in my mind with one solid *whomp*. Drake had lied to me; he had been lying to me all the time. He said dragons couldn't summon a demon, and yet here was Bafamal looking quite comfy and at home in his communications room. He said he didn't kill Mme. Deauxville and the Venediger, and yet here was the instrument of their deaths. The only thing I couldn't figure out was why Drake hadn't hidden the signs that he had used a demon to commit murder, but I was sure I'd figure out that last puzzle. Right now I had to get out of Drake's house before he found out I'd seen his demon.

I turned back to Jim. "Is there any way I can get rid of a demon I haven't summoned?"

"Sure. You draw a circle, say the words, and poof! He goes up in smoke."

"Words, what words?" I asked, wringing my hands. It was becoming a bad habit, but I didn't have time to take myself to task about it. I had a demon to send back to Hell. "I don't have my notes or the book I need."

"To send the demon back, you need its twelve words, the ones ruling it."

"If you think I'm going to stand here and allow this Guardian to send me back without breaking her neck, you're as crazy as she is," Bafamal said to Jim.

I didn't need Jim's warning to guess the demon was about to attack me. Without thinking, I opened the door in my mind, summoned Drake's fire, shaped it, and sent it to my attacker just as Bafamal lunged toward me, its hands outstretched claws.

"That shiny material sure does burn," Jim commented from the hallway as inside the room the demon shrieked, spinning in a circle, frantically trying to beat out the fire that erupted all over its body.

"Quickly," I said, running to Jim. "Where do I find the twelve words?"

"Each demon has twelve words binding it: six that identify it, six that define it. Usually the only way to get them is to capture the demon and torment it until it tells you."

"Usually?" I asked, glancing back over my shoulder at Bafamal. It had put out almost all the flames on its suit.

Jim smiled. "Yeah, usually. The exception is when you have an extraordinarily handsome and intelligent demon of your own who doesn't mind telling you the other demon's words."

"You just said you couldn't help me!" I yelled.

"I said I couldn't *name* him. That doesn't mean I can't give you other information about him."

I grabbed Jim's furry head and kissed its muzzle, jumping back into the room to search for a felt pen I could use to draw a circle on the cream-colored rug that graced the middle of a highly polished wooden floor.

Five minutes later I opened the windows to let out the last whiffs of demon smoke. "That was close," I croaked, rubbing my throat.

"Too close. You really do need to find yourself a mentor, someone to show you the Guardian ropes. There *are* binding wards you can use to keep from being throttled while you're conducting the ritual."

Jim followed as I ran back to my room. "I don't have time to think about that now. I have to get the proof that

Drake murdered Mme. Deauxville and the Venediger. Where did I put that extra plastic bag? There it is." I shoved all my new clothes and my soiled pantsuit into the bags, including the sandals. I opened the window, checking for anyone who might be loitering along the side of the house, then tossed the bag of my clothes out. "Come on. Drake will get suspicious if we don't show up for breakfast. As soon as we're done, I'll tell him I need to take you walkies again, and we'll hightail it out of here."

I fished a card out of my purse, stopping by the phone that sat on the nightstand.

"Where are we going to go? The police are going to be looking for you."

"I'm aware of that," I answered as I punched the buttons on the phone. "Rene? Hi, it's Aisling. Are you free in about half an hour? Jim and I are going to need a ride. We're making an escape."

"An escape? Yes, yes, I can pick you up." Rene promised to be outside Drake's house at the appointed time. "Has he hurt you? Should I bring my revolver?"

"No, he hasn't hurt me, and no, definitely do not bring any guns. I have a feeling Drake is a hard guy to hurt, and he can zap you. . . . Well, just don't bring it. See you in thirty minutes."

"That takes care of being seen on the streets by the cops, but where are we going?" Jim asked.

I opened the bedroom door and peered down the hallway. It was clear. "The only place we can go— Amelie's."

"OK, but don't kiss me again in front of Cecile. She's the jealous sort."

We trotted down the stairs only to meet Drake coming in the front door.

"Good morning. You look lovely. Pál has a good eye,"

he said, looking me over, flashing me a sexy smile. My fingernails bit into my palms as I tried to keep from throwing myself on him. Honestly, what was I thinking? How could my body know the truth about him and still not care? I was thoroughly ashamed of myself—he was a murderer! He had lied to me! He had stolen from me! He was amusing himself with me at my expense, and *still* I wanted him.

I didn't have to let him know that, though. I raised my chin and gave him a cool look. "Yes, he does. You were out?"

His eyes—lying, traitorous eyes—flashed puzzlement. "I had to get something. For you, as a matter of fact."

"Oh really?" I turned and walked with him toward the kitchen, Jim trailing behind us. "What would that be? Cyanide? Strychnine? Hemlock?"

"Nothing so exotic," he said, holding the door open for me. I stepped into the sunny, cheerful kitchen and mused on how a man could have such a black heart and yet appear so utterly droolworthy at the same time. But then, he wasn't really a man, was he? He was a dragon, and dragons loved treasure above all else.

With a flourish, Drake pulled a small container out of a paper bag. I blinked in surprise at the sight of it. "Lemon yogurt. I had an idea you might like it."

My cheeks burned with a blush at the flames of desire visible in his eyes. He had invaded my dream, the erotic dream I was having about him just an hour ago. The beastly man! "Thank you," I said thickly, taking the yogurt and claiming a seat.

Breakfast was difficult to get through. Drake clearly was puzzled by my reaction to him, but he didn't say anything beyond asking me what steps I thought we should take to find the killer or killers.

I looked him straight in the eye. "I think the best thing to do would be to talk to the witness."

"Witness?" His brows pulled together in a frown. "What witnesses?"

"The demon that was summoned by the person behind the murders."

"Person? You think it is just one person?"

"Oh, yes," I answered, my gaze steady on his.

"I suppose that makes sense. The two murders are obviously related." His brows smoothed. "Talking with the demon is one idea, yes, but I believe a more practical one would be to speak with Therese, the Venediger's mistress. She would be able to tell us who visited him yesterday."

Hmm, what was wrong with that picture? Let's start with Drake had already admitted he was at the Venediger's yesterday, not to mention his plan drew my attention away from questioning the demon he had used. Still, it wasn't wise to let him see I had figured him out. This was obviously a time when it wouldn't hurt to play stupid. "Good point. Very well, just as soon as I've taken Jim for his walkies, we'll go question the mistress."

I hurried through the rest of the meal, wanting nothing so much as to get out of there before my resolve cracked. Drake was using me, nothing more. He didn't really care about me. He didn't like me. He only wanted the lodestone; that's why he was protecting me from the police.

"Go out to the side of the house and get my bag of clothes," I instructed Jim quietly at the bottom of the staircase. "Take it around front, to the street. I'll meet you there." I glanced at my watch. "Rene should be there in a couple of minutes."

"Where are you going?" Jim asked. "You're not going

to let loose that dragon fire all over Drake's house, are you?"

"What do you take me for, an arsonist?"

"Well, you did burn the Venediger to a crisp—"

"We don't know that. I'm sure the fire department put the gazebo out before his body was torched. Besides, that was an accident. Now, go do what I told you to do. I'm just going to leave Drake a note that will hopefully buy us a little time."

I ran up the stairs to my room. I left a note on my pillow that simply said I was going to pursue another avenue of investigation on my own, one that Jim and I were better qualified to do than him. I ended with a request that he question Therese while I was doing my thing. I doubted if it would convince Drake to leave me alone permanently, but hoped it would give me a few hours' head start.

Rene was waiting by the time I made it, breathless, to the rendezvous point. I pushed Jim into the taxi, jumping in after it as I gave Rene the order to leave.

"Where do you wish to go? Why are you in the hurry so great? What has happened?"

I told him to take us to Amelie's. "Nothing has happened, except I found out that Drake is the one who murdered both Mme. Deauxville and the Venediger."

"Drake? He is a thief, yes, but a murderer, too? And who is this Venediger?" Rene asked, peering over his shoulder at me.

"Eeek!" I screamed, pointing at the parked car he was about to plow us into. "Eyes forward and I'll tell you."

It took the length of the trip through a morning rush-hour Paris to tell the tale of my experiences during the last twenty-four hours, but by the time Rene pulled up to

Amelie's shop he had the bulk of it, everything except the fact that Drake was a dragon.

"I would ask you to stay with me until it is safe for you," he said apologetically as I got out of the taxi, "but with five small ones running around, my apartment is filled to the overflow."

"That's OK, I totally understand. I didn't know you had five kids, though!"

He made a wry face. "Why is it you think I work so many hours, eh? Now, before you go, you repeat for me what it is you will say if that murdering thief comes to seduce you with his so-handsome face."

"Rene, Drake isn't going to—"

"Repeat it!"

"Chat échaudé craint l'eau froide," I dutifully repeated. (It meant "A cat washed with hot water fears cold water," which evidently was the French way of saying once burned, twice shy.)

"You forgot to add the sneer to tell him you are so high above him. That is very important. Ah, well, you are improving. *Bonne chance,* Aisling. If you need me, call. I will come."

"Thanks." I gave in to impulse and leaned forward to kiss his cheek. "You're a doll."

Rene looked embarrassed by the gesture.

"She's not gettin' any from Drake," Jim explained in an annoyingly confidential tone. "She's kissing everyone. You should have seen her this morning, she was all over me—awk!"

"See you later," I said with a wave to Rene, ignoring the squirming demon struggling to free itself from the twisted hold I had on its collar. After it made a few pathetic gasps for air around its tightened collar, I let go of it and headed for Amelie's shop. "Behave yourself and I won't command you to silence."

"You're assuming I can talk after you brutally crushed my windpipe."

"Jim, you haven't even *begun* to see brutal," I warned as I walked toward Amelie's shop.

"That's what you think," it muttered behind me.

I was careful first to make sure there were no lounging policeman on surveillance. My Uncle Damian's warning rang in my head: *Security every place, everywhere, all the time.*

Suddenly, I was overwhelmed with a sudden sense of homesickness. What was I doing skulking around the streets of Paris at eight in the morning when I should be home getting chewed out by my uncle for allowing the aquamanile to be stolen from me? Why hadn't I taken Drake up on his offer to take my passport and run? Why was I putting my very life at risk by staying in a city that the police were probably scouring for me? And why did I feel like my heart was crushed in a vise whenever I thought about Drake betraying me?

"Because I'm fool, that's why. But I'm a fool who's got to clear her name, and by heaven, I'm going to do it." I marched forward to the shop, only to stop and stare first at the closed door, then down at my watch. "Rats. She doesn't open up for another hour. I forgot how early it is. Now what am I going to do? I can't stay lounging around here—Inspector Proust might send someone to watch the shop."

Jim peed on a lightpost. "Why don't we go to her apartment? You can talk to her there, and be off the street so the cops don't grab you."

"Brilliant idea, only I have no idea where her apartment is."

Jim nodded upward. "It's above the shop."

I looked up. The second floor of the long building that ran the length of the block held what looked like apartments—at least they had the same black wrought-iron railings at the bottoms of the windows that I had seen on every apartment building thus far. "How do you know she lives up there?"

Jim started off down the street. I followed. "Because, Einstein, I'm courting Cecile. You think I'm not going to find out where she lives? How can I serenade her at night if I don't know where she lives?"

"Jim," I said as we turned down an alley that ran behind the building, "you do realize that it's not quite normal for a demon to be courting a dog, right?"

Jim shot me one of its disgusted looks. "Of course I know, but I'm not just any demon. I'm a demon plus. I'm superior to your average run-of-the-mill demon. Think of me as Demon: The Next Generation."

I didn't make a face at that thought, but it was near thing. Instead I climbed the rickety wooden stairs that led up to a small landing, pressing on the bell beneath the neatly written MERLLAIN.

"Oui?"

"Hi Amelie, it's Aisling. If it's not too much trouble, I'd like to talk to you."

"Aisling? *Nom de Dieu!* Stay right there. Do not allow anyone to see you!"

Twenty seconds later I could see a figure approaching through the wavery glass that filled the upper half of the door. Amelie hustled me into a dank, dark hallway. "Quickly, I do not want my neighbors to see you."

She gave Jim a sour look, but allowed it to follow me. I trotted down the hall to the open door I could see at the end.

"What a lovely apartment," I said, looking around. It *was* lovely, although surprisingly modern. I don't know why, but I didn't expect her apartment to be filled with pop-art, fiber-optic lights, neo-Baroque furniture in primary colors, and very pricey designer chairs that looked extremely uncomfortable.

"Baby!" Jim crooned, heading for a dog bed that was filled to overflowing with Cecile. "Daddy's home!"

Amelie waved my compliments away. "What are you doing here? No, you do not need to answer that—I can guess. You are seeking shelter, yes?"

"Yes, but—"

"You cannot stay here," she interrupted. "You must leave immediately. I cannot have you here!"

My shoulders sagged in disappointment. This wasn't quite the welcome I had expected.

13

"It is not that I would not allow you to stay here if I could," Amelie said as she closed the door behind me. "But the police, they visited me three times last night, searching both my shop and this apartment."

"Oy," I said, slumping down into a scarlet chair. "I'm sorry about that. I thought they might watch your shop, but I never in a million years thought they'd disturb you."

"They said you murdered the Venediger." Amelie stood before me, her hands held tightly, her expression strained.

"I didn't. I swear to you, Amelie, when I arrived at his house, he was already dead. His body was cooling."

She stared at me for a moment, then put both hands on my head. I didn't know what she was reading—my thoughts or my emotions—but I fervently hoped she would realize I was innocent. "It is difficult for me to sense your thoughts, but I do not believe you are a murderer." She whooshed out a sigh as she collapsed onto one of the uncomfortable-looking chairs. "I had hoped you hadn't done it. I know you were frightened when you left, and the Venediger can be very . . ."

"Scary?"

"Ruthless. You would not have been at fault if you were simply defending yourself against his attack. That could not *really* be considered murder." She said the words with just a hint of implied question that I felt compelled to answer.

"I didn't kill him. But I know who did. I just have to find somewhere safe where I can get the proof."

"Who would kill the Venediger?" she asked, leaning her elbows on her knees. "Who would have the power to kill him?"

I looked away. "I think it's better if I don't tell you. That way, if the police question you again, you can honestly tell them that I didn't give you any information." That was only part of the truth, of course. I felt so betrayed by Drake that I didn't quite trust anyone anymore. If Drake could prove to be false, anyone could.

She was silent for a moment, the only sound in her apartment that of Jim sucking Cecile's ears. "You are right. It is better if I do not know. As for a safe place for you to go—" She spread her hands wide. "—I cannot think of one. Most of the members of the *l'au-delà* have heard what has happened by now. They know the police suspect you of murder, and they will do nothing to protect you. It would not even be safe for you to go to G & T now."

My heart fell at her words. There was much to be said for not being a fugitive. "I thought G & T would be closed because of the Venediger's death."

"*Non,* it is to be open. The Venediger's second in command will make sure that all runs as it should. It is a very popular club, you know, the only club for *l'au-delà*. It makes much money. She would be a fool not to open it."

"She?"

"Perdita Dawkins."

"Perdita is the Venediger's second-in-command? Wiccan Perdita?"

"Yes, she is. That surprises you?" Amelie raised her eyebrows, then made an annoyed sound. "Oh, but what am I doing questioning you? My manners have flown to the cats. May I offer you tea? Coffee? I have some brioches. . . ."

"No, thank you, we've had breakfast, and speaking of that, I apologize for disturbing you so early. I was in such a haste to leave where I spent the night, I didn't think about it being so early. Are you sure about Perdita being the Venediger's assistant? Both she and Ophelia seemed to be a bit . . . harsh when they mentioned him. I got the feeling that being pagan Wiccans, they didn't approve of him."

"Why wouldn't they approve? Perdita owes much to the Venediger. It was he who first saw Ophelia and recognized her." Amelie flitted about a tiny kitchen that opened onto the living area, stepping into a tiny walk-in pantry.

"Oh, were they separated when they were babies? I have a friend whose parents divorced right after they were born, and she got her dad while her twin went with their mom."

"Yes, I am sure about Perdita. Jean, the Venediger's previous second, he met with an accident. Perdita was named in his place," Amelie said as she emerged from the pantry. She set a plate of brioches on the table and cocked an eyebrow at me. "What did you say about your friend?"

"Nothing, really. Had Perdita and Ophelia been separated for long when the Venediger found Ophelia?"

Her eyebrow rose a smidgen. "Yes, they had. Tea or coffee?"

"Tea is fine, thank you. Hmm. Perdita," I said, thinking about the sisters. They were Wiccans; maybe I could appeal to them for help? Perhaps if I pointed out that I was trying to bring the Venediger's murderer to justice, they would take me in just for a day or so until I got the proof I needed? I was about to ask Amelie, but didn't when I realized that to tell her would be to put her in a compromising situation with the police. "I think I know of someone who might put me up for a couple of days, but I don't want to tell you who."

Amelie set down a tray with a pot of tea and two mugs. She nodded. "It is better that you do not tell me. I will not volunteer information, but I will not lie to the police if they ask me."

"Thanks." I accepted a cup of milky tea, gnawing on my lip for a moment before coming to a decision. "If you have the time, can you answer a couple of questions for me? I promise they're nothing that you can't tell the police I asked about, although whether or not you'll want to . . ."

Amelie sat on the yellow couch across from my chair, tucking her bare feet beneath her. "I will answer if I can, but you must not stay too long. The shop, it opens in an hour, and for me to be delayed will derange the police."

"Well, I wouldn't want them deranged—Inspector Proust is pissed enough at me. My question concerns a set of three objects called the Tools of Bael. Have you heard of them?"

The quick intake of Amelie's breath pretty much answered my question. "I have, but I am surprised that you have, as well. Where did you hear of this?"

Time to pick and choose what I told her. "The object I was delivering to Mme. Deauxville was an aquamanile that I was later told was one of the three Tools."

"*Sacré!*"

I nodded. I didn't need her to translate; the shocked look in her eyes said it all. "I happen to know that the Venediger had in his possession one of the Tools—the Eye of Lucifer—and had hired someone to acquire the other two."

"Nom de Dieu!" Amelie said, jumping up to pace the length of the couch. *"Nom de Dieu.* It was Drake Vireo, the green wyvern, who was to steal the other two pieces, yes?"

"Yes," I said cautiously, not willing to tell her too much. "My question is how much damage could someone who used the Tools do? Say someone of the Venediger's power—are the Tools really so important?"

"Mon Dieu, they are legendary!" Amelie stopped pacing to sit on the edge of the steel and glass coffee table in front of me. "They were lost for many hundreds of years, sometimes one of the three surfacing, only to disappear, but never, in all the ages since they were created, have all three Tools been brought together. For them to be used, it would be *une grande catastrophe!"*

"How bad of a catastrophe?" I asked, the sick feeling of the day before having returned, making my stomach protest the yogurt and toast that had been all I'd been able to choke down in Drake's presence.

She waved her hands in the air in a gesture that was reminiscent of the shape of a mushroom cloud. "Most bad. It is not just the person using the Tools, you see. That person would be destroyed should he even try."

"Destroyed? Why?"

She got up and started pacing again, but slower this time, as if she was gathering her thoughts. "What I tell you, you are not to relate to anyone, yes? It is most important that no know the truth, else the whole fabric of *l'au-delà,* it will come apart."

"That's comforting," I said dryly. "Go on—I won't breathe a word of this to anyone."

"I know this only because . . . because I have a friend who is a Guardian. She sometimes tells me things of importance." I nodded, silently urging her to go on. "The demon lords, they are not easy, you understand. They struggle to rule Abaddon as we struggle to achieve greatness in our world. One lord dominates over the other seven; that is the way it has always been. The lord Bael has long been dominate, but recently the signs show that another lord is trying to topple him from power. In order to maintain his premier role, the lord Bael, he calls in his armies, his support, yes? His demons, the mortals he rules, all of them he calls to his aid to keep the usurper from gaining his power."

"OK," I said, more than a little puzzled. "But what does a battle to be king of the hill in Abaddon have to do with the Tools? Bael can't use them since they're meant to tap into his power."

"*Oui,* but the power, it can flow both ways, you see?"

A light dawned in the musty darkness of my brain. "Oh, I get you. You mean that if someone tries to use the Tools to draw power from Bael, Bael could flip the switch and suck power from that person instead?"

Amelie nodded. "Yes, but it goes deeper than that. Before he took all their power, Bael would command his servant to use his abilities to feed him power from those within the servant's reach. So it would be that not only the person who used the Tool was drained by Bael, but too everyone with the reach of him. For someone of the Venediger's strength, that would mean everyone in the *l'au-delà* would have been drained in order to feed his master."

"Bael is the Venediger's master?" I asked, distracted by that thought.

"Was," she answered with a wry twist to her lips.

"Ah." That would go a long way to explaining the uneasy feeling I had around him. "And this draining, I take it that it's not a good thing?"

She laughed. It wasn't a happy laugh. It raised goose bumps on my arms. "It is deadly, the process."

"Erg. OK, so the important thing here is to not allow the three Tools to fall into anyone's hands, right?"

"That is so."

Another thought struck me. "Can someone use just two of the three Tools?"

"Not to draw Bael's power. It is the three together that can tap into Bael's strength, a—what is it called—triumvirate. Just as there are people who bond with two others in order that the sum of their power be greater than the individual parts, so it is with the Tools. Separate, they can do little except summon Bael. Together . . . ," She shuddered.

"Hell on earth," I filled in the blank for her.

She stared at me with emotionless eyes. "Literally."

And lining up to take the fall for Bael was Drake. Either that, or he seriously thought he could keep from being sucked dry, but that was just as distasteful a thought, for it meant he planned to rule using Bael's power. It all came down to the lodestone. No matter what else I did, I had to make sure it did not fall into Drake's hands. Which meant . . .

"If I know where one of the Tools is, if I had access to it, could I destroy it?"

"You?" She shook her head. "A powerful mage, possibly, but not a Guardian."

"Wait a minute, I'm confused. I thought you said that Guardians command the dark powers."

"No, I said you manipulate them, and so you do. But command? Only those of Abaddon, or one who serves such a master, can command the dark lords."

"Obviously I need a little help understanding exactly what it is a Guardian does, because I thought it was all about summoning demons."

She smiled again, but this was a warm smile. "I think you have done magnificently considering that a few days ago you were just a naïve tourist." I grimaced, and she laughed. "It is true that Guardians may summon demons as they need, but that is not their primary role. A Guardian is exactly that—the keeper, the watcher of a portal to Abaddon. Each Guardian is assigned a portal to tend."

"Tend how?" I asked, wondering if there were any portals in Seattle. "I have a feeling you don't mean cut the grass and pick weeds, right?"

She looked thoughtful. "In a way, that is not so poor a comparison. A Guardian monitors the portal she is assigned. She watches for unusual activity, for inhabitants of the dark world who cross over. A portal, it is like a doorway, yes? Through it the dark creatures, they can come without being summoned. So it is that Guardians must watch, and prevent the dark powers from using the portal."

"Kind of a paranormal doorman? OK. Where does the demon-raising come into it?"

"It is more for their abilities to send demons back that Guardians are known. Not only must they watch their portals, they also must take care of any occurrences of dark beings which leave their dark world and enter ours."

"Like demons, you mean?"

"Yes, demons and their servants, as well as others such as incubi and succubi, doppelgängers, sirens, furies, werefolk—"

I held up my hand to stop her. "You're making my head spin. I had no idea all those creatures were real, but let's go back a step. You said demons and their servants—I thought demons *were* servants?"

"They are, but they themselves command servants of their own, such as imps and other lesser creatures."

I wanted to ask what the Venediger did with the scraped-up bits of imps that people deposited in the imp bucket, but figured it was probably better if I didn't know. "That sounds like a lot of work. I'm not saying I can't do it—although I haven't the slightest idea what most of what you're talking about consists of—but how do people go about finding a portal? How do Guardians . . . well, become Guardians?"

"You are born to it, just as you are born to be a wyvern's mate."

I made a face at that comment. Oh, how I loved knowing I was born to be the mate to a dragon who planned on claiming a demon lord's power to rule the world.

"Regarding finding a portal, it is more a case of the portal finding you. Most Guardians who have not yet found their place in the *l'au-delà* become involved in an unguarded portal. And do not worry that you do not yet understand all there is to know. You have not found a mentor. Once you find her, things will become much clearer."

I didn't bother to tell her that I wasn't entirely sure I was willing to sign on full-time as a Guardian. I couldn't think about that now; first I had to save the world from Drake and Bael. Super Aisling to the rescue. All I needed was a big red cape and a pair of blue tights.

"Thanks for the explanation. If you don't mind me looking through your phone book, I'll get the number of the person I think might be able to put me up, and then Jim and I will be out of your hair."

Amelie looked worried. "This person, it is someone you trust?"

I did a half-shrug. "No more than I trust anyone. Is there a particular person you want to warn me against?"

She said nothing for a few moments, staring at the mug of tea in her hands. "It is not so much a person about which I want to warn you, more that you should not be deceived by appearances. You are untrained, true, but you are a Guardian. You are a wyvern's mate. Your instincts may be buried and untried, but they are there within you, speaking to you if you would just hear their words."

"Sage advice indeed," I said with a smile as I stood up.

She tipped her head back to look up at me. "Tell me this if you can without it harming you—you have a plan, yes?"

"Oh, yes, I have a plan."

A faint frown tugged her brows down. "But to do what? To expose the murderer, or to destroy the Tools of Bael?"

"Certainly the first, and hopefully the last, although if I can't destroy one of the tools, at the very least I can make sure it ends up somewhere no one will find it."

"That is not so easy as you think. People will search for it."

"Yeah, I know. But I'm hoping to find a spot where no one will find it. Thanks for answering all my questions, and I'm very sorry about the police bothering you. With luck, they won't do so again."

I availed myself of Amelie's phone book before leaving the safety of her apartment. She offered to let me use the phone, but fearing a phone tap (or records of who was called), I thanked her and headed off to find a distant pay phone.

"I don't see why we couldn't stay there," Jim complained as I marched down the street toward an open market. "We could have hidden if the police came."

"We couldn't stay there because it wouldn't be right to ask Amelie to lie for us to the police. Besides, I don't think Cecile's ears could stand up to much more sucking. And while we're on the subject, that's really disgusting, you know."

"Don't knock it until you've tried it," Jim answered sullenly.

We wove our way through the early-morning shoppers at the outdoor market, finding a pay phone in a busy café. I called the number I'd written down from Amelie's phone book, wondering as the phone buzzed in my ear what the odds were of finding your missing twin.

"Allô?"

"Ophelia?" I asked cautiously, not able to tell if it was her or her sister. "This is Aisling Grey."

"Aisling? Perdy, it's Aisling! No, she's on the phone with me. Aisling? Yes, it's me. Where are you? You would not believe what's being said about you—"

"Oh, I bet if I tried hard, I could believe," I answered, smiling a jaded little smile of one who knows the police force of one of the world's largest cities is after her. "Listen, I'm about to ask a really big favor from you, but I don't want you to feel pressured into saying yes."

"As if you even have to ask," Ophelia scolded me. "Whatever it is, you know we'll say yes."

"I need a place to stay for a day or two, somewhere my . . . er . . . dog and I can lie low."

"We'd be delighted to have you," Perdita answered, having picked up an extension. "Absolutely delighted."

"Yes, delighted," Ophelia parroted.

"That's very generous of you, but you should both understand that . . . er—" I looked around to make sure no one was standing near enough me to overhear. "—I'm a wanted woman. The police want to talk to me, not that I've done anything wrong."

"We heard you murdered the Venediger," Ophelia said excitedly.

"Feelie!"

"Well, we did! She should know that, shouldn't she?"

"Yes, but you don't just say it so baldly. You ease into such things—"

"Maybe we can discuss this later?" I interrupted, nervous at being on the street, exposed to anyone who looked my way. "And . . . I hate to ask this, but I need to make sure. You're not . . . uh . . . planning on telling the police about me?"

"Merciful Goddess, as if we would do such a thing!" Ophelia gasped, her voice filled with honest shock.

"I'm very sorry to have doubted you, but I just can't be too careful anymore. If you really don't mind housing a fugitive, I'd be eternally grateful."

"Would you, indeed?" Perdita asked. "Eternity is a terribly long time."

"Er . . . yes." I looked around the café again. A man near the door was eyeing me. "Can you give me your address? I'll be over as soon as possible. I'm a bit nervous about being out where the police might see me."

Ophelia gave me the address and told me they would be waiting for me. "Buzz three times. We'll let you in then."

"Will do. And many thanks!"

"Oh, don't thank us now," Ophelia laughed, somewhat cryptically.

I rang off and retrieved Jim from where it was mooching off a kindly café patron and his small daughter, apologizing in badly mangled phrasebook French for my dog.

"Why was that little girl calling you wa-wa?" I asked as we headed for a taxi stand.

"It's *ouah-ouah*. It means 'doggy.' She liked me. Everyone likes me, everyone but you. Do you know the French have a phrase: *avoir du chien*. It implies someone who has charm and sex appeal, which makes absolute sense since it literally means 'to have dog.' What do you think about that?"

"I think you had better clam up. No talking in the taxi or in front of Perdita and Ophelia. They're kind of weird about things like demons and stuff."

"I thought you said one of them is the Venediger's lieutenant."

"She is," I said, stopping to stare in horror at a newsstand before dragging Jim forward to the taxi stand down the street.

"Hey! Where's the fire? You're choking me!"

"Shhh! Someone will hear you." I stopped abruptly and bent down to fuss with Jim's collar. "The newspaper had my passport picture! Right on the front page!"

"Oooh, cool. Let's get a copy for my scrapbook."

"You don't have a scrapbook, and we are *not* getting a copy. Come on. The sooner I get off the street, the happier I'll be."

We made it to the apartment on the Rue Ponthieu, which surprised me by being just a few steps away from the Champs-Élysées and all the luxury shops. The sisters' apartment was two floors above an upscale bakery. After

being buzzed in, we took the elevator up and were admitted immediately into an apartment that left my jaw
hanging around my knees. Amelie's modern taste in art
and furniture surprised me, but the glorious Louis XIV
antiques of Ophelia and Perdita's apartment left me
speechless. Beautifully worked Persian rugs dotted an in-
laid parquet floor, two rose-and-cream-satin embroidered
Baroque chairs complemented the matching rose-colored
couch, a huge brown marble fireplace dominated one
wall, while an intricately molded ceiling bearing a detailed Rococo mural fought with the museum-quality tap-
estries on the walls to hold the eye. They were all so
gorgeous, so elegant, and not at all the sort of things with
which pagan Wiccans would be expected to surround
themselves.

"What a beautiful place you have," I gasped, trying to
look everywhere at once. I felt incredibly gauche showing up with my demon and my plastic bag of clothing.

"It's home," Ophelia said with a shrug. "Come, let me
show you to your room. I hope you don't mind sleeping
in our workroom. "

"Not at all," I said, my eyes huge as she paused to
point out the bathroom (the tiles lining the shower unit
formed a lovely Turkish mosaic) and separate toilet before sweeping into a well-lit room done in a pretty yellow-
and-green floral pattern. The bedspread matched the
hand-knotted rug, which matched the upholstery on the
armchair next to the window, framed between lace and
yellow-and-green matching curtains. On the far wall was
a large bookcase that contained a number of books, several glass jars like Amelie's that I assume held the sisters'
Wiccan herbs and such, a variety of candles, a set of aro-
matic oils, a couple of chalices, three different-size bells,
and several items in bone that I did not recognize. I

turned back to the rest of the room. It was feminine, light, attractive, and made me feel even more like an interloper. "I can't thank you enough for being so kind to me, and I hope that I won't have to stay here more than a day, or two at the most. I need to . . . er . . . conduct a ritual, if you don't object."

"Well, you are a Guardian," Ophelia said with a knowing smile. "We would be surprised if you did not practice your arts. Oh, but you cannot do it today!"

"I can't?" I shot a quick frown at Jim as it sniffed around the bookcase.

"No, the room hasn't been cleansed yet."

I looked around. It was cleaner than my apartment back home, much cleaner. This apartment looked like dust wouldn't dare settle anywhere. "Oh?"

"Yes, indeed. We would never allow you to work in an uncleansed room."

"Ah," I said, gathering the cleansing was some sort of Wiccan ritual. "But I'm not going to be doing the sort of magic that you and Perdita do, so the cleansing isn't necessary—"

"It is," Ophelia said firmly, moving over to the bed to pull out my clothing stuffed into the bag. She shook out the dresses and hung them in a rosewood armoire, saying as she did, "We would never be able to live with ourselves if some negative energy from the uncleansed room interfered with your ritual. Perdita will cleanse it tonight, when the Moon Goddess blesses us with her light."

I gave in. What choice did I have? I was going to have to walk very carefully as it was since I would be summoning a demon into their home, an event I had a feeling they would not be terribly happy about, but I had little choice. I had thought to do the ritual that night while Perdita (and hopefully Ophelia) would be at G & T, but it looked like Bafamal would have to wait until the following day.

Perdita returned from doing some grocery shopping (which made me feel even more guilty since I had little money left to reimburse them) and sat down with Ophelia to hear my story. I told them about finding the Venediger's body, reassured them I didn't kill him, and sidestepped the issue of Drake altogether. I trusted Amelie just as I trusted Ophelia and Perdita, but in the wake of Drake's betrayal, my faith in my ability to determine who was trustworthy and who wasn't was shaken. It was just better, I told myself, to not involve them that deeply in the situation.

"The V got what he deserved," Perdita said as I concluded my tale. I stared at her for a moment, surprised by the strong emotion in her voice. There was almost a gloating element to it. She must have noticed the question in my eyes because she added, with a light laugh, "That sounds terribly wicked of me, doesn't it? But the truth is, he was not a nice man. More than once he fell victim to his desires and used the dark powers to gain that which he wanted. Oh, yes, a dagger in his heart was a justified end for the likes of him."

"Perdy, that's a bit harsh, surely? No one deserves to be murdered," Ophelia gently chastised her sister. She nodded toward me. "You forget our guest is the one who discovered the Venediger's body. I'm sure Aisling would prefer to forget that horrible experience."

"I . . ." I chewed my lip for a moment, trying to think of how to ask what I wanted to ask Perdita without it sounding offensive. "I was told that you were employed by him?"

Her chin lifted in challenge to my question. "Yes, I was, but that did not mean I was blind to the man's sins.

By using the dark powers, he wronged not only the people who make up the Otherworld, but the Goddess and nature itself." She slid a quick glance toward a fretting Ophelia. "That is why I took the position. We had hopes that we would be able to bring the Venediger back into the light, but he . . ." Her lips twisted.

"He mocked her and refused her offer to baptize him into the Old Religion," Ophelia whispered, placing her hand over her sister's and giving it a squeeze. "He was a bad man, Perdy, but he is gone now. He is paying for his sins. The Goddess has seen to that."

"Yes," Perdita said, collecting herself. She leveled a firm blue-eyed gaze at me. "He was a very bad person, but he will not taint Paris any more. The Goddess's will has been done, just as it will be done to every member of the Otherworld who ignores the True Path and gives themselves over to the dark powers."

I was more than a little uncomfortable with this sort of talk, what with the demon I'd summoned lying with its big hairy butt on my left foot. "Er . . . yes," I said neutrally, unwilling to commit myself to anything more. Jim, whom I had commanded to silence in order to relieve it from the temptation of making a snarky comment in front of the sisters, rolled its eyes at me. I searched my mind for safe topics of conversation.

"Aisling has a ritual she wishes to conduct," Ophelia said, saving me from resorting to inanities like the weather. "I told her you must first cleanse the workroom before she can perform it."

"I don't want to be any trouble," I said quickly. "If there's somewhere else, somewhere quiet I can do it—"

"We use magic only in the workroom," Perdita said, shooting her sister a questioning glance. "It must always be cleansed first."

Ophelia smiled at me, adding, "It will be no trouble, I assure you. Perdy is ever so fond of cleansing. She likes the incense."

"Cedar works the best," Perdita agreed, her eyes on Ophelia for a moment before turning to me. "What sort of ritual will you be performing?"

Rats. I was hoping to get by without having to tell them, but I supposed it was only fair to let them know. I had a bad feeling, though, they'd tell me I couldn't. The key was to present the demon-summoning so it meshed in with their own beliefs.

"I am seeking proof of the murderer's identity," I said slowly. "My idea was to summon the being that can give me information, question it about its role in the murders, and present the proofs to the police. It is solely in regards to justice that I take such a dramatic step, you understand. I don't perform such rituals lightly, but I feel very strongly that the deaths of Mme. Deauxville and the Venediger must be avenged, and the person rightfully responsible for them must pay for his crimes."

"A being?" Perdita asked suspiciously.

Ophelia gasped, her eyes big pools of shocked blue. "You're speaking of a demon? You wish to summon a demon here, to our haven?"

I nodded, offering what I hoped was a reassuring smile. "I know it goes against everything you believe, but you must see that the only way I can gather enough information to turn over to the police is to question the demon used by the murderer to commit the crimes. I swear to you that I will be as quick as possible, and I will be happy to conduct whatever cleaning rituals you like afterwards."

Ophelia and Perdita exchanged glances before turning back to me. Ophelia cocked an eyebrow. Perdita frowned, and I was convinced she would refuse permission until she shrugged. "Very well, you may summon the demon, but we will be present when you do so. We have responsibilities to the Goddess, you know."

I blew out a silent sigh of relief. I wasn't thrilled about having them witness me grill the demon, since it would mean they'd know Drake was responsible for the murders, but it would all come out anyway. It couldn't hurt to let them find out the truth. "No problem."

"Tomorrow, then," Ophelia said, clapping her hands together happily. "How very exciting that will be! I've never seen a Guardian summon a demon."

"Don't expect too much," I said with a little smile. "It's not very impressive."

Jim rolled over onto its back and presented me with its belly.

"Oh, how adorable, your puppy wants his tummy rubbed!" Ophelia squealed, getting down on her knees to scratch Jim's belly.

Perdita gave me a measuring look as her sister crooned over Jim (who ate up the attention, the big demonic ham), finally relaxing back against the lovely rose couch. "You have summoned many demons as a Guardian?"

"Not many," I said, pretending interest in Ophelia and Jim.

"I am always surprised how many Guardians do not appreciate the ways of the Old Religion. I would be happy to instruct you. You have no doubt offended the Goddess with your activities as a Guardian. To appease her will assure you of your place in the Summerlands."

"Uh . . . Summerlands?"

Perdita smiled a very intense smile. It made me even more uncomfortable. There was something about her eyes that made me think of a religious zealot. "You would call it Heaven."

"Ah. Well, you know, it all sounds fascinating, and I'm sure it would be very good for me to learn more about Wiccans, but I really just want to get this murder situation cleared up, and then I really have to go back home. My uncle is already furious with me—"

" 'Where the rippling waters go, cast a stone and truth you'll know.' That is from the Wiccan Rede, the words by which we guide our lives. You would do well to heed it, Guardian."

"It sounds lovely, but—"

" 'Mind the Threefold Law you should, three times bad and three times good,' " she quoted.

And so it went. I sat through several lectures on the sins of being someone who dallied with the dark spirits, all the while extremely aware of the soulless demon who alternated between rolling around begging Ophelia to rub its belly, and mooching in the kitchen. By the evening I was exhausted with trying to keep my tongue behind my teeth. I pleaded an all-too-real headache and escaped to my bedroom, Jim in tow. I surprised myself by falling asleep in a nap that lasted until well after dinner.

When Ophelia woke me, I felt refreshed, my mind made up as to what course it would take.

"You must come with me to G & T," Ophelia insisted, smiling a winsome smile that would have melted the heart of a misanthrope. "Perdy is already there, but I know she'd want you to get out, too."

"Considering my face was plastered across the newspapers of Paris this morning, I don't think clubbing is the wisest choice of how to spend the evening."

"Don't be silly. No one will harm you there—it is neutral ground," Ophelia said, opening the wardrobe to see what I had suitable for an evening out. "Besides, Perdy is in charge now. No one would dare cross her."

That statement made me shiver. "To be honest, I just don't think I'm up to socializing tonight, but there is something you can do for me, if you would."

She turned away from the wardrobe, a disappointed pout evident. "If I can, you know I will."

"Other than Drake, are there any other wyverns in Paris?"

Her pout faded as a puzzled look replaced it. "Wyverns? Yeeees . . . Fiat Blu is here. He is the blue wyvern, although I do not recommend you have anything to do with him. He is not only depraved and immoral; he is a psychic, too. All the blue dragons are, but he is the most powerful." Her voice dropped to a throaty whisper. "It is said that he uses his powers to make women do . . . do . . . unnatural things with him."

"Sounds like quite the guy. The blue dragons are psychics, then? That's their trait? Are they known for their strength?"

She grimaced and absently straightened a picture on the wall. "All the dragons are strong."

"Hmm." The plan I had been mulling over since I left Amelie's solidified. "Do you know where Fiat Blu lives?"

She nodded reluctantly. "Yes, but I counsel you not to see him, Aisling. Fiat is much different from your wyvern."

I reached past her and pulled out the fanciest of the dresses Pál had bought for me. "All the better! If you tell me where he lives, I'll be very grateful." Stricken by the disappointed look in her eyes, I added, "And if I finish up with him quickly, I promise I'll drop by G & T and say hi."

That cheered her up.

An hour later, Jim and I walked up the shallow stone steps of an elegant building in the very chic Place de la Resistance. (The Eiffel Tower was just a few blocks away; then again, so was the Paris sewer museum.) "I don't know why I'm surprised by such a luxurious address," I said as I pressed the bell beneath a gold engraved nameplate that read simply BLU. "By now I should know that dragons equal wealth."

"This isn't just wealth," Jim said. "It's an attitude. You should adopt it."

I was a bit surprised when rather than someone using the intercom to find out what I wanted, the black-and-silver-door in front of me opened.

"Uh, hi. *Bonjour. Parlez-vous—*"

"*Or!*" the man in front of me interrupted, sniffing the air just as Drake had done. It flashed through my mind that the French word for "gold" was *or*, but before I could explain my gold wasn't valuable, he grabbed my arm and jerked me inside the apartment house, the door slamming behind me with a grim finality.

14

"Hey!" I yelled, squirming out of the grasp of my captor for a second before he grabbed me again. "You left my dem . . . my dog outside! Let go of me! You can't just drag me around like I'm a sack of potat—mmrf!"

The man, blond and muscle-bound and looking just like the surfer types my ex hung around with, clapped a hand over my mouth and hauled my struggling self into a small elevator. I tried kicking him in the shins, but he just threw me against the wall of the elevator and leaned against me, all but squishing the breath out of me. I'm not a small woman, but this guy was big and broad and didn't seem to be bothered at all by the fact that I was clawing at his back.

The elevator pinged its arrival at a floor, the doors opened with a rush of air, and for a few seconds I was airborn as Muscle Boy jerked me forward. "Come," he said in heavily accented English.

I dug my heels in, raking both sets of fingernails down the arm that clamped tightly around my wrist, but it did no good. I was hauled into an apartment, and without another word, tossed onto a blue velvet sectional couch. While I was fighting my way out of a nest of velvet pil-

lows that served as the back of the couch, Muscle Boy
rattled off something in a liquid-sounding language.

I managed to get to my feet, and stood glaring at the
back of my abductor until the person he was speaking to
stepped forward into the room. I sucked in my breath at
the sight of him—Drake was handsome in a dark, sexy,
seductive sort of way, but this man looked like a Greek
statue come to life. Curly blond hair brushed his shoulders, pure blue eyes—a true blue, not a filtered blue like
you see in most blue-eyed people—glittered brightly,
adorning a face that was so beautiful, it almost made me
want to weep. The rest of the man wasn't bad, either, although I only had a chance to notice that he was a few
inches taller than me before he glided forward with his
hands outstretched.

"*Cara,* Renaldo did not hurt you? He did not know
who you are. You must forgive his very poor manners.
We have been in Paris too long; he begins to behave like
a Frenchman."

"Actually, the Frenchmen I've met have all been extremely polite and very helpful, not to mention loaded
with manners," I said with great dignity, straightening my
dress. Where Drake was all heat and smoldering sensuality, this man radiated coolness—literally. The apartment
had that silent swish of air that indicated expensive air-
conditioning, cold almost to the point of seeing your
breath. I could imagine this man's dragon fire was of the
frigid variety, a blue fire that burned cold rather than hot.

He took my hands in his, kissing the back of each.
Even his hands were cool to the touch. I assumed this was
Fiat Blu, the wyvern of the blue dragons. He certainly
oozed confidence and power . . . and I understood exactly
why Ophelia had warned me against him. He looked like
the very worst sort of rogue.

"You are fortunate, then, for we have found Paris to be a city filled with barbarians," he said, waving his hands toward the window before gently pulling me down onto the velvet couch next to him.

I glanced quickly around the apartment. It was . . . blue. Everything in it was blue—the ceiling, the walls, the carpet, all the furniture. There were varying shades from midnight blue that was almost black to a pale washed blue that reminded me of an early spring morning. I turned my attention back to the Adonis sitting next to me. "I take it you are Fiat Blu?"

He put his hand on his chest and made a courtly bow. "I am Sfiatatoio del Fuoco Blu, the wyvern of the blue dragons, and I am very much at your service. How may I be of help to the mate of my esteemed comrade Drake Vireo?"

I frowned. "How do you know who I am? And how do you know I'm Drake's mate, not that I have any intention of fulfilling those duties even if I did believe I am who he says I am, but even if I was, how is it you know? Am I like marked somewhere? Is there a big red neon sign over my head saying 'Wyvern's Mate' with an arrow pointing to my head? Did someone tattoo it on my forehead without me knowing it? How?"

Fiat chuckled. It was a sexy chuckle as chuckles went, but gorgeous as he was, it had nothing on Drake's dark, sultry laugh. "I know who you are because I make it my business to know what goes on with those who are important to me. I have seen you with Drake. I hear a rumor that Drake has found his mate, an American who is a Guardian. I hear also that the police are searching for this woman, and that Drake has lost her. An American Guardian shows up on my doorstep with a demon. Who else could you be but his mate?"

"Oh," I said, more than a little relieved that he hadn't browsed through my mind pulling out bits of whatever information interested him. I hadn't forgotten Ophelia's warning that the blue dragons were noted for their psychic abilities. "I suppose it does make sense, then."

"Also," Fiat said with the Italian version of the Gallic shrug, "I browsed through your mind pulling out bits of information that interested me."

"Stop that!" I yelled, jumping up to my feet. "Stop barging into my head! You're not allowed to do that."

"But, *cara,*" he protested, pulling me back onto the couch next to him, his arm draped casually over the back in the first position of that ole-time move guys have. "It was so easy! You did not have even one mind guard up to keep me from your thoughts. I assumed you must want me to read them."

"What's a mind guard?" I asked suspiciously, slumping away from his arm.

He shrugged again. "It is the barriers someone such as yourself puts up to keep people from her mind."

Instantly I envisioned a high brick wall surrounding me, a brick wall without doors.

"No," Fiat shook his head as he took my hand in his, rubbing his thumb over my knuckles. His hands were so cool, they seemed to leach the heat from mine. "I can still get in because you have not sealed your mind from me."

Rats. He was right. The walls were open above. I rearranged my mental picture to form a tall tower with shuttered windows that I could open or shut. I shut them all, and immediately I was aware of the brush of his mind against mine as he tested my new barriers.

"It was not wise of me to say anything," he smiled a bit ruefully, his fingers still rubbing over mine. "Now I have done myself out of the pleasure of visiting such a charming mind, but these things, they are best not done so easily."

I said nothing, too worried that if I dragged my attention from keeping the shutters in my mind closed, he'd be able to breach my defenses.

Fiat leaned forward, his fingers a cool whisper as they danced along my cheek. "It is the thrill of the chase, you understand, *cara*. If the quarry gives up too easily, there is no pleasure in the hunt."

I mentally arranged iron bars to hold the shutters closed, pulling my hand from Fiat's as I said, "I don't suppose we could do this without all the sexual innuedo and hunter double-talk, could we? Because I've had a long day, and my demon is outside peeing on who knows what, so if we could skip all the seduction bit, I'd be grateful."

He laughed and withdrew his fingers from my face, leaning back against the pillows with an almost feline grace. It was then I noticed he was also dressed in blue, but a blue that had an intricate black pattern swirled through both the shirt and matching pants. "I hope Drake appreciates the mate he has been granted."

"I doubt he does, but that's neither here nor there. Um . . . do you think someone could let Jim—that's my dog—in?"

Fiat's eyes narrowed. He pushed briefly at my mind. "Why do you need your demon?"

I smiled. "Trust me, I don't need it, it's a big pain in the—it's a big pain."

He pushed at my mind again. "Then why do you want it to be allowed into my home?"

I broadened my smile until it positively radiated innocence. "Not for any nefarious purpose. It's just that it's forever getting itself into trouble, and I don't like the thought of what it's up to out on the streets without me."

Fiat watched me silently for a few seconds. "Very well, it is done. Now, what payment will you give me for granting your request?"

My smile faded. "Boy, you dragons really do know how to drive a bargain. I offer you my gratitude, Fiat. I appreciate you allowing Jim into your home. If that will satisfy you—" His face was an unmoving mask, but he didn't say no. "—then can we get to business? I wanted to speak to you about a business proposition."

His heavy blond eyebrows rose in surprise as he waved a languid hand toward me. "Business? *Cara*, I am intrigued. Please proceed."

I had to watch my step here, or else I might not find myself leaving the dragon's lair at the end of our meeting. "I know of the location of an object that Drake covets. It's bound in gold," I added, just to make sure I had his attention. I needn't have worried, his eyes were glittering with avidity. They dropped to my breasts. His nose twitched. I heaved a mental sigh and pulled up the gold chain, exposing the jade dragon. Fiat's eyes darkened at the sight of it. "This isn't the object I'm talking about, this is a talisman given to me. As you can see, it's not very valuable, not worth stealing."

"Drake might not have thought so, but I do not agree," Fiat murmured. I quickly tucked the talisman away, a little worry of fear skittering down my back at the dangerously flat tone in his voice.

"Regardless, the object I have in mind is worth a great deal more. It's priceless, you might almost say."

"What is it?" he asked, his voice sharp even though his body was relaxed.

I shook my head. "I can't tell you what it is, only that

Drake is desperate to have it, and I'm the only one who knows where to find it."

"Why are you offering *me* such a prize?" Fiat asked, his fingers lazily tracing a serpentine pattern on a pillow. "Why do you wish to keep an item of worth from your mate?"

"I'm offering it to you because you're the only other wyvern in the area." Fiat stiffened at that. I hurried to smooth over the insulted look that flashed through his eyes. "But more important, I want the object to be safe, to be in the possession of someone who is strong enough to keep Drake from getting it, and from everything I've heard, you are."

His body relaxed as he inclined his head in a graceful gesture of acknowledgment, his fingers stroking the velvet pillow in a way that was extremely sensual. "It is true, what you say. I am very powerful. But I still do not understand why you don't want your mate to have this mysterious object, and since you have withdrawn access to your thoughts—" I felt him brush against my mind again, but my shutters held tight. "—I must ask you to explain."

I stood up, taking a little stroll around the room and admiring the objects Fiat had chosen to display on the occasional tables and walls. There was less gold scattered about than at Drake's house, and more of an emphasis on very old paintings, but still, the furnishings and artwork screamed serious collector. "My reason for keeping it from Drake is my own. I just want reassurance that if I tell you where to find the object, it will be safe in your lair where Drake can't steal it back."

Before I could blink, he was there in front of me, one extremely pissed-off wyvern. I took a step back as he leaned toward me, his eyes black, his voice a low hiss. "You insult me, Guardian. My lair is safe from all intruders, no matter how powerful they might be. I am *il drago blu.* No one takes what I hold!"

"My apologies," I said, adopting what I hoped was a submissive, nonconfrontational pose. The last thing I needed was to piss off the probably only person in Paris who could keep the Eye safe from Drake. "I meant no insult. I just needed to be sure. You've convinced me that whatever I give into your safekeeping you will keep safe."

Fiat straightened a small icon on a marble shelf. "And what it is you want in exchange?"

I smiled, pleased we were to the bargaining point with me in such a strong position. "Once I tell you where to locate the item, I will need your help to leave Paris . . . to leave *France.* The police have my passport and other things, and although I fully expect that they will see the error in their thinking, it could take some time. In exchange for you taking the item into your custody—and giving me your word you will never allow anyone else to have it—you will get my passport and things back, and help me get out of the country."

A calculating look filled his eyes as he leaned one elbow on the shelf. "I am no thief. For that you would do better to ask your mate."

I took a deep breath. "Does that mean you can't help me get out of the country?"

Fiat considered me for a moment. "The matter is insignificant. It is within my power to see to your escape. I am curious, though, why you ask so little for an object you claim is priceless."

I shrugged. "That's all I need."

His lips narrowed. "So you say, but I think that you are not telling me the entire truth. I do not like to be fooled, *cara,* not even by a woman I would enjoy taking. You come here presenting to me the grand explanation, but you shield your mind from mine, you insist on your demon being present, and you refuse to tell me much about this object. I was not born yesterday."

Jim chose that moment to stroll into the room, its leash trailing behind it. "Hey, nice digs! Is that Ming dynasty?"

"Jim," I said warningly as it put its paws onto an ebony table to examine a graceful Chinese vase.

Fiat stepped toward me, and my early-warning system went into immediate Red Alert mode. In a moment between two breaths, things had changed, going from me having the upper hand to Fiat posing a very tangible threat to me.

"Maybe you just need a little time to think about it," I said, sidling around him toward Jim. "There's no hurry. I can give you until . . . uh . . . tomorrow at lunchtime. I'll just be on my way now so you can think it over."

"You will give me as long as I care to take," he answered, all male arrogance and power seething just below the surface. Dragons! Unreasonable, every last one of 'em. "As for your leaving, that is quite out of the question, *cara*. You are here, in my house and in my power. Drake might have been foolish enough to let you slip out of his grasp, but I assure you I will not. You will oblige me first by handing over the talisman you wear."

It was worse than I thought. The hard look to Fiat's eyes told me that the time for negotiation was over. "Jim?" I asked quietly, backing up toward him.

Jim sighed. "I suppose you want me to do my trusty sidekick thing again?"

"If it's not too much trouble," I answered.

"*Cara*—," Fiat said, shaking his head, starting toward me.

"When?" Jim asked.

"Now!" I yelled, whipping around to grab the Ming vase, throwing it to the left of Fiat. He lunged toward it with a shriek while Jim and I dashed to the right, out of the room and down the hall toward the door. The blond behemoth named Renaldo who dragged me there stumbled out of a side room. Jim flung itself on him. I continued, yelling Jim's name as I threw open the door and ran out of the apartment, racing down a wide stone spiral staircase. Voices shouted after me, but I didn't wait around to see what they wanted. I leaped down the steps, my heart pounding, my breath caught in my throat. A black shape lunged past me as I threw myself toward the street door.

"You . . . have . . . the . . . stupidest . . . ideas . . . sometimes," Jim panted as we jumped down the front stairs, running pell-mell into the busy street.

"No . . . argument," I gasped, pausing for a minute to find a likely hiding area. A glance over my shoulder confirmed my fear—three men, Renaldo included, were dashing out of the apartment after me.

"This way," Jim shouted, running toward a small building that bore a blue and white sign that read VISITE DES EGOUTES DE PARIS.

"What is it?" I managed to ask as I ran toward the building.

"Sewers," Jim yelled, running under a barrier meant to keep people from entering without paying. I ran up to the turnstile, grabbing a wad of euros and thrusting them at the attendant, scattering apologies behind me as I vaulted over the metal bar. I sprinted into the building after Jim, just barely stopping myself when his cry of "Stairs!" warned me of the staircase just inside the door. I pounded down the metal stairs after him, well aware of the sounds of yelling behind me. No doubt Fiat's dragon squad had bypassed the ticket-seller, too.

"Why the sewers?" I yelled down a dimly lit staircase. As I turned on each landing, I could see Jim's black shape hurtling down the stairs in front of me.

I tossed another apology over my shoulder as I passed a family of four who were taking the stairs at a more sedate rate, the whole family looking in surprise as Jim yelled back, "Water! The blue dragon element is the air. They hate water!"

The smell hit me as I cleared the last steps and lunged through the heavy metal door at the bottom. We were in a huge stone tunnel lit by weak lights that glowed out of the curved ceiling, a long vista of tunnels opening before us. The smell was awful—don't let anyone tell you the Paris sewers don't smell like a sewer, because they do— but I didn't have time to do more than wrinkle my nose before Jim's voice called back to me from a tunnel to the left. I ran after him down a stone-lined tunnel. Above me, lights were set into the stone at regular intervals. Down the center of the curved ceiling ran a huge blue water pipe, while several smaller pipes snaked next to it down the length of the tunnel. I kept to one side as I ran after Jim, the center of the floor consisting of a steel grate that sat over a roaring river of water. Sewer water.

"Really? Why do they hate water?"

"It's opposite them—water and air, earth and fire. One cancels the other. The dragon septs each claim an element," Jim called back to me.

"Fascinating. I can't believe I'm doing this," I grumbled as I turned a corner, glancing behind me as I did so. At the far end of the tunnel one of Fiat's men appeared, spotted me, and yelled something over his shoulders.

"What the heck?" I stopped as I turned around. The

antechamber we were in held huge black wooden balls . . . and I do mean huge. One of them was seated up against the opening of a tunnel, the ball almost completely filling it. Other balls of lessening sizes were chained to the walls, the smallest probably about four feet high, the biggest about sixteen.

"Come on, we don't have time to admire the sewer's balls," Jim snapped as it took off down another round passage.

"What are they?" I yelled, one hand clutching at the stitch in my side.

As I passed a narrow opening in the side of the tunnel, something jerked me sideways. "They clean the sewer of debris. If you want me to play tour guide, I can," Jim said as it spat out the hem of my dress it had used to pull me after it. "Or we can escape the blue dragons. Choice is yours."

"Escape," I said. We ran. And ran. And ran. It felt like we ran down miles and miles of sewer, passed open waterfalls of sewer water pouring into another channel, past numerous huge pieces of machinery used to keep the sewers clear, down narrow stone paths littered with dead leaves and empty plastic bottles that had been caught in the sewers screens.

We came to another juncture. Jim leaped over a metal railing intended to keep people out of a tunnel. I lurched (less gracefully) after the demon, almost falling with surprise as I landed on a narrow stone ledge. Unlike the other tunnels open to the public, this one had no grating over the water that rushed through it at a tremendous rate. Behind me, a man yelled.

"Faster!" Jim cried as it raced across a wooden plank about four inches wide that had been set across the open channel.

"You're kidding me! I'm not crossing that!" I came to a screeching halt at the flimsy bridge, glancing behind me. Renaldo might be bulky, but I'll give it to him—he had a sprinter's speed.

"Merde!" I yelled as I shuffled across it, my lower lip caught between my teeth in an effort to keep from screaming. Renaldo was almost upon me when I stepped off onto the other ledge. Jim was clawing at the plank even as I spun around to help it throw the bridge into the water. Renaldo screamed what sounded like an Italian obscenity as he lunged toward the plank.

He missed it by inches. I stood, panting, my back against the curved wall of the tunnel, staring across nine feet of open, torrential water to where Renaldo stood pacing back and forth, glaring at me. He wasn't even breathing hard, damn him!

"What's wrong, afraid you'll get wet?" I taunted him, feeling a little payback was in order.

Renaldo growled something and looked for all the world like he was going to try to vault over the open water, but each time he got near the edge, he'd back up again.

"Didn't your mother teach you anything?" Jim asked as he turned toward the far exit. "It's not smart to bait a dragon."

Renaldo kept pace with us as we ran down the tunnel, snarling and swearing threats at us when we dashed off into a side tunnel that he couldn't reach.

We ran down more tunnels, some open, some with grates, until I lost any and all sense of direction.

Not to mention my breath.

"Jim, I have to stop," I gasped as we entered yet another junction that held machinery. Some sort of engine with big red gears sat atop what looked like a small railway handcar, behind which a sharp-sided black tender was attached. Both had metal wheels shaped to move along metal tracks.

"Can't stop unless you want them to get us," Jim said as it crawled underneath the coupling of the two cars. I sat on the coupling mechanism, swinging my exhausted legs over it, pausing for a moment to suck air into my lungs. "I don't care. They can have me. I just want to stop. My heart's going to burst."

"Just a little farther," Jim urged me as it scrambled over a railing marked with a red warning sign that read: DANGER! INTERDIT AU PUBLIC. I didn't need to understand French to know what that meant.

Just as I opened my mouth, I heard two men calling to each other in the tunnel we had just come from. I slammed my mouth closed and hauled myself over the waist-high railing, stifling a scream of surprise as I fell about four feet. We were in a small well, evidently some sort of unused overflow valve if the red metal cap beneath our feet was anything to go by.

I didn't need to be warned to be quiet as we crouched down, making ourselves as flat as possible. Because of the machine cars standing in front of us, unless Fiat's men were right next to us peering down into the well, they wouldn't see us. I sat with my arms around Jim, my mouth pressed up against its heavy coat to muffle the sound of my gasping wheeze for air. A moment later the men entered the tunnel intersection, calling to Renaldo. I didn't risk standing up so I could peer out at them, but even though I didn't understand a word of what they were saying—the blue dragons seemed predominately Italian in origin—the angry tones of their voices left me in no doubt they were not happy campers. After a consultation lasting about a minute, they left, each taking a different tunnel out of the area.

"Think they'll come back?" I whispered into Jim's furry ear.

"Don't do that, it tickles," Jim complained, butting its head against me to rub its ear. I rubbed it, scritching behind the ears the way I knew it liked.

"We have to leave," I said softly, aware from the echoes of other tourists talking and calling to one another that sound in the nonwater tunnels traveled very well.

"No! I figured we'd stay here until they started calling you the Phantom of the Sewers."

I socked Jim on the shoulder and hoisted myself out of the well with an audible grunt. "I'm too old for this. I want to go home. Let Drake have the Eye. Screw the world. I just want a hot bath and a nice comfy bed."

"Selfish, selfish, selfish," Jim said, jumping nimbly out of the well. "This way."

I turned around. "Oh, now you're an expert on the sewers? What makes you think you know the way out?"

Jim walked over to a corner and nodded toward a small blue sign that read AVENUE BOSQUET. A painted red arrow pointing up was nestled up against a line of metal grips set into the wall. "Oh. I suppose that leads to an exit?"

"That's the idea."

A couple of tourists wandered in as I was in the process of dragging Jim up the grips. It couldn't make it on its own, and after I summarily refused its request to carry it up, I ended up more or less giving it a piggyback ride as I dragged us up the vertical path. What the tourists thought, I can only imagine, but I sure hope the little girl with the camera sends me a copy of the picture she took just before I shoved the manhole cover aside and exhaustedly crawled onto the still sun-warmed pavement of Avenue Bosquet.

"Remind me," I said as I heaved my body out of the path of an oncoming car. I kicked the manhole cover back into place and collapsed on the ground between two parked cars, Jim sitting on the sidewalk watching me as I doubled over, gasping for air, completely mindless of the stares I was receiving from people walking by. "Remind me about this evening if I ever again get the bright idea to go visit a wyvern in his den."

"Do you think you're likely to be that stupid?" Jim asked, sotto voce.

I slumped back against the bumper of the car behind me, my eyes closed, too wiped out to move. "You never know, Jim. You just never know."

15

The unsettling realization that I had no idea how much of my thoughts Fiat had read before I erected mind barriers kept me on tenterhooks until the taxi I'd hailed dropped us off at Ophelia and Perdita's apartment. I wasn't sure if Fiat had been able to tell who was offering me shelter, but I hadn't thought he had—at least, I hoped he hadn't. And since no one was waiting for me outside the door or inside the apartment, I tucked the keys Ophelia had given me into my bag and slunk off to the tiled bathroom to wash off the stench of the sewers.

It was shortly after nine when I emerged from the bathroom in a plume of jasmine-scented steam, sore and scraped from crawling in the well, not to mention dragging a huge demon-in-a-Newfoundland-suit up the side of a wall. But at least I was clean.

I left Ophelia and Perdita a note explaining that I was too tired to make an appearance at G & T that night, and after taking Jim for his evening walkies in a nearby park, crawled into bed and slipped almost immediately into a deep, dreamless sleep.

At least it started out dreamless.

"I am *so* not doing this," I said as I walked into a pool

of light. I had no idea where I was other than there was the faintest sense of a tall, arched ceiling above me and a long narrow space that resembled the inside of a Gothic cathedral, but I knew Drake was somewhere in the shadows. I spun around, suddenly aware that I wasn't in the cream-and-lace nightie he had dreamed me into for the last two dreams. This time I was wearing a very tight red-and-black flamenco dress, complete with ruffled sleeves, low-cut bodice exposing a fair portion of my bosom and all of my back, and a slinky, hip-hugging skirt that clung to my thighs before flaring out to open into black and red ruffles. It was a very sexy dress, much more daring and seductive than anything I'd ever worn.

The tango music seemed to come from nowhere and everywhere as Drake sauntered out into the circle of light, clad almost completely in black. The light source above us shown down on his black satin shirt, turning it to liquid ebony as it rippled across his chest and arms. He stopped and held out his hand for me. Without thinking, I did a twirl toward him, clasping his hand and continuing to turn until I was flush against him, our hands locked together in the small of my back, the bloodred sash at his waist matching my dress exactly.

"I don't tango," I said, breathless as I always was in his presence.

"Now you do." His voice, deep and rich and filled with all sorts of erotic unspoken promises, stroked down my spine with a touch that left me shivering . . . but whether it was with fear or arousal, I was unwilling to admit.

I twirled away, Drake following me, our bodies coming together in a sensual dance that had no choreography other than the need to be near each another. The tango music demanded, we danced; his body asked, mine answered, my legs moving in and out and around his, my foot sliding slowly up his calf in a caress that almost did me in. We moved together, sweeping a sultry, sensual line down the pool of light, my skirt caressing his legs as we danced without words, without even touching, just a breath apart and yet bound tighter by our mutual passion than mere contact alone could promise. I swung around him to the left, he spun to the right, our bodies meeting again, moving off in another direction as the pulse of the music drove us harder. My eyes never left his glittering green gaze as his hands slid around my waist, holding me suspended in a moment so filled with tangled emotions that I couldn't speak; then it passed and we swayed into another sweeping pass through the pool of light, our hearts beating an identical rhythm.

"Why did you leave me?" Drake asked as he bent me backwards over his arm, his face shadowed. "Why did you run from me?"

I slid down his thigh, swung my leg through his, and did an amazing little turn that rubbed most of my back against his. He caught my arm, spinning me until my vision blurred, slowing me to stop with my back pressed against his chest, his fingers digging into my hips as he directed us in another pass through the light. "You know the answer to that, Drake. I don't have to defend my actions to you."

His breath was hot on my neck. Oddly enough, during the whole of our dance, I hadn't felt even a wisp of his fire, but suddenly it consumed me, raging through me until I realized that what I felt wasn't his desire, but his anger. I spun to face him, rubbing my breasts against his satin chest as we danced a line of intricate footwork that would have, had it been real, probably left me with at least one broken ankle.

"I don't understand you. I've tried, but it's impossible. I don't know what you want from me."

He spun me outward. I twirled back to him, wrapping his arm around my waist as I turned. "Would the safety of the mortal world be too much to ask?"

His fire raged through me, setting my soul ablaze. I embraced it, opening my arms to let the fire flow back to him.

"I don't know what you're talking about, Aisling, but whatever game you're playing is a dangerous one. Who is protecting you?"

I smiled as I did a provocative step around his body, the fingers of one hand trailing just above the slash of red at his waist as I circled him. "I don't have to tell you anything. We may have some strange metaphysical tie, and we might have had indulged ourselves in the last dream, but that doesn't mean we are meant to be together, nor do I have to listen to anything you say."

"You will answer my question," Drake growled, the deep sound thrumming in my blood for a moment before merging with the fire within me, growing hotter until it burned with a white flame.

I laughed and arched my back when his body got all bossy with mine in time to the music. "This may be your dream, but it doesn't mean I will do anything I don't want to do."

"We have mated. You want me even now."

"That doesn't mean we're going to do anything."

Outrage stiffened him against me. "Are you refusing me?"

I did a slow shimmy that left us both breathless. "Not refusing outright, just delaying. In fact, I need to be going back to sleep. I have a big day ahead of me tomorrow, one that involves making sure that you pay for the crimes you've committed, so you might want to get some rest, too. I have a feeling you're going to need it."

"Is that a threat?" His eyes were filled with so much emotion, they almost glowed green.

"A promise," I whispered against his lips.

The music came to a reluctant stop as I twirled one last twirl around the leg he forced through mine; then I backed away. I wasn't entirely sure that I could break off a dream that he had initiated, but I wasn't about to stay in his little nocturnal fantasy while he conducted an erotic third degree.

"Good night, Drake. Thank you for the dance. And the slinky dress. Maybe another time we can do the rumba?"

"This isn't over, Aisling. You're a fool if you think it is."

You're crazy if you think I didn't notice that not once did he deny doing anything wrong. Part of me wanted to stay and argue it out with him, to try to reason with him, to make him admit what he'd done, and wring a promise from him that he'd turn himself in to the police; the other part was sounding warning bells and counseling me to run like crazy from him.

Instead I drifted backwards into the shadows, leaving him standing by himself in the light, a mysterious figure in black, his face haunted, his eyes dark with shadows.

I would *not* fall in love with a murderer. No matter how much he wrung my heart.

I woke with that resolution echoing in my head. The clock at the side of the bed showed it was only two in the morning. I beat up the pillow until it was somewhat comfortable, and I lay awake for a long time thinking over what I had to do. An hour into my contemplation, Perdita crept into the room with a cone of cedar-scented incense and conducted the ritual cleansing by the light of the moon. It was a strangely unsettling experience, one that left me wondering just how right things were in my head that I suspected the two women who were risking their own safety by protecting me.

"All right, you and I are going to have a talk."

"Goody gumdrops. I'm slobbering at the thought."

I pulled out a fresh drool bib that Ophelia had kindly purchased for me the day before, and tied it around Jim's thick neck. We had done a quick walkies—quick because I was nervous about being on the streets where someone might recognize me, and yet hesitant to have either Ophelia or Perdita take the demon out for me since they might find out it was a demon—and had our breakfast with the sisters. Ophelia offered to run any of my errands as she was out doing her own, but I couldn't think of anything I needed until after she'd left.

She also asked that I wait to conduct my demon-summoning ritual until after she returned, so she could watch. I gnashed my teeth a bit at the delay, wanting to get the demon's interrogation done so I could turn the information over to the police as soon as possible, but there wasn't much I could do. She and Perdita were taking a big risk by putting me up; delaying the summoning of Bafamal for a few hours was the least I could do in return.

"I was being sarcastic rather than literal," Jim said snappishly as I tied on the drool bib.

I wiped up its moist flews with the dirty bib. "You don't have something caught in your teeth, do you? I heard that tooth problems can make a dog drool excessively. Maybe I should take you to a vet?"

"You could brush my teeth instead. A good owner brushes her dog's teeth. Cecile says Amelie brushes her teeth for her every night. She has a special dog tooth-brush and everything. Some people *care* for their pets."

I sat in the puddle of sunlight that was warming the edge of the bed. "Stop trying to distract me. You are a demon, *not* a pet. I want to talk to you, and I command you to answer my questions. Honestly."

Jim muttered something under its breath and looked away.

"What powers does a Guardian have other than taking care of portals and summoning and releasing demons?"

"Whatever powers she needs."

"That's no answer," I said with a frown.

Jim pouted. "It's the truth, and that's what you asked for."

Why couldn't anyone in this city except Amelie offer information when I asked questions? I sighed and tried again. "Give me a specific list of powers a Guardian has other than the portal and demon stuff."

"She can draw wards and curses, can conduct mind pushes on mortals, depending on the level of her training, and can recognize Otherworld entities no matter what their disguises."

"That didn't hurt to much, did it?" I asked as I thought over Jim's list. It muttered that it hurt a lot. "Let's start at the top, ward and curses, what are those?"

"Wards are magic in symbol form. Most, but not all, are used for protection. Curses are anti-wards, drawn the same, but with the intention of doing an action to some-one else rather than the drawer. Happy now?"

"Nigh on ecstatic. What's a mind push?"

Jim sighed a throaty sigh. "Remind me to make my next demon lord someone who knows his job. A mind push is just what it sounds like—you want someone to do something, you give them a little mind push to make them do it."

"Oh. Something psychiclike? ESP and all that?"

"Not the spoon-bending kind. It's just you reaching out with your mind and convincing the other person they really want to do what it is you want them to do. Mind push, get it?"

"Got it. Kind of. Now this recognizing beasties and such, you mean like demons?"

Jim nodded and started licking its shoulder.

I frowned, going back over everyone I'd met since I summoned up Jim. "If that's so common, why is it that both wyverns recognized that you were a demon, and yet Amelie didn't until I told her? And for that matter, Ophelia and Perdita don't know what you really are, either."

"Who said it was common? Only those mortals who have the ability to control the dark powers can recognize beings who originate in the Otherworld. Same goes with those beings themselves, like the dragons."

"Ah. So Amelie as a healer and O and P as Wiccans can't see you as you really are?"

"Yes. Are you done with the questions? Because it's past time for my spit bath, and it's going to take me at least half an hour to take care of my package."

I "Ew, ew, ew!"-ed my way out of the room and left him to his grooming. I spent a few minutes making up a list of things I'd need for the demon summoning in between watching Perdita as she puttered around on a good-size balcony. Most of the space was taken up by flower boxes and containers filled with various plants—herbs, she'd told me earlier as she walked by with a watering can.

"Finished already?" she asked as she came in with a handful of something green and leafy.

I nodded. "I think I'm going to have to go out. I need a couple of books that I know Amelie has, as well as dead man's ash."

"You're welcome to check our library," Perdita said as she rubbed a stalk of plant between her hands. "I'm sure I saw some dead man's ash in the workroom."

"Really?" That was a surprise. I'd thought I read somewhere that dead man's ash was only used in summoning ghosts and demons. "Thanks, I'll go look . . . er . . . in a few minutes." After Jim was done with its groin washing.

Perdita set her bruised leaves in a wooden bowl. "Dill," she explained as I watched her crush them with a pestle.

"Something for lunch?" I asked.

She frowned. "No, dill is a great protector against demons. I thought that as you were bringing one into the house, I would use it to protect every room but the workroom, just in case."

"Er . . . " Dill was demon's bane? I thought briefly of Jim. How on earth was I going to explain my dog's sudden inability to leave my bedroom? "How exactly does the dill protect you from a demon?"

"Demons hate it," she answered, still grinding away with the pestle. "They can't stand to be in the same room with it."

The door to my bedroom, which I'd left cracked so Jim wouldn't have to get the doorknob all slobbery, opened and my demon on four legs strolled into the room, making a beeline to me as it dropped its leash at my feet.

I watched closely for a moment, but Jim didn't seem to be disturbed by the dill Perdita was setting around the apartment in little pots. In fact, I doubt if it even noticed. So much for protection.

"I'll just go see if you have any dead man's ash, then be out of your hair for a little bit."

Perdita made polite noises about not minding me underfoot. I shot Jim a warning look to behave himself, and went back into my sunny bedroom, stopping in front of a glass-fronted bookcase. There were a lot of Wiccan books, a couple of Herbals, books on magyck, books on the origins of witchcraft, and the like. "Nothing I can use," I said to Jim as it followed me back into the room. "Which doesn't surprise me because . . . Hmmm."

"It doesn't surprise you why?" Jim asked, sharking the bed to rub itself along the edge of the mattress. Jim, I had discovered, loved to have its back scratched.

"Because they don't have anything to do with the dark arts. Is this what I think it is?" I pulled out a tiny volume, about the size of my palm, that had been tucked behind a larger book. "The *Steganographia*. Well, I'll be."

"Oh, that. Yeah, I saw that yesterday," Jim said, sounding bored as it continued sharking the bed. "I thought you preferred the *Liber Juratus*. Isn't that what you used to call me?"

"Yes," I said slowly, flipping through the book. "But it's odd that Wiccans should have a book of this sort."

"Not if they had anything to do with the Venediger," Jim said, still rubbing itself along the bed. "Think you could get me a brush? I want to look my best if we're going to see Cecile."

"The Venediger . . ." I'd almost forgotten that Perdita worked for him. "Of course, if she worked for him, she must have had some skills with the dark powers, don't you think? Hence the *Steganographia*."

"What I think is that I need brushing," Jim said pointedly.

"Hmm? Oh, yeah, I suppose you do. You're looking a bit ratty." I slid the book back into its spot and make a quick check of the shelving holding the various pots of herbs and such. No dead man's ash.

"Come on," I said, snapping on Jim's leash and grabbing my purse. "Let's make this fast. The least amount of time I have to spend out on the streets, the happier I'll be."

"Call Rene," Jim suggested.

I was about to say I wouldn't bother Rene for something so trivial, but rethought my strategy. With Rene serving as my driver, he'd keep his eye peeled for the police . . . that was assuming he'd want to drive a fugitive around Paris while she did her shopping. "Maybe I shouldn't get him involved."

"Are you kidding? He'd love it," Jim said softly as I opened the door. I signaled for it to be quiet, then pulled Rene's card out, explaining quickly to Perdita that I was going to use a friend to drive me around. I watched her out of the corner of my eye as I dialed the number, wondering just how deep in the Venediger's business she had become. A Wiccan who had a well-used copy of the *Steganographia* was definitely an oxymoron.

Kind of like a Guardian who was also a demon lord.

Fifteen minutes later Jim and I descended the stairs, peering up and down the street for signs the apartment was being watched before dashing into Rene's waiting taxi.

"Bonjour," I said breathlessly, grunting when Jim jumped into the taxi and landed on me. "Get off me!"

"Sorry."

Rene twisted around in his seat and glared at me. "Before we go, I must first lecture you."

"Um—"

"You said on the phone you did not wish to derange me if I believed those stories in the paper about you. Me, I am offended you would think that!"

I fluttered a hand at the window. "Rene, I'm sorry, the last thing I want to do is offend you, but I wanted to give you an out if you were uncomfortable with the thought of driving around someone who is wanted by the police."

Rene snorted. "You do not have faith in me, eh?"

"I have a lot of faith, I just don't want you getting involved in something that you'll regret."

He made a rude gesture out the window at the person behind us who was yelling at him, turning to face the front. *"Quand les poules auront des dents."*

"Huh?"

He put his foot on the gas. I clutched Jim as we were thrown backwards. "It means when female chickens have teeth. It is your phrase for today, but it also expresses what I think of your so foolish worry."

Evidently I was forgiven if he was giving me another phrase to wield during my time in France. I smiled and, while we drove to the Latin Quarter, gave him the latest on what had been happening since I last saw him.

"It is good you called me. I will watch with eyes most vigilant to be sure the police do not see you," Rene told me as I dragged an unwilling Jim out of a pet shop we'd stopped at to get a brush. Jim decided any store that had big open bins of dog cookies was more or less heaven, and had to be forcibly convinced to vacate the premises. "We will serve the reconnaissance on the Rue Ébullitions sur les Fesses de Diable. If we see the police, *hein*, we will leave. If not, I will drop you off and park down the street, yes?"

"Sounds like a plan," I agreed. And that's exactly what we did—Rene drove up and down Amelie's street a couple of time, but we didn't see any police cars, or strange men across from her shop who appeared to be reading newspapers, or women stopped in front fussing with a baby carriage, or any of the other many ruses cops take when on stakeout. There were a lot of people on the street, but none of them were loitering. It was nearing midday, and people were hurrying along to the shops or for an early lunch. Rene let me out about a block away, following slowly behind as I strolled up and down the street, watching for anyone who might be interested in me.

On my third stroll past Amelie's shop, he gave me the all-clear symbol and zoomed off to our rendezvous place a couple of blocks away.

"Operation Amelie is go," I told Jim quietly as I turned on my heel and headed back for Le Grimoire Toxique. As I approached the door to the shop I did a final scan of the street, but no one was paying the least amount of attention to us. "Whew. Looks like for once luck is with us."

I pushed the door open and walked right into Inspector Proust.

16

"Pardon me . . . Oh, holy *merde*," I said, getting a good look at whom I had careened into. For a moment I just stood in stunned surprise; then my fight or flight instincts kicked in and I turned to run.

Inspector Proust's hand clamped down on my arm, stopping me dead in the door. "Mlle. Grey, what a pleasant surprise. I was just having a little chat with Mme. Merllain about you. Madame declared that she had no idea of when you might stop by her shop, and yet here you are. How very timely your visit is."

My heart sank to my shoes (again) as I turned back to face him, flexing my arm experimentally. His grip wasn't painful, but it was extremely solid. There was no way I could get away from him unless I ordered Jim to attack, and I hesitated doing that, not only because it wouldn't look good for Amelie, but also because despite the fact that he wanted me in jail, I kind of liked Inspector Proust. At the very least, he was honest with me.

"Amelie was telling the truth," I said, briefly allowing my eyes to meet hers as she stood looking very worried behind Inspector Proust. "She knows nothing about my plans. I suppose you want to have a chat with me, too."

"That would be most agreeable," he said, gesturing toward the door with his free hand.

Somehow I doubted if *agreeable* would be a description that I would use. I shot a warning look to Jim as we left the store. It raised its eyebrows but kept silent.

"I'm innocent, you know," I said in a conversational tone as Inspector Proust walked me down the sidewalk in the opposite direction of where Rene was waiting for us. I figured I had a minute at best before he marched me into official custody. Now was as good a time as any to fill him in on a few facts. "I didn't kill the Venediger any more than I killed Mme. Deauxville, and you yourself admitted I didn't kill her. I do, however, know who did kill both of them, and I'm in the process of gathering proof you can use to convict the murderer."

"It is the job of the police to gather proof, mademoiselle, not you. I will be glad, it is true, to hear your thoughts on the matter. I am most interested in what you have to say about your adventures at M. Camus's house." He cocked his head as he glanced at me. "It was you who set fire to the gazebo, was it not?"

"Yes, but that was an accident, I didn't mean for it to happen. I was just a little careless with . . . uh . . . matches." I pulled on my arm. He didn't loosen his hold at all, just kept walking me down the street, Jim trailing behind us. I chewed on my lip for a moment, remembering what Jim had said earlier. Of all the powers a Guardian had, there was only one that could do me any good in this situation. If I could figure out how to do a mind push on Inspector Proust, I might be able to get away from him and make it back to Rene. I glanced at Inspector Proust from the corner of my eye. He lifted his free hand and gestured to someone, probably his driver parked down the street. It was now or never. "You want to let me go, don't you?"

He looked at me, clearly startled by my statement. "I beg your pardon?"

I curled my fingers into fists and opened the door in my head, ignoring the embers of Drake's fire that always seemed to be there, instead picturing Inspector Proust releasing my arm. "You want to let me go. You don't want to hold on to me. You know I'm innocent, so there is no reason why I should not just walk away."

His brown eyes looked a bit wary. "Mademoiselle, are you unwell?"

I took a deep breath, held the mental picture of Inspector Proust releasing me, and infusing my words with as much of my will as I could muster, said, "Let . . . me . . . go."

Something gave, a barrier that was there, then was gone, and with its absence the pressure of Inspector Proust's hand on my arm also disappeared. I looked down, surprised the mind push worked. He wasn't holding on to me. I took a step away, glancing up at him. His eyes were a bit flat, as if he were thinking some deep thoughts. Ahead of me, a car approached. I took a few more steps away from Inspector Proust. He didn't even blink.

"It works," I breathed as I yanked on Jim's leash. I didn't have to yank twice. As the unmarked police car zoomed up and stopped next to Inspector Proust, we walked away quickly, half expecting either the Inspector or his driver to yell after us, but neither did. The driver must not have realized his boss had me in custody. "Hot damn, it works! I can mind push! Now this is a skill I can use. No more speeding tickets, no more waiting for a table in a restaurant, at last, at long last, something practical!"

"Doesn't work on dragons, only mortals," Jim said.

"We can't have everything," I answered as I turned the corner, intending on doubling back to dash into Amelie's shop just long enough to grab a copy of the book I needed. "Why do you mention dragons, particularly?"

"Signora Grey," Renaldo said, popping out of a parked car to stand in front of me. "*Il drago blu* wishes to have a few words with you."

"That's why," Jim said.

I smacked it on the shoulder. "You couldn't have just said, 'Hey, Aisling, there're dragons sitting in a car over there'?"

"*Il drago* wishes for you to come with us now, signora," Renaldo said in a louder, more aggressive voice.

I didn't even try a mind push, not with Jim's half-assed warning fresh in my ears. Instead I jerked the gold chain with my jade dragon talisman over my head, yanking the talisman off the chain. "Look, gold!" I waved the gold chain in front of Renaldo's face. He sniffed the air, his eyes brightening as he watched the chain sway. When I was sure he was about to lunge at it, I threw it as hard as I could over his head. "Go get it!"

Unable to resist the lure of treasure—gold, I had discovered, generating an almost visceral reaction in dragons—Renaldo spun around and jumped for the chain. I ran in the other direction, down the street toward Amelie's, past Inspector Proust, who was still standing on the sidewalk looking distracted, this time with his driver waving a hand in front of his face. The driver didn't even glance at me as Jim and I raced past. I was almost to Amelie's door when two familiar figures ahead of me crossed the street to my side of the road, heading right for me.

It was Pál and István.

"What, *everyone* knows I'm here?" I grumbled as I thought quickly. Behind me, Renaldo was stuffing the gold chain into his pocket as he walked quickly toward me, giving Inspector Proust and his driver (who was now shaking the Inspector) a wide berth. Ahead of me Pál and István marched toward me with familiar grim looks on their faces.

Talk about being caught between a rock and a hard place.

I decided Drake's men were the least of my worries and beckoned to them, pointing behind me as I yelled, "The blue wyvern's man is trying to kidnap me so he can use me against Drake!"

Drake's red-haired duo stiffened at my words, both their gazes going over my shoulder to where Renaldo was bearing determinedly down on me. Renaldo saw them at the same time and paused.

"He has gold," I added persuasively.

It was all the urging Pál and István needed. They sprinted past me, their eyes lit with pleasure. Renaldo stood still for a moment, then he turned on his heels and ran for it.

I shoved Jim into Amelie's shop, following quickly after the demon. I had no idea how long Inspector Proust would stay mind pushed, or how long the dragons would take to realize that I had tricked them, but I wasn't planning on waiting around to see.

"Hi, Amelie, I'm sorry about all this, but do you have a copy of— Oh, bloody hell, that's all I need! What the devil are *you* doing here?" A shadow fell at my feet as Drake loomed up in Amelie's doorway behind me. He must have been following Pál and István, although I hadn't seen him. I turned back to Amelie, unsnapping Jim's leash as I asked, "Do you have a back exit?"

"Yes," she said simply, and nodded toward the bead curtain that separated the public part of the shop from the back.

"Jim, attack!" I said, pointing behind me.

Drake opened his mouth to say something, but Jim—for once—decided to obey me without argument and sprang at Drake before he could speak. They went down in a solid thud of tangled legs and black fur. I bolted toward the beaded curtain, jumping over cartons of books, heading for the door painted with a blue pentagram. I was through it and halfway down the alley that ran behind the building before I realized that Jim wasn't on my heels. I stopped, hesitating, unsure of whether I should risk going back for it, or trusting that Jim would take care of itself.

"Dammit," I swore as I turned my back on the shop and continued to run toward the parking lot two blocks away, telling myself that the probability of Jim's survival was far greater than mine if I went back. A few tears snaked down my cheeks, making me angrier still at myself. Jim might not be able to be killed, but its doggy form could be destroyed. I wiped at my cheeks, spinning around the corner of a café to the busy parking lot that butted up against it. Rene was leaning against the hood of his car, reading a newspaper. I yelled and waved my arm as I bolted into the parking lot. He evidently got the message, because he didn't wait for me to explain; he just jumped into the car and pulled out of his spot, stopping long enough for me to throw myself into the front seat next to him before he burned rubber getting us out of there.

"Where is the little devil dog?" he asked as I slammed

into the car door with the force of a highly illegal and completely death-defying hairpin U-turn.

I wiped angrily at the tears still streaming down my face. "I told Jim to attack Drake, but he must have done something to poor Jim, because otherwise it would have been on my heels. It's not normally very big on heroics."

The thought of Jim being harmed by Drake made my tears flow faster. What sort of a coward was I that I would so quickly abandon Jim like that? It was following my command faithfully. Jim might be just a demon, but it was *my* demon.

"Drake was there?" Rene whistled. "We will make a dashing escape right now."

"Turn around," I ordered, pulling up the hem of my skirt to mop up my face.

Rene looked at me like I had frogs in my bidet. "What?"

"Turn around—we're going back. I can't leave Jim to Drake's mercy. Drake *has* no mercy. He'll torment Jim. I just know it."

Rene slowed the taxi but didn't turn around. "Your bell is being rung," he said.

I sniffed and shot him a frown. "I what?"

He gestured a circle on his temple. "Your bell is being rung. You are not thinking right."

"Oh, I'm crazy? Yeah, I know, but I'm learning to live with it. Turn around, please. I have to get Jim."

Rene complied, but not without several comments about the immense lack of wisdom I was showing. "It is a little devil—you said yourself it cannot be hurt."

"That doesn't mean Drake won't make Jim suffer, and no one torments my demon but me. It's a rule I have. Stop here. I'll slip in the back way."

"I will drive around the block. You will wait for me

here, yes?" Rene asked as he pulled up at the end of the alley. We both peered around. No one was visible.

"Yes." I got out of the car, leaning in through the open window to give him instructions. "Five minutes. If I don't come out . . . go home. You won't be able to help me."

Rene gunned the engine. I pulled back as he waved. "Me, I do not abandon my friends, just like you, eh?"

He was off before I could warn him not to hang around. I slunk down the alley to Amelie's door and used my trusty credit card to get in the locked door, making my way silently through the back room to the curtain of beads.

Amelie stood at the open front door, looking out. There was no one else in the shop. She turned when I whispered her name.

"Aisling!" she gasped, closing the door quickly.

I slid through the beads. "Where's Jim? Did Drake take it? What did he do to it? Oh, lord, I never should have left Jim alone with him."

"Calm yourself—your demon was not injured," Amelie said, glancing nervously over her shoulder. "You must leave. It is not safe for you here. Drake and two of the green dragons are just outside. Inspector Proust is out there, too, although he appears to be in some sort of a daze."

"Oy," I said, backing through the bead curtain. "Where's Jim?"

"It ran off. Where, I do not know. I assumed it would follow you. Here—you will need this. Drake left it for you."

"Thanks," I said, snatching the dragon talisman she tossed to me, quickly making my way around the boxes to the back door. "If you happen to see Jim, would you tell it to come home? It knows where we live. And thanks for everything else, too."

I didn't wait around to hear anything else. I was at the end of the alley just as Rene came roaring around the corner.

"M. Drake, he is in the street, speaking to two men in suits," Rene said as soon as I opened the car door. I got in, Rene taking off even before I could close the door properly. "They are the police. I know they are—they have the look of police. We must get you out of here immediately."

I slumped back in the seat, worried, depressed, angry, and irritated at the sense of loss that I connected with Drake's sudden appearance. I stared out at the streets, watching for any sign of a big, lost Newfoundland. Rene shot me a questioning look when I didn't respond to a comment about Jim, finally settling back to drive me to Ophelia and Perdita's apartment without further demands for conversation.

I sent up a little prayer that Jim would have the common sense to return to the apartment as well. If it didn't . . . I shook my head wearily. I didn't want to think of what trouble my demon could get into without me to keep an eye on it.

Call me stupid, but I missed the big galoot.

"I'm so sorry you lost your dog, Aisling. Would you like me to ring up the animal-control people? They will let you know if they find Jim."

"No, it's OK," I told a sympathetic Ophelia. I had returned home to find that Jim hadn't found its way back yet, but that was no surprise. I was in a taxi, and poor Jim was hoofing it.

Three hours later, however, I had paced every square

inch of the apartment, no doubt driving both Ophelia and Perdita nuts, although both were too polite to tell me. I felt awful, not just guilty about leaving Jim to fend for itself, but physically drained and depressed, as if a horrible black cloud hanging over my head was leeching into my body. The apartment, at first so bright and lovely, was now oppressive and bleak, a prison rather than a haven. Perdita and Ophelia had offered to search the streets for Jim, but I knew that wasn't necessary. Jim was a smart demon; if it was at all possible for it to make its way home, it would.

"I just feel so helpless," I said, stopping before Ophelia to fret, trying to push down the rising sense of panic-laden despair. "Poor Jim is out there all by its . . . himself, facing who knows what horrors. Maybe he's been picked up by vivisectionists! Maybe someone will do a *Hundred and One Dalmatians* on him!" I paced past Perdita as she chopped up mushrooms for dinner.

"A hundred and one Dalmatians?" Ophelia asked her in a quiet voice.

"Skins," Perdita answered succinctly.

I waved my hands around, dread filling my mind at the horrible things that could be happening to Jim at that very moment. "Exactly! Jim has a lovely coat! Someone might want him for it. Or for . . . for . . . oh, I don't know, something awful. Someone might want to use him as a stud dog, ruthlessly breeding him again and again and again. Although to be honest, he probably wouldn't object to that too much, but dammit! He's *my* dog! He doesn't get to have fun unless I say he does!"

Ophelia set some apples in cinnamon to simmer, coming around the long marble counter that separated the dining area from the kitchen. She patted my hand, but it didn't make me feel any better. In fact, I felt worse, almost sick to my stomach with worry. "Aisling, if there is anything Perdy or I can do, any spell we could perform, you have but to ask."

I swallowed back a lump of unshed tears and tried for a smile. "Thank you, Ophelia. That's very generous of you, but I'm afraid spells . . . well, just they would be a waste of time." I had a feeling that if Perdita's dill was such a failure as an anti-demon protection, their herb-based spells would be ineffective, as well. "I'll just have to hope that he's lying low for a while until it's safe to come home."

She patted my arm. "You're distraught. Perhaps it would be best if you didn't conduct your demon ritual tonight. You can't focus if you're so upset. And didn't you say you needed a special book?"

"Oh, that's all right. I'll use Perdita's. It's a bit different from the one I'm familiar with, but I'm sure it will be OK. You don't mind if I use your book, do you?" I asked, desperately trying to distract myself with trivialities.

Perdita opened her mouth to say something, but a quick look at Ophelia left her shaking her head. "No, please use the book. I don't mind at all."

I squashed down all the worry, and sick fear, and a horrible sense of dread, and ordered my mind to focus on what was important. "There's no time like the present. If you both are free, I'll just go in and raise my demon, ask it a few questions, and send it back. Do either of you have a tape recorder?"

"Better than that, we have a digital video camera," Ophelia said, running for a closet. "We'll film your demon! Oh, this is so exciting!"

"That would be wonderful," I said in a voice that dripped unease. The two sisters followed me into the bedroom, newly cleansed and sadly Jim-less. I took the

Steganographia from the shelves and thumbed through it. I was vaguely familiar with the book, having read the translation (and decoding—part of the book had been written in a numerical code) a couple of years ago. I found the demon lord's symbols and sat down to draw a circle of ash made by paper I had burned earlier.

"I have no idea if this will work or not without the proper equipment," I warned both women. Ophelia sat on the bed behind me, filming me as I drew the circle widdershins with salt. I stopped halfway around the circle, almost overwhelmed with despair that welled up from deep within my heart. Why was I bothering? Why was I wasting my time? I'd just embarrass myself in front of Ophelia and Perdita when I couldn't summon Bafamal. They'd know I was a fake, a liar, someone who couldn't even perform a simple delivery without messing it up. I'd failed in that, just as I failed Jim. Even Drake was disgusted with me.

I fought back a sob and finished the circle, arguing with myself the whole while I traced the twelve symbols of Ashtaroth. By the time I had done the six symbols for Bafamal, I was very close to just rolling myself up into a ball and indulging in hysterical tears. Only the steady red light blinking on Ophelia's digital recorder kept me from giving in.

I pricked my finger with a pin Perdita gave me, then closed the circle with my blood. Nothing happened. There was no sense of thickening air as there was when I had summoned Jim. There was no tingle when I passed my hand over the circle. It was just a circle. I frowned, consulting Perdita's book, trying to recall everything I had done with Jim.

"Is something the matter?" Ophelia asked from behind me.

"Er . . . no, I guess not," I said, closing the book. I had done everything the same. Maybe the difference was because Ashtaroth was a different lord than Jim's former one? I shrugged, too upset and dispirited to care very much. I stood and called the quarters, aware not of the sense of something waiting to be called forth, but instead, a dread seemed to press in on me from all sides.

"I conjure thee, Bafamal, by the power of thy lord Ashtaroth, also called the keeper of the horde, to appear before me now without noise and terror. I summon thee, Bafamal, to answer truly all questions that I shall ask thee. I command thee, Bafamal, to my will by the virtue of my power. By my hand thy shall be bound, by my blood thy shall be bound, by my voice thy shall be bound."

One second the circle was empty; the next a handsome blond demon stood within it, watching me with a speculative gaze in its smoky gray eyes.

Bafamal had arrived.

17

The demon had changed clothes from the last time I'd seen it; now it was wearing scarlet pleated pants with a bright yellow shirt and azure tie. Very chic, very primary colors.

"Ever the fashion plate, I see," I said, taking a step back.

It smiled and made me a little bow. "You called me, oh master?"

I staggered over to a chair. The despair swamping me increased with the presence of Bafamal, draining me physically until I felt like a well-wrung limp rag. Behind me, Ophelia and Perdita stood, but I couldn't spare them even a glance. I had a horrible feeling that if I didn't keep my attention focused on the demon, it would break free of my control. "Bafamal, I command thee to answer my questions. Were you at the mortal Aurora Deauxville's house when she was killed?"

The demon smiled. "I had that pleasure."

"Were you there at the behest of the person who killed her?"

"I was."

My shoulders slumped. "Were you the tool for the death of Aurora Deauxville?"

Bafamal rubbed its hands, the open enjoyment on its face making my nausea increase. I clutched my stomach, fighting the urge to vomit. "Not the death, no. I strung the mortal up, though. That was fun."

My stomach lurched. I gritted my teeth. "Were you present at the house of the mage named Albert Camus?"

"Yes."

"Were you there at the request of the person who killed him?"

"None other."

"Were you the instrument of Albert Camus's death?"

"No. I heard you set fire to him later. Classy style you have, Guardian."

Behind me, Ophelia gasped. I ignored the demon's attempt at provocation, fighting wave after wave of nausea. My voice cracked as I asked, "Who summoned you, Bafamal?"

The demon's grin grew wider. "Drake Vireo, the green wyvern."

My heart turned to stone, fracturing into a million pieces. I knew Drake was guilty—I had ever since I'd found Bafamal lounging around in his house—but to hear the confirmation of it destroyed a part of me I hadn't known existed. Blackness swam before me. I clutched the arms of the chair and forced myself to breathe slowly. If I passed out, I'd lose control of the demon, and who knew what horrors that would unleash. "Who killed Aurora Deauxville?"

"Drake Vireo."

Pain stabbed through me. I turned my mind from it. "Who killed Albert Camus?"

"Drake Vireo."

Wetness streaked my cheeks. I lifted my hand to brush away the tears and found my fingers stained red. I was weeping blood. "Who ordered you to hang both Aurora and Albert?"

"Drake Vireo," the demon answered gleefully.

"Why?" I asked, my voice sounding like two rocks rubbed together. My mouth was so dry, I could hardly swallow. "Why did Drake summon you?"

"He needed my help to conduct the murders and escape undetected."

I closed my eyes and swayed, desperately trying to hang on to consciousness. "What does Drake intend to do with the Tools of Bael?"

Behind me, something glass crashed to the floor. I hoped it was the small bud vase that was next to Perdita rather than the video camera.

Bafamal buffed its fingernails on its shiny yellow shirt. "He wants to rule the mortal world, of course."

It was enough. I couldn't stand any more. With each word, another little piece of my soul was torn from me. I gritted my teeth and drew the symbols of evanescence. The demon didn't say anything, just grinned as I spoke the words that would disperse it back to its origin. With the final command, its figure blinked out as if a plug had been pulled.

"I can't . . . can't . . . " Without looking at the sisters, I leaped to my feet and raced for the bathroom, just barely making it to the toilet before losing my lunch.

When I returned, Ophelia was standing before Perdita, her hand on her sister's. "Please Perdy, please don't do it. It's wrong. You *know* it's wrong. You know well the penalty demanded of those who call upon the dark masters."

"I'm sorry, Feelie, but I have to. The Tools of Bael are not to be used lightly. I cannot allow Drake—"

A movement of awareness by Ophelia stopped Perdita from finishing her sentence.

"Aisling, are you all right?" Ophelia came forward, her hands outstretched. "You poor dear, what a horrible experience you've had. Did you know it was your mate who killed the Venediger and the other woman before the demon told you?"

I looked past her to where Perdita stood, her face grim. "What can't you allow Drake to do?"

Perdita started to say something, shot her sister an unreadable glance, and then shook her head. "I must leave now—I'm late. I have to open G & T. I will . . ." She paused at the door, looking back at us. Ophelia moved to stand close to me, a comforting hand on my arm. Perdita's eyes were hard and determined as she looked at us. "I will speak with you later about this."

I wasn't sure which one of us her words were meant for, but before I could ask, she left the room. Ophelia's hands fluttered at her sister's back as she left. "You'll have to excuse Perdy—she has been under a great deal of strain since the Venediger was killed, and she . . . she was . . . Well, to be honest, she and Drake Vireo were . . . were . . . friends before you came."

"Friends?" I blinked a couple of times while the emphasis she placed on the word sank into my fuzzy brain. "Oh, you mean *friends*. I didn't know."

"I'm sorry. That was tactless of me to blurt it out like that. I just wanted you to understand why Perdy is so upset."

I waved her apology away, rubbing the back of my neck as I sank onto the bed. The feeling of sickness and despair still clung to me, but it had lessened with the demon's disappearance. "It's all right. Drake might think I'm his mate, but it doesn't mean I have to accept that role. And we're not . . . *together.*"

She looked relieved.

I scooted up until my back was against the wall. "To answer your question—yes, I knew Drake was responsible for the deaths. I found Bafamal at his house. I knew there could be only one reason the demon was there. It was just a bit of a shock having it confirmed."

Ophelia curled up next to me. I closed my eyes, the nausea still holding me in its gut-wrenching grip. "How horrible for you to be deceived by a man you are so bound to. What are you going to do now?"

I rubbed my head. A headache was blossoming to life, making it difficult to think clearly. "I had planned to take whatever evidence the demon provided to the police, but now I'm not so sure. There was nothing it said that I could offer as proof positive, and if I tried to explain to Inspector Proust just who Bafamal was, he'd lock me away in a loony bin."

"Perhaps if you watch the video, something will occur to you," she offered, setting the video camera next to me. "I must go and make sure Perdy is all right, but then you and I will brainstorm a solution to this problem. There must be a way we can make the police understand just who is behind the murders."

I thanked her, lying quiet for a few minutes until I felt like I could move without my head splitting open—or vomiting again. I sat up and flipped on the video camera, wincing when the demon's voice came out just as loud as if it stood before me.

"Who killed Aurora Deauxville?"

"Drake Vireo."

I watched the recording all the way through, then

stopped it and thought about everything the demon had said. There was something that it mentioned that bothered me, something that was raising a red flag, but my tired, aching brain couldn't pin it down.

"Well, she's off," Ophelia said fifteen minutes later as she dragged the armchair over to the bed. "She's very upset, but determined to keep G & T open until the Venediger's will is read next Monday. He promised to leave it to her, you know, as a mark of his respect, and an acknowledgment of his debt to her."

"His debt?"

"Perdy has worked for him for almost a year. She's a very powerful Wiccan, and she has done much to teach him of the Goddess's power."

I rubbed my forehead. The headache was increasing in its intensity. "Now I really am confused, and not too proud to admit it. I thought the Venediger was a mage."

She nodded.

"Isn't a mage some sort of a magician? A wizard? Wouldn't that mean he knew magic?"

A frown creased her brow. "Do you not have any mages where you are from?"

I made a half-shrugging motion that committed me to no particular answer.

"I thought they were everywhere, but I guess not. A mage does indeed know magic, he's a master wizard in fact, but it's dark magic that he practices. You might have gathered that Perdy and I feel strongly that it's our duty to spread the word about the Goddess's love to those who make use of the dark powers"—I made a little grimacing moue. I had been on the receiving end of Perdita's lectures about the power of Wicca more than once in the last twenty-four hours—"and she felt particularly that the

Venediger could be turned from his path of destruction if only he would embrace the Rede."

"But he didn't," I said.

"No, and it was only last week that she finally admitted that nothing would turn him from the dark path. That's part of the reason why she feels so bad—she had intended on resigning her position, feeling it was wrong to stay working for him when he embodied everything we hold abhorrent, but now . . . now she feels she has to stay on, at least until a new Venediger appears."

I closed my mouth from where it had been hanging open, trying to at least appear as if I had a few wits left. "The Venediger is a . . . uh . . ."

"It's a position within the Otherworld, yes. You don't have them? No, you wouldn't, not in the States. Everything there is a democracy." She smiled. "Here we stay with the old ways. The Venediger is a position of power, a person who controls the Otherworld of each country."

"Sounds kind of like a paranormal Mafia."

She didn't laugh as I expected her to. Instead she looked troubled. "I'm afraid that's an accurate comparison. The Venediger—the one who died—long held France in his grip. No one challenged him, because of the power he held. Those who were foolish enough to cross him once never did so a second time. It was a virtual dictatorship. Our only hope of avoiding the same fate is if the next Venediger will be one of our own."

I couldn't keep my surprise from showing at that comment. "A Wiccan? A Wiccan can be a Venediger?"

She nodded. "Female Venedigers aren't common, but they aren't unknown. All that is needed to acquire the title is the ability to beat the other aspirants."

"How many people are there who are likely to try for the job?" I asked, wondering if Perdita had wanted the

Venediger gone not because of his history with Bael, but because she wanted his position . . . but that was stupid. Drake killed the Venediger; Bafamal admitted as much.

"Right now there are few people in France who have the power needed to control the Otherworld."

"The wyverns are powerful," I said slowly, my mind twisting and turning as it tried to work through a convoluted thought.

"Yes, but they are too bound to their septs to ever become a Venediger."

"Does Perdita—?" I hesitated, unwilling to put my thoughts into words. I didn't want to offend Ophelia with my question, but I had to know the truth. All of it. "Does Perdita have the power to become the next Venediger?"

"Perdy?" Ophelia's nose scrunched as she thought about the question. "I suppose she does. She's a very powerful Wiccan. Oh!" Her eyes went round as she clutched at my hand. "You don't think she intends to do it, do you? Become the Venediger? I hadn't thought she would, but you may be on to something. It is just the sort of challenge she would enjoy. She might just do it."

Every bell and siren that composed my mental warning system went into Red Alert double overtime. Ophelia's innocent act rang false, completely false. The question was, why did she want me to think Perdita hadn't considered the job of Venediger?

The answer to that was easy—she had to know I was beginning to suspect Perdita's motives. She would naturally be expected to cover up the acts of a dearly beloved sister.

And with that thought, a light clicked on in my head. I saw it all, saw the whole plan, each jigsaw piece of it fitting smoothly into the next. All those knowing looks between the two of them, Perdita's copy of the

Steganographia, Perdita's lectures about people who tapped into the dark powers, Ophelia telling me that Perdita had had a relationship with Drake—it all came into focus as I sat watching Ophelia wring her hands with pretend worry. Even the vague something that bothered me in watching the video of Bafamal dropped into place—Drake had told me that dragons couldn't summon demons. He might have been lying, but thinking back, I was of the mind he had been telling the truth. That meant that someone else had to have summoned Bafamal. Ophelia prattled on about how wonderful it would be with a Wiccan in charge while I wondered idly if she knew that I was familiar with the fact that a dragon couldn't summon a servant of Abaddon.

"What are you going to do?"

I started, drawn out of my own dark musing by her question. "About Drake?"

She nodded.

I leaned back against the wall, wrapping my arms around my knees. I knew what the solution to the problem of the murders was, but as yet, I had no idea how to prove it. "I suppose I'm going to have to have it out with him."

She sucked her breath in, her blue eyes wide with surprise . . . and perhaps a smidgen of pleasure. "A challenge? You're going to issue a challenge to him?"

I nodded. *Challenge* was a good word for what I wanted to do.

"How exciting! I've never seen a wyvern challenged."

"Yes, well, there's a first time for everything. A challenge might suit very well." I slid a glance her way. "It will allow me to reveal the truth."

"The truth is good," she said with a righteous nod. "I do hope I can help you. May I be your second? Perdy won't approve, but you are my friend. I can't turn my back on you when you're about to undertake something so terrifying as challenging a wyvern."

A tiny frown grew until my brows were pulled together, the awful suspicion bouncing around my head that there might be something more to a challenge than I had supposed. "Eh—"

She jumped up from the chair, turning to the cabinet of supplies. "I must cast a spell of clarity over you. Or no, perhaps one of protection would be best?"

"Protection?" I asked, getting a bit more worried.

"No one has ever challenged a wyvern and lived," she tossed over her shoulder as she rustled around the shelves. "Protection would be best, although clarity . . . Oh, why can't Perdy be here to help me? She would know what to do."

"Um—"

She turned around, her arms full of jars of herbs, candles, and other supplies. "I'll just whip something up for you just as soon as we return from G & T."

"We're going to G & T?" I asked, now seriously worried and moving straight into panic land. "What . . . eh . . . what exactly did you mean no one has ever challenged a wyvern and lived? You were talking about something a long time ago, right? Hundreds of years ago?"

"Goddess, no! Just last year someone challenged one of the wyverns—I believe it was Drake, although I was visiting my mother at the time. Perdy would know. She was still living with Drake then. One of the German mages accused him of stealing a very valuable ring, and challenged him. Drake killed the mage, of course."

"He did?" I squeaked.

She set her things down on the table next to the bookcase. "That is the way of dragons. It's one of the reasons Perdy and I have wanted the Venediger to see the True Path, so he would put his foot down about the violence that seems to follow the dragons." She drifted toward the door, her hands doing the usual graceful flutter that accompanied her conversation. "I'll just go get changed. Will you be ready in twenty minutes or so?"

I nodded, too dumbstruck to speak. Drake killed a man who challenged him? I stood up slowly and walked to the wardrobe, opening it to look at the face that stared out of the mirror hung on the inside door. My lips stretched into a suitably grim smile. "Out of the frying pan, Aisling, and into the fire . . . *again.*"

"Are you sure this is a good idea? Inspector Proust closed the club down once—what if he comes back?"

"Perdy won't allow him entrance," Ophelia said, flipping a clump of her golden ringlets over her shoulder. Despite my insecurity at the situation, she spoke in a comforting tone of voice as we stood at the top of the three steps that led down to the club proper.

I looked behind us at the door that led to the street. There was no doorman, not even a bouncer in attendance. "How can she keep him from coming in?"

"Wards," Ophelia said, tugging my arm as she descended into the club. "Didn't you feel them when you came in? Come on, we'll get a table and have Perdy help us with the wording of your challenge."

I looked around the club as I obediently followed Ophelia. It looked the same as the last time I was there— smoky, crowded, music pulsing at almost a subconscious level. It was also wyvernless.

Well, almost.

"Cara," Fiat cried as a group of people between us parted. "I had hoped that I would find you here."

Ophelia stopped and glanced back at me curiously. I made brief introductions. "A word of warning, Fiat—if you or any of your goon squad even looks like you're thinking of abducting me, I will scream bloody murder. I know for a fact that G & T is a neutral territory, and anyone who violates that neutrality will be in very hot water."

Fiat laughed, his blue eyes unreadable. "Ah, *cara,* you have such fire. You truly are worthy of being a wyvern's mate. Drake doesn't deserve you."

"No, he doesn't," I said dryly.

"As for violating the rules of G & T—" He smiled. "—who is there to stop me from doing whatever I desire with you? The Venediger is dead. No one has claimed his title."

"We will stop you," Ophelia said suddenly, pushing her way in front of me. "Aisling is my friend. Perdy and I will stop you from harming her."

Fiat dismissed Ophelia's declaration with a flicker of his eyes. He lifted my chin with one cool finger, taking a long moment to study my face. "So determined, so forceful. But still mortal."

"She might be mortal, but she is challenging Drake Vireo," Ophelia trumpeted. "It is not everyone who has the courage to do so."

As it had the night I had called Drake Puff the Magic Dragon, the entire room went silent.

Respect dawned in Fiat's eyes as he considered me. "So, the Guardian plans to challenge her mate for control of the sept."

"No," I said quickly, shaking my head to add emphasis. "It's not like that—"

"Yes, she is," Ophelia cut in, waving a hand at me to shut up. "She will challenge him, and when he fails, she will rule in his place."

"But, I don't want—"

"Yes, you do," she whispered, turning so Fiat couldn't hear what she was saying. "That's how a challenge is conducted. Ostensibly it's for control of the sept, but the loser must abide by whatever terms the winner sets. If you make one of the terms that Drake must turn himself in to the police, he will have to do so when you beat him."

"*If* I beat him," I pointed out.

She waved that away. "You will triumph. You will have me and Perdy in your corner."

I watched as she turned back to Fiat, wondering if I should tell her that I knew the truth about her twin.

"We are about to formalize the terms of the challenge. If you will excuse us," Ophelia said with lofty arrogance, pushing Fiat aside to stride toward the back of the club.

"I will see you later, *cara,*" Fiat said, imbuing the words with a dark promise that was echoed in his eyes.

"Not if I see you first," I murmured, wary of outright insulting him. I was beginning to see the folly in tweaking a dragon's tail.

"This way—Perdy's office is in the back." Ophelia was waiting for me at the entrance to a dark hall that led to the bathrooms. We walked past the bathrooms, turned a corner, and headed for the two leather-studded doors that opened off to either side of the hallway. One of the doors bore black-and-yellow crime scene tape.

"That's the Venediger's office. Perdy said the police have sealed it, but she has the Venediger's solicitor working on releasing the business papers to her," Ophelia said, nodding to the door on the right. She opened the door op-

posite. "This is Perdy's office. It's smaller, but it's—
Goddess above, no!"

I looked at the body hanging in the center of the room,
abstractly noting the fact that whoever killed Perdita had
used a rough rope as the binding that tied her feet and
hands together behind her back. Her body was suspended
sideways in midair, the same rough rope wrapped around
her waist several times before it was attached to a hook in
the black beam that crossed the ceiling.

"The Third Demon Death," I said, not even looking at
the circle drawn beneath the slowly rotating body. I didn't
have to. I knew what it would show.

Ophelia hit the floor in a dead faint.

18

I stood in the opening to the hallway and searched the club for a familiar face, wishing more than ever that Jim was with me. I needed someone trustworthy, someone who wouldn't take one look at Perdita's dead body and run screaming to the police, but how was I to tell who was who?

There was a slight anticipatory rustle to the crowd of people drifting around the club as everyone paused and looked at the front entrance. Drake sauntered down the steps in a show of masculine grace, István and Pál in tight wing formation behind him. I stepped back, into the shadow of the dimly lit hallway, not wanting Drake to see me. He was the last person I wanted to call upon for help with Perdita.

Even as I scanned for someone familiar, the crowd rippled again as Fiat approached Drake with languid grace. The two men exchanged cheek kisses; then Fiat leaned in to say something private to Drake, his hand gesturing toward the hall I stood in. Drake lifted his head as if to smell the air. I stepped farther back into the shadows, retreating to Perdita's office.

Ophelia moaned as I patted her cheeks in the approved "vague assistance to woman who has fainted" manner.

"Perdy?" she mumbled, her eyelashes fluttering.

"No, it's just me," I said, looking up when the door opened. "And Drake and Fiat, and Pál and István, and I think that's Renaldo and another one of Fiat's bullies in the hall, although it's a little hard to see with everyone in the way."

The two wyverns stood silent in the doorway, both staring with apparent surprise at Perdita's body as it slowly turned.

"Who?" Ophelia shrieked, pushing me back as she got to her feet. She pointed a finger at Drake, huge tears rolling down her cheeks as she stabbed the air in front of him. "It's him! He killed Perdy! He killed her just as he killed the others! He killed my . . . my . . ." She dissolved into heart-wrenching sobs, her hands covering her face.

I helped her to a chair, glancing back at the two men who blocked the doorway. "Unless you want everyone in the club to troop in here and have a look, I suggest you set your men as guards at the end of the hall and close the door."

Drake nodded at his men, who immediately left. Fiat was slower to send his men off, but eventually he did. The door closed with a soft click that was the only sound in the room. Ophelia was sobbing silently into her hands, her body shaking as she wept. I squatted next to her, offering what comfort I could.

Drake circled Perdita's body, his bright green eyes noting everything, I was sure. Fiat leaned back against the door as if keeping intruders out, but his eyes gave him away. They were coolly speculative . . . the eyes of someone truly surprised by what he saw before him.

I cleared my throat, the noise unusually loud in the

close confines of the room. "Drake, you've been accused of murdering Perdita. Did you do it?"

His gaze met mine over the slowly rotating body. "No more than I killed Aurora or the Venediger."

I smiled a sad little smile. Why had I expected I would get a straight answer out of him? I turned to Fiat. "You haven't been accused, but you were here when Ophelia and I arrived, so you had opportunity. Did you kill her?"

"I do not kill women," Fiat said stiffly. His shoulders made an odd sort of jerky motion of denial. "Well, not often do I kill them."

"How reassuring that is. Can I ask another question?"

"If it would please you," Fiat answered.

I stood up and yelled at the top of my lungs, "WHY CAN'T ANY OF YOU DRAGONS ANSWER A SIMPLE QUESTION WHEN IT'S ASKED?"

I'll be the first one to admit that I might have been showing a wee bit of stress what with people trying to kidnap me, and arrest me for murder, and steal things from me, but is that any reason for Drake to march over and slap me as if I were hysterical?

"Oh! You are going to be so sorry you did that," I snarled, making a fist and swinging it. Fiat plucked me off Drake, but not before I got in a really solid right jab to Drake's nose. "No one hits me, no one!" I yelled as Fiat dragged me backwards. Drake gingerly touched his nose, staring in patent surprise at the blood smeared across his fingertips.

"If I were you," Fiat said softly in my ear, "I would run."

Drake's roar of anger shattered the only two windows in the office. It also summoned both his and Fiat's men, all four of whom burst into the room just as Drake started toward me.

I didn't wait around to debate the issue. I ran. Straight through the men at the door, across the hall, and into the Venediger's office, trailing bits of crime scene tape behind me as I whirled around and locked the door a hairbreadth before Drake reached it.

It took him all of five seconds to kick it open. I backed away as he stalked into the room, pausing only to close the door behind him.

"Look," I said, my hands up in self-protection stance number seven. "I know you're a bit pissed right now, but—"

He was on me before I could even scream. One second he was at the door; the next he was fifteen feet across the room, dragging me up against his chest. For one brilliant, crystalline moment in time, I stared deep into Drake's eyes and beheld the dragon within.

My resistance melted into a river of passion.

I opened my mouth to remind him that he couldn't kill me without killing himself, but it wasn't death Drake had on his mind. He slammed his mouth against mine, his tongue not waiting for an invitation to come visiting; it just shoved its way into my mouth and took immediate possession, stroking, teasing, tasting every last square inch of my mouth, forcing me to submit. I fought him, not because I wasn't suddenly just as aroused and filled with desire as he was, but because I wanted him to know right from the start I would never again submit.

"You can woo me," I said against his lips as I grabbed the front of his dark green shirt, literally ripping it right off his body. "You can court me, you can seduce me, but you will *never* force me into submission again. What happened in the dream was a fantasy, a figment of our imaginations. This is real, and on *my* terms."

He growled into my mouth as he grabbed my thighs,

hauling me up until I locked my legs around his waist. I grabbed his hair, pulling on it as I gave him a taste of his own treatment, plundering his mouth as he had plundered mine. He tasted spicy, hot, like he had been drinking Dragon's Blood. He lunged to the wall behind me, smashing me between his body and the cool wooden paneling, his teeth nipping at my tender flesh as he buried his face in my breasts.

"Gold," he breathed as he licked the rise of one breast. I had just enough presence of mind to remember the Eye tucked into the lining of my bra.

"No! Not here!" I cried as his head dipped to the valley between my breasts. He brought his head up, the dragon talisman clenched between his teeth. I took it back, replacing it with an offering of my lips as I tucked the jade back into my bra, shivering at the look of molten desire in his eyes.

He jerked my dress up, his fingers hot and hard on my thighs as he shredded my underwear. I flexed my legs around his hips, squirming when his fingers parted me, testing me, teasing me, absorbing the burn his touch had started and building it to an inferno of desire, arousal, and consuming need. I dragged my nails across his back as he tormented me with his body.

"You're mine," he ground out through clenched teeth, the heated tip of him edging into me.

"Not even close. *You*, however are mine, mine, mine." I grabbed his hair and arched myself against him, desperate to feel him within me, desperate for his heat, his fire, his hunger. My soul burned for the touch of his; my body wept tears of passion that only he could stop.

"Mine," he snarled as he lunged, pinning me against the wall as his body became the invader, spreading me, impaling me, touching me in a way that no mortal man could. His fire swept through me as I moved against him, reveling in the feeling of his body moving in mine, embracing the conflagration of our souls, riding great waves of fire that spiraled around us, fusing us, firing us, binding us together until we exploded together in a million dancing sparks. Drake's eyes opened wide as ecstacy overtook him, and for a moment, for the breathless, endless length of time it takes to pass from one second to another, his form shimmered between Drake the man and Drake the dragon. His lips closed on my collarbone, and I jerked against him as a fire hotter than anything I'd felt yet burned the skin beneath his mouth. I moved against him, spun into another orgasm, my body tightening around his until he arched his back and roared his triumph to the heavens.

"We are sick people," I said later, after breath had returned to my lungs and reason to my mind. I unlocked my legs and slid down his thighs, various and sundry parts of me making me aware that Drake liked to play harder than I was used to.

"Sick?"

I straightened my poppy dress before managing to gather enough courage to look him in the eye. "What else would you call having this sort of a reaction to finding a dead body?"

His eyes were hot, remnants of his dragon fire still visible as his gaze licked down my body. "I would call it fated. It was inevitable that we would mate again."

I fussed with brushing out the newly made wrinkles in my dress. "Yeah, well, I have another word for it, but as it's not complimentary to either of us, I'll keep it to myself."

He retrieved the shirt I had torn off him, giving it an

odd look. Luckily only a few of the buttons were ripped off. "I take it this means you love me."

I goggled at him, a good old-fashioned "What the hell are you talking about?" goggle. "Not even close, dragon boy!"

One ebony eyebrow rose as he turned to retrieve his tie. I flinched when I saw the scoring my nails had left on his back.

"You said you engage in sex only with men you love. You refused me in the last dream. Thus, you must now be in love with me."

My face flushed as I adjusted my upper story, which had been dislodged in his quest for gold. "What happened a few minutes ago was an exception to the rule. It was purely a physical reaction to the stress of finding Perdita's body. Life asserting itself in the face of death and all that. I'm sure psychiatrists have a name for it."

Drake slipped into his shirt. "So do I—desire. It had nothing to do with Perdita and everything to do with our bond."

I turned to look in the other direction, unable to face the knowing (read: smug male) look in his eyes. "Ow! What the devil?" I touched the side area on my collarbone he had kissed. It was the same spot he had burned in my first dream. The skin was tender, very tender. I tried to look down at myself, but the sore spot was up too high to see. I glared at him as he tucked his shirt into his pants. "What did you do to me, bite me? Are you part vampire, too?"

He buckled his belt, giving me a look that went a long way to cooling the still-burning fires deep within me. "We mated. I marked you. It wasn't a bite."

"You marked me?" I said in disbelief, spinning around to see if the Venediger had a mirror anywhere. He did, I discovered after a few moments of searching in his top-most desk drawer. "You marked me like I was your laundry? Or a cow you'd brand? That sort of a mark? Oh, my God, you did mark me! Ow! It hurts!"

He took the mirror from me, gently touching the burn that stood out on the right side of my collarbone. It was curved-edged triangle with a line twisted around the three sides, a symbol that bore an enormous resemblance to the curved dragon's tail on my aquamanile. "It will heal."

I pushed away from him. "That's all you're going to say, it'll heal? I'm going to be left with a big ole herkin' burned hickey on my collarbone, and all you can say is it'll heal? Thanks a whole heck of a lot, Drake. If you don't mind, I think I'd like to return to the room across the hall where everyone is probably wondering what happened to us."

"They aren't wondering," Drake said with an arrogant look that my palm itched to remove from his handsome face. He grabbed me as I stormed through the door, keeping me from plowing into István and one of Fiat's men, who were standing in the hall. István started to grin, but looked away when I glared at him. Fiat's man outright smirked. Behind him, in the open doorway of Perdita's room, Ophelia stood clutching a box of tissues as Fiat and Renaldo lowered Perdita's body to a blanket on her desk. Drake's voice growled into my ear. "Aisling, much as it distresses me to say this, we must talk."

I jerked my arm out of his grasp. "What we just did changes nothing, dragon. *Nothing!* There will be no talking," I said loudly, turning to stomp into the other room. I went to Ophelia and put my arm around her. "You OK?"

Her cheeks were still wet, and her chin quivered, but she managed a nod. She plucked at my sleeve, her eyes filled with pain. "Please, Aisling, don't let him get away with this. Don't let him kill anyone else."

"Don't worry," I said, leveling a look at Drake that would give him something to chew over for a couple of days. "The person who killed Perdita will be punished. I swear that."

"Thank you," she whispered, and went to pieces again. I led her back to her chair and let her sob out her agony.

"We will not, of course, inform the police of this matter," Fiat said as Renaldo covered Perdita's body. "This will be taken care of by those in the *l'au-delà*."

"Agreed," Drake said.

"*Not* agreed," I said, marching over to where the two of them were warily watching each other. "We can't keep a murder from the police—they'll have to know about it. I just want to wait a day, until I have the proof to convict the person who killed her and the Venediger and poor Mme. Deauxville. Then we'll contact the police and tell them everything." I fingered the burn mark on my collarbone. "Well, almost everything."

Fiat froze as his eyes followed my hand's movement. His eyes narrowed. "You mated with him just now?"

I fisted my hands to keep from punching out his lights. I'm not normally a violent person, but the last few days were enough to make a sinner out of even the purest of saints. "I don't think *everyone* in the club heard you. Maybe if you used a microphone, then the whole of the Otherworld could know the intimate details of my sex life."

Fiat's lips quirked. Drake looked bored.

"You mistake me," Fiat said. "I am not surprised that you were in the other room mating with Drake—it is the way of dragons to seek their mate in times of strong emotions. I am merely surprised that you had not done so before this. If I had known that you had not yet mated with him when you were in my apartment, I would have been doubly careful that you not escape me."

"You were in his apartment?" Drake asked in a velvety soft rumble. It sent shivers of apprehension down my spine. "When was this?"

"None of your business. The question is, what are we going to do with Perdita until tomorrow?"

Ophelia moaned softly. One of the blue dragons was patting her on the back as she clung to his shoulders and sobbed into his chest.

"Sorry, Ophelia, I didn't mean that to sound callous, but it is summer, and . . . er . . . without getting too gross, things are going to start going stinky really soon if we don't get some ice or something."

Fiat said something I didn't understand to Drake. Drake answered in the same language. They both turned to look at me.

"What?" I asked, looking from one to the other.

"We agreed that you have a point," Drake said. He lifted his head, and Pál snapped to attention. "I own a butcher shop not too far from here, one that has ample cold storage. We can move the body there until such time as it can be turned over to the police."

Pál nodded and slipped out of the room, pulling a cell phone from his pocket as he left.

"You own a butcher shop?" I couldn't help but ask him. "Isn't that a long way away from gold and jewels?"

Drake grinned. My knees tried to melt, but I locked them in place. "I like meat," he told me.

"No wonder Jim loved your house." A sharp zing of pain went through me at the mention of my furry little demon. I pushed down the desire to pull an Ophelia and sob all over Drake's chest, instead concentrating on what I had to do next. "I'll take Ophelia home."

"No," she wailed, wiping her nose on the blue dragon's shirt. "You can't! Not yet! Not until you . . ." She gave me a meaningful look before shifting her gaze to Drake.

"Oh, right. Um. Ophelia and I need to have a few minutes of quiet time. Girl talk," I said, taking her arm and steering her past the guys at the door.

"Thank you, Aisling," Ophelia whispered as I escorted her down the hallway. "I knew you meant what you said when you swore you'd see Drake pay for killing Perdita."

"I'll need you to help me with the wording of the challenge. Are you sure you're up to that?"

She dabbed at her nose with the handful of tissue clutched in her right hand. "Yes. To see justice done for poor Perdy, I can do anything."

"Right." I paused by the women's room and made a little grimace. "I'm a bit . . . uh . . . I need to freshen up a bit. I'll be out in a minute. You find a table and get started on the challenge."

She nodded and I hurried into the bathroom, wondering just how much stranger my time in Paris was going to get.

Why do I even ask such silly questions?

"Look what the cat dragged in," a familiar voice came from the vicinity of Ophelia's lap when I returned and approached the table where she was sitting. "Hey! That's a dragon's mating mark on your chest. You didn't wait for me before you did the nasty with Drake?"

"Jim!" I yelled, and threw myself at the big black shape that was leaning against Ophelia's leg having its ears rubbed. I hugged it, quickly running my hands over its legs and back to make sure it was whole. "Are you all right? What happened to you? Where have you been? Don't you know I've been out of my mind with worry about you? Why do you smell like a compost heap?"

"It's Eau du Dumpster, and I'm glad to see you, too. You think you could stop strangling me now?"

I let go of the hold I had on its neck and hauled myself up to a chair. Ophelia gave us a watery smile. "I'm so happy your demon is back."

I stared openmouthed as I realized just what she said. "You knew about Jim? Before it spoke?"

"Yes, of course we knew. You don't think we wouldn't notice a demon in our house?" She shook her head and clicked her tongue against her teeth, giving a damp sniff. "Perdita recognized it first. Since you seemed so fond of it, we did not want to make you give it up."

"I'm sorry—I feel terrible having deceived you like that, but I'm kind of stuck with Jim. I didn't think it would hurt if I hid the fact that it was a demon."

"That's the cover story," Jim said confidently to Ophelia. "The truth is she's gaga over me."

"I might be delirious with joy to see you," I said as I ruffled its ears, "but that doesn't mean I can't command you to silence. Now, where have you been, and why were you in a Dumpster?"

"The blue dragon's men spotted me when Drake threw me out into the street. I took off and they followed. They're trackers, you know, and it took me half the day to shake them. I ended up in a Dumpster behind a restaurant, and decided I might as well have some dinner before coming home."

"Next time, call me and let me know you're all right," I said, realizing just how stupid that sounded.

Jim rolled its eyes, but gave my hand a quick snuffle.

"Right, well, now that the prodigal demon is back,

let's get to business." I filled Jim in quickly with the details of the last couple of hours.

"I made a rough draft of the challenge," Ophelia said, pushing a piece of note paper toward me. "I'm not sure of the wording. . . ." Her lower lip quivered for a moment as her eyes swam with unshed tears. "Perdy would have known it for sure, but I don't."

I gave her hand a squeeze and took the paper, reading it over.

"Is that what you wanted?" she asked, a worried cast to her eyes.

"It's perfect. I don't have to change a word. You said everything I wanted to say. Now, how do I do this?"

She dabbed at her eyes, bravely blinking back the tears. "You must make an announcement to as many members of the Otherworld as is possible. I would suggest you use the microphone."

I looked to the red-lit area where a band normally played. Tonight there was recorded music, but the sound equipment was still set up from the last gig. Drake and Fiat came into the room; Fiat in an elegant stroll, Drake with a sexy, coiled-power sort of glide that made various dark, secretive places in my body want to stand up and cheer.

"Looks like everyone is here. I'll just go get their attention."

"Let me, let me," Jim asked, almost dancing. I made a face, which it took for permission because it ran across the club, snaking in and out of people until it jumped onto a tall, high-backed chair in front of the mic.

I excused myself through the crowd, offering apologies to those people whose drinks Jim had spilled in its mad dash, finally making it over to the band area. Just as I arrived, Jim figured out how to turn on the cordless mic.

"Ladies and gentlemen, dragons, wizards, Wiccans, faeries, fellow demons, and citizens of Abaddon and the Otherworld, welcome to the Goety and Theurgy Starlight Lounge. For my first number, that timeless classic by the Oak Ridge Boys—'Elvira'!"

I snatched the microphone away from Jim just as it was crooning the opening lines. The silence in the room was almost deafening as I looked out at a sea of astonished faces. "Uh . . . hi. Excuse my demon, it's a bit giddy after dining à la dumpster. Um. For those of you who don't know me—and that's most of you—my name is Aisling Grey."

Several people gasped at my name. I sucked on my lower lip for a moment, unnerved by having the complete and total attention of so many people. "I . . . uh . . . have an announcement, so if you'll just bear with me a moment." I smoothed out the wrinkled sheet of notepaper, glancing up to locate Drake. He leaned against the wall, a drink in his hand. "In accordance with the laws governing the Otherworld, I, Aisling Grey, Guardian of the portals of Abaddon, do hereby issue a formal challenge of transcendence to the one who is mated to me, Drake Vireo, the wyvern of the green dragons."

This time the whole room gasped. I didn't wait for the excited chatter to start; I plowed ahead, even though Drake's unconcerned expression was worrying me greatly. Why was he looking bored when I just announced that I was going to battle him for control of his sept? Did he think I was that ineffectual? That clueless? Well, OK, I probably was, but it was still extremely insulting that he should let everyone else know he wasn't in the least bit stressed over our upcoming battle. "I charge you, Drake Vireo, to meet me here, tomorrow, at the time of the moon's zenith, when I will defend my challenge with my body. Should my power prove stronger, you will immediately turn yourself in to the police and confess to the acts of murdering Aurora Deauxville, Albert Camus, and Perdita Dawkins. How say you?"

Drake didn't answer right away, which was good because the people in front of me burst into startled conversation, some people claiming Drake's innocence, others making crude comments about how I was going to defend a challenge with my body, and still others already starting the wagering on the outcome. Finally Drake stepped forward, his eyes so dark, they looked black. "I, Drake Vireo, wyvern to the green dragon sept, will accept your challenge, body to body. I agree to your terms and offer my own: Should my power prove stronger, you will surrender yourself for judgment by the will of the green dragons."

I was more than a little surprised at his words, having assumed that he would ask for me to reveal the location of the Eye of Lucifer rather than agree to take whatever punishment the sept handed out for someone who challenged their beloved wyvern. I didn't even want to think about what that would consist of—as long as it couldn't be lethal, I would (probably) survive.

"How say you?" Drake finished.

"I agree to your terms," I said with an attempt at a quelling look at those people who swarmed forward around Drake to show him support.

Which pretty much left me, Ophelia, and Jim alone.

"Thank you," Ophelia said, her eyes shiny with tears again. "Let me just get my things and we can go home."

She moved off through the crowd. Jim looked at me, its lips pursed. "Think you're going to beat Drake?"

"Are you kidding? Even with the Eye of Lucifer, I couldn't beat him at checkers."

Jim thought about that for a minute as I continued to watch the crowd of people around Drake. "Kinda odd you challenging him, then, huh?"

"Not really. The purpose of the challenge is to draw the murderer out into the public eye. I have high hopes it will do just that."

Jim shook its furry black head. "He must have bonked the brains right out of your head, Aisling. In order to get Drake to turn himself in for the murders, you have to beat him."

"That would be true if Drake were guilty of the murders," I said with a pinch on its shoulder for the bonking comment. "But since he's innocent, the point is moot. Come on, demon mine, Ophelia is waiting. We have miles to go before we sleep."

19

Jim and I came in from doing his before-bed walk to find Ophelia sitting at the tiny blue-and-white-tile kitchen table, sobbing over a teapot.

"Oh, Ophelia, don't," I said, feeling utterly helpless to stop her tears.

Jim stood in the doorway, sniffing. "Demon was here. Bafamal?"

"Yes, I summoned it to ask it questions about the murders." I squatted down next to Ophelia. "Here, let me pour you a cup of this wonderful tea you made. Then we'll get you tucked into bed."

"It's not fair," she said soggily, clutching a damp napkin. "Perdy had so much to live for! Everyone liked her . . . everyone but Drake. He spurned her once he discovered she would not work magic for him. He threw her out. He's evil, Aisling, very evil. I know he's your mate, but you should know the truth about him before you commit yourself."

"I do know the truth about him. Why else would I challenge him so publicly?" I asked, positively oozing innocence.

Jim coughed a cough that started out a snicker. I stepped on one of its paws.

"You're so good to me," Ophelia sniffled. "You don't know what a comfort it's been to have you take up the banner of justice for Perdita. I don't have even half the power she had. I wouldn't stand a chance against Drake, but you—you are a powerful Guardian, his mate, the one person he cannot destroy. You can defeat him and force him to admit to the murders." She shivered, rubbing her arms as if she were chilled. "He's so frightening, his eyes so dark and cold. I don't know how you stood being around him."

Drake? Cold? Dark? My steamy, sexy, bright-eyed bringer of flames? "Mmm. Well, you won't have him to worry about any longer. I suppose I really should start thinking of the future."

"The future?" she asked, accepting the cup of tea I poured for her.

"Yeah, well, I assume I'm going to have to stick around here once I take over as wyvern for the green dragons. Can a woman *be* a wyvern? Would I be a wyverness?"

"Wyvernette?" Jim asked. "How about Wyvernina?"

I turned a gimlet eye to my demon. "Go to bed, Jim."

"Yeees," Ophelia said slowly as Jim left the room. "A woman can be a wyvern—the red dragons' wyvern is a woman—but I assumed you'd want to go home after it was all over."

"Home?" I said, pinning a bright smile on my face. "Why would I want to go back to a mundane courier job when I have the opportunity to rule a dragon sept here? In fact, I'm thinking I might just take over as Venediger, too."

"What?" Ophelia choked on her tea. I patted her back

helpfully before taking a seat and pouring myself a cup of tea. "You want to be the Venediger? But—but—"

"Yeah, well, I know you said that the wyverns are too bound up in their septs to be Venediger, but that's where I'm perfect for the job. I don't have any ties to the green dragons, so I'm sure I'll be able to do both jobs just fine." I blew on my tea before taking a sip. "Unless you know of a reason why I couldn't?"

Her gaze dropped to the teapot. "No, I know of no reason. I just assumed—you sounded as if you didn't want to be wyvern, and now you are talking of taking on a role of great responsibility—"

"The idea kind of grew on me," I said with another cheery smile that I felt far from feeling. "I have you to thank for that, too. If you hadn't mentioned something about Perdita taking over as Venediger, I never would have thought about it."

"Perdita . . . ," she said, her lips quivery.

I stood up and took the cups to the sink. "I'm sorry—that was cruel of me. Let's get you into bed. You've had a heck of a day."

She allowed me to escort her to her bedroom. I locked up the apartment, turned out the lights, and headed for my own room where Jim was lying in the middle of the bed. "About time! I thought you'd never dump the wet blanket."

"Shh! She'll hear you."

"Naw, the walls are thick. So. Drake's innocent. . . . Do I get to guess who did kill Deauxville and the Venediger and Perdy?"

I shoved my demon over so I could sit on the bed, too. "It's not that hard to figure out who. It's just getting the proof that's going to be difficult."

Jim eyed me for a couple of seconds, then got off the

bed and went to curl up on the pile of blankets I'd arranged as its bed. "I don't suppose you'd care to lend me a couple hundred euros?"

I pointed at the wall. It turned its back to me so I could get into the nightgown Perdita had lent me. "You are not going to bet on me. Or against me. No betting whatsoever. Got that?"

Jim huffed and settled down for the night. "You sure do know how to take all the fun out of life. Bet you even made Drake use a condom."

I sighed to myself and added STDs to my list of things to discuss with Drake at a later date.

Despite the events of the day, I had trouble getting to sleep, finally drifting off around three in the morning. I half expected that Drake would come and seduce me in a dream, but he didn't. I woke once, my body jerking with the remnants of a non-dragon dream, then relaxed into the solid, comforting heat at my back. Drake's scent teased my nose. An arm lay heavy over my stomach; hard, muscled thighs spooned tightly behind mine. The faintest breath of air ruffled the hair at my neck. I drifted deeper into sleep, not sure whether this was yet another type of dream, or just a fantasy my mind had arranged to lull me into security.

I awoke alone to find that sometime during the night Ophelia had been kidnapped.

"How could I have been so wrong?" I asked Jim as I paced down the length of the apartment. "How could I have been so stupid? Ophelia wasn't guilty of anything more than being a bit shallow and trying to protect Perdita. How could I think she was guilty of murder? Triple murder?"

"You had me convinced," Jim said. "It's always the sweet, innocent ones that you have to watch out for."

"Yeah, well, because of my stupidity, that sweet, innocent one is in the clutches of some evil person. You're sure it was Bafamal you smelled in her room?"

"Absotively. Baffie and I go way back. He was there, all right."

"Drat it all. There goes my whole big plan. How can I prove she was guilty of the murders if she's been kidnapped?"

Jim got to its feet and padded over to the bowl of water I had set down for it earlier. "You know, you never did explain to me exactly when you switched from thinking Drake was the killer to believing he was innocent."

"My conversation with Bafamal had a lot to do with that. So did something Ophelia said," I answered absently, looking out the window at a rainy June Paris morning.

"What was that?"

"She told me Perdita was Drake's girlfriend."

Jim raised its eyebrows. "And you didn't believe her? Honey, we need to have a little talk about dragons and their sexual drive."

"Don't be stupid," I said, watching the rain run down the window. "I know Drake's had girlfriends before, but I happen to know Perdita wasn't one of them."

"Really?" Jim tipped its head. "How do you know?"

"The night I first met her she made a comment about dragons being different sexually. They're not. She'd have known that if she had slept with Drake."

"So, that old saying about being hung like a dragon isn't true?" Jim asked with a leering lilt to its voice.

I turned around to glare at it. "I didn't say that. I'm just saying that there was nothing unusual in the groinal region. Nothing other than an . . . er . . . abundance."

Jim hooted. I ignored it as I stood indecisively in the middle of the living room. "Who would want to kidnap Ophelia? And why? And what am I going to do about getting her back?"

"Who says saving her is your responsibility? Last time I looked, you weren't the Lone Ranger, and I'm sure as shootin' no Tonto, even if I am the extremely cool sidekick type."

"I put her in this position. I have to help her," I said obstinately.

"Call the cops."

"I can't! Even if I had somewhere else to stay, my fingerprints are all over this apartment. They'd lift one print, figure out it belonged to me, and blame me for her kidnapping. Besides, I don't think this is an ordinary kidnapping. Bafamal was in her room—that means it has to be someone connected with the Otherworld who used the demon to nab her."

"Too bad you can't ask Baffie himself, but he's probably still in the power of whoever summoned him."

"I suppose it would be worth a try to summon it, although I don't have any hope that I could. It would be incredibly stupid of whoever was using Bafamal to release it so it could be questioned." I paced the length of the apartment, my mind back to being a hyper hamster on a wheel as it formulated and discarded various ways to find Ophelia. "I could hire a private detective. . . . No, I don't know any, and don't have enough money. Maybe I could offer to pay Fiat's men? You said they were good trackers. Maybe they could follow her trail—"

"You'd have to have a whooooole lot of treasure to get them to do that."

"Poop!" I kicked at the lovely antique armchair as I passed it. "OK, how about this—I get Drake to find her for me. He's smart, he's got lots of contacts in Paris, and I just bet you he's likely to know all the spots someone might have hidden Ophelia."

"He's also the one you've issued a formal challenge to, which means no contact until the challenge begins."

"Is that a real rule, or are you just trying to annoy me?" I asked as I passed Jim.

"Would I do that?"

"In a heartbeat, not that you have one. All right then . . . mmm . . . what if you track her scent—"

"I'm not a bloodhound!" Jim protested.

"You're a dog. You can follow a trail, can't you?"

It gave me a look of profound censure. "In Paris? City of a million smells? No."

I thought for a moment. "What if I summon up another demon? Couldn't I order it to find her for me?"

"Not if she's been taken by another demon, no. I told you, you need to learn the rules. We can't rat on each other that way. It's a brotherhood thing between the demon lords. Only a demon that was unclaimed—not part of a demon lord's legions—could squeal on another demon, and the only demons that aren't in a legion are like I was before you summoned me: cast out and power-less."

I refused to give up. Guilt lay heavily on me. I had drawn Ophelia into the situation; it was because of me that she had been snatched.

Jim watched me pace for a while, then finally said in a tone heavy with disgust, "You mortals, always doing things the hard way. I shouldn't help you, I just know I'm going to lose my union card over this, but have you considered that nestled up against your perky breasts is one of the most powerful lodestones known in all the ages of man?"

My hand went to my breast. "The Eye? What about it? Amelie said it couldn't be used without the other two Tools."

Jim put its martyr face on. "She said it couldn't be used by itself to draw the power of Bael. It does have power of its own, though. Surely you've felt it."

I touched the stone through the gauze dress and material of my bra. It's true that I had noticed a slight warmth connected with the stone, but I assumed it was just my body heat warming it. I realized now that the pleasant feeling had nothing to do with me, and everything to do with the energy of the lodestone itself. "Uh . . . sure I have. Of course. What do you take me for, an idiot? Don't answer that, just go on. What can the stone do?"

"You're the Guardian—you should know." I made a snipping gesture with my fingers. Jim got the mime and hurried on with a more helpful answer. "What is the stone famous for?"

I thought. "It's one of the Tools of Bael."

"And what do those do?"

"Aside from causing the destruction of the world as we know it when the demon lords take over?" Jim nodded. "Tap into Bael's power."

"Right. And who is the one being who can tell you what Bafamal was ordered to do with Ophelia?"

I blinked. "Um . . ."

"His demon lord! A demon can't tattle on another demon because they are both servants, but a demon lord is not bound by that rule. Honestly, it's like talking to a bowl of pudding. Let's make an effort here, Aisling. I can't be helping you out all the time—I have more important things to do."

"Like lick your genitals?"

"Yes."

"Can we get back to the point of this catechism, assuming there is one?"

"Where was I? Oh, yeah, the answer was Ashtaroth. So, given those two facts, you get . . ." Jim waved a paw in an expectant gesture.

I gnawed my lip. "Mmm . . . I don't see the connection. Ashtaroth is Bafamal's lord, but the Eye draws on the power of Bael."

Jim sighed. "Who's the first prince of Abaddon? Who's the primary spirit? Who's the big daddy of the Otherworld?"

It took a while, but I finally got it. "Bael is. So you're saying I can use the stone to summon Bael and use him to force the truth from Ashtaroth?"

"Give the girl a banana!"

I sat down with a thump. "There's just one problem with that idea."

Jim cocked its ears. "Really? I thought it was pretty foolproof, myself. What's the prob?"

I started laughing. I couldn't help it, the very thought of what Jim was suggesting was ludicrous. "You want me, the person who summoned up the only demon who'd been kicked out of Hell, to conjure up the most powerful demon lord around, the one so powerful, he plans on overtaking the mortal world, and ask him nicely if he will find out for me what another lord's demon has done with Ophelia?"

Jim made a face. "When you put it like that, I guess it is asking for trouble."

I sighed and stood up, heading for the phone, punching in the now-familiar numbers. "Unfortunately, it's also the only choice I have. Hi, Rene, it's Aisling. Are you up for a little excitement tonight? I have a feeling I'm going to need a bodyguard, and since you offered when you brought me home yesterday, I'd like to take you up if you're still willing."

"But yes, of course! I will be happy to guard you. I am very dangerous, you know? No one messes with me. They used to call me the Rambo before I was married. When do you want me?"

I put my hand over the mouthpiece. "What time will the moon be at its zenith?"

Jim flopped over on its back. "What do I look like, *The Old Demon's Almanac*? How about a tummy rub?"

"The next demon I summon is going to be falling over itself to be helpful to me," I warned, uncovering the phone. "Rene? How about eleven at the Jardin du Luxembourg, south entrance? I might need you for several hours. Is that going to be OK?"

"*Oui.* Eh . . . what is it we're going to do?"

"Oh, nothing much. Just challenge a wyvern, summon a demon lord, and figure out who the murderer is. Bring your gun," I said pithily, and hung up.

"So it's going to be another one of those plans, is it?" Jim asked. "A nonspecific, winging it, seat-of-the-pants sort of plan? The kind with guns?"

"If you're not part of the solution, you're the problem," I told it, heading for my bedroom.

"What are you going to do?" Jim asked as it followed me.

"Read. Keep quiet unless you have any demonic insights to where Ophelia has been taken."

I plucked the copy of the *Steganographia* from the bookcase and sat down to bone up on demon lore.

Four hours later I threw the book onto the bed in disgust.

"Don't tell me—the butler did it and you had money riding on the seductive neighbor?"

I sighed and gathered up my sandals, walking over to the wardrobe to examine my scanty belongings with an eye to what was best suited to the evening's activities. "I wish it was that easy. I read all the sections pertinent to demons, and I just don't understand how a demon I summoned could lie when I ordered it to answer my questions honestly."

"That's because it's impossible," Jim said, standing up and shaking, a flurry of dog hair floating down to the floor. I made a mental promise to tidy up the room later. "I can't lie to you unless you order me to do so."

I paused in the act of slipping into my now-clean linen pantsuit. It was the most dignified outfit I had. "Are you sure there's no way? No circumstance that would allow you to lie? Because Bafamal was lying when he said Drake murdered everyone, I know he was. I couldn't have—" I waved my hand around vaguely. "—with Drake if he was a murderer. I would have felt that sort of evilness in him, wouldn't I?"

"You mean while you were busy playing ride the dragon?"

"What?"

"You know, hide the forked tongue? Hoarde the treasure? Heh heh heh."

I shook a sandal at him. "You need your brain washed out with soap. I'm serious. I'm too new to all this Guardian stuff. Sometimes I don't think I have a very good grasp on it all."

"Sometimes?" Jim hooted. "Sometimes like maybe mind-pushing Inspector Proust into la-la land?"

"I called his office while you were AWOL. Whoever

answered the phone said he was OK, so the mind-push thingy must have worn off pretty quickly."

"How about walking into a rival dragon's lair with a powerful lodestone that any dragon worth his scales would kill to get his hands on stuffed down your bra? Or maybe summoning up a demon that lies was an example of you having a grasp?"

"There are times when I don't like you," I said stiffly. "Answer my question—would I or wouldn't I know if Drake had killed those people?"

Jim shrugged. "That depends on how tightly bound you two are."

"We're not bound at all. A little fling composed of . . . of . . . unadulterated lust is not binding in any way, shape, or form." Jim muttered something as I buttoned up the tunic and ran a comb through my hair. "I just have to assume the evidence is false. Bafamal lied."

Jim shook its head. "If you asked me a question, I could evade the truth a bit, but not outright lie."

I glanced at the clock as I stepped into my sandals, grabbing my purse before hurrying out of the room. "I don't understand. . . . Oh, come on, let's go meet Amelie. We have a couple of hours to kill, and she might know something."

"Hel-lo! You're like three eggs short of a potato salad, sister. You know everyone is watching her shop just hoping you'll show up again. Much as I want to see my beloved Cecile and do that thing with her ears that makes her go all squirrelly on me, I can do without spending another day on the run from the Brothers Blu."

I smiled and opened the door to the apartment. "That's why I'm not going to the shop—you are, my little carrier pigeon."

"Fires of Abaddon, what am I, your slave?" Jim

groaned as it followed me out. "Why don't you lop off my goodies and call me Lassie while you're at it."

I met Amelie an hour later at the south side of the Jardin du Luxembourg, one of the few parks that allowed dogs. Jim and Cecile came with her, Jim strutting alongside the crotchety Corgi, periodically giving her ears and head a swipe with its huge pink tongue. I made a mental note to have a talk with Jim about the propriety of ear-sucking in public.

"I was not followed," Amelie said by way of a greeting. "We took three Metros and walked through the shop of a friend to leave by the alley. No one could follow me."

I gave her a little hug and invited her to share my bench.

"Eh . . . Cecie and I are going to go check out a lovely stinky spot I found while I was on the run yesterday. We'll see you in a bit," Jim said as it nudged Cecile toward a low bank of shrubs.

"Don't go too far—we might have to get out of here quickly," I warned before turning back to Amelie. "Why do I feel like we're going to be in-laws?"

She laughed, shaking her head. "I will admit, to me it was at first most disturbing, but I see now that the demon is not a true demon, *hein?* It is *une petite* demon. Cecile, she seems to like it, so I say *ouf,* and let them be."

"Mmm. I have a feeling I'm going to have a sulky demon in love when it's time to leave Paris."

"Leave? Ah. You have solved the problems haunting you?"

"Not yet, but I hope to soon. You've probably heard about my challenge, huh?"

Amelie gave me a pitying smile. "Yes, I did. That was not so well done of you, was it?"

I think it was the experience and knowledge she had that made me feel like I was being called on the carpet by my grade-school principal. I squirmed a tiny bit and stared down at my hands. "Um . . . well, I had this plan, you see? I figured it would bring the murderer out into the open if I challenged Drake and lost. It's obvious that Drake has been set up as the fall guy, and I just kind of stumbled onto the scene and messed everything up. But then my chief suspect up and got herself kidnapped by the demon Bafamal, and no one knows where she is or how I can find out, and I can't ask Drake for help, because it's against some rule to talk to the person you've challenged, and I don't trust Fiat any farther than I can spit, and even if I did, I doubt if he'd order his men to track Ophelia because I don't have any gold left except the bit on the talisman you gave me, and that means I'm left with having to pull out Plan B, which between you and me, I'd rather not do."

Amelie gave me an odd look. "That was a great deal you said."

I sighed. "Yeah, well, it's been kind of a rough last couple of days."

"Ophelia Dawkins has been kidnapped?"

"Sometime last night, I think. She was there when I went to bed, and gone this morning. Jim says her room smells like Bafamal, so that can only mean someone conjured up the demon and had it snatch her."

Amelie did a pretty good impression of Drake's head tip. "You are a very linear thinker, are you not?"

I smiled at the praise. "I try."

She shook her head. "It will not benefit you. You have much learning to undo before you can step into the role you were meant to take. A Guardian draws her power from her understanding of the possibilities, not in linear order. You must shake yourself of the desire to see only those things that can be arranged to match what you know, and learn instead to embrace *all* the possibilities that exist."

"That sounds strangely like a quantum physics class I once took," I said warily.

She gave a one-shouldered shrug. "Quantum theory is just another way people have of ordering that which cannot be ordered."

"Ah. As I failed miserably in that class, I think I'll quickly change the subject to something I can think about without having to lie down in a quiet room with a cold wet cloth over my eyes. You don't happen to have any idea of why someone would want to kidnap Ophelia, or where they would take her?"

She shook her head. "You do not see, and yet it stares you right in your eyes. Do you have your talisman?"

"Sure." I plucked it out from where it rested between my breasts.

She took it from me, holding her hand open flat to show it resting on her palm. Slowly she closed her hand over it, then held up her other hand, also closed. "Now, tell me, which hand has the talisman?"

I touched her left hand, the one that I had seen holding the talisman. She opened her hand. It was empty.

"Uh . . . well, you must have palmed it to your other hand, although I don't quite see how since your hands never moved—"

She opened up her right hand. It, too, was empty.

"Now," she said, tapping me on the forehead. "Close your eyes and open yourself up to the possibilities. Tell me where the talisman is."

I felt a little silly doing this in the middle of a busy park, but I sensed she was trying to show me something important, and since I hadn't done too well trying to mud-dle through things on my own, I figured it was to my ben-efit to learn. I closed my eyes, pushed away all the noises and distractions that surrounded me, shoved down all the worry and panic and confusion that filled me, squashed even the faint burn that was my feelings about Drake, and opened the magic door in my mind. I pictured the talis-man, remembering what it felt like, how it felt beneath my fingertips, visualized the smooth, curved lines of the warm jade touched here and there with cool gold.

I opened my eyes. I knew where it was. "It's in my hand," I said, blinking in surprise at the hand that rested on my thigh. I turned it over, opened my fingers, and stared at the talisman resting on my palm.

"How . . . I don't understand. It was there all along, but I couldn't see it or feel it?"

"That is because you did not consider all the possibil-ities, only the one you believed to be true. In order to be a great Guardian—and I believe you have that within your ability if only you will seek it—you must learn to see not just what you know to be, but those things that also might be."

I absorbed that for a few seconds. "So you're saying that I should consider the possibility that Ophelia hasn't really been kidnapped?"

Amelie just looked at me, neither confirming nor denying that idea.

"If that's so, then it would mean she disappeared for some reason of her own."

She raised an eyebrow.

"Which would also mean that if Bafamal was in her bedroom, it was because . . ." Goose bumps rippled up my arms. "Because she summoned it there. And if that's the case, then I couldn't have summoned it when I thought I did. Oh, holy *grenouilles*—that's why it could lie to me! She summoned it before I could, probably telling it what I was going to do and what to say to me after it pretended to be summoned." I stood up and faced Amelie. "That's why the circle felt different! That's why I was so sick and feeling icky yesterday—it wasn't just a depression over leaving Jim behind—the demon was there all along. It was the demon's presence that I felt!"

I spun around, holding my talisman to the sky, suddenly feeling as if I were a hundred pounds lighter. "I wasn't wrong! I wasn't stupid! I was right about Ophelia! She *is* the murderer, wahooo!"

"That is a very strange thing you are celebrating," Amelie said with a dry smile.

I grinned and sat down. "I know, call me wacky, but it does make me feel better to know that I wasn't wrong about her. I've been wrong about so many other things. But I suppose I shouldn't be celebrating yet. I still have to draw her out and get her to confess before enough witnesses that Inspector Proust will be able to charge her."

Amelie smiled and looked out over the park. Dusk was setting in, but the rain had stopped some hours ago, and now the soft, warm summer air was luring people out to the park.

"It's going to be a long night," I said with a little sigh.

"The longest of the year."

I did a quick mental calculation. "Oh, that's right, today is the summer solstice. Midsummer."

"Litha," Amelie said, still watching the people strolling by us. "It is also the night of the full moon." She slid me an odd look. "You have chosen well for the night of your challenge."

"Pure happenstance. I didn't actually set it up this way. Ophelia kind of pushed me into it."

She shook her head. "You are not seeing the possibilities, my friend. But come, we have much to do if we are to ready you for the tasks you have chosen to undertake."

I stood up when she did. "We do? I don't want you getting into trouble on my account—"

"We won't go back to my shop," she said, putting her fingers to her lips and blowing a shrill whistle. "What we need we have here."

The shrubs near us rustled; then Cecile emerged at a stiff waddle, Jim following with a plaintive note in its voice. "But baby, it can work. I'll lie on my back and you can lower— Oh, hi. This isn't what it sounds like."

I glared at it with the squintiest eyes possible. "You are a heartbeat away from an intimate introduction to a pair of scissors and some rough twine, demon."

Jim had the decency to look abashed. It didn't fool me, however. I kept a close eye on my furry little friend as we walked up one side of the Jardin and down the other, Amelie talking the entire time, lecturing me on everything from the foolishness of linear thinking to a brief history of the Otherworld.

"This is all fascinating," I said an hour and probably several miles later, "but it's not terribly practical, if you know what I mean. I was hoping you'd teach me some wards or give me an idea of how to tackle one of the demon lords, something useful like that."

"Demon lords?" she asked, coming to a halt. "What do you need to know about managing a demon lord?"

"Eh . . . well, I may have to summon one of them."

"Which one?" she asked, going absolutely still, her eyes large and black under the soft yellow glow of a nearby lamp.

"Bael," I said, hating to say the name.

She shuddered and started walking very quickly, as if

to distance herself from the unpleasant idea. "No. You are not that foolish. You would not attempt to bind the most powerful lord in all of Abaddon, not you who does not even yet know the extent of your abilities. It is impossible what you say. You cannot control even the small powers you have touched. You are making the joke to me."

"This is not doing a whole lot for my self-confidence," I said as I trudged along. I was telling the truth. My stomach had knotted up into the size of a prune. A runty prune. One with a rotten core.

"This is not funny!" Amelie suddenly shouted, spinning around to pin me with a look that shriveled my stomach even further. "You have challenged a wyvern! You intend on summoning a demon lord! These are not trivial events you plan—they could destroy you!"

I made a placating gesture as I urged her forward. People had stopped to stare at her outburst, and the last thing I wanted to do was garner anyone's attention after having my face on all the newspapers. "I didn't mean to sound flip. I'm taking the matter of Bael very seriously, very seriously indeed. But you don't have to worry about the other thing—the challenge to Drake is just an excuse to draw Ophelia out in front of a bunch of witnesses. Drake won't mind if I cancel the challenge."

She stared at me as if I had cheese growing out of my ears. "You cannot do such a thing!"

"Sure I can."

Her head shook vehemently. "No, you cannot. It is in the rules—once a challenge has been made, the two combatants must see the challenge through to the end. One must be the victor, the other the loser."

I shrugged. "I'll just refuse to fight and let him be victor. I was planning to forfeit anyway, that's how I'm going to get Ophelia to show. And if she doesn't, I have a little chat with Bael and have him bring her forth to admit her guilt."

Amelie stopped, took a deep breath, and pulled on my arm until I was turned to face her. "You do not understand," she said slowly. "By the rules that govern the *l'au-delà*, the challenge must be fought. There is no losing by default. There is no forfeit. Either you fight or your opponent will destroy you. That is the law."

I shook my head. "He can't destroy me. To do so would mean he'd kill himself, too."

She just looked at me. "Yes, it would."

I chill rippled through me at the certainty in her eyes. "He wouldn't do it. He'd refuse. He's not stupid. He wouldn't kill himself over something like a little formality—"

She sighed again. "You do not understand even though I have told you our history. The laws that govern the *l'au-delà* are not ones you can break. You accept them, or you are not a part of our world. Drake was born to the *l'au-delà*; he is immortal. He knows the laws and he will abide by them, even if it means his own death. You *must* fight him."

"Oh, God," I said, my guts twisting with a new understanding of just what I'd set into motion. "What have I done?"

"That is a question you must ask yourself," Amelie said acidly as she continued on down the path. "For I do not have an answer."

Even if she didn't have an answer, she had a lot of opinions. The next hour was spent with Amelie telling me in exacting detail just how stupid my plan was, but by the time the moon was rising beautiful and cold in the velvety blue-black sky, I had heard enough. I glanced at my watch and waved my hand for Jim to stop sweet-talking

Cecile. "I'm sorry, Amelie, but there's nothing else I can do. I appreciate all your help, and your warnings, and all the information you've given me, but there's no other way out of this situation. Ophelia has us where she wants us—impotent. Justice for the deaths she caused aside, I can't let her blame Drake for her crimes. Or me. So that means I have to do what I have to do. If you'll excuse me, I've got to go to the south entrance and meet my friend Rene. He's promised to be my backup tonight."

"There is nothing I can say to make you see the folly of your plan?" Amelie said, her face twisted with worry.

I put my hand on her clenched fists and gave a gentle squeeze. "No. But I thank you."

She straightened her shoulders and started down the path to the south. "Very well. I, too, will be your backup."

"You don't have to—," I said hesitantly, not wanting her to get any more involved than she was, but aware of the warm fuzzy feeling I got thinking about her support.

"Of course I do not. But I wish to. It will be . . . interesting. Cecile? Come, *ma petite*, we march."

"I have a feeling *interesting* is going to be the least of it," I said with a morbid sigh.

I just hate it when I'm right about things like that.

20

It was standing room only when we arrived at G & T. We had opted to wait for Rene to find a spot to park before walking to the nightclub, but even before we got to the building, crowds were visible streaming in from all directions.

I felt a lot like a big, bad gunslinger coming into town as I walked down the sidewalk with my posse behind me. Rene was riding shotgun (literally, although in this instance the gun was a small snub-nosed .38 he'd tucked into his brown leather jacket) while Amelie and Jim were on my left. Cecile was left to snooze in Rene's taxi.

"I still do not understand how it is the man Drake is really a dragon," Rene complained. We had filled him in on everything, and much to my surprise, he had been amazingly accepting of ideas I was still coming to grips with. "He seems so human."

"Most beings use human forms these days," Amelie explained. "Some have been in human form so long, they have lost the ability to change back to their true form."

I made yet another mental note, this time to ask Drake if he was stuck in a man shape. Not that I was complaining—

I was just curious. Such trivial thoughts were quickly dismissed as we approached the club.

"I am confident," I said softly to myself as I slipped a hand into my pants pocket to touch the Eye of Lucifer I had placed there earlier. "I am a professional. I have power. I can do this."

"Talking to yourself is a sign of mental instability," Jim said helpfully.

I shot it a thin-lipped look.

"Just trying to break the tension a little. Sheesh."

As they had done before, the mass of people flowing into the club parted before me, people stopping to whisper as we passed through the narrow channel of bodies.

"You know," Jim said, looking from side to side as we walked the gauntlet, "I'd say this was really cool except I have a nasty suspicion we're all going to end up dead."

"One more crack like that, and you'll find yourself in solitary confinement with no hope of parole," I breathed in an undertone I knew it could hear.

We walked up the steps to the club, the mass of people closing behind us. I stopped at the door, confused by the invisible net that seemed to be strung across the doorway.

"What is it?" I asked, pushing against it. The net held for a few seconds, then reluctantly gave way and allowed me through it. It was like pushing myself through a dense mass of air.

Rene pushed his way through it without too much difficulty, Amelie on his heels. "It is a ward, a powerful one, intended to keep out all creatures of Abaddon."

I looked back through the door at where Jim stood, fifty or sixty people behind it. "Jim?" I asked.

It tried to step forward. For a fraction of a second an intricately drawn symbol glowed black on the air, then disappeared.

Jim shook its head. "It won't let me in."

I went back through the door, feeling no resistance as I left the club. "Here, let me help you. Maybe if I push, we can get you through it. I need you in there with me."

As I approached the door again from the outside, I could feel the power of the ward filling the door.

"I don't think this is going to work," Jim complained as I shoved him into the doorway. Its black body distorted as if a sheet of glass blocked its path. "Ow. Ow. Ow."

"Oh, for heaven's sake," I muttered, glaring at the door. "I do *not* have time for this."

I pulled the Eye out from my pocket, held it so it faced the door, and mentally envisioned a crack in the ward. The lodestone grew hot in my hand, drawing an answering heat from deep within me—Drake's fire, the fire that never entirely left me. I let the two blazes join together into one conflagration, then directed it toward the ward at the same time I shoved Jim through. There was a crack like thunder; then we were inside.

Amelie stared at me in horror. "Aisling . . . you should not . . . you should not have been able to do that! The ward, it was most strongly drawn!"

The crowd outside the door went absolutely dead silent at her words. Every hair on my head stood on end at the look people were giving me. I imagined it was the same sort of look the guys running the witch trials gave the convicted.

"Just warming up, folks," I said with a weak smile, trying to diffuse the situation.

"Oh, that's gonna make everyone feel better," Jim muttered.

"Come on, let's get this over with. The sooner everyone has Ophelia to focus on, the quicker they'll forget about me." I marched forward, my little gang of three following close behind.

The inside of G & T was packed, but still people poured into the club, squishing together like sardines. We pushed our way through to the dance floor, which had been cordoned off. At one end Drake stood with Pál and István. All three were wearing knee-length dark green silk tunics and black leggings, Drake's tunic embroidered with an intricate gold-and-black dragon on the chest. He looked incredibly handsome and absolutely dangerous. I stopped at the edge of the dance floor, aware that someone had squeezed forward to unsnap the black velvet rope to allow us onto the parquet floor. The surrounding crowd was so dense, it was almost impossible to see how deep they were, but I scanned them nonetheless.

I didn't see Ophelia.

Drake smelled the air, his eyes glittering black with anticipation. I knew without him even saying it that he was aware I had more than just the talisman with me, proving my suspicion that the talisman had indeed done well to hide the presence of the Eye. "You come to meet me in challenge, Guardian?"

I stepped forward two paces and spoke the formal words per instruction from Amelie. "I come to meet you in challenge, wyvern. Who are your seconds?"

Pál and István stepped forward. "Pál Eszes of the green dragons, known as the wise, and István Vadas of the green dragons, also named the hunter. Name your seconds, Guardian."

Uh-oh. Ophelia was supposed to be my second. "Um . . . I call a time-out." I turned to face Rene and Amelie. "Guys, this is probably going to get ugly later, so why don't you both find yourself a good place to watch and let Jim be my second."

Amelie spoke as she shook her head. "A demon cannot serve as second. It will be the greatest honor for me to serve you."

Rene nodded. "Me, as well. I do not understand it all, but I know you need me."

"You guys are just the best," I said, giving both their hands a little squeeze before turning back to Drake. "Team Aisling consists of Rene Lesueur, taxi driver, and Amelie Merllain, healer."

"I'm the mascot," Jim said, pushing itself forward. "And our cheer is 'Aisling rules, others drool,' so you can just stick that in your pipe and blow it out your—"

"Thank you, I think that will be enough." I glared Jim into silence.

I swore one corner of Drake's mouth twitched as he inclined his head toward me. "You are the challenger, Guardian; by what means will you meet me body to body to prove your superiority and claim control of the green dragon sept?"

Rene came forward at my gesture, holding out a dark blue canvas bag. I pulled out a round sisal and metal object, holding it up to show him, turning so the crowd could see it as well. "I, Aisling Grey, challenge you, Drake Vireo, to a game of darts. Winner takes all."

If I thought the crowd was silent before, it was positively breathless now. At least it was for a second or two; then everyone erupted into comment, most of them outraged yells of foul.

Drake stormed toward me, his eyes an angry forest green. "What are you doing?" he asked softly when he got close enough to me. "Why are you doing this? Why do you make a mockery of me?"

I clutched the dartboard to my chest, more to keep

from grabbing Drake than to protect it. "I'm not mocking you, Drake. This was the only thing I could think of."

"You issued me a challenge to meet me body to body. That is traditionally defined as combat. What you suggest is not combat—it is a game!"

I let my eyes caress him from his nose to his toes and back up again. "I'm not stupid, Drake. There's no way I want to try to fight you physically. I can't even arm-wrestle you, I've got girly arm muscles. I might be able to take you down with a few self-defense moves, but Jan, my instructor, told me never to use them except in life-threatening situations, and you can't kill me."

His hands made fists at his sides as he leaned into me, his breath feathering my face. "What you plan is ridiculous. I told you I was an expert at darts. You will lose."

"I know," I whispered back. "And I'd appreciate it if you could keep that fact in mind when your sept is dreaming up its punishment for me."

"Why are you doing this?" he asked again, his eyes losing a bit of their anger.

"It's part of my plan," I said, wanting desperately to kiss him. "Don't worry—it'll be over quickly. I have a horrible throwing arm. Is it kosher for the challenger to kiss the challengee?"

"No," he said, a startled look flickering across his face. "It is not done at all. What plan?"

"Just a plan I have. You'll find out about it as soon as this is over. Well, good luck. I mean, *bonne chance.*" I held out my hand. He stared at it for a moment, then shook it carefully as if it were made of glass.

Everyone watched as I gave Rene the dartboard. He hung it on the wall, pulling out the cheap blue and yellow darts from the cloth bag. István shot Drake a disbelieving look before reluctantly accepting the yellow darts.

"OK, so how do we do this? First one to hit center wins?"

Drake rolled his eyes, then grabbed me and hauled me up to his chest in the best arrogant, domineering wyvern manner. "You are impossible," he muttered just before his mouth descended upon mine, his tongue immediately invading, stroking the fires that burned so deep within me. Before I could do more than think about responding, he was gone. It took a moment for me to realize that the dull roar I heard wasn't just my blood pounding in my ears—everyone in the club was laughing and applauding.

"We will play the 501 game," Drake announced, ignoring the still howling crowd. He briefly explained the rules, showed me how to throw a dart, and even gave me a couple of practice shots before we started the match proper.

"Well, that didn't take long," Jim said when Drake beat me in record time. My score was still in the four hundreds when he made zero. "Almost anticlimactic, you could say. Too bad about István. You think he's going to hold that wild shot against you?"

I looked over at where István had a protective hand clapped over the edge of his groin. I'd missed the important parts, but just barely. He glared back at me. I grimaced. "I hope not. I also hope he doesn't get a say in the sept's punishment of me."

Pál stepped forward and held up his hands for silence. The audience, which had been loudly and vehemently discussing the outcome of the challenge (several people shooting me vengeful looks that left me making a mental vow to be sure I had Rene with me at all times), lowered their voices enough so Pál could speak. "By the laws of the Otherworld, Drake Vireo has met the challenge and proved the victor. The terms of the challenge call for the Guardian known as Aisling Grey to accept the punishment meted out by the green dragons." He turned to look at Drake. István limped forward and grinned an evil, anticipatory grin.

I decided right then and there that if I ever truly did become Drake's mate, István would be the first one to go.

Drake glided forward, interrupting his henchman's gloating look. "The punishment will be delayed until such time as the sept can meet to discuss the matter. The challenge has been satisfied."

He looked at me. I put my hand in my pocket and fingered the lodestone, turning to face the crowd. If my plan fizzled out, I'd have to do the one thing I was dreading—summoning Bael. "Drake is right, the challenge has been met and satisfied. He will not turn himself in to the police for the three recent murders that have stained the reputation of the Otherworld. He has no reason to do so even should he have lost, since he is not guilty of those crimes."

"You are the one wanted by the authorities," a tall black man said in heavily accented English. "You are the one who has caused much difficulty to those of us in the *l'au-delà*. Why should we not turn you over to the police?"

I raised my eyebrows. "Because I'm innocent, as well."

"And I say you lie," a voice called from the back of the room.

I smiled as I released the lodestone, breathing a sigh of relief. I had counted on Ophelia's need to witness the challenge to bring her out into the open. The throng in front of me shimmered, then parted slowly, revealing the figure of a woman in black striding toward me, her blond head held high.

The gasps of horror were eerie, but it was the woman herself who set my skin to crawling.

It was Perdita.

"You're — you're dead," I said, my flesh tightening along my back and neck. "We saw you dead." I turned to Drake, confused beyond all confusion. "She was dead, right? We saw her? Together? All of us?"

Drake nodded, his eyes on Perdita. He had that bored look on his face again that I was coming to learn was a warning sign. "I suspect it was a setup."

"Well, that's the understatement of the year," I said as I looked at Perdita. "Why did you pretend to be dead?"

Perdita laughed and spun around with her arms up, showing everyone how healthy she was. "Me? It was I who was drugged and made to look as if I had been murdered, but I am quite well, as you all can see. Your little plan to pin the murders on my servant Ophelia have failed. Now everyone will hear the truth of how you killed the Venediger and Aurora Deauxville in your attempt to serve your master Bael. Everyone in the Otherworld will know how you intend to rule them by wielding the Tools of Bael."

I gawked. There was just no other word for it: I gawked at her. "You what? Ophelia was your servant? You said she was your sister!"

Perdita laughed again. "Everyone here knows Ophelia is my doppelgänger, my servant to summon when I so desire." She appealed to the crowd. "Is that not so?"

Every single blasted head in the crowd nodded. "Well, poop!" I said, turning to Jim. "Did you know Ophelia was a doppelgänger?"

It shook its head, looking thoughtful. "No, but I've

been a bit off my game ever since my powers were stripped."

I looked over to Amelie. "A doppelgänger?"

She gave a little shrug. "I thought you knew."

"I didn't!"

"You see how she does not deny the truth," Perdita said. "You see that she does not dare refute her dark master. She does not even try to deny that she has in her possession one of the Tools of Bael at this very moment. Is this minion of Abaddon who you want ruling you? Will you let her destroy the Otherworld in order to gain power? Should she be allowed to kill our kind without punishment?"

The crowd rumbled an ominous negative, moving forward slowly until the space on the dance floor all but disappeared. Panicked, I looked over to Drake. He stood a few feet away with his arms crossed over his arms, watching me, making no move to interfere.

Drat his dragon hide.

"I do deny the truth," I yelled, the crowd pausing as I waved the steel pointed darts around. "I am not the minion of anyone, nor do I want to rule anyone. I just want my aquamanile back and the murderer of Mme. Deauxville and the Venediger caught so I can go home. Perdita is the killer. She summoned the demon Bafamal to help her set up the murders as a red herring to cover up her true plan to gather the Tools of Bael. She used her doppelgänger sister in order to give her an alibi. She's the one who tried to frame Drake for the murders because she knew he had two of the Tools, and *she's* the one who will tear apart the mortal world if she is allowed to fulfill her evil plan. Perdita is the only one here trying to escape justice!"

"Lies!" Perdita shrieked, turning back to the crowd.

"Do not listen to her lies—she has no proof to back up her wild accusations. We must take her now, use the Tool she possesses to destroy her before she destroys us. We must stop her!"

"You're right about one thing, you know," I told Perdita as I pulled the lodestone from my pocket. "I do have the Eye of Lucifer. The rest of what you're saying is a bunch of cow cookies, however. And I can prove it in the simplest way possible." I waited until everyone was silent, watching me as I held up the lodestone. "What say I summon Bael and we ask him just which one of us was working for him?"

Perdita screamed and lunged at me. Bafamal appeared out of nowhere in another of its shiny suits. Jim woofed as it threw itself forward, heading for Bafamal. I slashed the darts into Perdita's arm as she grabbed me, trying to twist with the motion of her body so I could throw her to the ground. We both fell as Ophelia shimmered into view, called by Perdita. The crowd surged forward around us as I struggled to keep the lodestone safe in my hand at the same time I tried to disable Perdita. Ophelia shrieked and grabbed my hair, making my eyes burn hot with tears. I kicked out at her at the same time I punched Perdita on the jaw. She wrenched my arm up, biting my fist in an attempt to get me to release the Eye. Behind us, Jim and Bafamal were locked in battle, each snarling and spitting curses.

Rene pulled out his gun and aimed it over his head, firing a few shots into the ceiling as he yelled, "Stop! I have a gun!"

The heavy lighting fixture above him fell, knocking him to the ground.

"Help. Rene." I gasped to Amelie as I fought to free myself. She hurried over to him.

The air was thick with cries and shouts of encouragement as Perdita and Ophelia and I rolled around in the catfight to end all catfights. "Aren't you going to do something to help me?" I yelled at Drake as I head-butted Ophelia into releasing my hair. Perdita kicked at my knee. I socked her in the stomach. Ophelia threw herself on my back, screaming blue murder in my ear.

Drake tipped his head to the side as we rolled around at his feet. "What will you give me to help you?"

Perdita punched me in the eye. Ophelia bit my ear. I kicked both of them, whipped open the door in my mind, and envisioned a hell of a lot of possibilities, most of which concerned both women cowering before me. The lodestone grew hot in my hand as first Perdita, then Ophelia let go of me to fall away, their faces covered. I crawled out from beneath Ophelia's legs to stand triumphant over them. My nose and mouth were bleeding, one eye was swelling shut, my tunic was torn, my kneecap had been wrenched sideways, I was panting, and I could feel one of my front teeth loose, but I hauled myself up. I wiped the blood off my face, stared at my bloody fingers for a second, then bent down and drew a circle. I turned to face east. "Guardian of the towers of the east, I summon you to guard this circle."

"No!" Perdita shouted, getting to her knees. "No, do not let her do this!"

"Guardian of the tower of the south, I summon you to guard this circle."

"Stop her! Someone must stop her!" Perdita was on her feet now, but when she turned toward me, I held the lodestone up, using it to protect me.

"Guardian of the tower of the west, I summon you to guard this circle."

"Ophelia! Stop her!"

Ophelia crawled toward me. I waved the lodestone, and she collapsed.

"Guardian of the tower of the north, I summon you to guard this circle."

With a cry that shattered every glass hanging in the bar, the demon Bafamal disappeared in a thick, oily black plume of smoke.

I took a deep breath. "I conjure thee, Bael, prince of all the legions of Abaddon."

"She will bring death upon us all," Perdita screamed, trying to lunge at me, but held at bay by the power I wielded through the Eye. "Stop her! Do not allow her to say the words."

Amelie stepped into my range of vision. Her face was drawn and pale, her eyes endlessly deep. She was trying to warn me, but I could not stop to heed her.

"I summon thee, Bael, to appear before me now." The air within the circle thickened.

"No! He will kill me! No one was supposed to know! He will take me with him! Stop, you must stop!" Perdita was sobbing now, on her knees before me in supplication. "Do not do this to me!"

"I command thee, Bael, lord of Abaddon, to my will by the virtue of my power." The air in the circle shimmered, a low howl like the wind in a storm filling the club. The people around us stood frozen, as if in fear of what I was about to do.

Perdita stared at it in horror. "Please! I beg of you, do not! I will be lost!"

"Aisling," Drake said, stepping forward. "Are you sure you want to do this?"

"I have no choice," I said, keeping my eyes on the woman at my feet. The air within the circle grew pearlescent, as if something was forming, the wind howling within the club growing until it was shrieking like a dying animal. My stomach tightened, my soul sick with dread. "She will not admit her guilt otherwise. By my hand thy shall be bound, by my blood thy shall be bound, by my voice thy shall be—"

"I confess!" Perdita shrieked. She clawed the air, dragging herself to her feet. "I will confess all, only do not bring him! He will take me with him if you do, and I will be damned for all time! I confess, please, I confess!"

"You confess your guilt to everyone here? You confess to the murders of Aurora Deauxville and the Venediger? You confess to arranging the crimes so that Drake and later I would be blamed? Do you confess to binding yourself to the demon lord Bael in exchange for bringing him the Tools of Bael?"

"Yes, yes, I confess it all. I threw suspicion on Drake. I arranged the murders to blame the Otherworld so as to confuse the police. I confess. I confess. . . ." She collapsed, sobbing hysterically as she writhed before the circle.

"I release thee, Bael, by my hand and my blood and my voice, thy shall return to thy dominion."

I rubbed out a bit of the blood forming the circle. The howling grew even louder, until everyone in the club screamed and clutched their ears. The air within twisted as if it were raging against my will, and for one horrible moment I feared I wasn't strong enough to send Bael back, but the lodestone burned hot in my hand with power. With a terrible noise that sounded like a thousand souls in torment, the howling abruptly ceased, the air in the circle slowly returning to normal. Perdita curled up into a fetal ball, rocking as she repeated over and over in a childish singsong voice, "I confess, I confess."

I walked over to Drake and stomped on his foot. Hard. "What will I give you to help me? What will I *give* you?"

He stood on one leg rubbing his foot, grinning a grin so steamy, it almost melted my underwear. "I never doubted you would defeat her. You are my mate. You could do no less."

I pointed a finger at him. "You are too arrogant for your own good. I officially de-mate you. Go away. I never want to see you again. Except maybe tonight. Naked. Your place. But after that, no more."

I turned back to the now-babbling audience. Rene was being propped up by the crowd; his head was bloody but he appeared to be OK. Amelie was fussing over him, instructing people to bring her water and herbs.

Drake's men pulled Perdita to her feet. She hung limply between them, her hands moving incessantly as if she were drawing something. I moved closer to speak to her, but Pál shook his head. I understood why when I saw her eyes. They were mad, totally mad. She had snapped under the strain of my threat to bring Bael forward to confront her lies.

I shivered, wrapping my arms around myself, chilled by the proof of what power the Eye could wield, my whole body shaking with the realization of what I had done to another human being.

Warmth flooded me as Drake's hand slid around my waist. I fought the need to lean into him for a moment, then gave in and allowed his fire to flow into my frigid blood. His voice stroked my skin like the sheerest silk. "You are not responsible for her madness. She walked that path long before you came. Is it not the work of a madman to kill for gain?"

"Yes, but . . . but I scared her by summoning Bael."

"She sold herself to Bael in exchange for power. She

made the decision to do so, not you. The price she pays now for that choice has nothing to do with you."

They were nice words, and they made a lot of sense, but they didn't ease all my guilt.

"Too bad we didn't have any Jell-O," Jim said as it strolled over to sniff Perdita. "Think of the money we could have made charging everyone to watch you three babes go at it!"

"You do what I think you're intending on doing, and you will be on nothing but dry dog food for the rest of your unnatural life," I warned it.

Jim lowered its leg and gave me a sour look as it walked away from Perdita.

"What will you do with her?" Amelie asked me, nodding toward the slumped figure.

I looked out at the dissipating crowd. "I don't know—it's not really my decision, is it? Why is everyone leaving? You all belong to the Otherworld, not me. It's up to you guys to decide what happens to her."

Amelie smiled a sad smile. "You have defeated the one who would be Venediger. By rights, that makes you—"

"No!" I yelled, dropping Drake's hand and backing away from them. "It's bad enough I'm a Guardian and a wyvern's ex-mate, and a demon lord. I'm not going to be a Venediger, as well! Jim, I command you, clear me a path! We're getting out of here before anything else happens!"

Epilogue

"Do you want me to castrate you right here and now?"

"Sheesh!" Jim flared its doggy nostrils at me and lowered its front from the overstuffed armchair. "I had an itch, that's all! I just wanted to scratch."

"In the last two days you've humped two pillows, the corner of my bed, and the vacuum cleaner the maid left while she was cleaning the bathroom. Drake's furniture is nice. I'm sure he'd appreciate it if it remained that way."

Jim threw itself to the floor. "My heart is breaking, and you won't even let me get a few jollies with a stupid chair. Fine. Be that way. You can tear me away from my beloved Cecile, but I won't forget her. Our love will last through all the long ages of mortals."

I patted Jim on its head. "I never said we weren't coming back—I just said I had to go home and explain to my uncle what all the fuss has been about. And whither I go, you go. So stop pouting."

"When I die, I'm coming back to haunt you."

"You can't die, silly." I strolled across the thick carpeting of Drake's private study and examined the painting hanging behind a monstrous mahogany desk. It was a simple pencil sketch of a seated woman holding an urn, but the casual line of it was pleasing to the eye, perfect in execution, as if each stroke was set down by a master.

"Do you like my da Vinci?"

Drake's voice wrapped me in a warm cocoon of tangled emotions that I did not want to examine. I smiled at the woman. "A da Vinci. I should have known."

I turned to watch him, my heart beating faster at the sight of his body moving with masculine grace, his power evident in every sleek movement. "You may have it in exchange for the Eye of Lucifer, which—" His head lifted as he sniffed, his eyes burning into mine with a familiar heat. "—you have tucked between your lovely breasts."

I raised my eyebrows. "You'd give me a da Vinci for the lodestone? A real da Vinci? As in Leonardo?"

"Yes, it is real. It is also uncataloged. It is what they call a cartoon, a sketch for painting. I found it in Germany after World War Two."

I let my smile go just the tiniest bit naughty. "You would exchange something that valuable for a simple stone bound in a bit of inferior gold?"

"Yes." His eyes were darkening even as I watched. He stood close to me, close enough I could smell his spicy dragon scent, the scent that had haunted my dreams for the last two nights, but he made no move to touch me.

I sighed. Even though my body might dispute the idea, keeping my distance from him was the best for both of us. We had no future together, despite his belief otherwise. I'd made my decision. I plucked the lodestone out from my bra, weighing its warmth for a moment before taking Drake's hand and pressing the stone into it.

He stared down at it in surprise, as if he never expected me to give it to him. Silly man, didn't he realize there was no one else to whom I could entrust it?

"You will trade?"

"No. I will give."

His hand closed over the lodestone, a little sensual shiver running down his body before he got control of himself. His head tipped to the side as I knew it would. "Why?"

"You're the only one who will keep it safe."

"I have all three Tools of Bael now. I've already told you that I will not give back the aquamanile. What is to stop me from using them?"

"Nothing. But you won't. I might not be your mate, but I know enough about you to realize you have all the power you need. It's treasure you seek, and treasure you guard. So I'm giving you the Eye of Lucifer, no strings attached. I figure with the three Tools hidden safely away in your lair downstairs, no one will ever be able to use them."

"You're right," Drake said, moving closer. His fingers skimmed along my jaw, his thumb brushing over my lower lip. I ground my teeth together to keep from sucking his finger into my mouth. "But only about one thing—I have no desire for more power. The Tools will be safe in my keeping. About the other things you are less prescient."

"Really?" I stepped back, feeling distance was a good thing. "You're not still thinking I'm your mate?"

"You *are* my mate. Nothing you can do will change that, but that is not what I was referring to."

I raised my eyebrows in silent question.

He smiled. "My lair is not the room you saw downstairs. That was merely a safe. In truth, I have no lair in Paris. Someday, if you ask nicely, I will show you what a true dragon's lair looks like."

"I'm going home this afternoon," I said, backing up

even more. "My uncle is still a bit pissed at me, but whatever you said to Inspector Proust when you handed over Perdita did the trick—he called Uncle Damian and explained that they had made a mistake about me. He also told him that the aquamanile was gone for good. Uncle Damian was less happy about that, but as I told him, that's what insurance is for."

"That's not all she said," Jim piped up. "She also told him that she would do anything he wanted, take any job he had, just so long as he kept her on the payroll. It was pathetic, really, the way she groveled. You'd think a Guardian would have a little more dignity—"

"One more word and you're a eunuch."

Jim shut up.

I tried to walk out of there, but my feet took me over to Drake, so I figured what the heck, a girl is entitled to a good-bye kiss.

"Good-bye," I breathed, allowing my lips to play over his.

"This is in no way over," Drake breathed back. "You are my mate. You are a Guardian. You cannot deny fate."

"I make my own fate, thank you," I said, slipping out his arms. I was calm. I was confident. I was a professional. "See you around."

He just stood and watched as I walked out of his study, out of his house, and out of his life.

"Fires of Abaddon, that was the best you could do? 'I make my own fate'? Man, when I left Cecile, she was crying in her kibble, and all you do is say 'I make my own fate'?"

I rolled my eyes and kept walking toward Rene's taxi.

"You didn't even kiss him properly. I didn't see one little bit of tongue action going on there, and I was watching. Rene, get this girl, she just gave Drake the Eye and walked out with the lamest line in the history of women walking out on men. She didn't even give him a good-bye grope. She just said, 'I make my own fate,' and left. Just what is that supposed to mean, anyway? 'I make my own fate'? Is that like making yourself an ice cream sundae? Hey. I'm hungry. Can we stop somewhere and get something to eat before we hit the airport? I keep telling you, you have to feed this form or else my coat goes all ugly. Sheesh, I hope my next Guardian at least has her training wheels, 'cause this business with having to tell you everything is getting a bit old. . . . "

Read on for a preview of

Katie MacAlister's

paranormal romance

Fire Me Up

Available from Signet Eclipse

I stood in the center of the Keleti train station in Budapest, surrounded by hundreds of people, nice, normal people, people who never once thought about things like demons, and demon lords, and Guardians, and all of the strange beings that populated the *l'au-delà*—the Otherworld—and I wondered for the hundredth time if I tried really hard, whether or not I could send Jim back to the fiery depths of Hell.

"No," it answered my unasked question before I could do so much as level another squinty-eyed glare at it. "You tried three times to send me back. The last time cost me a toe. My favorite one, too. How you can make a toe disappear right off my foot is beyond me, but the point is that I'm not going to risk another unbalanced paw just so you can play Junior Guardian. I'm staying put until you get yourself a mentor and figure out that whole sending me back thing."

"Will you stop answering questions before I ask them, stop telling me what to do, and above all, *stop talking*!"

As crowded as the platforms were, the air filled with not only the smell of diesel fumes but also the ripe scent of a couple hundred people who'd been crushed into a busy train on a hot August day, my words managed to pierce the miasma of sound, and echo with a strange piercing quality off the tiled walls.

Several heads swiveled to look back at us. I smiled some-what grimly at all of them. A hurt look filled Jim's brown eyes as it sniffed, with studied indifference, the butt of the man and woman in front of us.

We shuffled forward another few feet.

"So, *that* was an order?"

I sighed, my shoulders slumping in defeat. I was hot, tired, jetlagged from the flight from Portland to Amsterdam to Budapest, and to be honest, Jim's presence—although annoying in many ways—was more than a little reassuring considering just who else was occupying the same continent on which I now found myself.

The memory of glittering green eyes filled with smoky desire rose with no difficulty to dance before me, but was squelched with a much greater effort. "No, it's not an order," I said softly. "At least not until we're through this crowd. I doubt if anyone can even see you, let alone notice that your mouth is moving."

"I told you to get me that ventriloquist tape I saw on TV."

The crowd shimmered as a second exit was opened up, the mass of travelers undergoing mitosis as one part of the crowd headed for the new exit. Sweat trickled down my back, dampening the tendrils of hair that had escaped my ponytail until they clung to my neck. I was starting to get lightheaded from the heat, the pressure of so many bodies, and the lack of sleep during the twelve hours it had taken to get from Portland to Budapest. I had to get out of there.

"Come on, I think I see a break." I pushed Jim toward the slight opening next to a couple of kids decked out in Goth gear who were sucking the tongues out of each other's head, jerking the suitcase behind me, apologizing under my breath as I jostled elbows, backs, and sides as we squished forward. "Why I thought coming here was such a good idea is beyond me."

"Makes sense to me," Jim answered a bit distractedly as it smelled people, luggage, and the litter on the ground with the same unbiased interest. The crowd thinned dramatically as people scattered once they made it past the bottleneck exit. "You need training. Budapest is where it's happening. Hey, when are we going to eat?"

"I could have had a nice vacation in the Bahamas, but oh, no, I had to come—" My feet stopped moving. They simply stopped moving as my eyes bugged out of my head, my heart stopped beating, and my brain, usually a reliable and trustworthy organ, came to an abrupt and grinding halt. With no obstructing crowd remaining, the group of people standing just outside the floor to ceiling glass windows of the train station was perfectly visible to me.

Jim stopped and looked back at me, one furry black eyebrow cocked in question at my abbreviated statement. "You aren't using crude sexual slang, are you? No, you can't be, because I know for a fact you haven't been gettin' any since we left Paris."

Slowly, I blinked, my stomach turning somersaults, my whole being riveted on the scene just outside the station.

Jim turned to see what held me in such thrall. "Wow. Talk about speaking of the devil. I must be psychic or something. What's he doing in Budapest?"

It hurt to breathe. It hurt to think. It just hurt, period. I felt like someone had used me as a punching bag for a few hours, every atom of my body pulled so tight I thought I was going to explode into a million little pieces.

Outside the window a small clutch of people stood before a long glistening black limousine. The men wore black slacks with open-necked shirts in different shades of red, while the woman looked as if she'd just stepped from the cover of Beijing Vogue. She was tall, willowy, had long, straight glossy black hair that reached to her waist, wore a short black miniskirt and a red leather bustier, all carried off with an effortless grace that spoke of years spent in expensive Swiss finishing schools.

But it was one of the men greeting the VIPs who caught and held my attention. The wind rippled the dark forest green silk of his shirt so that it outlined the lovely curves of his muscular chest and arms. That same wind was responsible for his dark hair, longer than I had remembered it, ruffling back off a brow graced by two ebony slashes that were his eyebrows. Despite the heat of the August afternoon, he wore leather pants . . . *tight* leather pants, the garment glistening in the sun as if it had been painted on his long legs and adorable derriere as he made a courtly bow to the VIPs.

"Drake," I said on a breath, my body suddenly tingling as if it was coming to life after a long, long sleep. Even his name left my lips sensitized, the sound of that one word strange after its banishment from my life four weeks ago.

Four weeks? It seemed more like a lifetime.

Jim gave me a long appraising look. "You're not going to go all Buffy/Angel on me, are you? Mooning around bemoaning the forbidden love that cannot be? Because if you are, I'm finding myself a new demon lord. Love I can take, but mooning is not in my contract."

I started toward the window, unable to help myself, my body suddenly a mass of erogenous zones that wanted more than anything on this earth to place itself in Drake's hands. His lovely long-fingered, extremely talented hands.

"Aisling Grey," Jim said.

The sound of my name brought me out of the trance. Slowly I gathered my wits and determination, thankful that in the hustle and bustle of the train station, no one had noticed a deranged, lust-crazed woman and her talking demon in dog form. "I don't quite know what came over me."

It raised an expressive eyebrow. "*I* know."

I pulled my eyes from the sight of Drake and his men, dragging my wheeled suitcase forward and out the doors, purposely turning my back to the scene that had held such interest as Jim paced silently beside me. "I'm OK now. It was just a little aberration. I told you when we left Paris that things were over between Drake and me. It just took me by surprise seeing him here, in Budapest. I assumed he'd still be in France." Safe. Several hundreds of miles away. In a completely different country, living out his life without me.

"Uh huh. Right. Tell it to the tail, Aisling."

I ignored my smart-mouthed demon as we joined the end of a queue for taxis. The handful of people ahead of us laughed and talked, just as if their world hadn't come to a grinding halt, whereas mine . . . I glanced back at the limo. Drake was overseeing Pál, one of his men, loading the matched set of luggage in the back of the glossy car.

Jim pulled its head from the bag to look at me, its eyes opening wide suddenly as it made an odd combination of a bark and warning. "Behind you!"

I dropped its leash and spun around in a crouch, half-expecting an attack of some form, but finding instead that my suitcase had attracted the attention of three street gypsies, all of whom obviously had the intention of lightening the load of my possessions. "The amulet!" I screeched, throwing myself on top of the half-opened bag.

The biggest of the thieves, a boy who looked to be about fifteen, jerked the bag out from underneath me, his accomplices pulling on the outer flap so that it peeled back like a ripe banana. I lunged toward the small brown leather amulet bag that was stuffed into my underwear. "Hey! That's mine, you little wretch!" My fingers closed around the bag just as the youngest girl grabbed it, but I had not survived my Uncle Damian's wrath about losing a valuable antiquity for nothing. I had to save this one at all costs. I jerked the amulet free just as someone behind me shouted. The street gypsies snatched up handfuls of my things—pants, shoes, and my cosmetic case—before racing off in three different directions.

The wind, coming off the nearby Danube, flirted with the opened suitcase, decided it liked the look of my newly purchased satin undies, and scooped up several pairs, sending them skittering down the sidewalk. I left Jim to guard the luggage as I ran down the sidewalk, the amulet still in my hand as I plucked my underwear from a phone booth, a magazine stand, and a newspaper box. One last pair, trembling next to a garbage bin, suddenly spun upwards in a gust and flew a few feet down the sidewalk, its flight coming to a swift end as the pink satin and lace material wrapped itself in a soft caress around a man's leg

A man's leather-clad leg.

"Oh, god," I moaned, closing my eyes for a second, knowing exactly who owned that leg. Why me? Why did this sort of thing have to happen to me? Why couldn't anything ever be simple? When I looked again, Drake was holding my panties in his hand, his head slowly turning as he scanned the crowd until he saw me clutching a handful of underwear. Raising my chin, I marched forward, firmly pushing down the cheers of delight that several unmentionable parts of my body were sending up.

"I believe those are mine," I told him, holding out my hand for the underwear.

Heat flared deep in his emerald eyes, but I looked down at his hand, refusing to be drawn into that trap. I knew well the power of his desire.

"You have excellent taste in undergarments," he said, his voice a little rough around the edges as he placed the underwear in my hand. "Victoria's Secret?"

"No," I said, allowing my eyes to meet his for a moment. I swear a tiny little wisp of smoke curled out of one of his nostrils. "Naughty Nellie's House of Knickers. Amsterdam."

He inclined his head as I spun around, ignoring the disdainful arched brows of the woman as I marched back to where Jim sat next to my ravaged suitcase.

"Don't say it," I warned Jim as I squatted next to the suitcase, transferring to it my collected underwear and the amulet. A taxi pulled up beside me as I double checked the zipper and wondered what the street gypsies had done with the little padlock I'd used. "Just don't say it, OK?"

"Me? I'm not saying anything."

I waited. I'd lived with Jim for a month now—it was virtually impossible for the demon to let something as mortifyingly embarrassing as having my underwear scattered on my former lover go without comment.

"But if I was going to say something, it would be something along the lines of 'smooth move, Ex-Lax!'"

The limo pulled passed with a gentle, expensive purr of its engine, the tinted windows thankfully keeping the sight of Drake's politely amused face from view.

I didn't have to see him to know he was looking at me, though. I could feel it. There was just something about a dragon's regard that left the hair on the back of my neck standing on end.

PLAYING WITH FIRE

A Novel of the Silver Dragons

The first book in the scorching new series from
New York Times bestselling author

KATIE MACALISTER

Gabriel Tauhou, the leader of the silver dragons,
can't take his eyes off May Northcott—not even
when May, who has the unique talent of being able
to hide in the shadows, has slipped from everyone
else's sight. May, however, has little time for
Gabriel—not when she's hiding from the
Otherworld law, hunting down a blackmailer, and
trying to avoid a demon lord's demands. But her
ability to withstand Gabriel's fire marks her as his
mate, and he has no intention of letting her
disappear into the darkness she seems to prefer.
When May is ordered to steal one of Gabriel's
treasures—an immensely important relic of all
dragonkin—he must decide which to protect:
his love or his dragons.